Praise for *Bitter Fruit:*

"Achmat Dangor . . . has always delved beyond the surface of human relations, from the intimately personal to the societal and political. This took courage, risk to his own personal life, during the apartheid era. At the same time he did not compromise a dedication to high literary standards in the use of language—he has the invaluable imaginative instinct of expressing his varied themes through the one form of narration and character creation that, in each novel, is equal to the theme. Freshness and bold vividness are qualities of his writing. . . . In the post-apartheid era, he has tackled, in *Bitter Fruit,* as in *Kafka's Curse,* with the honesty of his insight, the problems as well as the promised fulfillment of the enormous change that freedom brings about."   —Nadine Gordimer

"Meticulously written and perfectly paced, the story . . . hints at an escape from history's tyranny."   —*Irish Times*

"Dangor's vivid prose, narrative fluency and facility for literary experiment make *Bitter Fruit* a considerable achievement."
—*Daily Telegraph* (London)

"The tensions, threats and insecurities of the new South Africa are refracted through the internal and sexual lives of the Ali family. . . . As this dense, painful and luxuriously written book carefully reveals itself, the racial conflicts still percolating through South Africa are pinpointed."   —*Metro* (London)

"The unremitting intensity of Dangor's focus is just as notable as its depth."   —*Independent on Sunday* (London)

"[Like] a ringside seat for witnessing the political, cultural and religious conflicts sweeping the Rainbow Nation."
—*The Guardian* (London)

Praise for *Kafka's Curse:*

"Dangor's prose swirls with all the undercurrents of political and sexual tension, regrets and personal disillusionment. . . . It's not often that a poet can turn his attention to prose and create a work that succeeds in such a subtle manner, without silly tricks or sentimentality."   —*Austin Chronicle*

"Entirely wonderful: delicious, moving, mysterious, wise and profoundly provocative."   —*Baltimore Sun*

"A highly original meditation on the politics of love."
                    —*Boston Book Review*

"Dangor's colloquial style is both immediate and poetic."   —*Booklist*

"Extraordinary. A dense surrealist fable . . . This is the essence of the emerging South African version of 'magic realism,' which could be described as 'realistic fantasy.' "
                    —Mike Nicol, author of *The Ibis Tapestry*

Bitter Fruit

Achmat Dangor

BLACK CAT
New York
a paperback original imprint of Grove/Atlantic, Inc.

First published in South Africa in 2001 by Kwela Books, Cape Town.

First published in Great Britain in 2003 by Atlantic Books,
an imprint of Grove Atlantic Ltd., London.

Printed in the United States of America

FIRST AMERICAN EDITION

Library of Congress Cataloging-in-Publication Data
Dangor, Achmat, 1948–
    Bitter fruit / by Achmat Dangor.
      p. cm.
    ISBN 0-8021-7006-4
    1. Johannesburg (South Africa)—Fiction. 2. Conflict of generations—Fiction.
3. Racially mixed people—Fiction. 4. Political activists—Fiction. 5. Married
people—Fiction. 6. Rape victims—Fiction. 7. Revenge—Fiction. I. Title.
PR9369.3.D26B58 2004
823'.914—dc22   2004059900

Black Cat
a paperback original imprint of Grove/Atlantic, Inc.
841 Broadway
New York, NY 10003

05 06 07 08 09   10 9 8 7 6 5 4 3 2 1

'It is an old story – ours.
My father's and mine.'

William Shakespeare

Part One

Memory

I will teach you that there is nothing that is not divinely natural,
. . . I will speak to you of everything.

André Gide, *Fruits of the Earth*

1

IT WAS INEVITABLE. One day Silas would run into someone from the past, someone who had been in a position of power and had abused it. Someone who had affected his life, not in the vague, rather grand way in which everybody had been affected, as people said, because power corrupts even the best of men, but directly and brutally. Good men had done all kinds of things they could not help doing, because they had been corrupted by all the power someone or something had given them.

'Bullshit,' Silas thought. It's always something or someone else who's responsible, a 'larger scheme of things' that exonerates people from taking responsibility for the things they do.

Silas watched the man, the strands of thinning hair combed all the way across his head to hide his baldness, the powdery residue of dry and dying skin on the collar of his jacket, the slight paunch, the grey Pick 'n Pay shoes, the matching grey socks. The man leaned forward to push something along the check-out counter, and turned his face towards where Silas stood, holding a can of tomatoes in his hands like an arrested gesture. Yes, it was Du Boise. François du Boise. The same alertness in his blue eyes. A bit slower, though, Silas thought, as Du Boise moved his head from side to side, watching the cashier ring up his purchases.

Silas went closer, accidentally jostling a woman in the queue behind Du Boise. Silas watched him pushing his groceries along, even though the cashier was capable of doing this on the conveyor belt.

Typical pensioner's fare. 'No-name brand' cans of beans, tuna, long-life milk, sliced white bread, instant coffee, rooibos tea, denture cream.

So the bastard's lost his teeth.

Silas pictured Lydia's angry face, were he to return home without groceries. Today's Sunday and the shops are open only until one o'clock. She'd suppose out loud that *she'd* have to do the shopping the next day, because his job was too important to allow him to take time off from work. All the same, he abandoned the trolley and followed Du Boise out of the store. Halfway down the length of the mall, past shop windows that Du Boise occasionally stopped to look into with familiar ease, Silas began to ask himself what the hell he thought he was doing, following a retired security policeman about in a shopping centre? What Du Boise had done, he had done a long time ago. Nineteen years. And Silas had learned to live with what Du Boise had done, had absorbed that moment's horror into the flow of his life, a faded moon of a memory that only occasionally intruded into his everyday consciousness. Why did it matter now, when the situation was reversed, and Silas could use the power of his own position to make the old bastard's life hell?

The man's smell, a faint stench of decaying metabolism, was in Silas's nostrils, as if he were a hunter come suddenly upon his wounded prey. Du Boise stopped at a café, pulled a chair out from under the table, ready to sit down. Silas stood close to him, facing him, and suffered a moment of uncertainty. Shit, this man looked so much older than the Du Boise he remembered. Then he looked – startled – into the man's equally startled eyes.

'Du Boise? Lieutenant Du Boise?'

'Yes?' he said, and looked Silas up and down, his bewildered manner changing to one of annoyance. He sat down, uttering a weary sigh, trying to draw the attention of other shoppers. Look, here was a youngster bothering an old man, a pensioner.

4

'Do you remember me?' Silas asked.

Du Boise leaned back in his chair, his air of open-armed, I'm-being-put-upon vulnerability quickly bringing a security guard closer.

'Should I?' he asked quietly, caught the eye of the security guard, then raised himself from his chair and pushed his trolley towards the exit.

Silas watched Du Boise disappear into the bright sunlight, watched the security guard watching him, and then turned away. The rage he felt was in his stomach, an acidity that made him fart sourly, out loud, oblivious to the head-shaking group of shoppers who had gathered to witness a potential scene. The guard spoke into his radio, the café owner pointedly dragged the chair back to its neat place beneath the table. Silas's rage moved disconsolately into his heart.

He drove home and, without saying a word to Lydia, took a six-pack of beer from the fridge and walked up Tudhope Avenue towards the small park. He found a tiny island of green in the bristly grass. A couple of hoboes, smiling generously, moved over to make room for him to sit down, legs sprawled out. He smiled back, but ignored the obvious hint. He placed the opulent, still-sealed pack of beer between his legs, and leaned back on his elbows.

Silas remembered how Lydia had looked up from the paper, then put it aside to watch him as he collected the beer from the fridge, walked out through the door. Her eyes had followed him as he passed the window where she sat, and when he turned to close the gate, he had seen the wariness in her face, and the tiredness. What unspoken trauma had he brought home, she must have been wondering. He felt guilty for a moment, then opened a can and drank, long deep gulps. He paused, burped, heard one of the hoboes remark that 'some people have it good in this new South Africa'. Silas turned and stared defiantly at them, then continued drinking, slow, slaking swallows, until his eyes

5

swam and his face flushed warmly. The hoboes got up and walked away in disgust.

At ease now, he stretched out his legs, smiled at passers-by. The park, even with its ragged lawn and fallen-down fence, provided some relief from the hot criss-cross of streets. Located on a busy intersection, it reminded him of those unexpected patches of green in the townships, where you could go without fuss. None of that 'let's go to the park' kind of ceremony that people so quickly acquired when they moved to the suburbs. Just tiny oases, where you could start off by yourself, a spontaneous decision to seek some solitariness, and the very peacefulness of you sitting on your own, sipping beer, would summon a whole group of bras to join you, all bringing along their own 'ammo'. Soon there would be a group of guys squatting in a circle and talking bra-talk, a mellifluous flow of gruff observation and counter-observation, no topic serious enough or dwelt upon sufficiently to maroon the hazy passage of a pleasurable, forgetful afternoon.

No one pressed you for answers or confidences, you soon forgot the problem that had driven you and your pack of beer into the street, you were just one of the 'manne', deserving of your privacy. Until a wife or a mother, or a formidable duet of mother and wife, came along to tell you that this was no way to resolve your problems, drinking in the street like a kid, or worse still, like a tsotsi who had taken to petty crime because he couldn't face life. And drinking in public *was* a crime, petty or not.

The worst was when the cops arrived, all cold-eyed and admonishing, revving the engine of their van until you and your friends slowly dispersed, a herd of dumb, resentful beasts being driven from a favoured waterhole.

Silas cracked open his third beer, lay back on the grass, resting his head on the three remaining cans. The sun pressed down on his eyelids, a hot illumination that would soon make him feel drowsy. This must be the way blind people absorbed light into their heads: raising their faces to the sun, to Ra, god of the blind. Everyone needed real light, not just the artificial, thought-up light of the imagination.

'God! You are so insensitive!' Lydia would have said, had he repeated this thought to her. An innocuous, light-hearted thought, born in a truly carefree moment. She would punish him for it. Lydia had an unforgiving mind. What went on in her heart these days? Well, he'd find out soon. Have to tell her about Du Boise. Not good at keeping secrets . . . well, not really. It struck him that he and Lydia spoke very little these days, and when they did, it was about something practical, the car needing a service, the leaking taps, the length of the grass at the back of the house.

And about Mikey. Speaking about Mikey was the closest she came to revealing herself. Not exactly pouring her heart out, but hinting at what was in there, the anxiety eating away at her calm exterior. She was always asking Silas to 'intervene', to take an active interest in his son. Hadn't he noticed how Mikey had changed, how he was no longer the easygoing kid they once knew?

'We all grow up, Lyd, and suddenly the going's not that easy!'

Words he would love to say, but dare not.

'Try and speak to him, Silas, try and find out whether he's got any problems, you know, a girl, drugs, things happen to young people.'

Meaning he doesn't speak to you, is that it?

Someone loomed above Silas, shutting out the sun. Served him right for falling asleep in a public park in the heart of Berea. Steal your shoes off your feet, people say.

'Dad?'

He opened his eyes and sat up. Mikey was smiling at him in that condescending way he seemed to reserve for his father's drunkenness.

'Dad, we have to be at Jackson and Mam Agnes's by three.'

This was Lydia's doing, sending Mikey out to find him, to humiliate him in public, lead him home, steering him by the elbow. Well, that hadn't happened for a long time. Silas imagined Lydia telling Mikey that his grandmother would be frantic. Mam Agnes was relying on Mikey to drive her to this wedding in Lenasia, because Jackson wouldn't go with her. Mikey's grandfather is strange, the way men can be. He doesn't like Mam Agnes's Lenasia friends, not because they're Indian, but because they gossip. More likely because they don't booze, and, in any case, Jackson was probably in his 'high nines' by now.

All of this would have been said in motherly tones, full of nagging intimacy. Mikey would have been reading, or listening to music, or sitting at the back staring into God knows what kind of nothingness. He would have looked at his mother, not pleadingly, simply to convey his annoyance, and then he would have strode out of the house to come and find Silas.

The way he looks at me, Lydia says. As if he were the adult and I the child.

Mikey extended a hand and helped Silas to his feet. It was a comradely gesture, Silas knew, a warning to expect nothing but cold scorn from Lydia when they got home. He farted loudly as he rose to his feet.

'Christ, Dad!' Mikey said, and walked away.

Silas didn't mind this anger. It brought the kind of understanding he needed and knew Lydia would not offer, a recognition of his ordinariness, his capacity for weakness, it drove the anger out of him, replaced it with a sense of fulfilment that was light, somehow, even if it was accompanied by a mortal belching and the sly emission of pungent farts.

Simple things that helped ordinary people to cope with life. Lydia asked Mikey to drive, as if to demonstrate the need for a 'man around the house'. Usually, she wanted to drive even when Silas was sober. Women are better at these things, we don't have egos to parade. Mikey, who had only recently obtained his licence, drove now, fast and resolute on the freeway, slow and careful when they took the off-ramp to Soweto. An afternoon haze of smog turned the sun to brass. When they pulled up outside Jackson and Mam Agnes's house, Silas said he would wait in the car. The vehicle wouldn't be safe if left unguarded, and, in any case, 'You're on night duty and we can't stay long,' he said to Lydia's disappearing back. Soon, Jackson, his face burnished the colour of dark wood by a day of drinking in the sun, swaggered out through the gate, his oversized shorts flapping around his sturdy legs.

'Sie*las*, Sie*las*, they'll steal you along with the fucken car,' Jackson said, delighting in the musical tone this emphasis gave Silas's name. 'Why don't you come in and have a drink?' Silas went inside to have a beer with his father-in-law. Mam Agnes gave the two men chiding looks, while Lydia became stony-faced. Mam Agnes, dressed 'like the queen bee in drag', according to Silas, made some remark about men who did nothing but drink beer all day, then handed Mikey the keys to Jackson's car (an old but stately Rover that 'needed a slow hand', in the words of its owner). The one thing she wished for her grandson, she said, was that he never became a beer-drinking slob.

Mikey and Mam Agnes drove off under Jackson's watchful eye, while Lydia strode away towards their own car. Silas gulped his beer much too quickly, and joined Lydia. They drove back towards the city. His loud, exaggerated burping brought no reaction from Lydia, who concentrated on her driving, glancing at her watch all the time.

'I saw Du Boise today.'

'Who?'

'Du Boise, Lieutenant Du Boise.'

Lydia said nothing. Her fingers gripped the steering wheel more tightly.

'Where?'

'In the mall.'

9

'Is that why we have no groceries?'

He looked out of the window. They had emerged from the township smog. Clouds darkened the sky. He opened the window, letting in a gust of moist, refreshing air.

'I recognized him immediately. Old and fucken decrepit, but Du Boise all right. It was his eyes. And that arrogant voice.'

Lydia looked at him, then returned her attention to the traffic. He tried to engage her eyes, but she stared straight ahead of her.

'You spoke to him?' she asked after a while, her enquiry casual.

'Yes.'

Again, he looked at her. She was steering the car down the off-ramp towards Doornfontein, bending her body with the curve of the road.

'I didn't mean to. I followed him out of the store, then suddenly found him sitting down, as if he was waiting for me.'

Lydia straightened her leaning body as the car straightened, peering into the side mirror as she entered the slow city traffic.

'Christ, Lydia, it just happened, I just ran into him. A fucken accident.'

She pulled the car halfway up the drive, switched off the engine and got out. Silas sat for a moment, then followed her into the house. She was already in the bedroom, pulling off her clothes.

'Lydia . . .'

'I'm going to be late, Silas, I'm on theatre duty tonight.'

He sat on the bed, watching her change her clothes. The white, staff nurse's uniform soon gave her a new and formidable freshness. She cursed her own distraction, as her pantyhose caught in the skirt's zipper. She hitched the skirt up, freed the hose and smoothed them upwards, over her thighs and buttocks. Her legs acquired a contained kind of sensuality. Then she pulled down the skirt, pinned on the gold-embossed nameplate that had once been such a source of pride to her mother, grabbed her bag and the car keys. She said a hasty 'Bye', and left Silas sitting on the bed. He heard the door close, the customary quiet click of the latch. She was always quiet, so precise in everything she did. He heard the car start, the engine rev, heard it settle down to an idle.

He went to the kitchen and opened a beer, slowly poured it into a tall glass that he tilted towards the bottle, until it was nearly full. He held the glass upright, continuing to pour, slowly, until a delicate head of foam gathered at the mouth without spilling over. But the pleasure he felt at pouring his beer so artfully quickly disappeared.

Overcome by a sudden, bloated feeling, he abandoned the glass of beer and the empty bottle on the long, austere dining-room table and sat down in the old easy chair that he had salvaged from his mother's house in Doornfontein, when the place was declared 'white' and the family was evicted. That had been his mother's last nomadic stop in her journey from suburb to suburb, singled out for pursuit, she believed, by the grey-suited men who implemented the apartheid laws. In his eyes, taking that chair from the ruins of his mother's home and life was the only sentimental thing he had ever done. Now it creaked under his weight, deepening the silence in the house.

The hot day and all the beer he had drunk made him feel drowsy. He raised his head and looked towards the sun, sinking behind the tall buildings that marked the boundary of Berea. He remembered the sun shining in through the high, square window of his and Lydia's first home in Noordgesig, a township on the edge of Soweto, recalled the small-house quietude of the day winding down, the noises in the street. There were many such half-drunken Sundays when Lydia refused to make love to him and he fell asleep, waking up when the sun in the square window gave way to cold shards of moonlight and she told him it was time for dinner. And then, one day, the moon was caught in the bars of a window that seemed familiar yet very different somehow, further away than even that distant township window that the architects had put in as an afterthought. Even bushies need light occasionally, they must have schemed. He heard Lydia's voice, different as well, hoarse and rich, vibrating like a singer's voice too deep to be played so loudly through a set of worn-out speakers. 'Naai her, naai her good!' another voice said, while someone laughed above the sound of an idling car engine, and then Lydia's voice was sharp, ascending into a scream, before fading into a moan so removed it seemed to come from his dreams.

Silas woke from his beery sleep, slumped in the easy chair, his mouth dry and the sky dark. He heard the car's engine running, looked out through the window and saw the empty seat and the door ajar. He stumbled outside, light rain on his face, switched off the engine, looked around, saw Lydia sitting in the wicker chair in the dark corner of the stoep. He must have rushed right past her. He closed the car's door and locked it.

'Lyd, you all right?'

'No, Silas, I'm not all right.'

He approached her with a sense of foreboding. She was in one of her inconsolable moods. Like the day Steve Biko was killed, and she mourned his death bitterly even though she was only seventeen years old, and had no way of knowing, Silas had said, what Biko stood for.

'Silas, it's the thought that they could murder people . . . just like that,' she had said, snapping her fingers the way the clevers do in the townships, and then had gone so quiet that he knew he had alienated her.

Then there was the day Silas's infidelity was revealed – his one and only, he insisted. He had slept with a woman, a comrade in the 'movement'. Lydia was angry, not only because he had betrayed the trust between them, which was all their marriage had going for it at the time, but because this was how she had found out that he was involved in the underground. She had to be told so that she would understand the 'context', so that her rage would not be 'misdirected'. Later, she learnt that the woman comrade was married as well and that her husband had been in detention at the time of the affair.

She confronted Silas about his callousness, and became even angrier when he tried to justify his actions. People in the underground were in constant danger, he said, and this created a sense of intimacy, it was difficult to avoid such things. She told him to stop using the struggle as an excuse for 'fucking around', there were many decent people who were 'involved' but did not go about screwing each other like dogs on heat. Then, too, her anger had hardened into something impenetrable, an invisible crust that made her skin impervious to touch and her mind deaf to even his most heartfelt pleading.

Now he put his arm around her and felt that same implacable coldness in her.

'Christ, Lydia, you're cold, let's go inside.'

She raised her legs onto the chair and hugged her knees to her chest. 'Silas, I'd forgotten . . .'

'I'm sorry, I didn't intend to run into him.'

'You chose to remember, you *chose* to come home and tell me.'

'You know I couldn't hide anything from you.' He took his arm away, went to sit on the wall of the stoep. 'It's not something you easily forget, or *ever* forget.'

'All these years, we never spoke about it.'

'There was no need to.'

She looked up at him, her eyes scornful. 'No need to? What do you mean, no need to?'

'It was a time when, well, we had to learn to put up with those things.'

'What did you have to put up with, Silas? He raped me, not you.'

'It hurt me too.'

'So that's it. Your hurt. You remembered your hurt.'

13

'Shit, Lydia, I didn't mean it that way. I was there, helpless, fucken chained in a police van, screaming like a madman.'

'So you didn't hear me scream?'

'Of course I did, how do you think I knew?'

'How do you know it wasn't a scream of pleasure, the lekkerkry and fyndraai and all that, the things you men fantasize about?'

'Fuck you, Lydia, I know the difference, I know pain from pleasure.'

She stood up, her angry reaction slowed by the coldness in her body. 'You don't know about the pain. It's a memory to you, a wound to your ego, a theory.' She thrust her face into his. 'You can't even begin to imagine the pain.'

They stood facing each other for a moment, then he slumped down in the wicker chair.

'Ja, I suppose imagined pain isn't the real thing. But I've lived with it for so long, it's become real. Nearly twenty years. The pain of your screams, his laugh, his fucken cold eyes when he brought you back to the van.'

'What else do you remember?'

'That Sergeant Seun's face, our black brother, the black, brutal shame in his face.'

'You don't remember my face, my tears . . .'

He closed his eyes almost as she closed hers. When he opened them again, she was inside, busy dialling on the phone. He followed her.

'Who're you calling?'

'The hospital, tell them I can't come in tonight. It's late to call, but a courtesy anyway.'

He took the phone from her and asked for the matron in charge, told her that Lydia was ill, that he'd call the next day to tell them how she was. 'I don't know, some kind of fever,' he said, then slowly replaced the phone.

Lydia stood at the kitchen sink, drinking a glass of water. He went in, leaned against the fridge.

'Lydia, we have to deal with this.'

'With what?'

'With what we went through, both of us.' He saw the smirk on her face. 'Yes, for fuck's sake, I went through it as much as you.'

'You're screaming at me, you know how I don't like being screamed at.'

'I'm sorry.'

She went into the front room, he wanted to follow her, but remembered that she didn't like being pursued when they were having an argument, even though fleeing from room to room was a sign of deep distress that she would need help to overcome. But he only made things worse by following her and trying to force on her his comforting arms and consoling voice. He leaned up against the fridge, felt its throb against his back, slid down until he was on his haunches. He remembered how the police had made them 'tauza', squatting with their legs wide open and frog-jumping, so that anything they had concealed in their anuses would drop out or hurt them enough to make them scream out loud. He closed his eyes and smiled.

'You're amused.'

Lydia was back in the kitchen. He got to his feet. 'I remembered how they made us do that.'

'What?'

'Tauza, when we were in detention, they would shout, "Tauza!" and you would have to hop about like a frog so that they could check if you'd hidden anything up your arsehole.'

'And did you?'

'Shit, what could you hide in your anus?'

'A penis.'

'Hell, Lydia.'

15

'Well, we have to, all the time, hide penises up our fannies, the recollection of them being there. Even the ones we never invited in.'

'Christ, Lydia.'

'Christ what, Lydia?'

'We have to do something about this.'

'What, talk to the Truth Commission?'

'Why not?'

'You think Archbishop Tutu has ever been fucked up his arse against his will?'

'What difference does that make?'

'The difference is he'll never understand what it's like to be raped, to be mocked while he's being raped, to feel inside of him the hot knife – that piece of useless flesh you call a cock – turning into a torture instrument.'

'Not all men are insensitive, Lydia.'

She stood close up to him. 'Do you want to know what sensitivity is?' She raised her skirt, pulled down her pantyhose, let them fall to her feet. 'Here, feel.' She took his hand and placed it on her vagina.

'No, no.'

'Go on, put your hand in, your whole fist, feel the delicate membrane, those child's lips that a woman's poes has, that is sensitivity!'

She took his finger and forced it into her vagina, winced as his fingernail touched something soft. He pulled his hand away, walked out onto the stoep, leaned back and thrust his face into the rain until it ran saltily into his mouth. When he lowered his head, she was standing beside him, barefoot, sipping his abandoned beer.

'Shit, Lyd, that beer must be really flat.'

'I want to taste like a man, all sour.'

'If you want to drink beer, I'll pour you a fresh one.'

'I want it to be flat, like a man's breath.'

She sipped, pulled her mouth in distaste.

'Would you kill him for me?'

'Who?'

'Du Boise.'

'Lydia . . .'

'If you were a real man, you would have killed him on the spot, right there in the mall, splatter his brains against a window, watch his blood running all over the floor.'

'You're joking.'

'Joking? He took your woman, he fucked your wife, made you listen to him doing it. I became his property, even my screams were his instrument. Now, you're a man, you believe in honour and all that kind of kak . . .'

'Lydia, stop it.'

'You know what he called me as he was fucking me?'

'For fuck's sake, Lydia!'

'He called me a nice wild half-kaffir cunt, a lekker wilde Boesman poes.'

Silas grabbed Lydia by the arms and shook her. The glass of beer fell from her hands. She kissed him on the mouth, held him close to her, and sucked his tongue into her mouth the way she did when she was really passionate. She tasted of hops, of bitter fruit. She gasped, then leaned up against him, her head against his chest, weeping, making gentle dancing movements with her feet. He cradled her head, astonished by how much taller he was. He glanced down the slenderness of her back, saw the slow pool of blood spreading on the floor, saw his heavy shoes immersed in its dark glow, saw her feet dancing, delicate little steps, on the jagged edges of the broken beer glass.

2

After what seemed like the longest hour of his life, Silas got Lydia to hospital.

On the stoep, she had clung to him, weeping silently, ignoring his pleas to stop dancing, she was cutting herself up badly, she would bleed to death. In the end, he had to heave her up into his arms, as if she was still the slender, weightless young girl he had carried to his bed, long before they were married, a romantic gesture that made her giggle and spoiled their sex, that first time, in his room in the backyard of his mother's house (he remembered now, of all things, how the hastily drawn curtains had kept the sun out, the way an animal is kept at bay). He staggered to the settee, where he laid Lydia down, exhausted by the dead weight of her limp body. He listened to her weeping, softly now, saw the blood slowly seeping from her feet into the white linen slipover covers that he had chosen and that she had warned were impractical.

Silas had to rouse himself, dispelling the memory of that miraculous young love. He wiped his mouth with the back of his hand, tasted the sweetness of the young Lydia's skin, then realized with horror that there was blood on his hands and on his clothes. He called an ambulance, told the woman on the emergency line that it was urgent, his wife had cut herself, an accident, that it was serious, she was bleeding 'profusely'.

The woman sounded dubious. How had the accident happened, she wanted to know, did his wife have any other injuries, was there anyone else in the house, children, domestic workers, any neighbours nearby?

'Please, lady, we need an ambulance!' he shouted, forgetting how his politics had drummed out of him the use of words such as 'lady'. It struck him that the woman mistrusted him, that she thought this was just another case of domestic violence and was trying to gauge the danger to the victim, and that perhaps he did sound guilty, an abusive husband filled with the usual remorse. He begged her to send an ambulance, she could interrogate him afterwards.

He put the phone down, listened to Lydia's weeping change its tempo, becoming slower, hoarser, saw the glaze in her eyes and was afraid she was going into shock. He went in search of something he could use to staunch the bleeding, bed sheets that he could rip up and wrap around her feet, towels, one of his crisp blue shirts perhaps. He realized vaguely that this was a desperate, mumbo-jumbo solution, subconsciously inspired by something he had seen on TV or in a movie, that she urgently needed real medical attention. Surprised at how very seldom he went into the linen room, a remnant of the house's once opulent intentions, he took two clean towels from a rack and swaddled Lydia's feet in their comforting thickness.

He watched the towels darken, a slow crimson seepage, and was filled with silent panic that he felt he dare not betray, not to Lydia the victim, not again. He could not – once more – scream and weep louder than her, just as he had done nearly twenty years ago, when his outburst of rage and futile horror had earned him a dismissive blow to the head from one of the cops. But once again he heard those deep, low groans, Lydia in agony, Lydia wanting to die, and he would not let her die here, in their home, before his eyes. He sat down on the settee, raised her feet onto his lap, and used his cellphone to call Alec. Brother-in-law, friend, cool, laconic Alec who never seemed to hurry but was so quick at everything.

'Lydia's had an accident, we need to get her to a hospital, the fucken ambulance is taking for ever!'

In his mind, the circumstances of Lydia's injuries were already being mitigated. Her wounds were not self-inflicted, not provoked by his obsession with remembering the past, it had been a freak accident, it had happened because she wanted to drink beer and hated the taste,

19

and he had criticized her for drinking flat beer. Ja, a small, trivial thing like that, and the glass went flying, fell, flung, who knows? You know how she is, bra, how they all are, the Oliphant women, with their anger, slow in coming but fucken volcanic when it's there, broer. Shit, you know what an Oliphant temper is like!

He addressed Alec mentally, not so much to rehearse an excuse, but to debate with himself how the whole thing had happened. The arrival of Alec and Gracie saved him from creating a lie in his mind. It had taken only fifteen minutes for them to get from a township west of Johannesburg to Silas and Lydia's home on the other side of the city.

'Drove like fuck!' Alec said, explaining the near miracle of making it there so quickly.

Jackson and Mam Agnes were on their way as well. Mikey was driving them, Gracie said, somewhat surprised that Mikey could drive and that Jackson allowed anyone else behind the wheel of 'his baby', that monstrous old car.

Christ, they always do this, mobilize the whole family at the first distress call from any one of them, Silas thought. They were hurrying indoors, and Gracie was still calm, politely solicitous, after all, what could have gone wrong that an Oliphant couldn't handle?

In the living-room light she saw that Silas was covered in blood, saw the congealed trail across the carpet, saw Lydia with her feet propped up on pillows, the steady ooze of blood staining the settee. Her eyes swept the room, searching for something hidden, some explanation – no matter how sinister – other than, 'Silas did this to Lydia.'

Gracie's shock immobilized all three of them, until she herself shouted at them to move.

Alec and Silas carried Lydia to the car, Alec's own grand old Mercedes-Benz that he would not sell, stretched her out on the back seat, a pillow propped up against the door to support her back, while Silas held her swaddled feet on his lap.

'Not to the clinic where she works,' Silas had the presence of mind to say. Too many questions, too much delay.

'Go to the Park Lane,' Gracie said. She knew her way around the city, in spite of not being native to it, knew where the private clinics were, where the 24-hour casualty would provide instant attention, at a price.

'How long ago did you call the ambulance?' Gracie asked.

'Twenty, twenty-five minutes ago,' he answered.

'Damn bastards – go left here –' she said.

In between giving Alec precise directions, she cursed the city and its forbidding unfriendliness, cursed the ambulances that never arrived, the police who weren't around when needed, the country that was going to hell, a government that didn't care, not sparing a thought for Silas's anguish, for the fact that he had helped to bring that government to power and now worked for it. She heard Lydia's weeping give way to a low, animal moan, saw her sister's eyes shut against a pain she could almost feel herself, unaware that this physical pain was Lydia's way of displacing a much deeper, unfathomable agony.

Alec got them to the entrance of the clinic's trauma ward within seven minutes.

'Seven fucking minutes flat,' he would say afterwards.

Lydia was to remain in hospital for three weeks. For the first few days, her plastered feet were raised in traction to prevent blood clots from forming, and having her limbs suspended in the air like that made her look gravely ill. The doctor said she was fortunate, she had not severed any arteries, but she had cut into one of the tendons, and this would require some attention. Mercifully, her blood loss was not that bad, given the severity of the cuts. Good that she had been brought in so quickly.

'But, God, she did need some stitching, over a hundred, you want to count them?' the doctor asked jocularly, addressing himself to Mikey, whom he thought capable of responding with quick empathy. In the circle of gloomy adults, the young man seemed most likely to bring some levity, make the poor suffering woman smile a bit.

Mikey feared that the doctor's attempt to cheer Lydia up would have the opposite effect, drawing them all into that ritual of mawkish intimacy that he had seen them sink into, especially Mam Agnes and Aunt Gracie. They were always looking for opportunities to 'let loose the waterworks', he'd heard Jackson say once. Give them a tragedy and they'll give you the tears.

'That's my father's job,' Mikey said, in answer to the doctor's question. 'In any case, I'm not sure when last my mom washed her feet.'

Lydia offered a muttered protest, in spite of her pain, Silas the merest smile. Both knew immediately that Mikey's offhand humour was an attempt to resist being drawn into any display of emotion, he had never been a 'hugger and kisser', even as a child. He had done what was expected of him when he arrived along with Jackson and Mam Agnes, he had embraced his mother and squeezed his father's shoulder. Now he stood up against the wall, so very obviously apart from the rest.

Mam Agnes, momentarily bewildered by this remote, aloof Mikey, tried to draw him back into their tearful fold. She wiped away a tear, and said, 'Get away you!' in light-hearted defence of her daughter. Gracie blew her nose, while Alec snickered in a mockingly effeminate way that Gracie vowed silently to make him pay for later.

'You're right, young man,' the doctor said, 'leave the details to the adults, you just enjoy your mom while she's a captive. She's a tough woman, she'll be all right.' And turning to Silas, he added, 'You know what, Mr Ali? Your wife has got such lovely feet, you should get a plastic surgeon in here to look at them, once the swelling's gone down and the stitches are out. Would be a shame to leave her all scarred.'

Lydia blushed, shutting her eyes to hide her embarrassment and to ward off a sharp pain, which came now in spasms, despite the constant doses of painkillers she was being given.

'Fokken busybody,' Gracie said under her breath, when the doctor had gone.

Mam Agnes straightened Lydia's pillow, while Gracie fussed with the flowers at the bedside, trying to fit the huge bouquet that Alec had bought – against her advice – into the small vase he'd found in the shop on the ground floor.

Each night, her family gathered around her, Silas and Mikey, Jackson and Mam Agnes, Gracie and Alec, all trying to maintain the cheerful tone that the doctor had set the night she was brought in. Mikey kissed his mother on the cheek and then took up his usual, sentinel position against the wall. One night, Gracie urged him to sit on the bed by his mother. 'What else are children good for but to comfort their parents?' He sat down next to Lydia, and impulsively she drew him close to her. He seemed to yield, relaxing his stiff body, resting his head on her chest with a tenderness that belied his tall, gruff appearance. With Lydia's feet still raised, they resembled an oddly chaste couple, awkwardly trying to be close.

Silas stood about uncomfortably, excluded by this uncharacteristic display of affection between mother and son. Soon his discomfort infected the others. Gracie, for want of something to say, repeated what the doctor had said, how lucky Lydia was. Alec still shook his head at the miracle of it all.

'All this damage was done by one of those glasses we gave you last Christmas?' he asked.

Silas nodded.

'Shit, it's that Swazi stuff, the walls are so thick they break them to use as weapons,' Alec said.

Gracie feared that her husband would launch into a long and inappropriate technical explanation of the Swazi glass-making industry

23

and cut him short with one of her glances. He grinned and kept quiet, stifling his impulse to say to Silas, 'Christ, a real cutting Oliphant look. I bet Lydia still snys you with them, hey?' But he had said this so often before, that everyone knew what he meant by the way he was grinning. The Oliphant women, Mam Agnes, Lydia, Gracie, and even Martha, who had married a Canadian and lived in fucken cold Toronto, had eyes so sharp they could slice the skin off your face. No one seemed to mention Mireille, the youngest daughter, any more. A silence had enclosed her name and her being, ever since she went to live with Martha, and even guileless Alec knew better than to ask why Mireille had vanished, in word and body, from the close world of the Oliphant family here at home.

As if prompted by Alec's unspoken curiosity about the accident – 'What really happened? Why don't you tell us?' his attitude implied – Silas said that it had been a freak accident. Lydia, freeing herself from Mikey's limp embrace for a moment, nodded her head in agreement. They both looked evasive, as if they had rehearsed their responses. They were avoiding something, trying to deny – even to themselves – that something dreadful had happened, something capable of precipitating *such* an accident. Mikey burrowed his head deep into his mother's breasts, trying to hide the scornful look on his face.

'Age nee,' Mam Agnes said, determined to change the subject. If Lydia and Silas wanted to discuss the accident, let them do so of their own free will. She gently chided Mikey, 'What is this, going on like a baby? You are eighteen now, nearly nineteen, in fact, and you still want to suck Mama's titties, hey Mikey?'

Mikey had always been friendly and respectful towards his grandparents, willingly doing chores and carrying out errands, but never close enough to exchange the kind of banter that Mam Agnes was inviting now. But he sensed that she wanted to change the subject, and that she wanted to rescue Silas from the silence he had fallen into.

'As long as they're not yours, Ouma, I don't like long-life milk,' he answered.

The brittle humour of their nightly visits was restored. His cheeky response evoked good-natured laughter from them all. Only Gracie gave Silas and Lydia quick, searching looks, wiping the involuntary smile from Silas's face and returning him to his sombre mood. Then Jackson said it was time to go, and kissed his daughter on her cheeks. This was the signal for the others to say goodbye, and leave Silas and Lydia alone for a while. Mikey slipped off the bed in the slanted, gangling manner of his youth, embarrassed in turn now that his parents wanted a few moments on their own.

Perhaps he thought they were too old to exchange private endearments, or feared there was something sinister in their closeness now, an avoidance of intimacy rather than its fostering. He sensed it in his mother, the way she held her body in the bed, warding off his father even as they embraced. At home, in the silent house, he felt it in his father as well, the fervour with which he tackled the household duties that Lydia's absence had thrust on him, cooking and cleaning until he was exhausted. And then sitting in his study until long after midnight, as if trying to avoid having to go to bed. It seemed that Silas did not like being alone in Lydia's bedroom or her bed.

Mikey stood outside the private ward with the rest of the family, listened to them saying yet again how lucky Lydia was that she and Silas had medical aid and could afford a private ward in a private clinic. She was being spared the horrors of a government hospital like the Helen Joseph. Jackson and Mam Agnes recounted their own travails in an even worse institution, the old Coronation Hospital, where you went in half-well and came out half-dead. At least now that apartheid was gone, black and white suffered equally.

Mikey smiled as if he had experienced and therefore understood the justice in all of this, how the awfulness of being a patient in a

25

government hospital united black and white. You smile too much, his grandfather Jackson had once said. When his father emerged from the glassed-in ward, Mikey knew that whatever it was that separated his parents – a shadow, a word, a name – was still there, and that it would be there the next night when they all returned to visit, and that sooner or later they would no longer be able to hide it from the others.

3

Dawn. Mikey lies in bed and observes the sun, still pale, feeble almost, on the dark rows of books that line the shelves in his room. 'And you are still so young!' Vinu had said, when she saw his books. He remembers the way she rolled her eyes, mocking, declaring herself 'forever chaste', saved from 'concubinage' because the Lord Vishnu was too busy with his books to 'truly' see her beauty. She had come, seeking not sex, but refuge from the carnage of her parents' broken marriage. Her language was a means of escape, its suggestiveness entirely rhetorical. But she did say that she smelled history in this house, too much history, and then promptly fell asleep.

Mikey thinks back to the debate they had in class a few days ago. 'Homer's *Odyssey* is the basis of the modern novel,' Miss Anderson had said, looking expectantly at her students. 'Well, *I* think so,' she'd added, when she saw the indifferent expressions on their faces. Lecturing in English literature is a sad profession, it seems, a refuge for failed writers. Miss Anderson once tried her hand at it, gave up, bored with the book she had 'lived with' for ten years. She has started writing again, in secret now, it is said, no longer discusses her 'work in progress' with friends. Now she confronts her class with the un-developed ghosts of last night's writing. Wasted on these spoiled, post-apartheid hedonists. She resorts to the desperate intensity of a writer still struggling with her words. Rumours of a tragic love affair with someone who is now in a powerful position. He – a Cabinet minister, it is said – divested himself of Miss Anderson, the 'white bit on the side', exponentially decreasing his involvement with her as he rose in the ranks. The inspiration of her creative rebirth is that she was 'gotten rid of', love abandoned for power.

Does some of her research among male students, and takes comfort there. Mikey can't see why they find her attractive. Thin, gaunt-faced, her shoulder-length hair flecked with grey. Perhaps some new vein of excitement has been opened, the promise of unleashed passion, it glows in her, the tender skin of love gone wrong.

He does not particularly dislike Julia Anderson, Mikey decides; well, perhaps only when she assumes the mantle of literary prophet and starts speaking in well-turned phrases. It makes her seem uglier than she really is, her emaciated features gathered into a fierce scowl. Who can kiss such thin lips? And she always picks on him, uses him as the sounding board for the answers she hopes to get from others. His diffidence, his obvious boredom, provokes her.

'Well, Mr Ali, what do you think of Homer's *Odyssey*?'

'It is clichéd,' Mikey answers.

Give her the poker-faced treatment, sometimes forces her to direct her venom elsewhere.

'Really?'

'Really.'

'Example?'

'"The pink fingers of dawn." Imagine the sun rising like that?'

'A metaphor for its time.'

'Clichéd,' he insists.

'No, worse,' Karabo Nkosi says. 'Eurocentric.'

'For God's sake! It's set in Europe. It's about Europe!'

'But the Greeks are darkies like us,' Vinu says.

'Clichéd, that's all,' Mikey says.

'Think about it, Miss Anderson: the pink fingers of dawn over Sandton!' Karabo says.

'Is that where you live?' Miss Anderson asks, looking at Mikey.

'Who me? No, I live in Berea.'

'The township in the suburbs, Miss Anderson, that's where Mikey lives.'

'Still, Homer Eurocentric and clichéd?'

'Dawn would have to be a white woman, then, with pink fingers, is that not Eurocentric?' Karabo asks triumphantly. He has Miss Anderson's measure, he thinks.

'Do *you* have pink fingers, Miss Anderson, can we see your fingers?' Vinu asks, her fervour false. Surely Miss Anderson must see the mockery of it all.

Vinu won the debate, no doubt about that. *We bring down the false gods/ All the gods/ Until there are none . . .* Mocking verse from the struggle era. Anonymous. Mikey turns onto his stomach, listens to his father in the bathroom, cleaning his teeth, blowing his nose. Will I harrumph-harrumph like that when I get to be his age?

He thinks now about his mother, her legs up in traction, the loveliness of a trapped animal. He has never thought of his mother as lovely before. Well, nothing wrong with that. Growing up means being able to recognize things such as the loveliness of people. Her family calls him 'ougat' because he recognizes the loveliness of people. But his mother's distance bothers him, the feeling that she is detached from her surroundings, that she is burrowing into her pain for comfort. Even he feels that this observation is facetious, that grown-up tendency to bury uncomfortable thoughts in 'constructions'. The Julia Anderson syndrome.

But he does not know his mother any more, he thinks.

'I do not know my mother,' he says out loud.

There is a sudden silence in the bathroom. Is his father listening, Odysseus eavesdropping, suspicious of Telemachus's loud musing about Penelope? Intellectual shit. Father is downstairs staring soulfully into his bowl of cereal. How senile does a man become when he is close to fifty, how sentimental, how fuzzy-headed and weak-hearted?

And my mother, what does she think about, does she think at all?

Of course she does. He has seen her sitting at her 'bureau', as she calls it, in the alcove between her bedroom and the door to the balcony, a haven created by an architectural miscalculation, writing in that diary of hers. Bent over, absorbed, an intensity that lasts for hours. What? A novel? A historical record of the lives they have lived? She and her husband, minor actors in the blockbuster movie *Liberation*! Bewildered rats, trembling with excitement, the pink-fingered dawn of history before them.

No, not a novel, hers is not the posture of a fictionalizer, never any amusement in her face, no smile of pleasure at an unexpected turn of phrase, no, something much drier, the details of their struggle, tales of petty heroism. Or is it something deeper, a delving into herself?

The silence in the bathroom endures, a quality of absence. His father is downstairs, fidgeting with the clock in the kitchen, always losing time, a genetic fault. Timepieces are like human beings, they have built-in flaws. Silas is waiting to hear if Mikey is up. There is no need for him to rise so early, varsity in recess, Miss Anderson on a beach somewhere, masturbating to the rhythm of Homeric hexameters.

The front door slams, the car starts, pulls out of the driveway with a loud, wet squelch. So it is raining out there. Silas wants Mikey to know that time is moving on, his oblique way of remonstrating with his son for his indolence. My father the stoic, can't tell you a thing when you look him in the eyes. And yet, there he is, dealing with the country's problems, trying to reconcile the irreconcilable.

Mikey rises, places Oupapa Ali's glowing fragment of Kaaba stone, which he uses to illuminate the desolation of urban nights, back in its soft receptacle of clean underpants, and pads to the bathroom. He urinates, watches the steamed froth with some satisfaction, shivers with delight at the end. How pleasing the simplest of our acts of gratification. But it is too cold to go about the house naked. Nature always getting in the way. He returns to his room, slips on a T-shirt and jeans over his chilled body, imagines the smell of coffee in the kitchen. The only indulgence he has detected in his father.

The sun breaks through the strangely sullen sky – this is a city of fierce thunderstorms, quick and transient, not used to this lingering greyness – and fills Lydia's alcove with a sudden brightness. Mikey pauses at her desk. A few unopened bills (does she owe people money independently of Silas?), a letter with a Canadian postmark. Probably Aunt Martha. Wonder how Mireille is? He tries the drawers, conscious of his own guileful posture, the sideways manner in which he pulls at each handle in turn. They are locked. His sense of intrigue grows.

Mikey rummages about in the old tool cabinet – an array of once immaculately clean screwdrivers, hammers, wrenches, grown rusty and blunt with disuse, testimony to Silas's changed station in life – and finds the bunch of keys. Once it must have been a simple collection of duplicates, but over the years, Silas has added stray keys picked up in the street, or abandoned by friends and colleagues when they moved homes and offices. Mikey remembers seeing Silas take the key from a cupboard in a second-hand furniture shop and slip it into his pocket, his face lit up with a shoplifter's secret enjoyment. Now the bunch resembles the jangling credentials of an ancient turnkey, the guardian of some vast, medieval dungeon. A marvellously practical habit, revealing of yet another obsessive side to Silas's bland character?

Mikey quickly finds a key that fits Lydia's desk drawers. Indeed, she had locked them as an expression of her privacy, rather than in any real hope of keeping out an intruder. He sifts idly through the memorabilia of a rather ordinary life. Entrance tickets to the Johannesburg Zoo (marked 'Non-White Day'), an invitation to Gracie and Alec's wedding, cancelled cheques, abandoned invoices for goods purchased. A solitary dried carnation, preserved, together with a florist's card simply inscribed 'Love', in one of those zipped polythene kitchen bags, provided a romantic touch. But whose love, whose *errant* love is being commemorated? Certainly not Silas's. His businesslike approach demands grand gestures, huge and overflowing bouquets, their imposing beauty transient and superficial. What is he like in the throes of passion, Mikey wonders. Then dismisses the image of bulging eyes and limbs clumsily entwined. He knows that Silas has spindly legs and that Lydia has hair under her arms, the sprouting of which she struggles to control.

Lydia's diary lies hidden, the only real attempt to conceal anything, underneath a sheaf of ancient legal documents: insurance policies, birth certificates, expired vehicle registration papers, the deed of sale to a house disposed of years ago, matters that are usually the preserve of husbands. Now Mikey begins to comprehend the extent to which Lydia, by default, manages the family's affairs. Anyway, collecting obsolete documents, in neat piles but without any obvious order or purpose, is the obsessive habit of people besieged by the constant fear of poverty. Do the rich preserve their past as assiduously?

With Lydia's diary on his simple breakfast tray, alongside the heated-up remnants of the coffee that Silas had made, and cereal soaked in orange juice (he cannot abide the taste of milk so early in the day), Mikey sits now in the rain-drenched garden at the back of the house. It is no more than a quadrangle of grass bordered by dying flower beds – don't plant exotics, not just before winter, he had heard Lydia tell Silas in a rare moment of domestic engagement (even if it was only to disagree). Mikey expects to glance, very leisurely, through the minor traumas of a life lived as best she could. Given Lydia's beginnings, parents like Mam Agnes and Jackson, a husband like Silas, what could his mother have recorded in her diary but the routine passage of life, births, deaths, petty cruelties and vain hopes? Nothing momentous in here, he tells himself, trying to dismiss the feeling of guilt that comes more at the remembrance of how easy it was to invade her privacy, than at the prospect of trespassing onto the secret domain of her life.

Yet, when he cannot bring himself to read the first entry, it is not a sense of decency that deters him, for 'every enquiring mind has the right to know even the forbidden', he rationalizes, but an unexpected foreboding. This diary has something to do with Lydia's accident, her subsequent hospitalization, with the name Du Boise that he has heard his parents whisper tensely between them in the hospital room.

A ghost from the past, a mythical phantom embedded in the 'historical memory' of those who were active in the struggle. Historical memory. It is a term that seems illogical and contradictory to Mikey; after all, history *is* memory. Yet, it has an air of inevitability, solemn and compelling, especially when uttered by Silas and his comrades. It explains everything, the violence periodically sweeping the country, the crime rate, even the strange 'upsurge' of brutality against women. It is as if history has a remembering process of its own, one that gives life to its imaginary monsters. Now his mother and father have received a visitation from that dark past, some terrible memory brought to life.

But Mikey's reluctance is also rooted in a fear of his own: he knows that Lydia would have written about the time she found him 'playing Gandhi' with Mireille in his room, she would have described the relationship between them as 'untoward'. Or perhaps this is not the muted kind of word that she would use, perhaps she uses the language of dread when she thinks back, still, to the moment she opened the door to his room and found her son and her sister, Mikey and Mireille, lying side by side, naked, only their hands touching, this somewhat chaste gesture in itself evidence of some dissolute ritual, the aftermath of a brutal . . . here she will hesitate, not say the word 'sex' in her mind, not acknowledge, the carnality of her incomplete thought, and immediately immerse its meaning in a cauldron of shapeless evasions.

Mikey remembers overhearing his parents talking, after Silas had questioned Lydia about the grave, tear-filled conferences she was holding with her family, Gracie, Mam Agnes and Jackson. At first, Lydia's response had been uncharacteristically vulgar; then, as if reminded of an injunction (Gracie, Mam Agnes, Jackson?) not to lose her dignity, she had lapsed into a matronly logic:

'It is obvious that Mireille has been sleeping with Mikey.'

'How can you tell?'

'You can see it in her eyes!'

'And him?'

'God, Silas, she is older, she is the woman, she should know better.'

Lydia's diary lies on Mikey's lap, forgotten for the moment. He remembers the day they asked them, all the 'young ones', what they wanted to be when they grew up. That's how it began, the game he started playing with Mireille. Christmas Day, Mam Agnes and Jackson's house in Soweto. When? Let's see, nearly five years ago? December 1993. 'The last undemocratic Christmas,' Silas had said, and everybody smiled, even though they didn't know what the hell he was talking about. It sounded so clever, Alec said afterwards, gossiping with his wife Gracie.

Around the lunch table, the turkey served, Mikey struggling with the rich pudding that the adults dug into with their forks, searching for the 'magical' old British tickey concealed in someone's helping, a portent of good fortune for whoever found it. They were bored, the grown-ups, or they had had too much to drink, or the prospect of life under the new democracy that Silas had heralded filled them with sudden and inspired hope. Anyway, they decided to interrogate the future.

'Tell us what you want to be when you grow up?' Mam Jackson asked her daughter Mireille, blind, as mothers often are, to the fact that her daughter had already 'grown up', that she had a gleam in her eyes, that the mystery of life was unfolding, a flower not only to behold, but to devour. Mireille, Mam Agnes and Jackson's 'baby', Lydia's youngest sister, Mikey's aunt, adored simply because she was the youngest, and beautiful simply because she was adored.

'A lawyer, like Silas and Alec,' Mireille said. Mikey knew she was mocking them, but they seemed not to notice, continuing to smile sleepily, their faces happy and sated; after all, it was Christmas, a time for getting drunk and forgetting.

Auntie Gracie and Uncle Alec's twins, Gregory and Devin, were next. No more than thirteen. 'Bankers,' they answered, no hesitation, no doubts. A vanity learned from their father. Just as they too would learn to fuck their wives without bothering to remove their socks. Aunt Gracie, in full swing now that her own children had answered so sweetly, pressed on: 'And you, Mikey?'

'A writer,' Mikey had answered, 'I'm going to be a writer.'

A simple, truthful answer, he didn't have to think about it for a second.

He remembers the silence, his mother's smile, the cloud that passed across his father's face, the way Uncle Alec laughed, Grandpa Jackson saying something about it being better to become a 'legal hijacker' like Silas and Alec.

Mireille, slightly drunk from the wine and the heat – adults and their ill-timed sense of indulgence: 'Let them each have a glass of wine' – took the wrong cue from Mikey. She giggled and said that if he could be a writer, she could change her mind. She wanted to be an actress. She let out the high-pitched, false laugh that she used to make fun of people who took themselves too seriously. Afterwards, when the adults retired to the garden, to play cards, doze off, get their psyches hyped up for the New Year, Mireille was left alone with Mikey, all surly and hurt by the way he had been mocked.

'Let's go to my room,' she whispered.

They often did that, took refuge in her room, their adolescence awkward and out of place with both the adults and the younger kids.

'What's the matter with you?' Mireille asked, when Mikey lay down on her bed, still morose and disconsolate.

'Nothing,' he answered.

She sat down next to him. 'You meant that, about being a writer, didn't you?'

'Yes,' he confessed.

'I'm sorry, we can be so insensitive,' she said, practising for when she had truly grown up. She started to undress, to take off the hot, satin-and-ribbon dress she had worn to church and had had to continue wearing throughout lunch because of the 'occasion'. Watching her undress was nothing new for him. They had grown up together, knew each other's bodies, each other's smells. He could tell her farts from her fanny-smells. Their intimacies were innocent and un-restrained.

Then he started telling her about this book he had read on the life of Mahatma Gandhi. Perhaps to show off, to demonstrate that he was not a child, even though he was only fourteen then, or to escape from the sudden consciousness that she was in her underwear, from the heat in the room, from the smell of her sweat. Anyway, in this book, he told her, the author describes how Gandhi put himself to the test by going to bed with young girls, soft naked girls (like you, Mireille, he may have wanted to say but cannot now remember).

'Do you think he was really testing himself or just being kinky?' Mireille had asked, making conversation.

35

'He was an ascetic, and for the ascetic there is no greater triumph than resisting the irresistible,' Mikey had said – or something equally facetious.

That was when Mireille gave him a strange look, standing there in her underwear, smiling her godless smile.

'Do you want to play Gandhi with me?' she asked.

Did he say yes with his eyes, did he nod, or did he stare at her with the wonderment of a child?

'Well, get undressed,' she said in her commanding tone, and slipped off her underwear. She lay down next to him, took his hand in hers. 'Is this how Gandhi did it?'

Mikey was no longer sure whether Gandhi actually asked the girls to undress or whether he touched them, even if only to hold their hands. But *he* wanted to test the ascetic side of himself. He breathed in Mireille's perfume, her sweat, imagined with his closed eyes the pulsation in her vagina, where her other hand rested. She giggled, fought to suppress her laughter. She did all she could not to laugh at the rigid way he held himself, his one free fist clenched, trying to ignore his erect penis, those vivid veins, the tremulous enormity. She laughed inwardly, he felt the tremors of her enjoyment, sensed that she was not mocking his Gandhi-like heroism. He had to detach his mind from the throbbing beast between his legs. She was celebrating that struggle.

Heaven knows, it took all his will-power, all the summoned-up tyranny of mind over body, not to rise up and plunge his tongue into Mireille's beautiful mouth, his penis into the mound exposed between her flung-back legs. He knows now that she would not have resisted, that they might well have satisfied an unspoken lust, quickly. And then, ashamed of their 'incest', realizing the sinfulness of this word, instilled in them by the family, the Church, their upbringing, the whole thing would have ended. They would never have done it again, or spoken about it, or even thought about it, for that matter.

36

Instead, they resisted. Maybe that's why they continued to 'play Gandhi' many times after that day. At first, Mireille was irritated by the 'mental masturbation' she said he was asking her to participate in.

'Either we fuck or we don't, but let's get it over with!'

But he convinced her that 'fucking' would destroy the true beauty of their relationship, that it was better to lie side by side, naked, bathed in sweat, moist all over, their love centred in their minds (yes, he had started using expressions like that, learned from books, from discussions with that solitary voice in his head he thought of as God – yes, blame Him too!). After a while, Mireille took part because, as she put it, this 'mind sex' really 'wound her up' and made sleeping with her boyfriend something unbelievable. Soon she went further, started craving those afternoons in the heat – his house mostly, there was never anyone home – as a substitute for fucking with her boyfriend. This wonderful 'nothingness', she said, gave her a sense of satisfaction greater than any penis. Fucking, she said, was like eating a rich meal, it made her feel bloated and nauseous. They often fell asleep, side by side, their faces empty, their minds serene.

One day, when he woke up, he sensed that someone had been watching them. A pair of eyes – adult eyes – had observed them for a few fleeting moments, transforming a scene of beauty into something vile and shameful.

The retribution was swift. Mireille was sent away, banished to Canada. When he first heard Aunt Gracie pronounce that word, slowly, painfully, Ca-na-da, he knew that it was truly cold there, as befitted a place of exile.

He grieved. He had lost Mireille and was alienated from his mother. She gave him fearful looks, constantly fighting back her tears. Soon, however, the whispering came to an end, a new and irresistible tension filled their lives, a force outside of their private lives, a fleeting moment when history became utterly important, inescapable, and compelling. Nelson Mandela became President, and the word 'freedom' took on an almost childlike meaning, so magical was its effect. Mikey heard Mam Agnes say, 'We're free,' when Mandela stood up to take the oath, her voice hoarse, filled with tenderness. Then, aware that Mikey was watching, she quickly reverted to her old, disbelieving self, her joy pressed like a dead flower between her unsmiling lips.

Still, Mikey could not believe the euphoria that swept through his family, cool Uncle Alec and laconic Grandpa Jackson, cold Gracie and an increasingly self-contained Lydia, their usual, crusty suspicion of life's good intentions flung aside like an unfashionable, worn-out coat. Until that enchanting April passed, and autumn came and the winter suddenly, and only Silas was left to walk about with a new sense of pride.

It helped Mikey too. He forgot about Mireille, discarded her along with the other adolescent obsessions, as the smell of her perspiration (how different it had seemed once – like incense) faded into the myriad of sexual odours he was encountering. That fragile spring, that cruel month of flowering liberty, allowed his mother to forgive him what she saw as his trespass, innocent and 'led-into', but a trespass nevertheless.

Mikey stretches his legs, wakes up, startled by the brightness of the sun. He had fallen asleep, allowing Lydia's diary to slip from his lap. He bends down, retrieves it and dusts it off. A sticky white pollen adheres to the cover. He looks up. The sun has penetrated the lush shade provided by the garden's solitary tree. It is a fig tree, dark and gnarled, and probably dying of old age, he thinks. He has seen it bud, a glory of delicate green leaves in early spring, but barren otherwise. It has not borne fruit, not since they moved in here, anyway. Now he is astonished by the unseasonal abundance of figs, large and coarsely veined, high up in its boughs, which are bent with their weight. Most are already overripe and have burst open, oozing a white sap on which ants have feasted and fruit flies died greed-filled deaths.

He stands on the stone table and selects a large fig, bites into the skin, then opens it with his fingers. He thinks of a woman's sex, ancient and eternal, no young girl would have such gritty sweetness. Was this not perhaps the fruit that got Adam and Eve thrown out of Eden? Who would want to give up an unblemished state of immortality for the insipid apple?

He goes inside, stands in the cool well of the house, contemplates the shadows cutting gloomy gashes across the polished wooden floors, remembers something else. People dancing, the old-fashioned way, one-two-three together, rapid swirl, backwards, forwards. The man leads, one hand resting authoritatively on his partner's waist, the other holding hers aloft. Subtle signals from his fingers dictate their movement, back, forward, sidestep, whirl.

The slip-slip of shoes on polished wood, the rustle of cloth, silk on a slender thigh. Mireille dancing with her father Jackson, with Uncle Alec, Silas, someone from Silas's office, the most danceable young woman at the party. One of Silas's rather hasty affairs, the guest list rapidly compiled, those most likely to be available, invited. Mireille tilts her head as she dances, her neck arched, its nakedness on offer, but she is held in this swan's pose by the music and not her dancing partner, her innate sense of rhythm slowly usurping his leadership.

The music ends, another piece starts, slower, an opportunity for bodies to be held much closer. Smilingly, Mireille walks towards Mikey, leads him onto the space cleared for dancing, takes him, slowly, swirling around in an adult world. He submits instinctively to her pace, until their movements flow with natural grace. The grown-ups slump down in chairs, sip drinks, observe the way the young couple hold each other, an easy, unforced embrace, and the watchers are suddenly conscious of their adult awkwardness when they dance. They watch Mikey and Mireille, nephew and aunt, friends, siblings almost, admire the shining innocence of their sensuality.

Mikey knows that this very closeness sets them apart, he dare not touch her neck, her gentle pulse, knows that he has to be content with their chaste game, played in secret, Gandhi putting himself to the test of soft flesh. Did Gandhi ever dance, ever inhale a woman's warm smell, did he ever desire her simply because of her womanly movement?

Impulsively, he decides now to call Mireille, even though he calculates, by counting backwards on his fingers, that it is close to six a.m. in Toronto, still dark, he may disturb Aunt Martha's ordered household. But Mireille has her own telephone in her room, he has seen the number in Lydia's telephone book, different from Martha's. North American obsession with privacy, or Martha older and wiser than Lydia, not wanting to know who Mireille speaks to?

He wonders what Mireille will sound like after all this time, still filled with sleep, secretive and mysterious, someone lying next to her, perhaps? No, Martha's generosity will not go that far, even though Mireille must be nearly twenty-one years old. The puritan gene inherited from Mam Agnes. Oupa Jackson has a certain gleam in his eye. Wayward when given the opportunity, Mikey thinks.

He stares at the ceiling, thinks of all the flaws he has deciphered in its ornate patterns. He has switched on the CD player, exploits its capacity to load half a dozen discs at once, idly switches from one to the other, back and forth at random, filling the room with a babel of music. Segovia sonatas, the hypnotic roughness of township kwaito, Samuel Barber's siren-like sadness, all disconsolately woven together. Finally, he flings the remote-control device across the room, allows the music to follow its own, more predictable sequence.

Feverishly, he writes in his head a sarcastic analysis of the prose translation of Homer's *Odyssey* that Miss Anderson has set as 'required reading'. He visualizes his words, their icy structure and sneering tone. Later he will type it up, word for word, copying from his mental text.

Still his anger at Mireille's response to his call will not soften. At first, her voice was as he had anticipated: innocent and unguarded, the phone answered precisely at the fourth ring, as if responding to a pre-arranged signal.

'Mikey, Mikey? Is that you?'

Then she had asked, 'What time is it?' and answered herself, 'My God, it's five fifty,' her tone harsher, the time read to the precise minute, a bedside clock dimly raised.

Her initial, sleepy response had reminded him how gentle and childlike she was when just awoken, and he wanted to explore her surroundings, establish his disembodied place in them, imagine himself there in her room, standing at her bedside, feel her cloistered heat.

'Describe your room, Mireille, tell me what you see . . .'

'It's not even six o'clock, everyone's still asleep.'

His taken-aback silence, the sound of him fumbling with the phone, evoked a coarse, whispered response.

'Mikey, let me call you back later.'

'Okay.'

'No, wait.' She had decided there was no better time to say what was on her mind. 'Perhaps we should not call each other, or write, or send e-mails. I would like you not to contact me, okay? Mikey, are you there?'

'Why?'

'Why? Well, perhaps what we did was wrong, we were so young, we didn't know what we were doing . . .'

'It was innocent.'

'Your mother doesn't think so . . . they made my life hell. I don't want to go through all that again . . . Mikey?'

He had quietly replaced the receiver and retreated to his bed, a slow, corrosive lassitude spreading through his limbs.

41

Mireille's betrayal – 'What we did was wrong' – is so easily explained, she has grown up, she has acquired an adult's sense of shame, the compulsion to confess, even if falsely, in order to obtain absolution. Is this how her memory will adapt, accommodating new realities, the need to get on with her life, disregarding the injustice of having been sent into exile by her own family, seeking no retribution? A man in her life perhaps, someone she loves, a clean-faced Canadian who has no need to know her 'shame', real or perceived. She has entered into a pact of silence with Martha and Lydia, made an accommodation with her past.

Is that how he, too, will grow old? Will he 'come of age' by creating memories that fade into loving forgetfulness, like old emulsion photographs, blurring, softened with time? This process started a long time ago, he acknowledges. He also has an inventory of things kept in mind, an index of important things to remember.

Now he tells the hour by the erratic slamming of doors, the radio being switched on, the ritual news-hour voices booming through the house. Silas is home, filling his soul with the numbing incantation of views, opinions, the dull beauty of reported life.

4

Mikey told his father that he didn't feel well – a headache, and his stomach was running – and so he was not going to the hospital, would Dad mind, would he explain to Mom? He said all of this in one quick breath, as he climbed the stairs to his bedroom, not giving his father a chance to question him, to feel his forehead the way fathers do – what can you learn by putting your palm to someone's head? – to offer medication, or simply to search his face for some signal – 'Tell me what's really bothering you.' The ridiculous – telepathic – things that fathers expect of their children, more so even than mothers, who are supposed to be clairvoyant when it comes to their offspring.

Silas stood at the bottom of the stairs, aware that when he went to visit Lydia, he would take with him the burden of Mikey's absence, that any attempt to justify his not being there – he was not feeling well, these things happen, you know everyone feels out of sorts now and then – would be transformed into something mysterious, even sinister.

'This is not like Mikey, what's the matter with him, *really* the matter?' her eyes would ask.

Constrained by her family's presence – hovering like members of an animal pride, alert to the needs of a wounded child or sibling – Silas would not be able to speak openly to Lydia. He would not be able to confess that he didn't know what was *really* bothering Mikey, except that he felt Mikey was staying away from the hospital not because he did not love her enough, but because he loved her too much. Silas did not have the gift of speaking with his eyes, with the way he held his body or with the gestures of his hands. His world was a verbal one, he had to say things to give them meaning.

The doorbell rang and he went to answer it in irritation, he could not contend now with a beggar's pleading voice or with someone selling brooms in order to survive, he was not responsible for all the poverty and misery in the world, and would they go away, for fuck's sake, as he was facing the crisis of an inscrutable son and an inconsolable wife.

Through the door's ornate glass pane, which depicted a flower of some sort held in place by leaden black roots – how had it survived for so long, being slammed in anger hundreds of times during fifty years of private wars waged by a succession of families? – he saw Kate Jessup and Julian Solomon. Suddenly happy and relieved, he hugged each one in turn, going beyond the brief and routine tactility that the exiles had brought home with them from cold and foreign cities, and that had now been adopted by all the comrades, as meaningless as the question, 'How are you?' No, they deserved a warm, almost passionate expression of gratitude. They were his friends, Kate in particular, and he needed their help. Not just because Lydia was in hospital, but because he would depend on their understanding when they learned the nature of her accident. And because of Mikey.

His calm and pleasant son had suddenly turned into a moody and reclusive stranger. Like that time, four years ago, when Lydia's family had taken to whispering among themselves and then abruptly sent their youngest girl, Mireille, away to Martha in Canada. This had aroused in Mikey a silent fury that Silas noticed and understood, because it was how he too reacted to the incomprehensible actions of others, allowing himself to be eaten away inside.

'What's going on?' Silas had asked Lydia then.

'God, Silas, you walk around with your eyes in your arse,' she had answered, despairing of her own vulgarity as much as his preoccupation with his work.

'Oh, for shit's sake, you Oliphants are befok!' Silas had said, when he realized that Lydia and her family thought there was something between Mireille and Mikey. Mireille had been born when Mam Agnes was in her forties, she was what Afrikaans people called a laatlammetjie, 'a late lamb', and was only two years older than Mikey. The two had grown up together, like siblings, intimate and conspiratorial in the face of an indifferent adult world. Secretly, Silas had been intrigued by the idea that they had experimented sexually, as young people do all the time, even though the fatherly side of him revolted against the possibility that Mikey was having an incestuous relationship with his mother's sister.

He used to lie awake at night thinking that Mikey and Mireille had more life and laughter between them than the whole damn Oliphant family put together. They believed in instilling in children a forbidding, puritan innocence. How blind he had been not to have observed the exchange of black looks, the frantic, hissed conferences, the sad and brittle silences that enveloped them all, bright Lydia and forthright Gracie, avuncular Jackson and jolly Mam Agnes (the description 'jolly' suited the Oliphant matriarch, not only because of her rotund physique, but because she was especially cheerful in times of adversity), when they discovered the real or imagined sexual relationship between Mireille and Mikey.

But Mireille's departure had had a terrible effect on Mikey. He had withdrawn from the family, suffered headaches and fevers, and seemed to be afflicted by an overwhelming lassitude. Tonight Silas had seen the same signs, except that Mikey no longer betrayed a childlike bewilderment, but the coldness of some terrible knowledge.

The arrival of Kate and Julian was indeed fortunate, he was just about to phone Kate anyway, he told his visitors. He had to go and see Lydia in hospital, but didn't want to leave Mikey on his own. The boy wasn't well at all. Kate readily offered to stay with Mikey, and Julian said he would keep her company.

'You have no choice!' she reminded him.

'Oh God, the lesbian queen doesn't have her car with her!' Julian said in answer. 'What a demanding bitch she can be.'

Silas, grateful for the sense of easy familiarity that their biting jocularity brought, hugged them both once more. 'You sure you can stay?' he asked Julian.

Julian was going through a difficult period in his marriage. His wife Val was resentful that her family still had to make political sacrifices, now, when the struggle was over. A specialist in tropical diseases, Julian earned a meagre civil servant's salary, because the fledgling government needed his skills and could not afford to pay him what he would earn in private practice. Anyway, it was an honour to work for someone like Nelson Mandela, Julian said. And – he told Val

– she was a banker and earned enough for both of them. What about their son, an ailing and sensitive boy, Val asked, did he, Julian Solomon, think he could simply sacrifice a boy's life in order to satisfy his own perverted sense of duty?

Repeating – verbatim – conversations that he had had with his wife, Julian reported to his close friends just how tense things were at home. Silas always responded sympathetically, saying in his mind that he understood, because he too lived with a person 'whose whole sense of the future was made up of a series of anxieties', but never dared to actually talk out loud about his relationship with Lydia. The two men ended up nodding to each other in silent solidarity, their sorrows no longer in need of articulation. Kate was more challenging. It had been rumoured that Julian was gay, and Kate said she had sensed it herself. She had confronted him about it. He should face the truth, and 'tell it', she urged Julian, for his sake as well as Val's.

Silas, who had been subjected to Kate's merciless brand of truthfulness, knew how difficult it was to live normally in the aftermath of having told an 'enormous' truth. But then, Kate had never lived a normal life, he rationalized. She would have made a great Catholic, finding as much pleasure in confessing a sin as in committing one.

'Late nights, no matter how noble the cause, do not help troubled marriages,' Silas said now in the ostentatious tone he sometimes lapsed into, especially when he was unsure of his arguments, and hugged Julian again, an exaggerated gesture of appreciation. Kate smiled her indulgent smile.

'How about me, what about my problems at home?' she asked, mockingly indignant.

'God, a lesbian triangle, I can't stand it,' Silas said.

The subject of Marguerite usually brought out in Silas a caustic, township humour. Marguerite was Kate's former lover who had turned up unexpectedly from Europe, after almost ten years, silently demanding the same hospitality of home and body that she had once offered Kate. A complicated demand, seeing that Kate now lived with Janine. Kate had been on the run when she first met Marguerite. It was just before the unbanning of the liberation movements, and she had fled to Belgium, where Marguerite had taken her in. Marguerite had a wiry body and the kind of hawk's face that Silas said could only be loved 'as jy daarvan hou om kraaie te naai' – if you liked fucking crows.

Although the Afrikaans meaning was lost on her, Kate saw the disparaging intent in Silas's bearing, his sudden, twisted smile, in Julian's complicit laughter. This kind of comment always earned Silas the approving smiles of black men in particular. How unkind we South Africans are, when we are on our own turf and not in need of refuge and bodily comfort, Kate thought. Still, having a reason for going home late, when both Marguerite and Janine, former lover and current partner, had retreated to the bitter sanctuaries of their own rooms, was attractive. She suddenly realized that she was having a conversation with herself, that Julian had fallen into a reflective silence, while Silas was going about closing windows and drawing curtains, like someone postponing an unpleasant task.

'Off you go,' Kate told him, ushering him towards the door the way one dispatches a reluctant child on an errand.

'Where is Mikey?' Lydia asked.

'He's not feeling well,' Silas answered. He had complained of a headache, and nausea, something he ate, perhaps. He had gone to bed . . .

'He's alone?' she asked, the alarm in her voice growing.

'No, Julian and Kate are there, stopped by on their way from work. They'll wait until I get back.'

'Who's Julian and Kate?' Gracie asked.

'Ag, Gracie, you know, the people Silas works with,' Alec answered on his behalf.

Gracie observed the exchange of looks between Silas and Lydia, saw his pleading eyes: not now, not here, we have no privacy, there are things we need to talk about on our own, not just for a few minutes while they wait outside, this family of yours with their gift for understanding unsaid things.

But Lydia either could not understand her husband's silent plea or chose to ignore it. He had not brought her son to visit her, her face said, that was the least she expected of him, and tears flowed down her cheeks. Mikey's absence was bringing out into the open the anger and unhappiness that both of them had suppressed, postponed for another time, the night Lydia danced on broken glass and experienced a physical pain momentarily more overwhelming than the pain in her heart and mind. Now, in that hospital ward, those agonies, physical and metaphysical, fused together into a blend of fury and grief. She wept silently, without trembling lips or blinking eyes. Jackson imagined what the stony face of the weeping statue of Our Lady of Fatima looked like (even though he had twice resisted travelling to Portugal with Mam Agnes to see the miracle).

It was Jackson who saw an equally immense anguish on Silas's face, his clenched jaw and rigid eyes. He was at Silas's side when he started sagging down as if his legs had suddenly lost their strength. He helped him into a chair, and sent Alec running down the corridor to summon help.

Mam Agnes wondered what her husband was doing when, after loosening Silas's tie, he took a pen from the poor, trembling man's pocket and wedged it between his teeth. She would ask him afterwards how he had known it was a seizure.

'It is the kind of thing you just see coming,' he would answer.

At first, Gracie thought that Silas was acting, that it was a case of 'green cheese' (a term she had heard somewhere to describe people who would not be outdone for drama). But then she saw how limp he was, slumped in the chair, and how his eyes seemed to have rolled up in his head, something that only happened to dead people.

'Oh my God!' she shouted. 'Come on, Alec, where are you?'

She too went running down the corridor, no longer trusting that he would find a doctor in time. Imagine the shame of having to tell people that Silas died in hospital, in full view of his sick wife, and that they could do nothing to help!

Lydia, when she had overcome her own feeling of helplessness, was dismayed at how quickly Alec and Gracie had panicked, and how this had infected Mam Agnes. She was standing over Jackson, hissing instructions, telling him to wait for the doctors to come. He tried to tell her that it would be better for Silas to lie down flat, even if it was on the floor. Sitting hunched up like that couldn't be doing his circulation any good.

When Gracie and Alec eventually returned with a doctor, it was obvious that they had been arguing, calling each other names, each saying that the other was 'retarded'. Lydia could not help smiling. They used that kind of angry language to ease the tension. But she seemed unbecomingly calm, 'grinning even', Alec would say later, under such grim circumstances. She was able to tell the doctor that, to her knowledge, Silas had only suffered one such attack before, almost twenty years ago.

'Yes,' she confirmed, when he asked if he had also been under severe stress then.

Silas was admitted to the hospital for observation. It would be wise to keep him overnight, they said, even though it may only have been nerves, the stress of his wife's accident and her being in hospital. Lydia, realizing that Mikey would be alone, lost her poise. She wanted to go home and take care of her son, she said. No child should ever be alone in this world. But Mam Agnes, her voice startlingly intense, said that the best thing the two of them could do now was to deal with *this* problem, *whatever* it was, so that they could stop *this* madness between them. She and Jackson could go and stay over in Berea.

For the first time, someone had mentioned 'this problem'. Gracie, Alec and Jackson looked away, while Lydia leaned back and shut her eyes. She meekly accepted the sedative that the nurse shot into her arm and soon fell asleep, propped up like a living corpse. Her visitors left, each glancing back, sad that this should be happening to someone like Lydia, who had always been the strongest one in the family. Their panic had subsided, and they were confident and querulous once more.

They would have to go home first to collect some things, Mam Agnes said, before they went on to Berea. That meant driving all the way back to Soweto. 'It's because you children want to move to the suburbs,' she said, as if expressing a thought that had been preoccupying her for a long time, 'the township's not good enough any more. I mean, in the past we had all of you right there, close to us. Once, we could just walk over to where Mikey was.'

'Why did you offer if you're going to moan about it?' Jackson said.

'Listen –' Gracie interrupted '– don't the two of you start arguing now!'

They walked down the corridor, people standing aside for them, their quarrelling reduced to whispers by the sudden hush that had descended, as if at the command of a silent voice. Alec imagined that people were staring at them, signalling that visiting time was over, people pay for the peace and quiet here, this is not one of your township hospitals where you can make as much noise as you want. Gracie tugged his sleeve, pulling him away from the confrontation she saw building up in his eyes.

As they walked, she took out her cellphone and called Mikey.

'Hello, Kate speaking.'

Gracie, forced by the atmosphere in the hospital to lower her voice, and desperate not to lose her own composure, resisted the temptation to berate the woman at the top of her voice. 'How is Mikey?' she asked instead, matching Kate's cool voice with an iciness of her own.

Mikey was asleep, Kate said, and Julian had gone home.

Gracie explained what had happened to Silas. 'Mam Agnes, Mikey's grandmother, will be coming over to look after him,' she concluded.

'I could stay the night,' Kate said, 'and see that he's okay.'

'No, we can't ask you to do that,' Gracie protested. Then, conscious of her raised voice, lapsed into a whisper again. She saw Alec's smug smile, gave him one of her stern looks.

'Oh, it's no problem,' Kate said, 'I have my toothbrush in my bag.'

'What about Julian, won't he mind?' Gracie asked.

'Julian? Oh no, we're not . . . partners or anything like that, he's a colleague, both of us work with Silas.'

'Are you sure about this?'

'Yes, it's no bother at all.'

'What's the matter?' Alec asked when Gracie snapped shut her cellphone.

They were out in the courtyard by now, a sudden breeze brought a chill to the air. Gracie breathed in deeply, searching for the oxygen she had suddenly started struggling for in those cold blue corridors.

'Kate, Silas's colleague, nogal, she's staying with Mikey. She's got her toothbrush in her bag.'

Gracie took Alec by the arm and walked ahead of the others. 'Is Silas jolling with her?' she asked, when she thought that Jackson and Mam Agnes were out of earshot.

'Who, Silas with Kate? Nah, she's a dyke.'

But Jackson, a few feet behind them, overheard their conversation.

51

Trained to pick up gossip, he always joked. Live with someone like Mam Agnes for more than forty years, and you acquire the knack.

'She's a what?' he asked.

'A lesbian,' Gracie said.

'How do you know?' Mam Agnes asked.

She too had kept pace with Gracie and Alec, suspecting there was something going on, something that Gracie thought she shouldn't hear. Gracie gave Alec another of her scalpel looks.

'Yes, how *do* you know so much, mister?' Gracie asked.

Alec shrugged. 'I do lots of work for the government, and you know, people talk.'

'You, you're too diep for your own good,' Gracie said. Her voice was full of admonishment.

Tongues as sharp as their eyes. Ja, my bra, Alec said mentally to himself and to his friend Silas, lying drugged in a bed somewhere, we married into the cavalry, you and I. And then, out loud, in his jester's voice: 'Have a little more grace, Gracie.'

5

No, Silas and Kate had never 'jolled', which was a township way of describing an affair, though many people were firm in the belief that they must at least have slept with each other, just once, as an experiment. After all, he was a black man and she was a white woman, and when they had been active in the movement, breaking the racial barrier was like breaking the land-speed record or shooting an AK-47 for the first time. It created the same fleeting excitement, sleeping with someone of another colour.

Alec had once told Silas he found it incredible that he had never tasted a 'nice piece of silverside', and that Kate being a 'double adapter' must have made it all the more exciting. Silas's angry response had only reinforced Alec's suspicion that he was being devious and unnecessarily coy. 'Shit, everyone knows that white cherries want black ouens because white ouens don't know how to naai.'

The fact was that Kate and Silas had reasons greater than their own morality for not having sex with each other. They had been in the same MK counter-intelligence unit, and their job was to identify infiltrators and informers, a very difficult task, if they wanted to be objective and retain their integrity. There was no room for clouded judgement, it could allow an enemy in your midst to go undetected or condemn an innocent person to being cast out like a leper.

Once suspicions had been aroused about someone's reliability, it was difficult to redeem them. The enemy went around spreading rumours about comrades, planting suspicion about the best of MK's soldiers, hoping to sow disarray in the ranks of the underground army. Counter-intelligence's biggest challenge lay not in the unmasking of traitors but in proving the innocence of those who had been falsely accused. Good and loyal comrades were subjected to isolation and scorn, unspoken but obvious. They could end up being assassinated by some overzealous and misinformed MK infiltrator from abroad, alongside the askaris – MK soldiers who had been captured and 'turned' – or impimpis who sold their comrades for money, or even those who had been broken by the security police and could not help being traitors.

Being in counter-intelligence gave you a certain amount of power, and it was tempting to use this power to get rid of rivals, real or imagined. Generally speaking, having affairs inside MK was bad enough, fucking with someone in your own intelligence unit was fatal. Infidelity among comrades, jealousy, the suspicion that your wife or husband or lover was sleeping with someone else in MK, often achieved what the state could not: it turned a loyal soldier into a traitor. In their quiet, intimate moments, Silas and Kate often whispered about a notorious case where one of their bravest operatives, a close friend, secretly started working for the cops because he had discovered that his wife was jolling with her unit commander. The cops trapped the errant lovers and shot them both, while the traitor himself was 'fed' to MK and killed as a consequence. A lot of good people dead, a whole network smashed, 'All for a fuck!' people would say.

Kate and Silas always stopped short of such summary condemnation, as both remembered how close Silas had come to being 'compromised' because of an indiscretion, a moment of weakness ('Don't make it sound so *Christian!*' a scornful Lydia would tell him). He had had an affair with another MK comrade, a courier, not in their unit, but it was still dangerous. And most of all, his timing was wrong.

One day, must have been about December 1988, Lydia would say if you asked her, Kate had turned up at the clinic where Lydia worked, and asked to speak to her alone, somewhere private. They went out into the garden, and sitting down next to Lydia, on a bench under a tree, Kate leaned close, like an old friend, only to reveal that she and Silas were members of the ANC underground and that he had a problem.

'What kind of problem?' Lydia demanded.

Kate looked around, as if to say, 'This is not a game, not just idle gossip I'm bringing you, it is a matter of life and death.' Silas had been 'indiscreet'. He had had an affair with a comrade, a woman who did sensitive work for MK. They now had to prevail on this woman to leave the country, without her two young children. They were afraid that she was susceptible to pressure because of her children, and because her husband was a respected 'up and coming' lawyer who did lots of sensitive political work. The woman might break, reveal things.

'Who are *they*?' Lydia asked.

54

'We,' Kate answered coldly, lit a cigarette, and went on speaking as if lecturing an innocent child about the dangers of life. 'We think the cops know of the affair and may try to exploit it, use it against us.'

'So they *know* that Silas is in the underground, as you call it?'

'Yes. Among other things.'

Lydia realized that Kate was testing her, wanting to see how much she knew, whether Silas was a talker, someone who confided in people close to him. She said: 'Then why don't they simply arrest both Silas and this woman? That's what they usually do.'

'Because Silas is untouchable, at the moment. Involved in something so important that they dare not arrest him. They would prefer to compromise him.'

Lydia shook her head in disbelief, the bewilderment of suddenly finding out that her life, her son's life, that of her mother and father, her whole family, was fragile, subject to someone's whim, their freedom dependent on how much people thought they knew or did not know.

She did not pursue the many questions that arose in her mind: How long has Silas been in the underground? How long has he been sleeping with this woman? Who is she? She did not like Kate, and saw no point in having a long conversation with someone who was unlikely to see the world from any perspective but her own. She also resented her, not because she was jealous of her, not in any physical sense – indeed, she saw in Kate a ruthlessness, manlike and brutal, that would have prevented a sexual relationship with Silas. No, Lydia resented this woman, this white woman with her nicotine-stained fingers and wiry looks, because she shared secrets with her husband, because she had the kind of relationship with him that she herself had never been able to develop. Imagine people sharing the intimacy of deadly knowledge, confiding in each other, in secret places, at designated times. They may as well also fuck each other.

But above all, what incensed Lydia was Kate's simplistic righteousness, her clear definition of right and wrong, not so much of who was a comrade and who an enemy, but of who was useful and who was not. Her unspoken assertion that this distinction justified any kind of behaviour added insult to the hurt of Silas's 'indiscretion'. What mattered to Kate was how the problem was resolved, the need to protect the 'movement' at all costs. The morality of Silas's actions and their effect on Lydia were immaterial.

'I have to get back to my work,' Lydia said, and got up.

Kate laid her hand on Lydia's shoulder, then abruptly withdrew it.

'Listen, Lydia, in six months, a year from now, none of this will matter, people will no longer be hunted down, there will be no need for an underground. Silas is too deeply involved in that process to be pulled out now. Help him stay there, please.'

It was not a plea but an order, as if she had rehearsed the words and, like any good actor, was improvising their sequence, trying to produce the maximum effect on her audience.

Gradually, Silas began to talk about the 'incident', more as a way of justifying what he had done, Lydia thought, than out of any real sense of remorse. The fact that his lover, whose identity was still a secret, had been sacrificed and sent into exile, weighed heavily on him. It also threatened his career. She would return, reunite with her husband, or divorce. Silas's selfishness, and the underground's cruelty in separating her from her children, would be revealed. After '1990', when 'the war' had ended and 'comrades' were able to associate with each other openly, Lydia heard Silas's MK colleagues casually boast how difficult life in the camps had been, as if gratified by their own suffering. She imagined what it must have been like to be sent out in disgrace, as it were, for having been indiscreet, for having slept with someone in a senior position, how it must have created the image of a shamed woman, a soldier 'fuckable' for the cause. How much leering this nameless woman must have endured.

Silas later told Lydia that Kate, who remained his commander, even though he had been seconded to the political structures, had counselled him, had vouched for his 'stability' and saved him from the ignominy of being taken off a vital task. He was then helping to prepare for the negotiations between the movement and the government. He could have been expelled from the unit, or worse, sent to Angola or Zambia for 'consultation'.

What Lydia could not forgive, she told him, was the fact that she had only found out about his underground activity because he had been unfaithful. He had endangered their lives, hers and Mikey's, because of his secretiveness, his inability to trust her, his own wife.

Silas was indebted to Kate, and by implication, so was Lydia. Lydia hated being beholden to people, owing them anything. It was a principle instilled in them all by Mam Agnes: never get into debt, and if you must, let it not be to white people! Especially thin white women from Natal. Lydia's family were also from Natal, but they were coloured, and that made the world of difference. Lydia knew that there was little she could do to repay Kate the debt of her husband's freedom.

She endured Silas's increasing insensitivity to her feelings about Kate. He constantly invited the woman over to their house for dinner, drinks, Sunday tea even, sitting in the back garden like those geriatric white couples in Durban's posh areas where Mam Agnes had worked as a cook. Lydia recalled the disconsolate pride of Martha, her eldest sister, when she abandoned her ambition to go to university and found a job instead, so that her mother could be released from the humiliation of privileged servitude – 'Don't ever tell me again how well they treat you,' Martha had scolded Mam Agnes. The only time one of her children had ever raised a voice to her in genuine anger.

At first, Lydia recognized that the social occasions were pretexts for

57

Kate and Silas to talk about their work; negotiations were under way and both served on various 'commissions'. When the meetings continued after the first elections in 1994, Lydia bitterly understood that there was a genuine bond of friendship between them. One night, Kate brought her 'friend' Janine along to a dinner party and announced in a monotone over coffee and dessert that she was a lesbian, that bisexuality had been an 'experiment' that had yielded her a child, 'the only gratification of penetrative sex'.

Lydia's dislike for Kate turned to detestation.

Here was a woman born into privilege, white, rich, educated. Without forswearing the fruits of her millionaire father's much derided 'greed', judging by her expensive clothes and the quiet opulence of her jewellery, she was always the one with the most radical view: the 'fat cats' were merely enriching themselves, liberation should not mean that only the few got rich. Even though most of the people present at that dinner were Silas's friends, his colleagues, his kind of people, this was *her* house. Lydia knew they were used to this kind of talk, confessing with great bravado the secret lusts of their rather timid souls – who (other than their current partners) they wanted to sleep with, what part of the covertly desired person's anatomy turned them on, and so forth – but observed how even they fell silent, uncertain how to respond to Kate's 'revelation'.

That night Lydia found Kate's 'directness' particularly offensive. Mikey was present at the dinner table – he had just turned sixteen and this was supposed to be a sort of birthday celebration for him – and he had to sit there, silently enduring his father's experiment in 'letting him be a grown-up'. Julian had tried to restart the conversation by making light of Kate's serious tone, saying that it didn't matter at all, since all life revolved around the principle of the 'universal orifice'. Lydia rose from the table and asked her son to come and help her in the kitchen. He wiped his mouth, stern and unsmiling, a young puritan scornful of the adult stupidity being enacted around the dinner table, and followed his mother out of the room.

Lydia knew that somehow Kate's injudicious pronouncement had been prompted by Mikey's presence. It was as if she was trying to protect herself from his cool and unsmiling countenance. Earlier on, Lydia had seen something stir in her son's mind, a shadow passing across his calm features, a twitch in his cheek, and he had looked directly at Kate for a moment. Kate too had noticed, looked up, smiled at him, then looked away flustered, like a young woman taking pleasure in being scrutinized by a sexually interested man.

Afterwards, with all the guests gone and Mikey in his room, Lydia and Silas had had a huge argument of words hissed and words shouted. Painful memories were traded. There was something she had wanted to tell him a long time ago, Lydia said: 'You have no culture of your own, Silas, no belief that is yours, just yours alone. All you stand for and believe in was picked up along the way. Well, ideals are not formed that way, a little idea found here and a little thought found there. These fancy friends of yours go home to their families, their religions, their damn traditions. And you, where do you belong?'

'God, how long have you been saving up that little speech?'

She stared at him, seeing for the first time the bitterness in his eyes, the way some long-suffered, patient silence had given way to an utter weariness.

'You married the wrong person. Perhaps you should have married someone like Kate.'

'Don't start, Lyd.'

'Start what, Lyd? She would have thrown you out long ago. She would have demanded the fucken fairy-tale life you promised at the beginning, the idealism you offered, the dream you wanted to share. Remember, Silas? Or was that just naai-talk, designed to seduce this starry-eyed little Durban girl? And now? You are one of them, the grey men you always mocked, look at you, you've learned how to lick arse, maybe even suck some cock. God! You are just as lifeless as your friends.'

Lydia's sourness had astounded Silas, and her gift for rhetoric, her knowledge of books, this quiet wife of his, the woman in the white tunic going off to work, to tend to the ill and the maimed, uncomplaining Lydia with the long sexy legs. When did she read, when did she listen to music, when did she think about these things? Of course, behind the earphones when she did her chores at home, and probably in the dead of night, a book balanced on her knee in a pool of blue light, while her patients slept, her mind learning the schizophrenia of divided attention. One half of her alert to the noises of the ward, to the texture of people breathing, the regularity of heart-monitoring machines, always ready to drop her book or rip away her earphones. The other half absorbed in the brilliant edges of words quickly read, fragments of music held in her ear to be reunited afterwards, when an urgent task was done, into a continuous, melodious stream.

Silas sat crestfallen in a chair next to the bed while Lydia went to the bathroom. He heard her crying, and wanted to go in there and embrace her, touch her intelligent face, try to recapture the warmth they had lost between them a long time ago.

And then he remembered that Lydia, too, had never been the same since the night she was raped. Somewhere inside of her that *other* Lydia was hiding, shielding herself from the memory of being raped and from his response to it. It would take too much energy to find her, and he felt tired, drained of all his enthusiasm for the struggle this would demand. He buried his face in his hands, remembered the way his father, Ali Ali, used to sit in his chair and pray, moving his lips, shutting his eyes when it came to beseeching God, begging some favour, the bestowing of serenity perhaps, or simply asking for a longer life or to be spared a slow and lingering death. At the end, the old man erased the burdens of his life by wiping his face, carefully moving his palms from the crook of his nose across his cheeks, until there was only a ruddy emptiness in his dark features.

When Lydia came out of the bathroom her face had been scrubbed, the evidence of her tears removed, and she shone with the brightness of a new outrage building up in her. She was not yet done with her discourse on his friends.

'Another thing,' she said, 'you make sure that Kate keeps away from Mikey.'

'She declared herself a lesbian, she prefers girls,' he answered sarcastically.

'Don't be so naive, Silas. Did you see how she came on to Mikey, sixteen-year-old Mikey?'

Silas groaned out loud, told her to stop being so suspicious of people, that perhaps she was betraying her own fantasies about young boys. He was slightly drunk, and she let his remark pass, even though it burned in her, this grossness of her farting and belching husband, who could think that she had sexual fantasies about children as young as her own son.

For a few years, Silas's social life subsided, and he stopped imposing on Lydia the frequent dinner-and-drinks parties with his friends. Kate seldom came to the house now, and Silas spent more time at home. But his presence was subdued, aloof, slowly filling the hours with an atmosphere of restraint that both Lydia and Mikey found oppressive. So their time spent together passed quietly, each one reading on their own, or listening to their own music through earphones or in their separate sanctuaries. Lydia loved to watch movies, but she would stop the video she had obtained from the library at the hospital as soon as Silas settled down on the settee. Being idle made him restless, and his shifting about soon spoiled her own, leisurely enjoyment.

Intrigued by Lydia's eclectic reading tastes, a small library collected as if by careful design, modern classics and novels by avant-garde writers (whose titles were admired by the occasional 'intellectual' visitor from his office), Silas tried to engage her about a particular book. But the conversation rapidly faded away, because, as Lydia once observed, he was more interested in why she had bought that book than in the book itself. The music that she so obviously loved (an absent, contemplative mask slipped over her face, a euphonious sound seeping into her head like water into an underground well) also set them apart. One wintry Sunday afternoon, their suburban house having acquired the same end-of-day peacefulness as their old township home, his loneliness got the better of him – or was it nostalgia, for they used to share such moments, a glass of wine, a record playing on the old turntable. He picked up a CD cover and tried to talk to her about the music she was listening to.

'Who is Philip Glass?'

'Does it matter? An American.'

'Can I listen?'

She switched off the earphones, allowing the music to play through the speakers. The house was filled with an eerie musicality, polished and cold, that somehow seemed suited to its irregular angles.

He picked another CD, looked at the cover, and began to browse through her collection as if it was a catalogue of her mysterious inner selves. Names like Samuel Barber, Aaron Copland, Leoš Janáček deepened his sense of her distance from him, names that exuded a feeling of frantic energy but also of infinite sadness.

'At least I know who Leonard Cohen is,' he said, in an attempt once more to engage her.

'Just listen to the music, just *listen*,' she answered through closed eyes.

He mumbled something about 'all this being too intellectual for a simple man' and retreated to the blandness of his study, to conceal the grudging love he felt for this 'new' woman, someone he was discovering as if for the first time, to retreat from her demand for a love that could not be moderated by words, or even through touch, and that could only be experienced in the imagination. He knew then, several years before he encountered Du Boise in a shopping mall, that Lydia really wanted to explore some hidden pain, perhaps not of her rape, but to journey through the darkness of the silent years that had ensued between them.

He was not capable of such an ordeal, he acknowledged. It would require an immersion in words he was not familiar with, words that did not seek to blur memory, to lessen the pain, but to sharpen all of these things. He was trained to find consensus, even if it meant not acknowledging the 'truth' in all its unflattering nakedness.

Hell, he had an important job, liaising between the Ministry of Justice and the Truth and Reconciliation Commission. It was his task to ensure that everyone concerned remained objective, the TRC's supporters and its opponents, that they considered the law above all, and did not allow their emotions to sway them. What would happen if he broke his own golden rule and delved into the turmoil of memories that the events of those days would undoubtedly unleash?

He sipped a whisky, slowly swirling the ice around in the glass, listening to its meaningless tinkle. He stared at the dull spines of the legal tomes that lined the wall, was comforted by the sombre, solid phalanx of precise wisdom, and forgave himself the rationalization that stopped him from going into the living room, asking Lydia to turn down the music that he himself had prompted her to set free in this house of restraint, and taking her into his arms, holding her, without needing a reason. And when questioned: 'And now? What's this?' He would be able to give a simple answer: 'Out of love.'

But Silas didn't get out of his chair that day, not until the music died away and shadows swarmed through the house, bringing their own peculiar, vibrating darkness, until he too felt the empty peace of having left things undisturbed. How strangely like their inhabitants homes become, he thought, how equally idiosyncratic this one was in its rapid crossing from light to dark, like the transitions of Lydia's moods, frontiers of emotion without any twilight.

And now Kate was in Lydia's home, alone with Mikey. The result of Silas's ancient insensitivity, not deliberate, a lapse in judgement, but cruel nevertheless. He did not think about the things that hurt Lydia, repeating old stupidities because he could not help himself.

'God, Lyd, I work with Kate and Julian, they are my colleagues,' he would have said, had she given him half a chance. 'They heard about what happened and stopped by to see if you were okay, and if we needed anything, if you *needed* anything.' Lydia imagined Kate at the door, smiling her bright and brittle smile, heard her ask in that breathless, white woman's voice – 'How *is* Lydia, do you need anything, does Mikey need anything?'

Silas must have fallen into her arms, 'Thank you for coming, I was going to call you anyway.' How Lydia wished that there was something sexual between them, then at least she would have been able to explain why they were so close; but more importantly, it would have protected Mikey. No, she did not think that her son would be an innocent, exploited party, should anything happen, but Silas – and Kate – should have known better than to expose a boy like him to such temptation. God help the women in Mikey's life. His beauty will prove to be a curse. Ask Mireille.

It will start off innocently, with mundane things, a meal being prepared, a bed made, lights switched on or off, waiting for a bathroom to be free, a question asked, 'Where are the towels, does your mom have any shampoo I can use?' Somewhere in this humdrum process, the encounter will take place. Mikey's green eyes, the brightness of his skin caught in a yellow glow of light, his arms flung lazily behind his head, Mikey the irresistible 'innocent' waiting for his prey, setting his trap, conscious of his own intentions once his mind has been made up, deliberate, dramatic almost.

God help us, Lydia thought. Give Kate the strength of character she does not have.

6

Kate called Janine to tell her that she would be home late, started explaining, without being asked, that Silas had a problem and needed someone to be with his son Mikey, who was not well. She ended the conversation with a pained expression that Julian said made her look old. She confessed inwardly that she had called to keep herself occupied and not because Janine would be waiting anxiously for her to come home. Janine was not given to such routine anxieties. She was a water engineer, energetic, self-contained. Her blue eyes seemed deeply hued against her tanned skin. Many hours spent in the sun. You could feel her beauty in the dark, it was calm and liquid, the day's heat still alive within her. She offered Kate the best of both worlds: a woman's patient, absorbing love, and the freedom to explore, as an equal, the ruthless, thrusting selfishness that men offer.

But Kate could also feel Janine beginning to withdraw; perhaps loving her so unquestioningly was becoming too much. She remembered how perplexed Janine had been in the beginning by her many contradictions, her bisexuality, her equally comfortable relationship with her wealthy family and her radical friends. Inevitably, one part of her always undermined the other, and it was usually her lover Janine and her daughter Ferial who suffered most. But Janine had never probed or moralized, she had never seemed to doubt her love, until now.

'What's eating you?' Julian asked.

'I need a drink,' Kate said.

This was the time of day when she most enjoyed a glass of whisky, standing in the garden, enjoying the fragile suburban quiet. Her one solitary moment before Ferial came bouncing in from art or drama classes, whatever fad it was her father's indulgence was able to afford, tossing her mane of black hair from side to side ('Mom, when do we eat?'), and then Janine, sleek, ferrous, back from her jog, still bathed in sweat. Soon Kate would be drawn into the contrasting worlds of daughter and lover, of women at ease with their femininity, the sway of dark hair, bright laughter, almost European in its icy, gay quality.

'But I *am* European: I'm from France, remember?' Janine would protest.

Until Marguerite arrived, with her manly timbre, the bristling blonde hair on her pale arms. Belgium, her skin, her French intoned, whereas Janine's French was still spontaneous, as volubly Parisian as ever, despite her many years away from home. But it was in their eyes that you could tell the difference. Janine's showed the slow emptiness of empty spaces, long hours spent peering at dry landscapes, delicately wrinkled from constant narrowing against glare and wind. Marguerite's eyes were quick, lupine in their alertness.

Once, Kate could have loved them both, but not now, not now that she had struggled to create a normal life for herself and Ferial. The liberation struggle was over.

Julian handed her a glass.

'Pure malt,' he said.

She sipped. 'God, it's strong! Where did you find it?'

'In Silas's study, where else do you think you'll find whisky but in the man's den?'

66

'Silas has a den?'

'Almost in the American sense.' He sipped, ran his tongue over his lips with satisfaction. 'And his son was lurking in there,' he went on, as they watched Mikey walk up the stairs.

'How do you mean "lurking"?'

'You know, surreptitious, secretive, that's what it means.'

They watched the news. Nelson Mandela beaming, the nation's talisman against a world relentless in its demand for the continuation of a 'political miracle'. They eerily observed the world they worked in as if it was foreign, fictional. As soon as he could, Julian switched off the TV and searched for some music to play.

'For goodness' sake, let's at least watch the weather report,' Kate protested like an irritable wife. He responded with one of his smirking, disdainful looks: can't you let us get away from our jobs even for a moment?

The biting sadness of one of Lydia's CDs filled the room. After a few minutes, he switched it off. 'If I want to listen to such screeching laments,' he said, 'I can go home.'

Two hours later – after nine already – and still Silas had not returned. Kate tried calling him on his cellphone, but it had been switched to an answering service. She should call the clinic. Perhaps Mikey knew the number? She started to go upstairs, then realized that she could look the number up in the phone book lying right there on that old-world telephone table.

'I'm hungry,' Julian said.

Kate saw Mikey come down the stairs and go into the kitchen. 'Mikey must be hungry as well,' she said, 'want to order a pizza?'

'You think the delivery service will come out here?'

'This isn't Sarajevo, Bo, this is Berea, Johannesburg, South Africa!' Very few people close to Julian still called him by his nickname

'Bozo', or one of its many variations. He had acquired it at varsity. A Jew studying at the predominantly Afrikaans University of Stellenbosch, he had insisted on playing rugby – to demonstrate his manhood, he always said in rueful recollection. These days only the media called him Dr 'Bozo' Solomon, the President's adviser on HIV/AIDS. Julian was an unsentimental man, whose one rule in life was to consider the facts above everything else.

'Don't romanticize, Kate, this place is dangerous. Quite frankly, Silas and Lydia should get out of here as soon as they can.'

'Maybe they can't afford to,' she said. 'Anyway, what's wrong with living in Berea?'

'It might have been okay for you in your bohemian days, but you didn't have a child then. They do.'

He looked into his empty glass, contemplating the prospect of another drink. He resisted the temptation, remembering the weird effect that alcohol had on his mood lately. He said: 'You know, Kate, the only people that young Michael there has to look up to are drug dealers, gangsters in flashy cars, what kind of example do you think they set? You think Silas can compete with them?'

'Why do we always have to compete, and why always with people worse than us?'

'Listen, sweetie, Silas is just a civil servant now, a plain and simple lawyer in the Justice Department, someone who – as far as his son is concerned – speaks some mumbo-jumbo language about truth and reconciliation, and will end up driving that Toyota of his until it's a clapped-out old wreck. The days of the MK hero are gone, he has nothing romantic to offer his son.'

'God, Bo, you sound like my mother's therapist! No wonder your wife wants to leave you.'

'Don't be cruel.'

'I'm sorry.' She went over and kissed the dome of his balding head.

'Here's the Mr Delivery menu. You see, Silas and Lydia know how to make the ghetto work for them!'

'Shit, Kate, I'd like to see you move back here, bring your lovely daughter Ferial to live in Berea, to imbibe all this wonderful local colour! Put your money where your mouth is.'

'Hush now and order the pizza, I'll see how Mikey is doing,' she said, her tone placatory.

She found Mikey in the kitchen, standing at the sink and sipping a glass of water. He was staring intently at something through the window.

'Hello, Mikey, how are you? Do you know the number of the clinic . . .?'

He raised a finger to his mouth, signalling her to be quiet. She could not see what held his attention in the darkened yard. She observed his calm face, the intense, adult expression, and marvelled at how he'd grown. He had been – what, sixteen? – the last time he was in her company. Since then he had been just a boy in a school uniform, smiling from the passenger seat of his father's car, on the rare occasions they passed by her house. She remembered that horrible dinner party three years ago, here at Silas's house. Mikey's birthday, and Silas's belated house-warming dinner, the township kid moved to the suburbs. Two celebrations for the price of one.

'You are so thrifty you should have been Jewish,' Julian had joked.

'Good mixture of abstemious Muslim and puritanical Dutch Reformed,' Silas had answered.

Mikey was the only child present that night, and yet how adult he had seemed, Kate remembered thinking to herself, alienated, aloof, disdainful of his father and his father's friends, their forced attempts to be irreverent, trying to find release from the seriousness of their new young democracy, gleefully displaying the 'anything goes' spirit they could only let free at dinner parties, sacrilege, profanity, elevated to an art. How ordinary they had become, just like people everywhere, grappling over coffee with the humdrum woes of the world. Of all the adults, only Lydia had shared Mikey's scorn for this childlike self-indulgence.

It began, that night, her folly, with Julian reciting some lines of poetry, he could not remember the poem's title or the poet's name – what did it matter, he said, this is the Age of Anonymity:

What will become of you
now that there are no crowds to marshal
no ovations to pluck
like flowers from the air?

Then each one had to declare what had become of them – personally, of course, none of this public doing-my-duty shit – since Mandela had walked out of prison. Julian in charge, stage-managing their responses, their sometimes uncomfortable shifting about, yelling, 'You lie! you lie!' whenever their body language betrayed that something was being concealed.

Kate was the boldest, apart from Inga, the Swedish journalist, who stroked her husband's thinning blond hair and said she would like to try a black man, now that it was no longer forbidden.

Kate announced that she was lesbian, irrevocably. That she desired only a woman's flaming tongue and not the limp little weenies that men these days had to offer. Everyone at the table had fallen silent, including her latest and most enduring lover, Janine. Julian failed to restore the flow of light conversation by declaring that, in that case, he too would become lesbian – 'Who wants a limp weenie?' In the end, Janine reached out and touched Kate's cheek affectionately, providing testimony to her newly announced sexual orientation. Julian made some comment about orifices – trust him – and Lydia froze.

Then Lydia had risen from the table, summoned her son to join her in the kitchen. Kate remembered the horror on her face and the way she looked at Mikey, at his eyes filled with mocking laughter. And Kate realized that she had said all those things for the boy's sake, that she had been addressing him, trying to tear some web he had been weaving around her. Rubbish! she told herself afterwards, there is no such thing as mental communication; probing, daring glances, yes, but that was akin to physical contact, being addressed by someone's eyes.

Now Mikey, no longer a child, his aged demeanour already betraying a kind of coiled-up decadence, the sloe-eyed hardness of men as ruthless as her father had been, evoked in her that same urge to say and do something completely out of place. Again he held a finger to his lips, silencing her before she could say anything. My God, he is directing my mood, just like he did that night, she thought.

His strange, rather sallow skin was tinged with blue, as if he had no colour of his own, as if his complexion was created by absorbing light from elements around him, from the fluorescent tubes above them and the darkness into which he stared. When at last he did turn towards her, it was to convey a passing acknowledgement, to reinforce the fact that there was something more mysterious and exotic out there. His beauty was sinister, she thought, then smiled to herself. How crude that was! Demonizing his good looks in order to justify her desire for him. Ferial would tell her to keep her hormones in check, boys like Mikey belonged to *her* generation, not to rapacious older women.

Where did her daughter, just turned sixteen, get language like that from? A 'rapacious older woman' indeed. She winced, remembering how Ferial had recently asked her whether she was a 'double adapter'. Telling her that the word was 'bisexual' had made it worse. 'You mean you are?' she had responded, her heavily pencilled eyebrows held in a perfectly stern, straight line, evidence of the fact that she was growing

71

up, of encounters at parties, things discussed, boys kissed, and hopefully of enduring – or enjoying? – nothing more than being felt up.

The thought of Ferial, nearly three years younger than Mikey, but his generation really, restored Kate's sense of adult hierarchy, of authority over this 'young snapper' – her mother's words, a way of putting things in their proper place, dismissing the feelings that blur lines. She turned to go in search of Julian. Mikey, like one of those sham magicians, she would later reflect, awaiting his cue, reached out and opened the window. A tiny bird hopped in and stood on the marble sink, looking about it in its vigilant, but not fearful fashion. Mikey gently extended his hand and the bird hopped into his palm. He tilted the glass towards the creature, allowing it to drink with ease. It was more than thirst – it seemed to Kate – it was a libation being offered and accepted.

Julian came into the kitchen, clumsily trying to set down the hot pizzas. 'Dinner's here!' he announced.

The bird flew from Mikey's hands, crashing into the window in its attempt to escape. He picked it up, cradled it in his cupped palms, and walked out onto the back veranda. Kate and Julian watched him bend his head and whisper to the bird, something indecipherable, a prayer, Arabic perhaps, or, who knows, some made-up language that young people use to distance themselves from the adult world. Then, in one swift motion, he propelled the bird into the air, giving it the lift it needed to take off. It flew into the darkness, though its wings seemed hesitant and shaky.

'What was that all about?' Julian asked.

'A sublime moment.'

'Oh God, the Bird-boy of Berea.'

'Don't mock.'

'Okay, I'm sorry. I was just bringing in dinner.'

'Mr Delivery was quick,' she said, peering into one of the boxes.

Her eyes, though, never left Mikey, who continued to stand on the back step, staring out over the hazy Johannesburg skyline.

'Mr Delivery my eye! I had to go out into the jungle to get this dinner for you and St Francis over there. Have I offended him?'

'Who knows?'

Julian found a knife in a drawer and started cutting one of the pizzas into slices. 'Shall I offer him some pizza? Kids love pizza, forgive anything in the face of a greasy offering.'

He spoke with his mouth full, and searched for a napkin in another drawer. 'You're going all silent on me, Kate.'

'Sorry,' she said, 'I was just wondering.'

'What about?'

'About Mikey. What goes on in the head of that kind of child?'

'Kate, he's not a child any more, he must be nineteen years old. And what's more, there is no such thing as a Mikey kind of child, birdman, person, whatever you want to call him, just as there is no such thing as a Kate kind of person! Humans are not types, we are individuals.'

'Am I about to get a Freudian lecture? Oh, I forgot, you're a Jungian.'

His cellphone rang.

'Oh God, there is such a thing as a Val kind of person,' he said. He walked away, speaking into the phone in hushed and anxious tones.

'I have to go,' Julian said, when he returned to the kitchen.

'Problems?'

'Nathan has a fever that won't subside.'

'Then you'd better go.'

'Nathan always has a fever that won't subside. When Val says Nathan has a fever that won't subside, Nathan gets a fever . . .'

'Bo, don't be crass. Maybe your son really is ill.'

They both looked at Mikey, who was sitting on the wall outside, pensively swinging his feet.

73

'Perhaps I should have had a soulful son like Mikey, grieving over birds that the pizza man frightened away.'

'You wouldn't know how to deal with him.'

'And you think I know how to deal with a child who gets a fever when the stock market drops? Just like his damn mother, always worrying about being poor. You know what Val says?'

'As long as it's not crass, Bo.'

'She loves to tell the tale of wrong choices made. Of all the Jews in the country, she had to marry the meschugener who is named after a murderous Pope and has a black man for a God.'

'Borderline, Bo, go home.'

Kate and Julian exchanged their chorused greetings, high-pitched and somewhat frantic, a final attempt to release themselves from the daily camaraderie that their jobs imposed on them. It was said that the President had set this tone of farewell, infusing into his nightly greetings ('Ah yes, Julian, Kate, goodnight, goodnight') a musical solemnity that belied his calm, dignified nature.

Mikey came in and said, 'Auntie Gracie is on the phone, she says it is so urgent.' His voice had taken on a mocking lilt, the emphasis on 'so urgent' charged with false intensity. Julian went away feeling foolish, and resolved never again to greet his colleagues with so much passion.

President or no President.

As Kate spoke to Gracie, she watched Mikey walk up the stairs. He gestured with his cupped hands against his inclined head to indicate that he was going to sleep. A child again, devious, coquettish, asking for a warm embrace, a 'cuddle' even. Kate marched out onto the veranda, into the cool air where she could talk to his aunt without betraying just how distracted she was. Something had happened to Silas, Gracie said, he was being kept in hospital overnight. It was nothing too serious, they didn't think, probably just stress and exhaustion. Kate expressed her concern, offered to stay with Mikey, brushing aside Gracie's mild protests. She made a joke about carrying her toothbrush with her for all emergencies, without a thought about the effect this might have on Lydia's sister. She remembered her, pert and upright. She had an almost feline wariness about her, Kate recalled, but she did not have Lydia's searching, intelligent eyes.

'God, I hope the woman doesn't think I'm having an affair with Silas,' she thought.

But it was too late to do anything about Gracie's perceptions. What could be wrong with Silas? Gracie had probably discussed it in more detail with Mikey – but perhaps it was something best kept between family. She needed a drink. Not Silas's whisky, heavy on the tongue. She found a bottle of wine in the fridge, poured herself a glass and sipped, winced at its acidity, but continued to drink, idly wondering where she would sleep.

She called home again. This time Marguerite answered, and Kate had to add Silas's illness to the story about his wife being in hospital and his son all alone, and not too well himself, apparently, wondering why she had to explain any of this to a guest. Then she asked to speak to Janine, who came onto the phone after an interminable wait. Kate started telling her why it was 'vital' for her to stay over, but Janine stopped her and said: 'You don't owe me an explanation, Katie, but you should speak to Ferial.'

Janine the Logical, deserving of a martyr's title like Joan of Arc or Helen of Troy. Shit, Helen was no martyr, she was the floozie of a thousand ships; the little Kate could remember about ancient Greece, she had read in literature classes at university what seemed like a century ago.

Ferial came on the phone, her voice deep, wounded, manipulative. A gift inherited from her father. It struck that guilty chord that Janine had been unable to reach, and Kate wanted to get a taxi, go home, leave

Mikey a note, Christ, he was eighteen, a man already, full of carnal stratagems. Her place was with her daughter, and later, lovingly remorseful, in bed with Janine, immersed in her clean odours. She started to explain what had happened to Silas and that Mikey was alone, and Ferial's tone changed, as she loudly exclaimed her concern for Mikey, asked her mother to pass on her love.

In the end, affections were exchanged, goodnights said. Ferial let go of her artifices, her ability to arouse all those disempowering maternal instincts that Kate feared. The young woman knew when it was time to withdraw her punishing tone, restoring her mother's equilibrium.

Kate climbed the narrow staircase, glass in hand, more to enhance her mood than anything else, as the wine was undrinkable. It was as if she knew exactly where to go, even though this was the first time during her many visits to Silas's house that she was venturing beyond the 'living quarters' below. The house was tall and narrow, a survivor from Berea's grander days, designed to look like an apartment building in Europe. High ceilings made of pressed steel that a succession of less ostentatious, or simply much poorer, inhabitants had painted over in plain white until elaborate floral patterns faded, becoming gloomy reminders of lives left behind.

Kate's own grandmother, Catherine, had always lamented: 'This is what Africa does to you, it smudges your features.' As a child, Kate used to go around their home shouting, 'It's the light, the merciless light!', imitating her crazy old grandma, who had spent half her life in a state of demented nostalgia, remembering the shadowy beauty of the childhood home in Farnham, wherever that was in 'pretty' little England. Suddenly Kate was lost in a swirl of recollections about her own childhood and the house she had grown up in. Yes, *this* house was not unlike the Jessup home on Muswell Hill in Durban. But Paul Jessup had designed his monument to greed on a grander scale, probably because the fruits of his greed had been greater than what the entrepreneur who built this one could amass.

Kate stopped at the top of the staircase and turned to look down into the dark, cramped well of the house. This was exactly what you imagined when you looked at it from the outside, a poor man's palace marooned in a seawrack of flats, warehouses and whorehouses.

On the landing, she was confronted by four doors. One would be the master bedroom, another would be Mikey's, and a third should be the guest-room. She hoped that it had not yet been turned into a study for Lydia or Mikey. So many of her black colleagues and friends sacrificed this 'extra' space the moment they moved out of the townships, in order to create small havens of intellectual privacy. The ultimate symbol of their new-found freedom, a place where their once forbidden collections of books, paintings and photographs captured at memorable events could be displayed with pride. The anti-utilitarian instincts of people deprived of 'Lebensraum' for so long.

The fourth door – yet another ornate glass pane, another angled and distorted glimpse of the street beyond – led out onto a balcony that extended all around the upper part of the house. This was the door one saw from the street, an elegant touch that revealed the kind of house this was intended to be. Kate tried the handle, found the door unlocked, absently marvelled at how uncharacteristically trusting this was of Silas, and stepped out into the night air, always crisp in Johannesburg.

A spine of yellow street lamps marched rigidly down Louis Botha Avenue towards Orange Grove, Norwood, and Alexandra Township beyond, places that Kate found exciting and alive but that others avoided. Not safe for a woman. More women were raped in this city than anywhere else in the world. The hyperbole of our new struggles.

She heard someone muttering, and listened more closely. A lisping voice, saying a prayer, or singing in a low murmur, a feverish incantation of words, varying in intensity, at once staccato and melodic, today's rap music given a hallowed tone. The door to what must be Mikey's bedroom stood open.

'Mikey?' she called out softly.

There was no answer. The house was quiet, a stillness that accentuated the sound of the traffic on the main road, and the city's distant noises. She peered in through a narrow window, no more than a tall glassed-in slit in the wall, and saw Mikey dimly outlined, lying on his bed. In the darkened room, his naked body was illuminated by a blue glow emanating from his stomach. His arms lay languidly across his body, his hands cupping his genitals. Kate stood at the window, trapped in its monastic narrowness, watching Mikey's lips move like those of a novice priest ferociously asking his God to forgive him the ineluctable sins of his young body.

She was intruding on some kind of ritual, stumbled onto unwittingly, glass in hand like a typical bored, northern suburbs madam, Kate thought. Her trembling fingers signified both fear and excitement, she should draw back now, turn and walk away to safety. In the good old days, among the righteous people of the old country, her mother, gin-soaked and genteel, tall and statuesque, would have been able to enter the young man's room and command him to get dressed, make himself decent. Or with equal ease, instruct him to lend her the use of his beauty. But the young man, dark, sinewy, would have been a servant or the son of a servant, and the relationship would have been proprietorial. Vicky Jessup ('Victoria,' she always corrected people) and her male servants: the celebrated sins of Durban society.

And now Kate, too, the daughter doomed to be like her mother, could not turn away from such beauty. But fuck, she thought, I am no lavender-and-lace lady from the suburbs in search of danger and mystery, and this, this terrible need to stand here and stare at Mikey's ritual of nakedness, has nothing to do with being black or white. Age, yes, and curiosity. She had never slept with someone so young. A nimble animal, not fully grown, still some evidence of the cub's softness he was rapidly shedding.

'Ingwe!' was the word she had been searching for.

A game-viewing trip, long ago. A private estate close to the Kruger Park. Belonged to some business partner of her father's. A word hissed by a game ranger: 'Leopard!' His excitement was real, not just dredged up for the benefit of the visitors. 'It hits you in the stomach, every time you see a leopard up close,' the head ranger would say over dinner, later on.

That morning: light cutting through the shadows, trees gaining shape, the bush taking its mysterious, mute form. Like something from the Hemingway books that her father read. The animal lay stretched out on the branch of a tree, breathing heavily, obviously recovering from some strenuous exertion. 'It has just killed, dragged its prey up into the branches,' the young game ranger said in a whisper.

Kate, thirteen, fourteen then, remembered the bristling blond hair on the ranger's tanned forearm, white (those were the apartheid days, after all), adolescent in his good looks. And exotic in those surroundings, his Shangaan smooth, native almost, foreigners said. He conversed easily with the black guide sitting in the pilot seat up front, practising the mock democracy that comes with half-knowledge. The Shangaan guide decided where to go, which turn to take, when to slow down, when to speed up. The young white man always remembered his place, though, and the male preening for the sake of the young, fuckable white women on the safari was reserved for himself and the blond clones who drove the Land Rovers.

All around Kate, the transfixed eyes of her parents, of other adults, enthralled by their closeness to the animal. Only the children, she among them, seemed truly fascinated by the leopard, by its intrinsic beauty. The Land Rover inched forward, testing the animal's territorial sense. It rose, its yellow-green eyes losing their indolence, revealing a cold and naked capacity for savagery that someone would be stupid enough to describe as 'noble'. The leopard bared its fangs for one fleeting, petulant moment, causing a ripple of held-back bodies in the Land Rover. Kate remembered thinking that there was nothing noble about the leopard's ability to tear them apart, nor would there be anything noble about being torn apart. It descended from the tree, a casual, vaulting motion, and loped off into the bush.

'It is trying to draw us away from its kill,' the ranger said. His practised wisdom sounded false, banal in the hushed morning air. Elsewhere in the bush they heard the echoed shouts of 'Ingwe!' as other viewing parties spied the animal. *Ingwe*. How it transformed a simple leopard into something mystical, a thing of legends.

Mikey, harbouring a savagery of his own, that manipulative surliness, a 'mystique' created by his quiet, withdrawn manner, needed a name more dignified than that. 'Michael, Michael,' Kate whispered, as if testing the sound of his name, trying to picture him fully grown, his soft, skinny build giving way to something harder and fleshier. She stopped herself abruptly. Shit, she knew that in the end, if someone found her here, peering in through a window at the young man asleep on his bed, all this romanticizing, this mythologizing, would count for nothing. It is like game viewing, watching a sleek and wondrous animal in its own habitat, she could say, but no one would see the innocence, the beauty of observing beauty for its own sake. She would be a voyeur, a dirty old woman watching a teenager play with himself.

But that was what fascinated her. Mikey lay completely still, not masturbating or even caressing himself. He could be dead, for all she knew. She pressed her face up against the window pane, looked closer, at the detail of his languid, flung-back nudity. She saw some kind of stone nestling in his navel. That's where the weird blue glow came from. It was not a diamond or some other precious stone. A gem that big and Silas would have a fortune resting on his son's belly. Must be something bought from one of those 'New Age' trinket stores. The things they trick young people into buying. He seemed to be breathing, she could see the steady intake and expulsion of air.

He stirred, raised himself on his elbows. Kate pulled away from the window, hoping that he had not seen her, though she imagined his eyes searching for the intruder, for *her*, his slow 'ingwe' eyes returning to their barbarous purpose of hunting down prey. She stood immobile for a few seconds, then retreated to the end of the balcony, emptied her glass in one gulp, and stood watching the stealthy, solitary traffic of people hurrying through the darkness in the street below, her stomach turning from the rancid wine. She would be safe now, consumed by the battle against the rising acidity in her abdomen. Nothing like bitter wine, drunk to the dregs, to save you from an infinite folly.

7

Gracie could not sleep. What a hot night, she thought, then corrected herself: it was not the night, it was this room, this house, this township-house that kept them here, trapped by the nostalgia of people like Alec. Walls built of ash brick were economical, cheap – but they *breathe*, they told us when we bought these places. What they didn't tell us was that they breathe the wrong way, they suck air out of the house, then clog up like the lining of some diseased lung that can't suck any air back in.

She turned onto her side, lay close to the wall, finding a perverted attraction in its putrid smells. Just like when she was in boarding school. Funny how Lydia said the same thing: she too had found the stench of those austere convent toilets irresistible. And *these* odours were her own, fifteen years of accumulated sweat, children's sour vomit, her own smell of washed-off lavender, Alec's groin when he was 'in the mood', his farts after a long day of feasting. The ingrained reek of cooked food, toilet smells subtly enriched by the disinfectants ritually splashed down the bowl.

The history of their sojourn here, preserved within these walls. An archive you browsed through with your nose. And they knew – those men in their grey suits – they knew when they sold us this cheap dream, a house, a garden, a dog, a place you can call your own, that we'd build on it. Additional rooms, second storeys, swimming pools, rock gardens, water features, they knew that we'd make this slum liveable. And now we can't sell, we can't get out of here. Ja, they call us apartheid's astronauts, trapped in this damn twilight world. Let Mr Mandela come and live here, and then tell me about his miracle.

'Ag tog, Gracie, kry nou rus,' Alec said.

She absorbed Alec's Afrikaans and resentfully translated it into English.

'Oh please, Gracie, settle down.'

When you lose your language, you lose your soul. But English isn't your language, he would retort, Zulu is. Gracie was tired of explaining to Alec – and his sceptical Johannesburg township kind – that the name 'Oliphant', sadly, was Scots in origin and not an Anglicization of 'Ndhlovu', the isiZulu word for 'elephant' and a common African surname. If it had been, perhaps we would belong! Here we are, in our twilight zone between black and white, trying to be both and ending up as neither.

Alec was half-awake, she knew, and would not want to debate the origins of her family name, not at two o'clock in the morning, anyway. But he would ask over breakfast what the problem was, why she kept on tossing and turning like a 'sucklet on a spit'. Alec had his way with words. Abused them with great abandon. Wonderful entertainment at drunken braais, but not worth a damn when it came to discussing things calmly and coherently. Like why we don't just cut our losses, sell while we still can, and get out of here.

She was tired, and longed to sleep, but some malignant spirit pressed down on her. She turned towards Alec, faded body cologne sharpened by sweat. Alec the fancy man, he didn't believe in taking a shower before bedtime. It washes away the sleep, he says. He turned to face her.

'Don't get any ideas,' she said.

'About?'

'Sex.'

'What's bothering you, bokkie?'

'You!'

'Again? What about now?'

'Tonight, what you said about that woman Kate . . . being a dyke.'

'Jurre, Gracie, I've forgotten about that already.'

'It's, you know, an intimate thing to say.'

'Shoo! You've got some big words now, hey? – intimate, nogal.'

'Don't mock me.'

'Gracie, *lovey*, it's past two in the morning, you can't sleep, and now you want conversation, about nothing at all. Sex would be better than talking about Kate the dyke.'

'I want to know what you know.'

'About Kate?'

'No, about what's going on between Silas and Lydia.'

'How should I know?'

'Alec, Silas was looking at you tonight, when you were speaking, then he went out like a light.'

Alec was quiet, his eyes open, staring at nothing in particular. Gracie sensed his alertness.

'Look, I know that you and Silas are friends . . .' she said.

'We know each other since we were kids in Newclare.'

'Yes, I've heard that story, so tell me what he's up to.'

'Why should he be up to something?'

'Lydia didn't just cut herself on a broken beer glass. Or at least the glass didn't throw itself onto the floor! Think about it, Lydia has at least a dozen different lacerations, like she was cut repeatedly. How does something like that *just* happen?'

Alec sat up. 'Why don't you ask Lydia?'

'She won't speak about it.'

'She won't speak and Silas won't speak, but I'm supposed to know what goes on in their heads?'

'I know it has something to do with the past, something that happened soon after they got married.'

'Ja, well, lots of things happened after they got married . . .'

'I don't mean all that political stuff, I mean between them. And you can't remember anything?'

'No, I can't remember anything.'

'God, Alec, you're always remembering how things were in the old days; not a week goes by without you telling one of those "when we were young in Newclare" stories.'

'But you're looking for a revelation. Well, God hasn't come down yet to talk to Alec and reveal to him what's going on in the heads of Silas and Lydia. Maybe God doesn't do townships.'

His voice was clear, his words freed from their camouflaging tangle of colloquial expressions. She wanted to explain that her only motive was her concern for Lydia, who was her sister, after all, but he was out of bed and out of the bedroom already. This was the furtive Alec who surfaced now and then, cold and hard and unreachable, a stranger who talked differently from the man she knew. Even the way he walked at such moments, upright, without his practised township 'bump', made him seem like someone else.

Alec walked through the house dressed only in a pair of shorts. It was too hot for pyjamas, even in winter. Walls that incubated their own heat. Would make a fortune in cold places. Maybe he could persuade Martha's Canadian husband – what's-his-name? John! – get him to invest some dollars in leftover apartheid technology. Make something out of our suffering, true spirit of free enterprise. Land of opportunity. Love it. Unlike Gracie, who still has the phobias inherited from some stuck-up old ancestor with a hatred of Africa. Why did he come here if it was so wonderful in Scotland?

Alec loved the sensual feel of sweat on his skin. It made him think of the 'grand' days in the old townships, where people slept with wide-open windows, nights balmy, the breeze cool, life going by softly, shadows gliding along the street. The term 'grand' had nothing to do with grandeur, but with goodness and simplicity. The ability of people to understand each other and empathize – even when someone was doing things they disagreed with. Back then everyone recognized that the need to survive was paramount, so that breaking the law, dealing in stolen goods, running fah-fee or owning a shebeen were all acts of survival, and every occupation had its own dignity.

And survival in those days – if you were black – meant having to accommodate forces more powerful than yourself. Now moral zealots were running the world. They were always judging others, looking for something corrupt even in the efforts of ordinary people struggling to make a living. These fucken holier-than-thous have the luxury of jobs and good positions in government. Love to see them come and live – and survive – out here in the lokasies! The world was being fucked, all for the sake of some vague principle. Law and order, it's the joke that whites sold us. Gave us the government, kept the money. Now we police ourselves. Look at the high walls and the barbed wire. Just to protect the misery we had all along. No wonder the crime rate's going through the roof.

Alec made himself a cup of tea and sat down at the table, stirring in the sugar. Don't drink any caffeine after four in the afternoon, Gracie said, it keeps you awake. And there she was, unable to sleep, and here he was, driven from his bed by her obsessions, trying to sweeten this bitter brew. Overcome by a sudden rage at Gracie, at Silas and Lydia, at Mikey for not coming to the hospital, at Kate for her intrusion, at Nelson Mandela the political saint, at the whole 'beloved fokop' as he called the world, he stirred the tea violently, until it began to spill over the sides of the mug, staining the newspaper he had unconsciously placed it on, until the pounding of his heart was so loud he feared it would stop, and the world began spinning along with the swirling, tepid liquid.

Then the ancient clock in the kitchen gave its hourly 'bong' and he was able to push the tea away from him, cold and undrinkable. It was 3 a.m. He realized that he was still stirring the tea, which had gone cold, and felt foolish for having spent so much time worrying about things that were beyond his control.

Heaven help him, he didn't want to go mad, like those old bastards in Tara, off their fucken heads because they were always discontented about something. They were either too black or not black enough, they had lived too much or lived too little, they remembered everything or had nothing worth remembering. Ja, he always said that a happy nation has no memory. That's the problem with this country, we want to forgive but we don't want to forget. You can't have it both ways.

He padded back to the bedroom, his feet loving the touch of the cool floor. His anger at Gracie for driving him from his bed had calmed as well. Not good for her to see him like this, all twisted up inside, just like the rest of them. He would get into bed, make his peace with her, hold her breast in his hand, perhaps she'd be remorseful enough to pull him close, open her legs in that quick way of hers, let him in with a sigh, always helps him to sleep, this making-up sex in the middle of the night. He searched the darkened room, trying to read her mood, her posture, her eyes, trying to figure out whether she had softened.

He climbed sheepishly back into bed. 'Sorry about that, liefie, I didn't mean to be so abrupt,' he said gently.

She was grateful for the smoothness of his contrition (even though she knew that in his heart he wasn't sorry about a damn thing) and she didn't want to lie next to him all night trapped in her own lonely discontent. He would soon fall asleep anyway, and in the morning look at her in surprise, say that she 'shouldn't let things get to her like that'. The truthfulness of his statement would hurt. She would remember all over again that people felt she was too educated for her own good, that she had married below her station, that both she and Lydia had not fulfilled their potential. It was as if this failure was genetic, a defeat of the blood, ugly and sinister like a disease.

Alec's hand was on her breast and she loved him now for his very deviousness. She pulled him close to her and slid her legs around his waist, granting him her rare submissiveness. This way he would come quickly, fall away from her with a happy sigh, letting her drift off, unaroused, into her own exhausted sleep.

Alec made it possible for life to go on.

He does not know how to pray, Mikey realizes. He does not have a religion, there is no ritual he can follow to lull himself into sleep, there are no words he can utter, formulaic and patterned, to relieve himself of the responsibility of his thoughts. He tries to dispel his unease by rationalizing: we are at the end of the twentieth century, this is the Age of Reason, life is determined by logic, not the irrational magic of divine beings. But this sense of not belonging, of being unmoored, is the fault of his parents. Neither Silas nor Lydia ever thought to offer him the choice of following one of their faiths.

Anyway, Silas is a half-hearted Dutch Protestant, his soul confused by the omnipotence of Ali Ali's Islam, by the purity of its whispered music, its ability to conquer even a proud woman like Ouma Angel. Lydia's Catholicism, of course, is intact, fierce even, but secretive and personal. Christ the Redeemer reduced to a private refuge.

Silas and Lydia had brought Mikey up as a Christmas Christian. Celebrate that one glorious day and your Christian name is justified. The mystery of God laid out on a platter, turkey well-basted, crisped skin, cranberry sauce poured like blood, and afterwards, a dulling libation of wine. Easter: hot cross buns. No wonder the voice of God is silent in his mind.

He peers down at the fragment of purloined holy Kaaba stone nestled in his navel, its blue glow imbuing his body with an ethereal beauty. Ali Ali is someone he can identify with. Oupapa Ali, a man who knew the tools of his trade. Pray in hushed tones, a language they do not know, the meaning in its lyrical incantation, bathe it all in hallowed light. Give them something they can feel, almost, the enticement of visible salvation, the conjurer's ability to transform the ordinary. Take this puny flesh, O Lord, and render it irresistible. Perhaps he should take up a charlatan trade, Michael Ali, inspired by the mighty Ali Ali, his progenitor.

Mikey senses an intrusion, a disbeliever – looking for chinks in his holy armour – glances up through heavy eyelids. He sees Kate peering in through the tall and narrow window, designed perhaps for voyeurs. He resents her for having disturbed his slow descent into sleep, but does not move, watches her draw away, her retreat reluctant. The glass of wine brought to her lips – to show nonchalance, to deny the intensity with which she has been watching him – gives her a half-drunken allure.

When she is no longer within view, he struggles to retain his sense of drowsiness, to continue sinking into that mystical moment that precedes sleep. He recalls something he has read, the description of a woman, naked, strong dark shoulders rising from . . . water, a well of darkness? He remembers the first time he met Kate. Christmas, a holiday, a cottage on the banks of the Bushman's River, at the foot of Giant's Castle in the Drakensberg. Paul Wilson's house in the woods. Liberal, white, defying the law, esteemed lawyer, ceremonial bravery of allowing a 'forbidden' family to holiday on his exclusive property. Kate is drowning, waving her arms, screaming. Only Mikey is there to observe her watery death. He is young and powerless, and detached, watching a preordained rite. Who is he to interfere with the cycles of life and death? After all, he is only a child. The thought of her dead, naked, forbidden, fills him with pleasure. She has known his father for many years. Comrades in MK. Secrets shared. Nothing is sacrosanct in the struggle. The wisdom he has seen them wear like threadbare mantles, over and over.

He wakes from his dream of swirling water, shivers, and thinks: what was Kate doing there, at that secluded refuge which Paul Wilson once offered Silas and Lydia? She was the intermediary. Natal high society, everyone knows everyone else.

'Mikey, say hello to Mr Wilson. Paul, this is Mikey, our son.'

A warm greeting, the smell of old leather, his coat, his boots, his face. Now Mikey recalls that Kate's shoulders are white, not dark. Freckles on her back. That day, she carried her child cradled on her stomach, like an ornament, something to display. The cool, clear water lapping around them. The child screamed. Delight, fear, he can no longer remember. Kate's thrust-out pelvis comes back to him, the child being swayed about, the startling clarity of her unblemished sex contrasting with her mother's pubic hair, heavy, sinister, extraordinarily like a man's bearded face.

Mikey is aroused, a skin-hunger is awakened, pure, brutal: that erection of the mind he associates with Mireille.

It was three in the morning – *precisely*, Kate would later reflect – when she saw Mikey standing in the doorway of the guest-room, his nakedness having lost its lustrous blue glow. A pale and sinewy youth, gaunt almost, and even more beautiful now that he had rid himself of the 'exotic animal' posture he had so deliberately cultivated (for her sake, she thought). She quickly dismissed this discordant notion and raised the covers, letting him slip into bed beside her.

His mouth upon hers was warm, and the hour so opportune, his coming to her designed for the moment when her restlessness, that drifting in and out of sleep, legs crossed and uncrossed, was becoming unbearable. It was as if he knew exactly when she would be ready to receive him.

Afterwards, he lies awake, thinking that the image of a woman's strong, rounded shoulders comes from Kafka's *Diaries*. September 1911, Kafka reading Goethe's *Diaries*, is distracted by some or other woman. He imagines her rising in an 'ash-grey-coloured bodice'.

It is not Kate, but his mother.

8

Silas awoke from his own dream of death.

Mikey and Kate, naked and gleaming with sweat, watched from some distant shore, as Silas was swept away on a bier of floating flowers to an exotic burial at sea. The eyes of the living would have perceived the two watchers as specks on a rocky outcrop, braving the waves crashing around them, but to Silas's dead man's vision they were discernible in minute detail, their faces most of all, and it struck him as his bier reached a narrow river mouth, that they were singing, that he could not hear them, nor could he hear the noise of the waves. Being dead meant nothing more than entering a state of profound deafness.

His rational, living mind intruded: the geography was all wrong, no river has waves like that, huge, foaming breakers. And Mikey too was all wrong, his hair a long flowing blond that would thin to a frail baldness when he grew old, like Du Boise, dry patches flaking off from his exposed scalp. No, *his* Mikey has wavy hair that will go grey with age, but retain its fullness. He will have the silver-headed lustre of African sages. What kind of heritage is it that dooms young men to acquiring that scraggy, white man's hairlessness?

A distant fear came back to Silas, one that he rarely allowed to take shape in his mind – *Mikey is not my son, not physically* – and he struggled to rouse himself before the dream of death flowed into his life.

He was alive, that much he knew, it was five o'clock in the morning. A luminous clock on the wall told him the cheerless time. On either side of him, two old men breathing heavily, pipes stuck up their noses, watched on raised elbows and with frowning eyes a struggle against death taking place across from them. It was obvious that they too had been woken abruptly. A group of doctors and nurses surrounded someone's bed, whispering earnestly, one of them issuing instructions in God's ghostly voice, or so it seemed to Silas, still hovering between his sedated sleepiness and the sudden, urgent need to be awake.

Finally, the medical staff abandoned their attempts to revive the stricken patient. They stepped away from the bed for a moment, revealing a body already cold and curled up like a dead foetus, blankets having been flung away in its moment of ultimate despair. Some poor bastard who thought the expense of this private clinic would save him from the inevitability of death. Must have been dead already when they discovered him. A nurse turned and saw the audience. Silas and the other two patients had settled comfortably up against their pillows, as if ready to watch a movie on television. She gave them a steely look, then hastily pulled a screen around the dead man.

The nurses worked surreptitiously behind the screen, until men in white coats came and wheeled the shrouded body away. The screen was whisked open and tied back into its normal position. The disarrayed womb of the deathbed had been tidied, all freshly made up and stark in its white neatness. Ready, Silas thought, for the next diseased body. Somewhere a blue light was switched on, and heaven – or hell – had the same blue glow that was given off by Ali Ali's holy stone, the one that had gone missing from the velvet box in Silas's desk a few years ago.

Suddenly Silas had an unbearable need to urinate, to get out of this bed and out of this hospital. Fragments of his dream came back, Mikey and Kate on that distant shore, laughing with an intimacy that he could only interpret in his mind, because he could not hear them. Somehow Kate's mouth formed soundless laughter in the same way Lydia's did, in her rare moments of mirth. He pictured Lydia, how beautiful she was when she laughed, her stern face all lit up and alive, and when she made love. He dismissed the unsettling combinations he was creating in his mind, Mikey and Kate, Mikey and Lydia. The leapfrog logic of a mathematical equation.

Who had stayed with Mikey last night, he wondered absently. But pressed by the dire need to find a toilet, he forgot his anxiety. Gracie and Mam Agnes would have taken care of the problem. Sane and sober people, the Oliphants, they would have made sure the child was not alone and feeling abandoned. But they, Silas and Lydia, the whole damn family in fact, must stop thinking of Mikey as a child. A misjudgement that could have serious consequences.

He was padding through the ward when he realized that the surgical gown he was wearing was open at the back. Yes, he thought, they always do this in hospitals, rob you of your dignity. Private or state, it didn't matter, there was a mentality that went with these places. He was wearing this gown because some nurse had decided it was the regulation wear for anyone who didn't bring along his own sleeping clothes.

So now we must go around with our pyjamas handy. You've been in an accident, mister, where's your pyjamas? Anyway, he needed to piss, and couldn't help it if his arse was on show. He went in search of the toilets.

'Mr Ali, you shouldn't be out of bed,' a voice called.

He turned and saw the two nurses who had tidied up after the dead man, standing in the corridor. He had interrupted their conspiratorial whispering.

'I need the toilet,' he said.

'All you have to do is buzz, there's a little buzzer above your bed,' the one with the steely eyes said in a jarringly sweet voice.

He disliked her instinctively, her false, honeyed tones grated the sense of gravity still inhabiting him after his dream. He felt pure somehow, vulgar and ugly and totally without pretence.

'What, were you going to do it for me?' he asked.

The nurse stiffened, her companion stifled a laugh, then quickly masked her amusement behind a cold demeanour as rehearsed as her colleague's melodious politeness. Again Lydia's face intruded, hung its stoic mask over the sweet one's features. Lydia ready to come off duty after a long night of the dead and the dying, being abused by an ill-tempered patient. Going through her mind would be the futility of their profession. Some of them had become nurses only because they had no alternative. He remembered her bitter contemplation of having to go to nurse's college because she had no choice. She was black and could not find a place in a university, and even if she had, her parents had no money to pay the fees. Perhaps she had married him because he also represented the lesser of many evils (in her community, a single woman who wanted a child and the occasional companionship of a man was seen as no better than a whore).

But he also remembered the simple generosity with which she had loved him. No more than sixteen she was, much younger than he, and she had offered her slender beauty with an instinctive, knowing grace that made him think – in his jealous moments – that she was 'experienced'. Yes, back then he did think of women who were no longer virgins as soiled and passed around. He recalled how he could not help but search for the bloody evidence of her virginity's denouement. Ah, how insufferable we must all have been back then, oppressed and oppressive, dark-faced and dark-minded because we could think of nothing but our suffering, the hallowed torment we wore like badges of courage. Your skin colour determined the colour of your soldier's uniform.

Except for young people like his brother Toyer and that other fellow, the poet, what was his name? Never mind, the memory is allowed to fail at this hour, the circumstances, the need to piss.

'Lydia was born to be a courtesan,' the poet said (fuck, what is his name?). Crazy as hell, read his dry, painful verse to the dead in Croesus Cemetery on a cold winter's night, refusing to go home and face his dying father. 'Nothing more tedious than someone who is about to die. Always asking you to forgive sins you didn't even know about.' The first time he ever said something directly. He was Lydia's friend, no one knew how or why. She loved his madness, his low mocking voice, as gentle as this nurse's. Shameless in his effort to seduce her. But she had spurned the poet's body – 'Love me for my mind,' the swine said, 'I'll show you the greatest erection a mind can have' – because she was young and believed in the fidelity of love. He made Silas suffer. The hectoring beauty of his verses, the deadly patriotism that corroded the soul, but he had a way with words that made it impossible not to love him publicly. It made one look churlish not to rejoice in the way he celebrated even their cruel township life.

Did Lydia know his secret loathing of the man? What would she do if he came along now, drunk, dissolute, with that wine-soaked lure of lyrical words, and offered her an escape from the dull tragedies of her life? Would she succumb, has she ever done so, heaven knows she loves words so much, so does their son. A mortal affliction? No, she has never betrayed him, Silas says to himself, no, it is something she would not be able to hide from him.

He urinated. At this age you feel more relief than pleasure. The simple triumph of being able to discharge your bodily waste. The nurse had handed him his clothes and a towel, punishing him for his boorishness with a disciplined display of professionalism. He felt a sharp regret at the way he had treated her. Then, standing under the shower, enjoying the flow of water over his body, contemplating, as he did each morning, the things that needed doing, ordering them in his mind, setting priorities, things left undone, accomplishments savoured, he gradually found absolution in the cleansing flow of heat. Would have made a good Catholic, the ritual of trespass and forgiveness, the solemnity with which human frailty is dealt with.

He would atone, as soon as he was dressed, for having spoken to her so sharply, for the brutal abuse of his position as a paying customer. How things have changed; in the old days, his behaviour would have earned him a scolding. A matron summoned from some higher sanctuary in the hospital. Rubber soles squealing murderously on the linoleum floor, beware, Matron Augustus, with her august bearing and blazing eyes, coming to mete out justice. No need for all that now, this new liberated Age of Truth and Confession. He rehearsed how he would say, 'I'm sorry for being so rude,' and she would smile and say, 'It's all right, Mr Ali,' and he would go away feeling virtuous.

In his coat pocket, he found a plastic bag containing his car keys, watch, wallet, fountain pen and silver card-holder – the contents of a man's pockets betray his station in life – and wondered what the nurse thought of him, of people like him, the new elite who governed the country?

He remembered her face, delicate wrinkles at the corners of her mouth. Mid-thirties, old enough to remember the 'struggle', even to have been part of it. Demonstrating student, nurse who helped tear-gassed marchers, refused to record a name in a register because the cops would use it to trace dissidents.

Out in the dark corridor (a short respite before the place came to wheel-screeching life) he saw the nurse seated at her station. Blue light from a lamp, the tilting shade pulled down like a policeman's peaked cap. She was staring at the papers on her desk, at nothing at all, her arms resting idly before her. Under the desk, her legs hung apart in an attitude of utter weariness. Black stockings gave her thighs a youthful slenderness. He stood in the shadows observing her sadness. He bent down to retrieve the keys he had dropped, and glimpsed the faded 'v' of her underwear. He raised himself much too quickly and suffered a moment of dizziness. The soiled garment, evidence of her toil, stayed with him, even though he tried to dispel its image behind his closed eyes. He berated himself silently for this sordidness. Still, it would be wonderful if she did have a secret sex life, even if it took place in dingy rooms or up against walls. Anything would be better than that slumped-forward resignation, chance encounters with strangers included.

She was Lydia, she was his mother, she was every woman he had ever known and whose suffering made it impossible for him to truly love her. Even Betty, whom he had once loved simply for the sake of it, for her smell, for the way she slept, for the nightmares she spoke out loud, which made him an unwilling accomplice in her intrigues. And for the danger, ah, the blerry edge that the threat of death once brought to his dulled flesh.

'Mr Ali? Are you all right?' the nurse said, interrupting his reverie.

Shit, what the hell is going on with me? Have to pull myself together, take charge of this fucken body, not allow it to do these unexpected things.

'I'm fine, I'm fine,' he said, his cold manner restored, tempered by a ritual politeness.

'You have to sign this form,' she said.

'What form?'

'Refused Hospital Treatment.'

'An RHT? Christ, I didn't think they still existed.'

'They exist, for patients like you, sir,' she said quietly.

He signed the form, glanced up at her, turned and walked away.

Silas drove through the early-morning traffic, thinking about how things had changed. Now the lanes were clogged with people like him, black and white, travelling in contradictory directions, just like a normal city anywhere in the world. But ten years ago, he would have been one of the few black people driving on his own in a sedan like this, going home to a place in the suburbs after a night of revelry or whatever it was that had kept him out all night. Everywhere, there would have been buses and Kombi-taxis ferrying black people to their jobs – domestics, power-station workers, railway clerks, hospital order-lies, policemen coming on duty. Around the Johannesburg central station, the takeaway cafés would have been busy selling pap and steak, roasted mielies, the kind of fast food that nevertheless sustained workers all day. Ja, in many ways it was great back then, a simpler, more wholesome life.

On an impulse, he swerved off at an exit that would take him through the city centre itself, past the West Street taxi rank, where the armada of careening vehicles forced him to slow down. Even when he emerged from the congestion of what was called 'murder mile', he continued to drive slowly, along Market Street, past the City Hall and the abandoned old Post Office, turned into Von Wielligh Street and then into Jeppe, stopped outside Anstey's Building, where he and Betty and shared a secret apartment, sub-let from a film-maker friend who was never home. In those days, the streets had a kind of lived-in peace-fulness, the first joggers braving the smog and the erratic drivers,

hung-over revellers in search of a recuperative breakfast, street clean-
ers who followed in the wake of the watering tank that left the streets
damp and fragrant for a few minutes. Life in the city was strangely
normal then, given how abnormal the whole country was. Now the
place was busy in an overwrought sort of way, drivers clutching their
steering wheels, shoulders hunched and eyes vigilant.

He remembered that there used to be a Brazilian Coffee Shop on
the corner, and the thought of having a cup of coffee seemed
immensely attractive. But the quiet street made him feel uneasy, and
he recalled that the Brazilian had closed down even before he and Betty
split up. Anstey's Building itself had been invaded by squatters and
now had a derelict air about it. Betty was gone, moved with her
husband to Australia or England, wherever it was that embittered white
people moved to these days. They had loved each other absolutely, he
and Betty, once when it was dangerous to love like that, selfishly, ruthless in their disregard for others.

'I am going to see my husband in detention today, you know,' she
said.

Then she knelt down and took his penis in her mouth, and when
he ejaculated, she swallowed, and asked, 'Will you do something for
me?'

'What?'

'Take my taste home to your wife?'

She took his hand and guided him into her vagina, helped him to
gather its secretions on his finger, took the finger to his mouth and
made him suck it, and sealed the salty taste with a musty kiss that was
sweet, still so sweet.

Silas realized the sentimental objective of his detour, and chastized
himself aloud, 'Come on, Sielas! You can't go on like this!' Using
Jackson's intonation – Siel*as* – reminded him that his son was alone at
home. Lydia, awake now and lying in her hospital bed, would be

anxious, and if she did not hear from him soon – 'Hi, I'm home and Mikey is all right' – she would react. Anger made her unpredictable. He could see her signing a Refused Hospital Treatment form – Christ, that RHT thing really brought back memories – going home in a taxi, sitting at the back, legs stretched out on the seat.

He accelerated, drove quickly through the narrow streets, slowing down only when he entered the busy main road leading to Berea.

Mikey was in the kitchen, standing before the sink, eating cereal from one of Lydia's prize dinner-set bowls. He acknowledged Silas's questioning look, held up the bowl and appraised his transgression, smiled calmly, the Mikey of every day.

They exchanged greetings, hugged, asked each other in turn, 'How are you?'

Then Silas said: 'Were you alone here last night?'

'No, Kate stayed behind, but she's gone now. Listen, Dad, you'd better call Mom at the hospital.'

'She's called already?'

'Ja, but I think *you'd* better call and tell her I'm okay.'

He looked into the already inscrutable depths of Mikey's green eyes, contemplated challenging the obvious deflection of the questions looming in his mind – 'Were you okay, did Kate make supper, why didn't you go and stay over at Mam Agnes's or Auntie Gracie's?' – then turned away to call Lydia, making up a placatory speech in his mind.

When he arrived at his office in Pretoria, after the hour-long drive on the freeway, Silas graciously received expressions of concern from his Director-General (Kate had called to tell them of his sudden collapse in hospital) and from colleagues. His very presence at work 'after such an ordeal' reinforced the sacrificial proportions of his dedication.

Belatedly, he remembered to call Mam Agnes and tell her that he was all right. Yes, yes, Mikey was okay as well.

Then he had to deal with the first crisis of the day. Someone from the ruling party had accused Archbishop Tutu of naivety, saying that no one, least of all a black man like him who had suffered so much, should dare to equate the inevitable excesses of the liberation struggle with the organized murder of the apartheid state. So now the party – the liberation movement, the entity that should *embody* truthfulness, as Tutu had said with rather pious sarcasm – was at loggerheads with the Chairman of the TRC. Tempers had to be cooled, conciliatory statements made, denials issued. '*There is no rift between the government and the TRC.*'

Finally, Silas was able to retreat to his office, take a painkiller for the headache that had distracted him more than once that morning. 'You're not listening to me,' that fucking difficult woman from the SABC had said during the daily press briefing, when he ignored one of her questions.

He stood at the window, stared out over the tree-lined streets of the capital. There had been too much rain and the jacarandas had blossomed early this year – the El Niño weather system, some minor office sage had said. Anyway, the place had lost its softening purple haze much too soon, quickly reverting to the nakedness of its carefully laidout criss-cross of streets, the usual array of triumphalist squares and shat-upon statues spawned by all pretentious political minds. The world over. Through the ages. From Alexander the Great to . . . God, hope that fate never befalls Mandela. Bronze likenesses burning in the African sun, stench of bird droppings, pigeon shit the worst, people say.

Usually, he had to make an effort to shake off the trite, imperious feeling that this vantage point brought. Very few in the new government had the privilege of such a towering office window, it depended not only on your formal position, but on the role you played, the sensitivity of your work. How much your Minister needed you. This morning the view evoked only sadness in him.

Lydia had sounded strangely content when he called, accepting his assurances that Mikey was okay and that his own health was fine. Was her real concern for him and his health, or was she worried that Mikey would be left to his own devices? He could no longer think of Mikey 'being alone', if this implied abandonment.

He went over the previous night's events in his mind. Lydia's power of artifice had not been at its greatest, he had not been taken at flood by her grief, it could not have been enough to disable him so abruptly, to blow a fuse in his brain. It was Alec's voice that had brought back some uncontainable memory, a grey-black photo of that day, the incident with Du Boise. Alec was saying something banal last night, he recalled. Alec was always saying something banal these days, but the timbre of his voice last night, its vibration, metallic, brittle, had resurrected a long-suppressed detail from the night of Lydia's rape.

Silas closed his eyes and listened to Alec's voice again, and there it was, a voice among many voices. Christ, what was he thinking? Voices like that come from a vast genetic pool. Millions of us, bastardized, hybrid, but still cut according to a pattern. The son of a slave-owner takes as his bride a captive slave child, they produce a bastard child, this bastard marries yet another child of master and meid, miesies and boy, and so forth, ad infinitum, basic piel-en-poes history. Any one of a hundred thousand men could have a voice exactly like that.

But Alec's voice *was* distinctive, his township 'bry' unique, tongue pressed against his teeth so that he pronounced 'trow' for throw. When he was a child, he always ended up saying 'Treesa' for 'Theresa' when calling out to his mother. In times of real stress, it came out as an exaggerated, hissed 'Treesssa!' Yes, that flaw marked him, Alec whispering, Alec praying, Alec baying like a hound at soccer matches; the same way Silas's own childhood betrayed him when he was excited, bringing out the 'dem' and 'dose' of his heritage.

If Alec had been present that night, it could only have been as perpetrator, or conspirator, at best. Not as victim, no, everyone would have been made to know. Alec was never one to keep his suffering silent.

'Alec was one of them? Fuck off, Silas, fuck off, what are you thinking?' Silas said to himself.

Speaking the unspeakable out loud had saved his sanity in the past, confused his interrogators, and, above all, allowed him to retain his sense of space (solitary confinement disoriented you, made you think you were among friends, that the questions being put to you, casually, in well-practised, jocular township voices, were part of some innocent banter among buddies).

He called Alec on his speakerphone, wanting to hear him speak through the echo that the device created. A sudden inspiration: that's what a voice magnified by darkness and the metallic barrier of a police van would sound like. Clear up another mystery at the same time.

'Alec?'

'Siel*as*, hey bra, how are you?'

Silas flinched at this eccentric play on his name. We are defined by the way our names are pronounced. Can't people see what a simple man I am?

'I'm fine, I'm fine, bra, I'll live a little longer.'

'You should take it easy, seriously.'

'Ja, ja, listen Ally, you remember that weird, thin little guy who used to write poetry?'

'Shit, bra . . .'

'Back in Newclare, lived in Pollack Avenue, up there near the Chinaman's shop.'

'You mean that ou who married Fanny Dip?'

'The poet married Frances Dip! That skinny guy with the rat's eyes?'

'Well, you certainly got his description right down to a fucken T. His name was Amin, Amin Something-or-Other . . .'

'Amin Barfi! His father was that old guy who went around talking to himself. You know what, Alec? I was thinking about him this morning, just couldn't remember his name.'

'He was after Lydia, wasn't he? Chased her mal, didn't he?'

'And you and I had to go and drag him from the cemetery . . .'

'Because Lydia begged us to,' they said in unison.

Alec laughed, and Silas pictured him, head thrown back, business on hold for a precious moment. The only one among them who had become his own boss, and could afford to put his feet up on his own desk and take raucous pleasure in his memories.

'You trying to find him?' Alec asked, his voice moving smoothly from laughing spontaneity to grave seriousness. From the moment Silas had started talking about Amin Barfi, Alec had wondered whether they were looking for him. 'They' was the TRC, always looking for people whose names had turned up in files, in confessions, in accusations, memories of minor characters brought back to life by the retelling of the big events. Do you know who drove the police van that took Steve Biko from Port Elizabeth to Pretoria? Christ, some boertjie with a boertjie name. Silas never called simply for the sake of it, to say hello or chat about the past; he always had a purpose for everything he did.

'No, no one's looking for him, specifically. Just that I was in the old part of the city and suddenly thought about Amin Barfi, and couldn't remember his name. And what do you know? He married our Princess.'

'Hey, shit, you were really in love with her, not like the rest of us, we simply wanted her fanny.'

His secretary knocked and motioned with her hands that there was a call waiting. He nodded, told Alec he would call him back later, and rang off. When he lifted the receiver, it was the Minister, apologizing in an agitated voice for interrupting his conference call: something urgent had come up and he needed to see him immediately. Silas put the phone down and closed his eyes for a moment.

He turned the memory of Frances 'Fanny' Dip over in his mind, the way you lovingly examine a yellowing photograph, saw her skin caught in the half-light of her father's storeroom. Sunlight penetrated through holes in the corrugated-iron roof, igniting the shadows around them, as she raised her dress just high enough for him to see the startling contrast of black public hair. 'Remember, you can look, but you can't touch,' she said. And afterwards he told Alec, Bruno and Toyer (curious but bemused at their heterosexual obsession with wanting to know what Frances's fanny looked like) that he couldn't tell them whether it was crosswise, that he couldn't tell them anything, because he had sworn on his mother's life not to tell anybody what he had seen, and no one broke an oath made on his mother's life.

A legend grew up around this encounter. Silas Ali, 'that fucken lightie', had seen Fanny's golden sideways poes, some even said that he had made love to her, lying across her body. There was talk around the street-corner braziers, salivating, salacious, animated discussions on God, sex, manhood and oppression, vivid speculation about what it was like to screw someone so strange, postulation that it went in just like any cock entering a doos, but the angle had to be right and the guy's aim dead on.

Silas would never be the same, marked for ever by the fame of his prowess, his ability to seduce women – the mother of a close friend, it was said, and the daughter of the white stationmaster. A gift endowed on him by the great doos-goddess of the townships because he had conquered 'a left-to-right Gong poes'. A bushie lightie, a fucken moegoe and weakling in everything but sex.

He remembered how his resolute and saintly silence felt like a burden at first, how he wished he had not seen Frances's nakedness. But after a while, he began to enjoy the sense of mystery that went with the legend, how it gave him a 'rep' and how this became a talisman, protecting him from petty gangsters. He had an aura of mystery that made the young thugs avoid him (except the Vikings, of course, for whom nothing was sacred). They went about the township looking for fights, so that they could 'raise their score' and enhance their notoriety. But who wanted to fight over a cunt, even if it was a Gong cunt, one that had perhaps only been looked at and not even touched?

When he had asked Frances to show him her vagina (that was not the word he used, but already his adult mind was asserting its language of distance and detachment), she had looked at him in disappointment. 'I thought you were different,' her eyes said.

'Okay, I'll show you my poes, on one condition,' she told him.

'What's that?'

'You have to swear on your mother's life you'll tell no one what you saw.'

He thought about her stipulation for a moment – being unable to speak about what he had seen would spoil his triumph, deny him the reward he deserved for having the nerve to even ask such a thing of the most beautiful girl in the township – but agreed in the end. He was intrigued, too young to understand the full meaning of the voyeurism he was indulging in. Thinking back to what happened when he left Mr Leong Dip's warehouse, full of aromatic dust rising from sacks of dried malt, he remembered that Alec had been there waiting for him, along with Bruno, part of the sepia-coloured photograph in Silas's mind, beaming with innocent lust, shouting in annoyance, 'Fuck you, Sielas, you can't do this to us, we're supposed to be bras.'

No, Alec was safe, there was no need now to try and match Alec's voice to another, more sinister memory. Ridiculous to have thought that about Alec in the first place.

Another painful memory intruded. He had feasted silently on his fame for a long time, until he met Lydia and it was suddenly something he had to live down.

'Silas, how could you?'

'How could I what?'

'Perpetuate such racial stereotyping. Imagine letting people believe you had actually seen a crosswise vagina on a Chinese girl!'

'Christ, Lydia, we were just boys then.'

'And now? You still reminisce, take pride in that filthy memory, wallow in your petty fame?'

Alec was there on that occasion as well, looking sheepish. Lydia was always probing, asking questions, telling Silas's friends that she wanted to know what he was really like.

'Don't make it sound like I murdered someone. It was a childish, schoolboy thing, it hurt no one.'

'What about this girl Frances, what about her, standing there before you with her knickers around her ankles, while you ogled her?'

'I was sixteen, maybe even younger, a damn boy, do you know what boys are like?'

A pause, some new thought entering Lydia's subtle mind. She would have made a great plotter of palace revolutions and cabals, would have gone far in today's political system.

'Silas, why did she agree to do it? I mean, why would she willingly degrade herself like that, just to be observed, if, as you say, you swore beforehand not to touch her?'

He remembered Lydia's words in great detail, and her quiet manner, sensed her doubts about him, about who he was – as a person, she always added.

'Maybe she wanted to prove that Chinese people are no different from others, maybe she wanted to be looked at, maybe she . . .'

Lydia got up and walked away, Alec smirked because he could not help himself, and the newly-weds' household was hot and quiet, its smallness making it impossible for them to escape each other physically. They had to create interior spaces of their own, private rooms of the mind in which to hide their emotions. When Alec had gone, Silas had to start the painful process of making his peace with Lydia. Her language again, defining his responses, changing his ancient way of dealing with things, which was to hug and make up, say nothing further about the problem, no matter how serious.

'Make your peace with me, Silas,' was a command to atone. And for her, the wounds of betrayal and the alienation of angry words could not be dissolved in the tenderness of a touch; she needed words of reconciliation, spoken out loud. She would already have decided to make up. But there would be a price to pay: an evening's silent purgatory, or a day's or a month's, as long as it took him to speak about their 'problem'. Newclare was not the kind of township where effusiveness was tolerated, even at its most poetic. Ask Toyer, ask Amin. One was dead and the other enslaved – Silas guessed – to a woman whose sex had been deified by brutal legend.

That day marked a change in Lydia. There was a small but discernible hardening of her gentle love for him, she recoiled subtly when he touched her. Did the slow crumbling of their relationship begin there, the relentless tides of their different histories start their corrosive wearing away of love?

That's what we did not know or want to know, he thought: that we were not necessarily the same, just because we were both coloured; that we were not necessarily compatible, just because we both came from some kind of bastard strain. We were different. She virtually grew up in a convent, among dry-titted nuns and paedophiliac priests, while I grew up in a magnificent township jungle like Newclare.

The phone rang again. His secretary said that Alec was on the line, but Silas should remember that the Minister was waiting.

'Listen, broer, you think you can break that vow?'

'What vow?'

'Silas, what did you see in Mr Dip's shed?'

'Fuck, you still want to know, after thirty-five years? How many cunts have you seen in your lifetime, come on, tell me?'

Alec's laughter had a ribald quality that Silas easily imagined – tears streaming from his eyes, his glasses removed and placed on the desk before him. He would go for a piss afterwards, double the pleasure of his release.

'Well, okay then, she had a scar,' Silas said.

'A scar?'

'Yes, ran from inside of her groin right around her leg. Fell on some rocks at a picnic, she said. A real bullshit story. That was a wound, you know, a knife wound that hadn't been properly stitched. It was so deep. If she had allowed me to touch it, I guess my whole fingertip would have gone in. Fuck, Alec, she was trying to tell me something, but I was too stupid to know.'

His heartbeat was racing again, like the night before, he had to slow down, take a deep breath, slow down his pulse.

'Silas, are you orright?'

'Ja, I'll be fine. Listen, I got to run.'

'Sure ting, broer, we should have a dop together.'

'Ja, I'll give you a call.'

With Alec's parting laugh ringing soothingly in his ears, Silas walked down the corridor, able to fight off yet another dizzy spell and make it into the lift that would take him up to the ministerial suite without having to lean against something. He won't reveal his weakness to these people, leftovers from the old regime, enjoying constitutional protection to mock and undermine. They don't understand us, what we struggled for and why. Yet so many of them have a beguiling influence over their Ministers. They know their way around the system, it's comforting for the newcomers. His resolve was strengthened by the resonance of Alec's voice lapsing into his township-speak. Silas would show the Minister 'a ting or two'.

He prepared himself to confront that ageing face, the baggy-eyed seriousness that made him seem so sincere in front of the TV cameras, a veteran of the struggle anxious not to offend anyone. The public argument between the party and the TRC was growing, Silas's earlier intervention had not stopped more and more high-profile people from having their say. Freedom of expression was the kind of pain-in-the-arse price you had to pay for democracy. Listen, Silas's cold demeanour would tell the Minister, we're caught in the middle of a moral war, we're walking a tightrope, and you must have strong nerves.

'Now,' Silas rehearsed his approach, 'the party is quite right to be indignant about being branded a violator of human rights, but we must not give the wily old Archbishop an opportunity to bring the government into it. Let him say, "Torture is torture is torture," and let the party say, "It was not systematic and structured the way it was in the old regime." Let them use their words, we stay aloof. You know, separate the party from the state? Wonderful philosophy at a time like this. As Minister you should simply say that the TRC process must be allowed to run its course.'

Silas would have to find the right kind of words – when they went public – to extricate his Minister from the web of his own ambiguity. The best thing would be to spin even more elaborate webs, words and meanings that turned in on themselves, full of 'nuance and context', keep the media occupied with trying to figure out what we're up to. He would summon up what one of his colleagues had called 'the wisdom of a devious Solomon', prepare a statement for the venerable old fuck, and hope he stuck to the script. Sit next to him at the press conference, give him the iciest glare – 'Just read what is in the statement!'

Silas felt relieved that life had such immediate burdens, it allowed him to deal with a momentary feeling of guilt about not being able to visit Lydia again that night. He should have been with her, trying to revive their marriage. He must get his secretary to call Mikey, persuade him to go and stay over with Mam Agnes and Jackson. Then call them to pressure their grandson. God, that he had to be so devious with his own son!

Anyway, he would also get flowers sent to the hospital, a big blerry bunch, and a note saying, 'I'm sorry, big crisis here.' Hope she sees it on the news, get her to appreciate just how difficult his job was.

9

Lydia received a letter from her sister Martha in Toronto that filled her with anxiety. For some reason, Martha had used her maiden name on the envelope, and it took the hospital administration some days to work out who 'Lydia Oliphant' was. When a clerk delivered it to her ward, she knew that it had been opened. The envelope had been resealed with tape, and the clerk had that look of grim dignity Lydia associated with the delivery of mail that had been tampered with. There was no point in complaining about it. An honest attempt to establish her identity, they would argue, when all they needed to do was send it back marked 'Person Unknown'.

She recalled the mystery of the postman's averted eyes when he delivered the mail to their township home, back in the days when Silas was in the underground. Ignorant of his political involvement, she had been puzzled by the shy, almost coy friendliness of the meter-readers, telephone technicians, municipal inspectors – all men, self-conscious in the presence of a woman – as they went about their work. Afterwards, she had asked Silas whose side they had been on, these strange men with their secretive eyes?

Who knows? he answered. Ours, theirs, not on any side, just men doing their jobs.

She realized, later on, that she had been exposed, she and her child, to potential assassins, rapists, men who would do anything to intimidate people working actively against them, all because Silas hadn't confided in her. But she also thought: there is no point in starting another argument about this. It is men's nature to hide things from the people they love.

Now Martha was doing the same thing, hiding her pain, some anguish coldly acknowledged in her own mind but buried here in a gush of loving words, hopes for Lydia's recovery, for Mikey's well-being and Silas's success. The three of them, Lydia, Mikey and Silas (in that order), symbolized the future of the new South Africa, she had written some time ago, more than Alec's business accomplishments, more than the image of a smiling Nelson Mandela. Even the bits of news about John's business, about her three children and their youthful travails – 'Growing up in a city like Toronto isn't easy' – seemed to be hasty diversions that helped her shrink away from something ugly that needed to be said.

Lydia looked up, saw the doctors gathering outside for their morning rounds. They were like vultures in white coats, their craned necks moving about with the authority of weather-beaten scavengers. Why do the nurses always look like frightened storks?

She returned to Martha's letter. What was Toronto like, she wondered, beyond the eternal coldness, the dark and icy beauty that Martha unconsciously incorporated into her letters. She sensed that somewhere in her sister's brave, even daring heart, some kind of fear was growing, a presentiment of loss, a knowledge of impending grief.

It showed even in the description of a lingering summer: 'The trees are already bare, Lyd, but the heat just won't go away. The city seems so strange.' Mireille, taking advantage of the weather, was off to Nova

Scotia with friends, fellow students, one of them is her boyfriend, Martha thinks. Mireille was doing so well, but she's been moody again, these last few days, withdrawn, doesn't speak much. Received a call from home, early hours of the morning, not Mom or Dad. Martha thinks it was Mikey.

'But anyway, she's off with people of her own age. And we are going to the country for ten days, John has bought a share in this lovely cottage about two hours' drive from Toronto.'

Martha veering away from Mireille's troubled, intrusive presence, the exile that she bore silently, grieving not only because she was far from home, but because of the unspoken mistrust of those who had sent her away, the mild but ill-concealed shame with which she had been received. How generous and understanding of John – kindness was expected of Martha, after all, she was family – how good of them to 'give Mireille another chance'.

Lydia looked up, surprised that the doctors had moved off. So they were not seeing her today. A good sign. Means they have made a decision. Years of experience in hospitals had taught her to look out for details. A nurse poked her head into the ward and said, 'So, we're going home today!' Lydia smiled back diffidently, folded Martha's letter and asked to be told when the doctor had signed the discharge forms.

'I can see that you're a nurse, you know the routine! Anyway, Dr Scott will see you soon. He likes you, you know,' the nurse said in the gossipy sing-song expected of her profession, and closed the door.

Dr Scott came in and appraised her with his hovering eyes. He was releasing her, he said, his tone solicitous, sounding very much like Jackson in one of his mawkish, paternal moods. As if she were Dr Scott's charge, someone he could detain or release at his discretion. She felt an immense irritation. She had not had time to fully absorb the apprehension in Martha's letter. There was a subtle warning contained in it: 'No point in scratching up dead ash.' Was Mikey doing that, stirring up old memories? Now Dr Scott had interrupted her thoughts. But something stilled the sarcastic, mended-Lydia voice that rose sharply to her mind, ready to tell him that she was too old to be 'flirted at' by the likes of him, perfect in her imitation of his Irish accent, which seemed especially exaggerated today.

How ready she had been to mock that caricatured lilt, to remind him that he had been in South Africa for over twenty years, and that summoning up a Belfast brogue now and then wouldn't restore the Irishness he had abandoned for the love of apartheid money – hadn't he been enticed out here by the old government, trying to increase the white population by bringing in the flotsam and jetsam of Europe? Well, he could go home now and fight his own country's battles!

Dr Scott stared at her, aware that a huge torrent of words had passed through her mind, glad that he had heard none of it, to judge by the sharpness of her eyes, the blackness of their sparkle. She was a truly lovely woman when stripped of the placidity that seemed to envelop her very being. But no, he thought, he would never be able to pay a woman like her that kind of compliment. There was a hurt he ought to recognize, a 'woundedness' that was almost unreachable. He busied himself with making notes. Use them in his lectures to the new interns. Come and see how toughness heals itself.

He stood with his back to her, looking at X-ray plates raised to the sun. The nurse joined him, a slight breeze from the corridor stirring her white tunic, and also looked up. A crucifix had been hung there on the wall, because Silas had written 'Catholic' on the questionnaire, and the two of them appeared to be gazing up at it. What do they do for Muslims and Jews?

Memories of Sister Catherine flashed through Lydia's mind. The cool halls of the seminary at Mayville, buildings splendid in that crumbling colonial way, stark against the green Natal countryside. Prayers being sung and incantations repeated by solemn-faced monks, brothers of the Order of St Francis. Close to midday, and soon a bright but gentle sun would shine through the high windows of the school, burnishing the whiteness of the books and papers, over which the students sat with bowed heads, because that was what they taught you at the seminary, to be bent down and obeisant in all your endeavours.

But Dr Scott was not Catholic, she could tell by his voice, not only its lack of music (we know the songs of God even before we know God Himself), but its faint disdain, a prejudice he could not help. The nurse left, taking with her one half of Sister Catherine's aura.

She was fine, Dr Scott said, still with his back to her, and she would 'live long enough to sin'. She had some scars, but they would heal, even without the help of her Jesuit God. A man bred to smell out Catholics, she thought. He had sniffed the convent carbolic on her skin, breathed in its indelible essence of the forbidden. To fuck a Catholic, just the idea of it, must be exciting to a Catholic-hater. Had she aroused all the secret desire – cast-off bride of a God, dark-skinned and dark-souled, dressed in frilly Roman lace – that his Belfast upbringing had imposed on his paltry Protestant soul?

He snapped shut his notebook (what does he record in there, always scribbling, crablike, with the devil's left hand?), turned, and said in a voice once more so very Irish, 'Well, I'll be off then, and tell that husband of yours to look after you or he'll feel my Irish wrath!'

She could not begrudge him a warm smile, even though she knew that her silence was sending him away spurned, according to his logic, tail between his legs, overcome by the surly, canine humility of thwarted men.

What was Belfast like? Much greener than Martha's Toronto, and more squalid perhaps. She remembered descriptions of a sea, of rivers, of narrow streets and rain driven by a slanting wind, of songs and passions that outsiders simply could not understand.

'Except you South Africans, perhaps.'

Sister Catherine confiding in herself, muttering her thoughts out loud, thinking that her young wards would not understand her sorrows, drawing forth an internal voice the way water is drawn from an ancestral well.

There was another phrase that Sister Catherine repeated all the time, in a declamatory tone: 'Being Irish is God's most beautiful curse!' How mysterious it had seemed then. Now it was as bitterly superficial as all the slogans we preserve as memorials to our own struggles. Still, Sister Catherine's 'hard weave of words' had a steely virtue that held together her disparate parts, while Dr Scott's was merely a parody.

In spite of Lydia's resolve never to dwell on the past, to avoid being seduced by imagined 'happier times', Sister Catherine's image came back to her in all its contraband grandeur, sweet Sister Catherine, full lips with a ruby of their own, stern beauty and insinuated sensuality. Lydia had to close her eyes to constrain this secretly conceived creature. All the hours, the months and years of hours spent imagining the whore's legs and taut buttocks underneath the shapeless nun's habit, breasts held in nightly penance by arms crossed in honour of God, had not prepared her for the ferocity of the woman who was now conjured up behind her eyes.

And yet Sister Catherine was so serene. She had a quiet loveliness, a sensuality that she renounced because of her calling. Lydia had once told Silas that he and his gang of would-be revolutionaries would never know the true meaning of 'self-denial'. Now she knew why she had been so sure of this.

But no, she said to herself, don't let this *man's* image intrude, remember yourself as that child who wanted to marry God, and love him upon his cross, in order to love Catherine, his bride. Ah, how she longed to touch that agonized face on the crucifix, how she dreamed, every night for one whole year, of Sister Catherine's purity and Christ's sorrow all fused together, of her lips searching out this hallowed union,

115

dreams of desire that she dared not speak about, knowing instinctively that they would be seen as wrong, and would therefore become wrong. In the early hours of each morning, unspeakable love faded away into fitful sleep, only to surface again at dawn, a pale streak upon that dreary dormitory wall, dirty, faded green warmed by the Durban sun.

Time was marked by an army of cockroaches in full scuttle, on their way to do battle with each other in the slovenly kitchen, by beds creaking and covers slipping to release odours dulled by hours of entrapment. Faded intestinal gas, sharp, menstrual smells, Petronella, her neighbour (endowed at birth with a nunnish name, her destiny foretold) breathing her halitosis out into the already putrid air. A bad-breathed snorer, fit only for penitent dormitories such as these. The first rays of sun illuminating the rust on the steel beams of the roof gave the signal for doors to be flung open and left swinging on dry and squeaky hinges. A chorus of moans provided evidence of other dreams around her being lost, and always, at this lucid hour, the knowledge that God the Father and God the Son could read her thoughts, that nothing in her mind was sacrosanct. Nothing need be suppressed, especially when absolution was so easily offered.

To rid herself of the silence, she knelt before her father confessor, on the eve of the Easter recess, inspired perhaps by the hallowed atmosphere of ceaseless chants and prayers. He was a monk with a thin, threaded smile, on loan from Rome, and he brought penance to the very act of breathing. Dr Scott's fearsome Jesuit.

Perhaps it was the monk's sly smile, or perhaps it was the pleasurable prospect of a sin's telling (who knows what goes on in that part of the brain where words like 'cunt', 'suck', 'suckle' gather in their hordes, waiting to invade the innocent realms of the heart?), but Lydia found herself unable to speak. She flung her head back and raised her eyes to the flawed roof of the chapel, the sun a searing kaleidoscope through millions of tiny holes, and started laughing, a frail girlish laughter that grew into a man's baritone. It was a sound that caused the congregation of novices and live-in students, still considering the call to God, to pause in their own prayerful duties and see the Demon himself erupt from sweet little Lydia's throat.

The monk leapt out of his confessional box and prayed over her, feverishly pleading with God to expel Satan from the frail, young vessel before him, leavening her with holy water even as his mouth sprayed hot spittle. At last, her demonic laughter subsided into a giggling fit and he was able to carry her to Sister Catherine's office, where he laid her down upon a couch. It was Sister Catherine who pulled down Lydia's school tunic, which had somehow been raised when the monk lifted her (did she imagine then that Sister Catherine's eyes had lingered for a second on her slender thighs, whose loveliness Silas would moaningly proclaim the first time they made love?). 'No, Lydia is not possessed,' Sister Catherine said, 'this is a civilized country. In spite of all its problems, it *is* Christian, and no one should believe in such medieval things as possession.'

Lydia opened her eyes, saw the monk give a thin-lipped sign of acquiescence – he was a guest here, why should he care if the Devil went about in a girl's wispish guise? To Africa its own pagan curse. He backed away from the supine young girl and the gentle, attentive nun. 'A little too attentive,' he would perhaps have attested in another age.

In the quiet of her study, surrounded by books, by the serenity of knowledge, Sister Catherine counselled Lydia. It was rather sad, she said, but Lydia had to think carefully whether she was suited to God's calling. It was a 'solitary devotion', not for everyone, and there was no shame in acknowledging this. The important thing was to 'remain in the faith'.

Afterwards, a whole troupe of fresh-faced novices appeared as if from the wings of a stage – had they been watching all the time? Lydia wondered. Then one of Sister Catherine's assistants escorted Lydia through the mayhem of students getting ready to go home, down dank corridors to the courtyard, where her father waited anxiously.

Now Lydia inserted a CD into the portable player and clamped the earphones over her ears. Leonard Cohen's ragged voice silenced the screech of the hospital's life, the squealing misery of beds being wheeled about. She remembered Jackson speaking to her in the car that day. 'I have bad news, the business isn't going well, we can't afford to keep you here at Mayville.' Whenever he had something unpleasant to tell his children, Jackson would hunch his shoulders, as if trying to make himself as inconspicuous as possible. Lydia had not answered him, had turned instead to look back at the school, its white walls receding into the surrounding hills. 'We may even have to leave Durban, go and live in Johannesburg, where there's more work for a poor trucker like me,' Jackson had added in an almost desperate voice.

Back in Durban, when their relocation to Johannesburg, to mythical, frightening Soweto, had been confirmed ('They refuse to recognize my coloured identity card,' Jackson had announced in a monotone), Lydia wandered along the forbidden stretch of Butcher Road, just off the new freeway, watching the prostitutes ply their trade, wanting, just once, to love one of those women, with the same head-thrown-back pleasure of a beautiful sin confessed. She chose a young Chinese woman as her fantasy lover, named her Cathy, imprinted this Cathy's shape on her mind, the colour of her skin, her shiny black hair, removing the blemishes (a tired face, the varicose veins in her thighs) the way a clever photographer edits out the flaws in his composition.

Cathy became the phantasm projected before her each time she had sex with a man (only three different men, including her husband, her rapist, and, years later, a transient doctor, up against the wall of a darkened hospital ward, just for the illicitness, to remind herself that she was alive).

Cathy helped her wrench some pleasure for herself from her encounters with Silas, their lovemaking having followed the course she feared most when she was young: from love to lust to conjugal routine. Usually, her response was ritualistic, even when he did succeed in arousing her, in reaching that pure subterranean river still unsullied by the memory of being raped. Sometimes, she deliberately summoned Cathy, allowing herself to be filled with an almost malevolent knowledge of her own sensuality. The image of Christ and his bride Catherine, entwined with Cathy, snake-like and amber-skinned, always succeeded in bringing her to a climax.

Lydia had realized long ago that Silas, perhaps sensing the consubstantiality of the divine and the demonic in Cathy, had fused her, Lydia, with one of his own fantasies, the girl who had stripped for him on condition that he did not touch her. That girl had grown into a woman in his mind, and he called her name out loud when he needed to overcome Lydia's indifference or contend with the fierce, set-apart passion that occasionally seized her, when it seemed that she was participating in some distant sexual act, while he and his body were mere instruments of pleasure.

Frances Dip, 'Fanny' Dip, what a ridiculous name, Lydia often thought, lying next to Silas, Cathy gone, dispelled by the sobering power of her logic, its ability to reduce these carnal dreams to their basic, grotesque dimensions. She knew that in his eyes, her sexuality was defined by her status as a rape victim. Brave, stoic image of violation, grave-faced symbol of women in the struggle. Because Du Boise had abused his power over her, the policeman abusing his captive, a ritual as ancient as history itself. He had hurt her, Du Boise, yes, but more than in the mere brutalizing of her vagina, he had violated her womb with the horror of his seed. He had driven her to seek salvation in myths and invoked spirits, to deny herself the reality of her body, its earth, its power to conceive. She knew instinctively, the moment he rose and pulled up his trousers, that she was pregnant, and that she would thereafter refuse her body its right to bear more children.

She prayed each night, yes, to the God she had desired, but prayed to him virtuously now, in supplicant reverence, prayed that the power of her own unfulfilled love, its very unconsummated purity, would overwhelm Du Boise's dull rapist genes in her son Michael.

She remembered smelling Du Boise's scent on the baby, a faint stench, the premature decaying of a man who harboured some dreaded disease. A kind of cancer, she thought, something that would one day slowly eat away at his core. And she continued to sniff at Mikey, until he was old enough to say no with his eyes and his demeanour, all through his childhood, even though Mam Agnes gently chided her and Silas stared suspiciously at her, his fear and jealousy unspoken.

The door opened, rubber squealed on linoleum. The nurse was back, all smiles, happy to see someone being released. Making way for a new face, a new trauma, but still, a change in routine. Lydia removed the earphones, heard Leonard Cohen's distant, plaintive voice:

Now the flames they followed Joan of Arc,
as she came riding through the dark . . .

'Here we are,' the nurse said, waving the discharge papers, 'shall I call your husband?'

'No, I'll do it.'

Her feet were still heavily bandaged, and she put on the soft, tiger-striped slippers that Mam Agnes had had the foresight (but bad taste) to bring along. She made her way to the nurses' station, hesitantly, like a child still trying to memorize the rhythms of walking, stopping when she felt unsure, when the cushioning bandages and garish slippers made her feel she had lost touch with the ground. The nurse hovered at her side, ready to support her, but saw the determination in her clamped jaw ('Don't do that,' Mam Agnes used to say, 'it makes you look just like your father's scrawny family!').

She dialled Silas's cellphone number, surprised at how easily she recalled the ten digits.

'Mr Ali's phone,' a voice said. His secretary, Glynnis, or something like that. Her formality quickly changed to a nervous friendliness when Lydia told her who was calling and that she shouldn't bother Mr Ali. She would take a taxi home, seeing that Mr Ali was 'in conference'. She had not intended to be sarcastic. Am I going to become a sour old woman? she asked herself.

No, no, no, she would get a message to him right away, the secretary said. She had instructions to interrupt him if his wife called, no matter how important his meeting. Lydia left the hospital's number and made her precarious way back to the ward. Within minutes the nurse came in to tell her that the secretary had called back: 'Mr Ali' would end his meeting right away and come and collect her.

And why not? Lydia thought. Let him come and fulfil his patriarchal duty, let him play the role of a man among men, the measure of his devotion a willingness to race from Pretoria to Johannesburg. Can't let *his* wife take a taxi home from hospital. He wants to make my inconvenience his, the husband who feels my pain as his pain.

A sudden anger betrayed her calm exterior. She sat muttering to herself, seething with a vast feeling of irritation, into which her consciousness of the past few weeks sank, blurring the pain in her feet, turning it into a dull ache that was harder to deal with than the earlier fiery pangs. Her wounds were healing and so too must the memory of their infliction, that's what everyone would tell her. The wisdom that helped people to get on with life, no matter what traumas they had lived through. Gracie's way of dealing with things, and Mam Agnes's, and Jackson's.

Silas's as well, even though his 'forgetfulness' was not natural, was not an unconscious, pain-induced suppression of things too agonizing to remember, but a deliberate strategy, something thought out behind a desk, whisky in hand, ice tinkling, golden liquid contemplatively swirled. That's why he was so good at his job, helping the country to forget and therefore to forgive, a convenient kind of amnesia. For her to 'come to terms' with what had happened, she would have to seek some inner serenity, lock all her disturbing recollections into that secret crypt in her memory, along with Cathy, and Catherine, and Catherine's God.

But Silas had betrayed that place of refuge, unknowingly, because of his ego, his concern with *his* suffering.

She sat down in a chair, afraid of the passivity that she would have to immerse her mind in if she was to overcome this inner rage. She wanted to be content, happy to have recovered from her self-inflicted wounds, with no more than scars 'that any good plastic surgeon could conceal', but it was too late.

Silas had bought her the portable CD player – so thoughtful of him – that had become her source of silence, a filter through which she could screen the world. He had also brought along what he thought was her favourite music, discs by Leonard Cohen, Narciso Yepes playing all those Spanish classics, Schubert's *Death and the Maiden*.

But where's Santana or Lauryn Hill, what about Erykah Badu, she wanted to ask, or is the music you chose part of the sad and long-suffering image of me that you carry around in your head? What subtle and unconscious machinations were behind her husband's benign gestures? He was sinister without knowing it. Take the huge bunch of flowers he had sent on the day he got out of hospital: an apology for not being able to visit later that night, a manly gesture of affection, or a celebration of his own survival? He hadn't suffered a stroke or a heart attack or anything that could incapacitate him, and so he had celebrated by sending her a grotesque arrangement, roses, carnations, violets, all dressed in frilly fern. Though the card simply read 'Love, Silas', he had phoned to apologize, 'Sorry I can't visit, some big story about to break, watch the news.' The simplicity of his affection, his 'love' destroyed. See how important my job is, he was saying, understand my suffering.

That night, she had actually asked the nurse to turn on the TV so that she could watch the news. She saw Silas, cool and distinguished-looking next to his badly dressed and fidgety Minister, Silas quick and to the point in his evasions of the real issue – *Why were senior government officials attacking Archbishop Tutu?* – while the Minister fumbled about in the froth of his meaningless platitudes.

'Isn't that your husband?' someone had asked.

'Yes, it is.'

Yes, the smooth and devious one, handsome in his own way, he is my husband. You should have left Du Boise alone when you saw him, Silas, you should not have brought my rapist home. I can't rest peacefully with both of you around, your bodies, your smells, even your sounds have become all mixed up. It's like he raped me on your behalf, so that one day I would live with him through you. When you are inside me, and around me, it feels like Du Boise. He made you his instrument. Is it not enough that I have to deal with the thought of his seed in Mikey, his genes, his blood, his cold and murderous eyes?

Lydia got up from her chair, slipped the crutches she had been offered under her armpits, and started walking towards the exit, her head filled with the last of Leonard Cohen's bitter lyrics, 'Sing Another Song, Boys'.

A nurse asked her something.

'What?'

Lydia remembered the earphones, took them off and asked if they

123

could call a taxi. A clerk behind the desk looked dubious when she said she was going to Berea.

'They don't like going there,' the clerk said, realizing her unintended cruelty too late.

Lydia gave her the name of a taxi service. 'They'll take you to hell for a price. Glad for the custom.' She limped away on her crutches, a good-looking woman in her late thirties, slim and wiry. Ja-nee, probably of durable Malay stock, Creole perhaps, from Mauritius? You can hear the Durban in her. That's where they all ended up. But something other than her lithe bastard appearance held their attention. It was the lightness in her movement, despite her swollen feet and the uncertainty with which she used the crutches.

They saw Dr Scott watching her as well, and smiled to themselves when she turned, conscious that she was being scrutinized. He gave her a feeble little wave, then shuffled away down the corridor, trying to hide his blushing face in the dull blue light.

She steadied the crutches, making plain her dislike of how cumbersome they were, and went towards the exit.

'There's a woman who knows what she wants,' one of the nurses said.

'Ja,' her colleague answered.

But then their moment of leisure, the opportunity to take pride in another woman's resolve, was gone. Another patient was being wheeled in from the trauma unit below.

10

A week before his essay is due, Mikey sits down to read the book Miss Anderson has prescribed for the literature course. It is a prose translation of Homer's *Odyssey* by someone called Walter Shewring. He dislikes the book and the translator's name, perhaps only because of their association with Julia Anderson. He has also chosen a course in autobiographical writing, a choice Miss Anderson tolerates ('Why don't you concentrate on the formal programme, heaven knows it's difficult enough?') because Professor Graham, the head of department, loves autobiographical writing. She gives Mikey access to her library at home.

A volume of Kafka's *Diaries*, a handsome first edition published in 1948, lies on his desk waiting to be read. 'The finest example of how great books are born!' Shirley Graham says. '*Please* call me Shirley.' But the image of his mother's diary intrudes. A simple, black-cloth exercise book, worn where she has held it contemplatively to her chest, her thumbs pressed into the cover, pondering the entries she has just made, the wisdom (or is it vanity?) of committing her innermost thoughts to writing.

He puts aside both Shewring's book and Kafka's journal, dull duty and ambiguous pleasure. He recalls how flustered Professor Graham was when she handed him this prized edition, rare, and irreplaceable, you can tell even by its feel. Her husband's, Mikey thought, he is the collector of old and rare things. Shirley Graham was showing him their collection of first editions, a wall of leather-bound volumes, arrayed in rich and sombre rows, when a lock of hair fell across her brow. Instinctively, he paused and brushed the hair from her eyes.

'Not here,' she said, holding his hand as if to restrain any further trespass.

Then, looking around in a frightened, somewhat theatrical way, since she had told him earlier that there was no one home, she took the Kafka book from a desk and thrust it into his hands. An excuse for him to return, a gifted student bringing back a valuable book. But this book seemed so strategically placed, as if ready for such a moment, a worldly-wise older woman knowing just which gestures would deflect the young man's advances. Something to consider when he visited Professor Graham at home again.

He retrieves Lydia's diary from its hiding place: a secret compartment created by a flaw in the design of the built-in cupboard, the carpenter having been forced to construct a false panel to accommodate the art deco facia. Some day he will have to clear out the things he has hidden in there, including those secret TRC records that Silas brought home and seems to have forgotten about.

Sitting at his desk, his body slumped down in the chair and his legs stretched out before him, the posture he assumes naturally when there is a need to concentrate, he begins to read. The first entry in Lydia's diary is dated 6 December 1978. It takes the form of a justification for starting 'this journal'. The writing has an erudition that surprises him. She must have been eighteen then, a student nurse, destined for nothing more than humble service in a noble profession. Because she was black, because she had married a man more than ten years older, serious, sober, because she was the daughter of Jackson and Mam Agnes, whose own disenchantment imposed on their children a dutiful sense of restraint, Lydia had developed another world inside of her. A domain of books and music, other lives furtively explored, making the world outside seem reassuringly dull. Her secret life (like Mikey's own) must have started when she was much younger still.

That first entry reads:

'Three nights ago, I was raped. By a policeman, in a veld, flung down on the grass, the darkness above his head my only comfort. I will recover from the physical act of that rape. We always do, women have this capacity to heal themselves. But I also know that I am pregnant. Inside of me is a rapist's seed. My child will be a child of rape.

'Ever since it happened – yes, it seems like an eternity ago, something unreal, a nightmare from which I shall awake – I have tried to pray, tried to coax the voice of God back into my mind. I sang hymns I thought I had forgotten, even hummed those grey and sombre Gregorian chants that Father Michael got the choir to sing each Sunday morning, for years, until the church in Randles Road became really oppressive to me. But God is silent. Is He offended because I inserted Cathy into my knowledge of Him? But the God of salvation should not be offended by such thoughts, which are usually born in the minds of those who most need His love.

'I cannot speak to Silas, he makes my pain his tragedy. In any case, I know that he doesn't want to speak about my being raped, he wants to suffer silently, wants me to be his accomplice in this act of denial. I also cannot speak to my mother or father. They too will want to take on my pain, make it theirs. If they suffer on my behalf, that will be penance enough, they believe. They will also demand of me a forget-ful silence. Speaking about something heightens its reality, makes it unavoidable. This is not human nature, but the nature of "confession" that the Church has taught them. Confess your sins, even those committed against you – and is rape not a sin committed by both victim and perpetrator, at least according to man's gospel? – but confess it once only. There true salvation is to be found. In saying the unsayable, and then holding your peace for ever after.'

Mikey leans back in his chair. It is no longer the vast fiction of great histories he is reading, or the marvellous beginnings of stories in tormented minds, but the reality of his own birth. He reasserts control, smothers a cry, the need to weep that rises primitively inside him. He sits forward, resumes reading.

Lydia's prose is clear, translucent almost. It has the transcendent quality of pain captured without sentimentality. She describes the rape in cold detail, Du Boise's eyes, his smell, his grunts, the flicker of fear when he reached his climax and, for a moment, was not in control. Silas's rage, his wild screaming, which did not lessen her terror but enhanced it, his fists hammering against the sides of the police van, giving rhythm to Du Boise's rapacious movements.

Afterwards, the casual talk among the other cops, an ordinary, everyday event. How one of them told her to be glad that they had no time for a 'tournament', calls were coming in from all over the townships, they had to go, the 'fucken youth are going wild'. He hoped that 'this' would teach her a lesson. A verbatim quote: 'You fucken terrorists must think again about what you're doing. Otherwise, we'll naai you every time we see you.' Words embedded in her consciousness.

When she is returned to the van, she finds Silas lying dazed at the back, his forehead swollen. To shut him up, one of the cops had hit him with a baton. 'Just a klap,' the cop tells her. Then the journey home to Noordgesig, where they live in a small, two-roomed, government-scheme house.

'I crossed a divide that night. Soweto's lights in the distance, darkness all around. Silas groaning, weeping. I remember praying, calling on God to strike me dead, but knew instinctively that He too had fled somewhere. I also knew that something was stirring in me. I am pregnant, God, I am pregnant, I kept on repeating to myself, as if to exorcize the horror of that thought. But I knew it was true, and that I would have to conceal the moment of conception from everyone.

'I debated with myself: I could end the pregnancy. Abortions could be bought, even then. But I was already beginning to separate the child in me from the father's ugly, fleshy features, his grunts, his groans. Must the one life be damned because of the other? Yet, was I going to nourish, with my body and my life, the child of someone like Du Boise?

'In the end, I compromised, told myself to wait until it was born. I would decide then whether it would live or die. I did not think about what judgement. I would use to determine this. The way the child looked or smelled? I don't know. Nor did I think what I would do if I decided the child should die. Smother it when the nurses were not looking, break its tiny neck and proclaim to the world that I could not bear the thought of rearing a child of rape?

'They dropped us off at the edge of the township, and Silas and I walked down the quiet, peaceful street, both of us silent. He had stopped moaning, but did not know how to reach out and touch me. Perhaps if he had, my mind might have been made up: I would have aborted the child the moment the pregnancy was confirmed. Perhaps his touch would have drawn me closer to him and to his struggle. Yes, he could have made me loyal to his affronted manhood, turned me into a soldier, perhaps, a fearless bomb planter or a ruthless arms smuggler. But his fear, that icy, unspoken revulsion, hung in the air like a mist. It would enable me to give life to Mikey, my son. At that moment, in Smith Street, Noordgesig, I crossed over into a zone of silence.'

Another dawn. It comes red with blood, another savage day being born. No African could ever describe daybreak with delicate, Homeric beauty, Mikey decides, pink-fingered, a glowing nymph dispersing night's shadows before her. Not even Léopold Senghor at his most sentimental. African poetry hammered out on the anvil of brutal savannahs. Now there's theme for a dissertation. Drive Miss Anderson out of her mind.

He is calm, detached now from the full import of his mother's words: 'Mikey is a child of rape.' During the night, when he had first read this sentence, he had been overcome with horror. It stood on its own, a realization that must have come to her in all its finality years later, after her son was born. The starkness of the statement tried to conceal a hysteria that was absent from the rest of her writing. He had stopped reading for a while, fighting off the desire to weep. Suddenly, every tender touch, hug, or kiss on the forehead she had offered him no longer seemed like a spontaneous, simple, motherly gesture. He remembered the anguished look in her eyes when she held him, and how she often embraced him so fiercely that he feared she wanted to tell him about some great wrong she had done. Lydia had loved him out of pain and guilt. Yes, she too suffered the inverted morality of other rape victims, accepting the blame for what had happened.

Then Mikey had heard his father come home. Not wanting to talk to him just then, he had switched off his light and waited until the restless criss-crossing of creaking floorboards ceased, and the leaky plumbing stopped shrieking, signalling that Silas had washed and climbed into bed. There would always be a weary sigh, his day being considered and then relinquished. Does Silas grapple with his memories when he's alone? No, he blunts their impact by declaiming them loudly, and usually when he is drunk. Even this is often a pretence, Mikey suspects.

Eventually, he switched on the light and took up his mother's journal again.

He read through the night. From December 1978 to 16 May 1994, when the entries stopped abruptly. A random date, without any significance, after the country's first democratic elections. Why stop there? Perhaps history had dwindled away. Their lives, Lydia's and Silas's, the whole country's, had become ordinary things. Not worth recording any longer, not worth the few precious moments of her busy day.

His father is up.

'Mikey? Are you there?' Silas calls.

He slides into the blankets, a warm, rather unkempt womb, answers in a voice filled with feigned sleepiness. When Silas comes into his room, Mikey explains that he has been up all night, reading, preparing for an overdue assignment. He watches Silas's quiet, angular face, its expression of perpetual concern, and tries to reconcile this familiar image with his own, new-found knowledge that this man is not his father. He has always been there, kind and generous in the main, even if somewhat preoccupied, a *good* father, Mikey would testify if the need ever arose.

But so different from Lydia, and from himself, for that matter. I am the child of some murderous white man, Mikey thinks, a boer, someone who worked for the old system, *was* the old system, in fact. For the first time, the alien nature of this thought strikes him. Why think of the man as white, as a boer, there were many black men who worked for that system, and they too raped women, sowed their venomous seed in the wombs of their enemies? Being fathered by a traitorous black man, that would have been different, poetic almost, some sort of salvation in ambiguity.

But were they all traitors, the many black people who collaborated with the old regime? The subject for an inquiry, a job for some learned academic. Decipher those unspoken, ambivalent shadows of our past.

Silas's car pulling out of the driveway disturbs the debate Mikey is having with himself. The house sinks into its creaking stillness. The cleaner who comes once a week (the Alis have never kept a domestic worker, a matter of principle) is only due the next day. He is glad there is no one he has to speak to, even if only to exchange pleasantries.

He rises abruptly. He is determined not to sink into the melancholy that comes with reliving the past. He knows that it will not be possible to apply his golden rule – look to the future, always – with the same single-mindedness as before. He can no longer think of the future without confronting his past.

Christ, he thinks, I am beginning to sound like Archbishop Tutu. And what does *he* know? He has never been raped, nor is he a child of rape.

He replaces his mother's diary in her desk drawer, deftly uses a knife to slip the rather simple lock back into place. He picks up the phone and dials the number Kate gave him.

'Hello, Miss Jessup, it's Michael.'

11

'Michael, my Michael, you are my Michael!'

Mikey has already detached himself from Kate, and lies next to her, his hands resting on his stomach. Then he suddenly removes them, repulsed by his own sweat (the 'silkiness' that Kate says she loves, that she kisses and seems to drink in, luxuriating more in her own conception of his sensuality than in its reality), and firmly presses his palms down onto the bed, careful not to touch her.

This is the fifth or sixth time they have met to make love – to 'fuck', she insists. She is perceptive to his change of moods, the way his lust – back arched, eyes closed, buttocks tightened to allow him an absolute, almost menacing physical empowerment over her – quickly turns to faint disgust, a regret that is born deep inside him and forces him to thrust himself away from her, his climax wild and isolated, oblivious to her needs, her desires.

At first, she attributed this to an innate shame in him. After all, she is as old as his mother. It is understandable for him to be disgusted with her ageing body, yes, her breasts are sagging and her thighs are heavy (what do you expect when you get close to forty?). But she has since realized that it is not some crude comparison with the lithe bodies of young schoolgirls that makes him draw away. It is a struggle with some other moral image inside of him. His mother perhaps, or his grandmother, even that prissy Aunt Gracie with her Joan of Arc attitude. Who knows, who cares? This is becoming tedious.

She turns to look at him, ready to tell him that if he finds 'all this' so repulsive they should stop it. No problem. I have a life. I like the sex, your humour, your laughter when you're not being such a little damn martyr, but I can do without this demonstration of self-righteousness every time we've finished fucking.

She sees him lying there, his young, wrought loveliness, his beak-nosed, serious face, his limp penis still sheathed in the condom (that she insists he wear, helping him when his trembling ineptitude makes it difficult for him to slip it on at the height of his passion, her only moment of control), and feels the same sense of helplessness that over-comes her each time she wants to confront his displays of distaste.

She touches him with the tips of her fingers, then leans over and takes a tissue from the box he has so thoughtfully placed beside the bed, and removes the condom from his penis.

'There, now I don't have to touch a wet little weenie when I try to make up to you,' she says.

He laughs, breathes easier, is able to receive her with warmth again.

Will he bother to remove the condom from the bin, Kate wonders, or will he leave it to some hapless domestic worker? But she's not seen any domestic help around. Surely Silas doesn't do such chores, as preoccupied as he is? She tries to picture Mikey going about removing the evidence of their meetings here, not just disposing of used condoms, but washing lipstick from cups, putting sheets into the washing machine, opening windows to dilute her odours. She has the sudden image of a sly, calculating Mikey acting with angelic guile, purpose to everything he does.

She remembers the first time he called, after that first night (that night *is* a blur, a montage of images, smells, feelings she is still trying to put together into a coherent sequence). 'Hello, Miss Jessup, it's Michael. Can I see you?' Bold, to the point. She was lost.

What passion he had that day! Gaunt and hollow-eyed, the soft stubble of a boy in transition to manhood. A dissolute beauty. And that day he started a gentle aftermath of conversation – asking about her job, about Ferial, about how she'd come to know his father – that he now seemed to have disavowed. The second time, also at his behest, a breakfast 'meeting' during which he fed her pieces of orange, all sliced and ready, neatly arranged on a plate next to the bed.

Kate suspects that there is a great deal more purpose to their encounters. His questions are too precise, too detailed to be a mere part of conversational flow. She remembers him asking about an event, a specific date. What happened on the sixteenth of May 1994? She, of course, couldn't remember whether there was anything significant about that date. Afterwards, out of curiosity, intrigued by the exact nature of his enquiry, she looked it up on her computerized calendar. The marvels of modern technology.

'A party,' she told him the next time they met.

'What?'

'The sixteenth of May, you asked the last time. Well, we had a party at my house.'

'Who was there?'

'Oh, lots of people.'

'My father, and my mother?'

'Why, yes.'

'Was my father drunk, did he tell any of his stories?' His tone was sharp, inquisitorial.

'Yes, now that you mention it. That was the day they completed the TRC White Paper, ready to go to parliament.'

What is he after? she thinks to herself. Today, she decides to do some interrogating of her own.

'Has anyone ever called you "Michael"?'

'Like seriously, as a name? No, only when I'm being scolded, like when my dad wants to make a moral point. "*Michael*," he says in that lawyer's voice.'

'Lawyer's voice?'

'Yes, you know . . . look at how serious I am.'

She laughs. 'I'm a lawyer too, you know. But let's talk about this "Michael". So no one just uses the name for the sake of it, affection-ately? It is your name, after all.'

'Only my Uncle Toyer.'

'Oh, I've met met him.'

'Dad's brother, he's dead.'

'Oh, I'm sorry.'

He shrugs. 'Happened a long time ago.'

'Your dad never speaks about him.'

'Well, I don't think they were close. He was too young for my father's family.'

'I don't understand, what do you mean "too young"?'

He screws up his eyes, tries to picture his Uncle Toyer. 'He was full of fun. And he was gay.'

'Your father had a gay brother?'

'Yes.'

'Nothing unusual about that.'

The smile on his face is ghostly, another image being recalled, she thinks.

'In our community? You know that's not true,' he says.

'Your community?'

'Yes . . . coloureds.'

She is unsure whether or not he is using the term mockingly, the way his father does, calling himself a 'bushie' with exaggerated self-affection.

'But were things really that bad?'

'Kate, Uncle Toyer was found with his throat cut, and . . . he'd been castrated.'

'Oh God, I'm sorry.'

She hugs him, runs her hand over his smooth chest, his flat belly. Will he become fleshy, will this young body lose its suppleness, will he end up like all the rest? She dismisses this intrusion into her warm sense of peace. But now she thinks again about what she is doing . . . what *we* are doing, she corrects herself. Will the thought of him ageing force her to confront the transience of this 'affair', an ugly but apt word? Worse, will it force her to think about Janine, about her own sexuality, about the vague and theoretical concepts that cannot explain her attraction to this young kid and her simultaneous love for Janine.

Why can't I have the best of both worlds, Mikey's and Janine's, complex youth and warm, simple adult, enjoy them both at the same time? Would it have been different if I was heterosexual instead of bisexual?

'Kate?'

He is facing her, caressing her neck, her breast, the palm of his hand just brushing her skin. Something he discovered accidentally, how to arouse her by barely touching her. Kinetic energy, he explained afterwards. Ah, the mischief in his voice.

'Sweet Michael, I have to go soon. Don't start . . .'

'I need your help.'

'What with?' He props himself on an elbow, pensive and serious. She recognizes the machination.

'I need some documents from the security archives.'

'Whose?'

'An ex-cop called Du Boise.'

She stiffens, sits up. 'Mikey, please don't ask me to do things like that, it's illegal.'

'I'm sorry.'

He is contrite, takes her in his arms, soothes away her abrupt, cool manner by kissing her, slowly, meditatively, his eyes shut like those of a wounded child. They make love, gently, then fall asleep, Kate cradled in the crook of his arm.

When she awakes, she sees him standing before the narrow window, trembling, looking intently out into the distance. Then he turns and starts to get dressed.

'You'd better go, my mother is on her way.'

'How do you know?'

'I just know. Hurry, she'll be here in a few minutes.'

She slips her dress over her head, covering her nakedness rather than getting dressed. Pushed by his silent sense of urgency, she stuffs her underwear into her bag. She feels dirty, something drips from her vagina and runs down her thigh. God! We made love without a condom that second time!

She walks towards her car, and thanks heaven for having chosen a long dress today. He seemed to have disapproved, giving her clothing a disdainful look. The moment they were upstairs, he said, 'Please take off that dress.'

She gets into her car and slumps forward onto the steering wheel, feeling humiliated and angry with herself.

'This is so sordid!' she says out loud. She'll put an end to it, phone Michael – Mikey – and tell him not to call her again, not to say in his child's voice, 'How are you, Miss Jessup, when can I see you?'

She pulls away just as a taxi turns the corner. She sees Lydia in the car, sitting in front with the seat pushed right back, her legs stretched out. Kate hesitates for a moment, watches the taxi go past, sees Lydia's face, masked and cold, devoid of the suffering she somehow expected to find.

Then she dismisses the sudden wave of empathy she feels for Lydia, and drives off, resisting the temptation to look back. Angrily, she flips the rear-view mirror askew so that she can't glance at Lydia pulling up at the kerb. She does not want to know whether Lydia is looking back, and it no longer matters whether or not she has seen her speeding away from the house. Kate knows that Lydia will suspect something the moment she walks in, that she will see it in Mikey's face, sense it in the atmosphere, the air of disturbance that all such hasty departures create.

What confession will she demand of Mikey? Will she call Silas and say: 'Your son has been sleeping with your friend Kate. Yes! Kate, Kate the dyke!' Silas will call, speak in his hushed, I-am-so-shocked tone of voice, they will have a tearful discussion, followed by the usual recrimination. Janine will ask, 'Was it worth it, seducing someone so young, all for the sake of some cock?'

I'll survive, in the end, she tells herself, weighing up the consequences of this 'worst-case scenario'. More likely, Lydia and Silas – and Mikey – will learn to live with the fog that is about to descend on their lives. We'll learn, all of us, to live in our spheres of silence, not saying the unsayable, denying everyone the pleasure of seeing us suffer the divine virtue of the brave new country: truth. We have to learn to become ordinary, learn how to lie to ourselves, and to others, if it means keeping the peace, avoiding discord and strife, like ordinary people everywhere in the world.

She is still not reassured, but is rescued from her own sense of guilt and shame by having to focus on a more pressing, practical dilemma. She is late, and might just make it for a meeting with the President if she drives like a maniac. The freeway to Pretoria is hectic at this time of day. There is no time to go home and wash the semen from her thighs. Perhaps she'll find time to slip into the toilet at the office and pull on her panties, at least. This nakedness, this aura of just having had sex, she would not be able to conceal.

She smiles to herself. She could play a game, see how many of those present at the meeting are able to guess what's different about her today? Will they deduce that her bold, open-faced manner is because she is naked, that underneath her long dress there is a carnality, fulfilled but not yet spent, that when she breathes in deeply it is to inhale Mikey's smell, musty youth, that unwashed warmth? Or will they be deflected by this very out-of-character way of dressing. 'So unusual for you to wear such concealing clothes,' Julian might say.

Will it arouse her, this private knowledge of her own nudity, the consciousness of just having fucked a nineteen-year-old kid? Risky, though. The President has uncanny instincts. He may guess, and he'll begin to probe, first with those quizzical looks, then with the clarity that comes from his knowledge of women. His long years of incarceration have sharpened his ability to imagine us as we are.

'We tell him things about us simply by the way we hold ourselves,' she once told Julian.

'Your infatuation with the Old Man is dangerous,' he had warned.

Not infatuation, she now thinks, but admiration. He is a man who truly loves women. Mikey has something of that quality, the ability to manipulate her with his worshipful eyes. And, of course, those words of adoration, elevating her to a goddess when they make love! She remembers his hands on her skin that morning. The pleasure she feels dispels her sense of remorse, her self-loathing becomes a kind of bravado.

She will go to their weekly policy meeting with the President, her underwear stuffed into her bag.

12

When Mikey thinks of his mother, the word 'Mama' no longer comes to mind. Gone is the softness, the warmth of that word. It is no longer capable of absorbing him, the way it did when he was a child. He knows that Mama cannot offer him refuge in her motherly smells, gentle, milky, a blur of undefined generosity. There is a sharpness to her now, a sweetness of oranges, tangerines, he searches for the word – citrus! – that was not there when he snuggled into her as an infant, feeding on her breasts, or as a little boy, simply seeking love.

When he was a child and woke up to the silence in his room, his mother out of sight, he searched for her by raising his nose and smelling the air, tracing her movements along the passages of the dark and narrow houses they lived in. He noted, without knowing the cause, his father's discomfort and his grandmother Agnes's horror when he and his mother sniffed at each other, affectionately, with the innocence of animals. When he was fourteen, he went on his first date, to the Zoo of all places, and saw a wild dog exchange smells with her litter of whelps, a perfect, beautiful act of recognition that made him ashamed of the way he had discouraged his mother from leaning her face into his body and inhaling his odours, pulling away from her abruptly because others were watching.

He had been able once to read her mood long before she entered his room, enabling him to prepare his response, sometimes finding a way to blunt her anger at him, and, when it was unjustified, to confront it with a righteousness of his own.

But whatever passed between them, her love always won, permeating through the skins of their mutual resistance, until her touch regained its old, pure quality, something so simple and unambiguous that his father had once teased him about stealing his wife. He was ten years old and was puzzled by the idea of stealing love from someone else's beloved. Silas didn't even understand – then – the kind of love that mother and son had between them. Yes, it was full of silent tests and contests, but capable of shielding both from their own pain. Silas's love for Mikey veered from doting to indifference. In any case, the boy didn't like his father's smell. Beer and sweat, and a stale, acrid smell of smoke that clung to his clothes and his hair.

Like most children, he heard, and instinctively understood, the noises that adults make when they have sex. It would be too simplistic to call these sounds animal-like, because it is so intrinsically human to groan and sigh and suppress one's screams. Mikey also knew when his parents had just made love, even if he did not hear their primordial noises, by the intensity of the distance between them. Dad's face showed satiation, Mama's emptiness. She flung herself into a flurry of physical activity, scrubbing floors, cleaning, cooking, as if that emptiness would suck her in if she did not fill it with the most mundane and tedious of achievements.

When Mama touched Silas (still his father, in Mikey's mind), when she made love to him, hugged him, all those gestures immediately belonged to the past. It was as if she were living her life so that the seconds could speed up, and her time with his father could be brought to an end sooner. No, it was not a death wish or a desire to flee from her husband, it was a race against something unseen that seemed to pursue her whenever she was close to him.

When Mama touches Mikey, time changes to the present. He experiences what he describes (with growing intellectualism) as a 'nowness'. Time slows down, he feels its every movement. This immediacy can cause great joy and great pain. It makes it impossible for him to escape from his mother, or want to escape from her.

Now, as he is about to search for Uncle Toyer's photograph, he senses his mother. A strange impulse, to see the photograph of a long-dead uncle, to refresh his recollection of the smiling, secretive face. He needs to show his older-woman lover the uncanny resemblance he bears to Uncle Toyer, especially now that he knows there were no blood links between them. He remembers how Uncle Toyer moved with the agility of a dancer, his almost feminine elegance, a caricature of a gay man. The 'moffie', deviant, aberrant, loved by his family the way a retarded child, who cannot help what he is or does, is loved.

His mother is close by. Not in the house, not even in their street yet, but close. A strong citrus smell in the air, oranges today. But she will be here soon and he has to get Kate to leave. Mama will not understand. He can hear her chastizing him, 'You will be the death of me,' that same anguished voice with which she conveyed her shock when she found him and Mireille 'playing Gandhi'.

Now Kate is gone, hastily dressed, the evidence of their fucking still on her skin. Her resentment, a kind of rancid anger, stays with him. He dresses, washes his face, tries to remove the residue of her body from his own, expunge the memory of her pubic hair, but that is possibly the most beautiful part of her. It is an image that he can only erase through an act of utter brutality. He finds Oupapa Ali's glowing fragment of Kaaba stone, grasps it in his hand and smashes it against the wall. The stone does not break, instead it cracks the plaster and cuts into his palm. He wipes the blood from his grandfather's ill-gotten booty, his faith in the authenticity of the sacrilegious trophy restored, wraps a handkerchief around his bleeding hand, and prepares to go downstairs. He has succeeded in eradicating from his mind the image of Kate's nakedness, and knows that he will never again be able to bury his face between her legs, burrow into her hair with his mouth, an intimacy she loved.

Mama has an extraordinary way of knowing when Mikey has been in contact with a 'foreign' presence. When he was a child, she used to come home from work, lift him up, and say in that cooing tone she adopts when she is anxious, 'So who was here today, who held my baby?' A friend of his father's, his minder's sister, Mam Agnes, Aunt Gracie – Mama knew when someone other than his father had lifted him from his cot and held him to their chest.

When the door opens, he is there to meet her.

'Mama? Are you all right? How did you get here?'

She says nothing beyond a somewhat hoarse, 'Hello, Mikey.'

'It's so wonderful to have you home.'

They hug. Her response is cold, even when she is freed from the inhibition of the crutches, which she allows to fall away from her. Her stance, body leaning back, pelvis thrust out, demarcates the void between them, a chasm created by a lifetime of intimate knowledge. He draws her to him, pulls her head to his chest, suddenly conscious of how frail she seems. None of the Oliphants are tall, except for Auntie Gracie. Perhaps his angular, gangly body has its origins in some or other throwback gene? Not Du Boise, whom Lydia's diary describes as rather short. His hand touches a damp patch on his mother's back, she is sweating, and today her citrus is sharp.

They stand like that for a moment, until the heat of his body, and the child's smell that his defences have somehow secreted onto his skin, soften her silent fury. He hatred for Kate – whom she knows was here, even though she could not see the face of the woman speeding away as the taxi pulled up – is held in abeyance, to be resurrected at an appropriate time. She feels feeble against his youthful body, and it may seem to him that she is clinging. This is unseemly, she decides, and frees herself. She hobbles the short distance to the settee, sits down and says, 'Mikey, oh Mikey, I am so afraid for you.'

He knows that she will not mention Kate, that her mood will swing between anger and sorrow for days, that there will be a huge but unspoken barrier between them. That he will feel the silence, even as they talk about mundane things, about her health, about how he is doing at university, about how overgrown with grass the garden is. Everything is going to pieces around the house. Why doesn't his father do something about it all?

He goes to her, kneels, and lays his head in her lap. It is an inborn gesture, one that Mikey the baby, the child, used to make when he wanted to ask forgiveness for a transgression undiscovered as yet. He is quickly conscious of the subterfuge in his actions, of trying to dilute the disturbed stillness already beginning to set inside of her, and thinks how much he is like his father – Silas – after all, a man capable of crossing emotional divides only through touch.

Mama's smell is so sharp it shoots up into his nostrils, like the menthol spray he uses when he can't breathe. But it is a different smell, heavy, and makes him feel drunk. He knows that if he raises his head and tries to get up, he will be unsteady on his feet, that this will make her even more anxious, and that she has enough on her mind as it is. He worries too that she might feel rejected, that she might think he is recoiling from her odours, but starts to compare this strong reek with Kate's, and with Mireille's, long ago, when she lay naked alongside him, aroused by their game of abstinence.

He stays there, with his head in his mother's lap, even though he is frightened by his own thoughts, and his head throbs as he detects, for the first time, a different interpretation – inside his body – of the quality of Mama's smell. She too is rigid, holds herself as if she is afraid of what she may do if she moves, compensates by taking away the hand she had placed on his head, tenderly, when he first knelt down before her. He feels her fear as well, entering her skin and her mind.

Then he senses another presence. Silas is outside, staring morosely at the house, unable to walk up to the door, slip the key into the latch, push it open. Mikey rises abruptly, his mind sober, his hand aching where the stone cut into it, and he is able to push away the other image of his mother. She looks at him with her eyes narrowed, he looks straight back at her, and then at the door. When he walks away, there is an acknowledgement, for the first time, of a conspiracy between them, shapeless and undefined, the shadows of two complete strangers cast in their images, shadows they are unlikely ever to explore with words, and so to reveal their cruel meaning.

13

The view from the top of the hill at Tudhope Avenue always reminded Silas of the time he used to visit his father in Coronation Hospital. Ali Ali was dying of cancer, and his mother said that visiting him was the decent thing to do, even if he hadn't always behaved like a real father.

'You can't blame a man for his religion,' said his mother, she who had once been the beautiful Angelina Pelgron. She had taken on the name 'Mrs Ali', even though it had no legal standing and marked her with the stigma of a second-hand, Christian wife, because she didn't want Silas to be known as a bastard.

Dutifully, Silas did not blame his father's religion, and learned to control his anger at the open contempt his father's Muslim family had shown towards him and his mother. So he went to visit his father every day after school for six whole months. He saw more of the old man during those sombre afternoons than he had in the previous sixteen years of his life.

The crowded ward was somnolent after lunch, patients dozing. Weighed down by the heavy fare – boiled potatoes, boiled fish, boiled peas, everything boiled soft and set in boiled-off fat – they whiled away the slow hours until the doctors made their evening rounds.

His father did not speak much, either because he was too weak from the cancer – Hodgkin's disease, someone told the boy – or had nothing to say to his son, really. When he was well ('Up and about!' he used to say, in a poor imitation of Superman's slogan), Ali Ali visited Angelina and Silas because it was his duty to do so, a Koranic injunction to treat all his wives equally. He sat in their living room, drinking tea, staring at the pictures on the wall, perhaps because he was not allowed any in his real home, which he shared with his Muslim wife, or because it gave him something to fix his eyes on, so that he did not have to look at Silas's solemn, expectant face.

At the hospital, they shared that same silent hour of discomfort, apart from the most perfunctory exchange of pleasantries: How are you today? How was school? How is your mother? How is that Iblis of a brother of yours? At three-thirty precisely, Silas would rise, kiss his father on the cheek, and go out into the bright sunlight.

145

One day, the new patient next to Ali Ali spoke to Silas.

'Hey, what's his problem?' he asked in his brash, township-clever voice. One of the Saturday-night intakes, a trauma case, the ward was overflowing with casualties from the latest gang war in the western townships.

'It's called Hodgkin's disease.'

'Ja? And who's that?'

'It's a kind of cancer.'

'Cancer? Listen, take the old guy home, leave the beds open for the ouens . . . it's war out there. You want to see sick, look at me.' A living cadaver with pipes stuck into every conceivable orifice. 'Twenty-seven holes, they used a jungle knife, the swine!'

Tsotsi bravado hissed through a clenched mouth. Bad teeth, stench of the doomed.

Ali Ali had smiled at the young thug, and then at Silas, and said, 'He's right, you know.'

One day, Silas arrived at the hospital and found Ali Ali's bed empty. A kindly nurse told him that his father had died early that morning, that he was coherent right to the end. He even had the presence of mind to ask the staff to give something to his son, 'Silas, the quiet one who comes every day.'

That's how Silas acquired Ali Ali's Kaaba stone. He marvelled for a while at how it glowed in the dark, then forgot about it, his life filled with more pressing needs. Where *was* that stone, Silas wondered now? Maybe he should search for it, probably in that old box of useless things acquired over the years. Treasured heirlooms, the old people used to think. Nothing but rubbish to him. Except that stone. It had some strange effect, hypnotic almost. He could give it to Mikey, he had that kind of curiosity. Get him interested in his grandfather's rather mysterious life.

But Silas dared not go to the door and open it, say in his usual, calm voice, 'Lydia, are you home? Mikey, Mikey, where is your mother? She didn't wait for me, even though she knew I was on my way. I was only a few minutes late.'

A slight exaggeration, half an hour late, but hardly serious. Drove like mad. Literally insane to do that on the N1 freeway. Imagine being stopped by a cop. Ministry of Justice man arrested for speeding, doing 160 kilometres an hour, weaving dangerously through the traffic. 'My wife came out of hospital,' says Truth Man. The media so newly vigilant. Where were they when we were being murdered?

Silas realized that he was addressing Mikey, as if he was practising to live with the silence that was bound to envelop his relationship with Lydia. It was also his way of not thinking directly about what he feared was happening beyond that heavy wooden door. Reinforced oak, keeps out the unwanted of Berea, illegals from Nigeria, the Ivory Coast – or should he say 'Côte d'Ivoire', like some fancy perfume? The music of fugitive tongues. All shiny suits and flashy cars, the legend goes, drug dealers and currency smugglers. Where was the fabulous wealth the xenophobes kept talking about? Not here, not in Berea. Here there is only dark sin and incest.

He sat down on the kerb, felt the heat through his trousers, his civil servant's suit, purchased off the peg from Woolworths. Ill-fitting at the best of times. What would he say if he opened the door and found them together? No, he must not think the unthinkable. Can scarcely think of Lydia with another man, let alone . . . If there *was* another man, what would he do? Respond with dignity, resign this miserable job, petty heroics, drudgery of the intrigue, do the things he'd always wanted to, quietly go away. If the worst came to the worst, he could angle for an ambassador's post; now that the Old Man was about to retire, he had some hope. It would be just reward for all the years of struggle. Somewhere warm, though, none of those frostbitten places for him. Mauritius maybe, bachelor ambassador on the loose, white beaches, brown bodies, at home among his bastard kind. Getting tired of this 'not-black-enough shit'.

But Betty is in Canada. Yes, go and find Betty. Or was it Australia she fled to with that misery-guts of a husband? Stop holding onto such futile dreams! All grey hair and sunken tits, she must be by now.

And what did he suspect was going on in there? Mother and son being intimate? Well, that's the nature of relationships between mothers and their male offspring. But there was something different about Mikey, an arrogance, strutting about like a cockerel. It started when Lydia was in hospital.

Shit! Kate, he's been sleeping with Kate!

The sun began to dull in the haze of smog. Silas felt thirsty, he could do with a beer, take a six-pack and go and sit out there on the grass verge, the border between the past and the future. Where the township joins the suburbs, where Africa has come home to roost. Enough of this nightmarish obsession with Mikey's sex life. Life was going on, sins were being confessed, murder, rape. Assassins confessing to the Truth Commission. Imagine this: in that distant past, they had made plans to kill his Minister by substituting his heart pills with stimulants. These days, getting that slow heart to beat faster would be a noble gesture, not a murder.

The TRC report was due to be handed over to the President on the twenty-eighth day of October. We'll make that date, no matter what, the Archbishop had said. Piety and determination. That's how God made this crazy fucken world in seven days.

He rose at last, his anguish deadened by the sonorous voice of his everyday muse, the clerk of the soul, telling him that it was better to deal with the prosaic affairs of the world than with the poetry of his heart. He walked stiffly to the front door. You grow old and your arse grows cold. Now whose words was he perverting? he asked himself.

God, he hadn't read anything in years, not a stirring poem or a novel steeped in a slow ferment of words.

What does Nelson Mandela do when he goes to bed?

14

The day had passed uneventfully. The President had had to leave the meeting early. A confrontation brewing between 'the Arch' and people in the movement. He was to meet with all sides, try to find a dignified way out of 'the mess'.

'Silas Ali, he works for the Minister, he's a good man, is he?' the President had asked no one in particular, but everyone around the table had nodded their agreement. The Old Man's way of confirming something he already believed.

In the end, no one had mentioned Kate's dress, and she had begun to feel uncomfortable. Cold semen did not feel sensual on the skin. As soon as she could, she left work, drove home and lay in a hot bath for an hour, trying to stem her renewed feeling of disquiet. Before leaving the office, she had asked Van As, the President's security chief, if he could locate security records on 'François du Boise, a Lieutenant in the old Special Branch'.

Major Rudy van As had been in the old security police himself. His transformation into loyal guardian of the new order was complete, and fierce. Du Boise? The name did not sound familiar, he said. There had been thousands of foot soldiers, but he would see if he could get anything out of archives. Major Van As's smug voice, his neutral smile. He was living up to the cliché of the inscrutable old security policeman.

Afterwards, she regretted having asked him at all, bewildered by her own impulsiveness.

Draped in the loose gown she wore when there was no one home, she lay sprawled out by the pool, sipping a glass of wine. Her dogs, three huge German shepherds, clamoured for attention, pressing their noses against her. So much to be done, and here she was lazing about, breaking a house rule: no alcohol before five on a weekday. A gesture of restraint meant to impress Ferial. We lead by example. She quickly dismissed her guilt. She worked hard, put in many hours, this bit of indulgence was deserved.

Her thoughts drifted back to the morning's events. How had Mikey known that his mother was coming? There had been no warning, no phone call, no knock on the door, just this crazy kid standing at the window, *sensing* his mother's imminent arrival. Michael the Phenomenal. Always probing, lately, asking questions about the amnesty process, things he should ask his father, not someone he's just had sex with. Perhaps trying to demonstrate his intelligence, not just a young kid only good for fucking.

There was no doubting how bright he was. She saw the evidence of it all around him, the books on his shelf (without order, a random collection of truly intimidating titles), the music he listened to. Once, she'd glanced at some notes on his desk and was startled to read the beginnings of an analysis of the liberation struggle: there had never been an 'armed struggle', the movement had had more of an armed propaganda ability than any 'real capacity to wage even a limited war'. He had removed the notepad abruptly, locked it in a drawer, his eyes telling her that he did not want to discuss what she had read.

He had all the hallmarks of a driven person. A quest for truth, or justice, that grand kind of thing. She'd seen that ruthless gleam in people's eyes before, the holy, malevolent clarity of someone obsessed.

15

Somehow, out of expediency, through collusion, because of the sheer need to re-establish the surface continuities of their lives, things returned to normal. From the moment that Silas opened the door, on the day Lydia had come home from the hospital without waiting for him, they established a code of silence, a set of mutual understandings – Silas and Lydia, Lydia and Mikey, Mikey and Silas – striking separate compacts with each other: whatever had happened on *that day* would not be spoken about or even hinted at. No matter how bitter their disputes. What had passed between mother and son, and whatever it was – instinct, premonition, intuition – that had kept Silas out of the house for those crucial hours, was to remain buried. All families have secrets that they conceal for ever.

They would think of it as *that day* in their minds, independently acknowledging that their relationships with each other had started their real transformation when they sat trapped in their separate spaces, unable to reach out to each other, unable to express outrage or assert innocence, unable to accuse, justify or recriminate. Silas on the pavement, Mikey lying on his back in his room, Lydia on the settee, her feet raised up on pillows, the way they had been after she danced on the broken glass. Each set in the gravel of their emotions, an individual resolve never to raise the subject of *that day*.

Lydia: 'Let Silas suspect what he wants to, I know in my heart it is not true.'

Silas: 'Let Lydia hide whatever there is to hide, it is not my shame, it is hers.'

Mikey: 'Nothing happened, nothing.'

Silas did call out 'Lydia?' when he walked in, saw her on the settee, her eyes closed. He went closer, saw that she was asleep, leaned down over her, and smelled the sedative on her breath. A homeopathic formula he had bought to help him sleep. It contained a minute quantity of laudanum, that's what gave it this powerful smell. Upstairs, his feet pounding on the treads, loud, deliberate, a warning to Mikey to compose himself, should there be a need to.

He found Mikey at his computer, surfing the Internet, the website of an on-line bookstore on the screen.

'Mikey?'

'Oh, hi, Dad!'

'Is Mom okay?'

'Isn't she downstairs?'

'Yes, asleep on the settee.'

'She asked me to get her some water and that stuff you take, found it in your medicine cabinet. She looked tired, Dad.'

Mikey's bland face, concealed and concealing. He was beyond his father's reach, beyond any paternal love or revulsion or regret.

Silas asked Mikey to come and help him. His mother would have to sleep down there for a while, until her feet were completely healed. It would be difficult for her to climb the stairs each time she wanted to lie down or bath. Together they transformed Silas's study into a bedroom, the sleeper couch moved in from the living room and made up with white linen, which Mikey immediately thought of as 'fine', as if someone else had planted the word in his head. Silas brought Lydia's bedside lamp down from their room – 'She likes the light it gives her when she reads' – and set it up on an old 'smoking table' next to the bed. The neat piles of paper, briefing notes, press cuttings, pamphlets on the Truth Commission were unceremoniously scooped up into a cavernous old canvas bag and dragged to the storeroom at the back. Two vases of flowers – roses and daisies – brightened up the gloomy bookcase: sombre tomes that he hardly ever touched and that Mikey occasionally pulled out in order to inhale the musty fragrance of dust and leather binding.

Lydia could not help smiling when she woke up at last and was shown her 'bedroom' for the coming weeks.

'So this is where I am being exiled to?'

'Lyd, you still have stitches in those feet, you can't climb . . .'

'I know, I know. Thank you, both of you.'

The equity of her gratitude, distributed with such quick grace, helped them overcome the first hurdle in their quest for a forgiving truce. Peace through amnesia. Afterwards, they ate a late-night supper of pasta and an 'exotic' sauce that Silas jovially concocted, then settled down to a quiet cup of tea before the time came to go to bed. This would be the next test, their ability to part quietly, retreat into their divided intimacies (it was clear that Silas would sleep upstairs in their bedroom, while Lydia would be alone in his study) without betraying any hurt or suspicion, avoiding extraordinary gestures, a weighted glance or lowered eyes. Mikey, as was his custom, kissed his mother on her cheek, touched his father on the shoulder, before going to his room.

Lydia used her crutches to get to the small downstairs bathroom, allowed Silas to help her undress, but insisted on washing herself. She sat on a chair before the basin and sponged down her upper body. She could not wet her feet just yet, not until the stitches had been removed. He observed her nakedness, but suppressed his unexpected arousal. She had the squatted-down resolve of a woman not ready to be loved.

In the days that followed, they were helped in their reconciliation by the many real crises that Silas faced. Days before Archbishop Tutu was to present the TRC report to the President, the ruling party tried to obtain a court order to stop its publication. Silas spent hours shuttling between Ministers and lawyers, priests and politicians, trying to persuade them to reduce the scale of their demands, soften the almost tyrannical belief in the justness of their various causes. He mobilized friends and family of the adversaries, called in favours, threatened and cajoled. In the end, he preached, yes, he too was reduced to the gospel of his own beliefs, as pragmatic as they were: 'Let them all say what is necessary for them to say, let us follow the law to the letter,' he counselled his bewildered Minister. Desultory days and tedious nights of bargaining, until there was nothing left to barter with, neither principle nor compromise.

In the meantime, Lydia's feet were healing and Mikey was preparing for his exams. They spent their lonely hours in the different levels of the house, vaguely aware of each other late at night, when she could not climb the stairs and he dared not go down to her makeshift bedroom. His mother's smell – *that day* – still clung to him. He also remembered the silence in the house immediately afterwards. Now the house was just as quiet. He thought of Lydia, down there in the well of the house, aware of the unnatural distance between them. Mother and son should not be avoiding each other like this.

He suspected his own motives when he felt the need to go downstairs, to drink water or simply sit in the cool recess of the stoep, staring out at the comforting meaninglessness of the street's activity, people walking by, voices, music, the blurred hum of traffic further down the hill. The summer was already unseasonably hot.

He met Kate on one more occasion, at her house. Her daughter Ferial was away, and so was Janine. Marguerite had returned to Belgium. 'This is not Africa,' she had told Kate haughtily, 'it is your illusion of Africa.' Nevertheless, her departure contributed to love's grand coincidences. Kate and Mikey were alone, except for the dogs, which milled around him, smelling his manly foreignness, his odour of lustfulness. They made love in her study, on a chaise longue with an upraised back. Perhaps this influenced his passion. He was fierce, violent almost, and she winced with pain once, ready to withdraw from him. His rhythm was different, his passion dark and hard, no longer young and joyful. He has been spoiled for young people, doomed to seeking out older women for the rest of his life, she thought, when he finally leaned back, drained of colour and life.

She did not mention their last encounter, her hasty and humiliating departure, nor did she joke about his 'dammed-up' passion. He was restless, even as he reclined by the pool, stroking the backs of the dogs, offering themselves greedily to his attention. They took naturally to him. He had none of the fear of dogs that usually possessed kids who had grown up in the township. Thoroughly freed of his past, she thought.

It was obvious that there was something he would ask for, perhaps as he got dressed, or when he was about to leave. She went into her study and returned with a thick manila envelope. 'Here's what you asked me for the last time,' she said.

He smiled, thanked her, kissed her on the mouth, softly. A farewell? she asked herself. She watched him walk away, hands in his pockets, the envelope tucked under his arm. She did not offer him a lift, although it was a long way home on foot. But he was young and full of energy, ferocious in fact.

And is that not what a woman wants in a man – vigour? Or else it's not worth it!

That night, Lydia lay on her bed and looked around the sombre room. This was her husband's world, filled with recorded knowledge, a desperate orderliness of catalogued books and research papers. A history of the world, a *containment* of history, of civilizations won and lost through the rule of law. That was his true north, the rule of law. Swore by it. Saved him from the 'vagaries' of the rich and the powerful, he was telling her just the other night. Yes, he was beginning to speak to her again, about his work, about mundane office politics, his Minister's floundering. It was good to have a rule to live by, but how little his rule – if you make a law, then apply it, to the letter, there is no other way – had helped all those 'victims' who had told their stories

before the Commission. The brave victims and the wise Commissioners, the virtue of both defined as if by divine decree.

It would not have helped her to appear before the Commission,
even at a closed hearing. The offer had been made, a special session on
abused women. 'Of course, everyone acknowledges that both sides
used women, exploited them, this is an opportunity to bring the issue
out into the open, to lance the last festering wound, to say something
profoundly personal.' A young lawyer from the TRC had brought the
offer. She looked into his eyes and saw an evangelist's fervour. When
she refused, she saw in Silas (whom she'd asked to remain with her in
order to inhibit the young emissary's eagerness) a brief moment of
disappointment. Her appearance would have given him the opportunity to play the brave, stoical husband. He would have been able to
demonstrate his objectivity, remaining calm and dignified, in spite of
being so close to the victim.

Nothing in her life would have changed, nothing in any of their
lives would change because of a public confession of pain suffered.
Because nothing could be undone, you could not withdraw a rape, it
was an irrevocable act, like murder. Once that violating penis, that vile
cock had been inside you, it could not be withdrawn, not by an act of
remorse or vengeance, not even by justice.

For the first time in many weeks, she thought of Du Boise. In the
hospital, she had recalled his face every night, his small and dull eyes,
not beady, but transparent in their blueness. She remembered the
horror of his climax, the way he shuddered, his eyes closed only for an
instant, as if he was afraid she might murder him in his moment of
glorious incapacity. Is that not what all men feel? A sense of glory when
they come inside a woman, whether in consensual love or uninvited
imposition?

And now Du Boise was inside this house, this house of shadows,
ensconced in those high eaves through which the wind howled, a noise

audible only from down here. There, there it was, as if on cue, as if summoned by her awareness of it. A few more days and these stitches will come out, she'll be able to return to her bedroom, above this fatal flaw in the house's architecture. This brought home another realization. She'll be back in bed with Silas, her husband. And will he expect her to have sex with him, and will she desire him? Almost as if to test her ability still to desire, she touched her vagina, slowly caressing herself. She was fifteen the last time she had masturbated, the image of Sister Catherine hovering above her, and then Christ and Catherine, and then swarming apparitions, faces of delight and shame. Now, even the appearance of Cathy, the Butcher Road whore, in all her silken finery, could not excite her. She gave up and lay back, tried to sleep. Again that noise. Wind in empty space. The architect must have been a sadist, or a bored artist. A door closed somewhere.

'Mikey?'

Silence.

She climbed out of bed, took up her crutches, and made her way to the door, which she gently pushed open. She was able to observe the staircase, the living room, the dining room beyond. A light gleamed upon the long table they rarely used now, and she saw Mikey in his shorts, a glass of milk in his hand, emerge from the kitchen and stand at the bottom of the staircase, ready to ascend. He paused, looked around, slowed the circle of his sweeping eyes when he saw the study door ajar, then went up the stairs.

Hastily, she shut the door, retreated to her bed and sternly took up the book at her bedside, adjusted the lampshade and tried to read. A paperback edition of *Madame Bovary* that she had found in the otherwise barren hospital bookshop. Perhaps it had come to be there because of its cheap appearance, or because it seemed like a romance – 'Unabridged,' the cover proclaimed. Was it no more than a romance, after all? She pushed these thoughts aside, knowing they would lead her back to thinking about her son, up there alone in his room, and to contemplating how unnatural it was for her, no, for both of them to impose this preposterous lack of intimacy upon each other. A chaste distance had to be maintained between them, as if something unholy would happen if they had a cup of hot milk together.

She would take the milk to his room, or call him down, since she could not climb the stairs. They would hold the steaming mugs to their lips, sip the hot sweetness, the way they used to, long ago, talk about the day gone by, about tomorrow, about his exams, about her decision not to go back to being a nurse. She could explore his increasingly adult mind, talk about things she no longer felt comfortable discussing with Silas.

Abruptly, she halted this train of thought. He had grown up, wanted company his own age, probably surfing the Net right now, participating in chat rooms with people his age all across the world. What need had he of an ageing mother, flecked with grey, worn down by a lifetime of drudgery? She could become one of Silas's case studies, if he ever decided to write a book about how the 'law' prescribed not only the lives of nations, but of individuals as well. She had lived according to one immutable law: self-containment.

She read: *Madame Bovary had opened her window overlooking the garden and watched the clouds.* Then she snapped the book shut and got out of bed.

She stared at the crutches for a moment, as if imagining how awkward it would be to climb the stairs using those damned things. Mikey would listen, charting her progress, counting each weary thump. What would she say to him when she reached his room? 'I just want to talk.' And that was the truth. All she really wanted was some warm, intelligent company, not these cold books, their spines held in rigid hostility against her presence. She closed her eyes as if to ward off some wayward vision, put on her gown and slowly made her way into the hall, leaning up against the wall when she felt unsteady.

She heard a key in the door, Silas's rasping way of shoving it open with his foot, so that he did not have to put down the accoutrements of his trade, briefcase and computer. They stared at each other for a moment, Lydia in the darkened well of the house, Silas in the island of light at the door.

'Lydia, you should not be walking without your crutches.'

'I need to practise, when the stitches are removed I may find I've forgotten how to walk without those stupid things.'

She saw the unasked question in his eyes.

'I need to find your sleeping drops, and a glass of water.'

'I'll get it for you.'

'A woman has to do things for herself, especially when the men of the house have abandoned her.'

'Where is Mikey?' he asked, bringing her the water.

'Up in his room, I think.'

He sat down in a chair opposite her, measured out the prescribed fifteen drops into the glass. How imprecise homeopaths are! She sipped, grimacing at the slightly bitter taste, glanced up at him, hating him for having intruded, but relieved that he had arrived at such a crucial moment, before she had started her journey up those stairs. No, it was not the prospect of the embarrassment she would have felt, being caught like an errant schoolgirl, halfway up a staircase she had 'no business' ascending, it was the unconscious thought of what might have happened had he not come home when he did.

Silas had something to tell her, she could sense his urgency, the way he was tapping his fingers on the edge of his chair. Her self-reproaches would have to wait, the shame of how easily she had lied would have to be dealt with in the dead hours of the night, in spite of her inevitable exhaustion. For now, the moment of self-judgement was postponed with some relief.

'Lydia, the TRC is done, they've completed the report.'

'Oh, does that mean you're out of a job?'

'No, no, I work for the Ministry, remember, not the Commission.'

His art of evasion, something oblique, deflected in his eyes, even as he looked at her so directly. Just like the time he had to come and talk to her about his affair with that woman, Betty, his 'comrade in arms'. A joke in poor taste, she had to remember not to repeat it, even to herself. But what infidelity had he to confess now?

'So it's all over?'

'Yes and no.'

'Oh, Silas, can't you ever come straight to the point?'

'Well, the damned report is done, they hand it to the President next week, thank God.'

'You mean there was a chance they wouldn't have?'

'Touch and go, as they say.'

He described the tension, the intrigue, told her which of those who pontificated in public about truth and justice actually believed in 'the principle of the thing', and which were the expedient ones. 'They'd sell their mothers for a Cabinet post under the future . . .' He stopped in mid-flow, brought to a halt by his observation of her cold face, composed and expectant. She knew that he was turning something over in his mind, some fearful revelation he did not know how to slip off his tongue, despite all his glibness, his smooth gift for unsayable things.

'Lyd, the TRC hearings are over, but the amnesty process continues.'

'So, it is not over?'

'For a lot of people, it will never be over. For many, it will go on, for a while yet . . .'

He was reading a speech he had prepared in his mind, she thought. How long had he delayed before driving home, before getting out of the car, thinking about what to say to her?

'Come to the point, Silas.'

'Du Boise has applied for amnesty, he and three, four others, for rape, assault, on women mostly. He has named you as one of the cases he is asking amnesty for.'

She remained silent.

He leaned forward. 'I saw the brief, someone involved in the TRC's investigation recognized your name. The hearings will be in public, some time next year.'

'Stop them, Silas.'

'I can't, not even the President . . .'

Her hand trembled. He reached out and took the half-consumed sleeping draught from her, held her hand in his. Beneath her limpness, a tension concealed with brutal effort, her pulse was racing, the minuscule throb sensual against his finger. He caressed her hand, tracing long, blue-veined lines along her slender wrist, those arms with their incongruous, golden down of hair. He was on his knees before her, kissing her face, running his hands down her body, over her breasts.

'No, no,' she said, and pushed him away.

He fell back onto his buttocks, stared up at her, his humiliation fuelled by regret. 'I'm sorry, I'm really sorry, I just felt overcome . . .'

'It's all right, you are my husband . . . you have every right.'

Silas shook his head. 'God, that's not what I meant . . .'

'You *are* my husband.'

He got up. His dignity reasserting itself, his damn manly pride, he would later say to himself, recognizing the opportunity missed, the tender gesture some part of him wanted to make, to cradle her head, let her weep, wrest back her affections.

'And that is what it has come down to? All there is between us are my rights?'

She started crying, a soft, childlike, whimpering sound that she had hoped no one would ever hear again. Silas stalked away, his jacket flung over his shoulder. He hadn't done that in years, walked out into the night, away from her anger and her terrifying grief. And Mikey was

161

with her now, having bounced down from the top of the stairs, where Silas had seen him, wondering how long he had been there, listening, watching, and it was Mikey who put his arms around her, whispering, 'It's okay, Mama, it's okay.' It was Mikey she turned to, because Silas had walked away into the humid night, escaping to a bar, to the sweaty warmth of a dark-wooded place, full of late-night drinkers, an atmosphere of softened belligerence. He would confess his sorrows to them, the tragedy of his life, 'this wife, you see', then sink into a head-shaking silence, his tale unfinished.

It was Mikey whom she held now, and drew to her, and kissed, the way she had always wanted to draw a man to her, at her behest, for her own comfort and pleasure. Her lips on Mikey's lips, her tongue touching, just touching, the wetness of his mouth. She led him to her bed, and he lay down almost dutifully, his eyes closed. And then he was gone, fallen through a trapdoor into a haven of unconsciousness.

Lydia wept with sorrow and relief. She observed his slender body, saw in it a fragility she had not noticed before, and longed to reach out and touch him, tenderly, as a mother would touch her son, but knew that that was impossible now.

Already he had about him the gruffness that some men acquire later in life. He will be incapable of loyalty to any one woman, he will be the kind of man who comes and goes without warning. How difficult it will be, from now on, to love him only as a son.

16

The drama in their lives is gone. There is no need for it or its gaudier sibling, melodrama. They live truly secret – and secretive – lives. They are as concealed from each other as they are from the world. No one shouts or remonstrates, Silas does not storm out of the house, even when he is angry. He hides his anger, leaves quietly, and has learned how to shut doors noiselessly, to start his car and drive off without the squeal of tyres, without even revving the engine. He is the only one able to escape in this way. Lydia takes buses, or walks down to Louis Botha Avenue to catch a Kombi-taxi when she needs to go and see Mam Agnes and Jackson in Soweto. It is a brave thing to do, Jackson says, 'And foolish!' Mam Agnes adds.

Mikey walks, endlessly, strides away, long, loping steps that take him down Munro Drive to Orange Grove, to the Radium Beerhall, to the Health and Racquet Club, where he works out, mixes with friends. Suddenly, he seeks out the company of young people, who welcome him, absorb him into their circle, fiercely, the way compassionate people take in a refugee. Mikey also – Lydia discovers – catches Kombi-taxis to Newclare, where his father grew up. He returns from these trips drained of energy, and is often distracted and listless, without appetite. Both Silas and Lydia worry that their son is taking drugs, but say nothing. Lydia's guilt is particularly acute.

But they continue to live together, in proximity to one another, a family unit whose names seem more and more incongruous when said together. Silas Ali, Lydia Ali, Mikey Ali. Mikey dislikes the sound of his own name most of all, he has come to understand that it is an 'oxymoron'.

Vinu, from his English class at university, is celebrating her parents' divorce. She dyes her hair bright orange and invites Mikey out for a drink. Her tall body flung down in a chair, she tells him that his name is even worse than hers.

'Vinu Viljoen,' she says her name out loud. 'Bastard people are beautiful, bastard names are not.'

They laugh, and then she starts crying, and Mikey hugs her, stares fiercely at the curious people around them, until they are forced to look away. He tells her that he understands.

163

'Why don't they marry their own kind?' she asks. 'That way, they won't have to *discover*, years after they've brought children into the world, that they're culturally incompatible, and the children won't have to suffer.'

Mikey says that from now on, he is to be addressed as 'Michael', that is his name. It is a declaration of loyalty to her. He doesn't know why he is making this decision; after all, if you want to change what people call you, you should choose something more appropriate, a first name that goes with the family name.

'Something like Moosa Ali,' Vinu says, 'or better still, Mohamed Ali.' She laughs, dries her tears, kisses him tenderly, says, 'I am going to find a half-Hindu boertjie to fuck,' and goes off.

He remembers that Kate calls him 'Michael', that her use of this name has a possessive tone, but he dismisses the vaguely troubled feeling he gets when her name is mentioned or when he, on the odd occasion, thinks about her. He does not return her calls, and once turned back at the university gates when he saw her sitting in her car, waiting for someone, a friend or a colleague, maybe even him. He has no desire for her, for her body, her hoarsely whispering voice after they have made love, her smell, which he has begun to regard as 'typical of an older woman'. Yet he is grateful that she obtained Du Boise's records for him.

The Alis remain together in their middle-class home in Berea, perhaps because they have no choice, perhaps because they realize that for any one of them to move out would require an acknowledgement of the 'thing' that has divided them, for ever. They do not speculate about their fate, they each find a way to deal with the reality of the 'thing'.

Silas thinks of the past, increasingly summoning up happier times, epochs of greater clarity, times without this ambiguity he sees everywhere. In his home, in his office, in the country, in the grand scheme of things, in the religions of God and in the godlessness of politics, there is a growing area of grey, shadowy morality. He is a 'progressive', an epithet that distinguishes his generation from the older members of the liberation movement. He knows the value of being pragmatic, he welcomes the freedom 'even to be wrong', but it cuts him adrift, sometimes sending the needle of his personal compass into wild swings. The rule of law is no longer the keen knife-edge of all meaning, he is losing his 'true north'. He has a grudging sympathy for his Minister, and for the Old Man, the President, both of whom embody, in their personal integrity, the 'value system' of the liberation movement. Being in government, having to make decisions that accord not with their own wishes but with the 'needs of the country', makes demands on their personal principles.

The President has decided to make way for the inevitable future, the Age of the Manager, with deals being struck and countries saved over a companionable glass of whisky, in the hush of dimly lit rooms. His Minister should consider retiring, and so should Silas. After all, he is only a township bushie. What future does he have in the government?

Lydia lives in the present, self-judging, brutally honest. These once self-evident instruments of purgatory do not lessen the dull pain that besieges her consciousness. She is back upstairs, in the main bedroom, while Silas has taken over Mikey's room. It was Mikey's initiative to move down to Silas's study, so that both Lydia and Silas could have 'proper' bedrooms (they all avoid the guest-room, with its bare walls and gaping cupboards). This is the only change to their newly established routine. Lydia sits on the narrow balcony outside her bedroom, close to the precipice of an encroaching street, protected only by a rusty railing. She sips endless cups of herbal tea (for the health of body and mind), stretches her legs, admires her slim ankles.

She takes up her diary again, opening it one day with a sense of trepidation. She suspects that someone has read through these pages, but cannot imagine that Silas would do such a thing. Perhaps it was Mikey? She dismisses this thought and continues writing. Now it is a true journal, a record of daily events. Her feet are healing. The stitches have been removed, the cushioning (and deforming) swathes of bandages are gone. She thinks of her enduring loveliness, in spite of her remorse and guilt, and prays that her attractiveness will fade, that she will quickly crumble into a premature middle age of grey hair and sagging thighs.

She thinks: I kissed my son, carnally, on his lips.

Then softens the harshness of this thought, the cat-o'-nine-tails lash of her own confession, by placing it all 'in context'. She is a survivor, after all, or so she has been told. She kissed her son carnally, *she thinks*, and he did not respond. *Did* she then kiss him with carnal intent? This objectified language helps. She kissed him, he started to kiss her back, then withdrew. She held him to her and felt his hard body, no, felt the hardness of his sex. For a moment, a mere moment. She was weeping, that was why he held her. She was distraught, she felt weak. Is that not how all women are described under such circumstances: weak? But it was she who led him to her bed, that narrow, borrowed bed meant for guests, but in which a guest has never slept.

Yes, he lay down next to her, but seemed immediately to retreat. Some kind of trance, a state of practised absence, his body withdrawing into a cool cocoon of a world, no, it was not womb-like, it had no heat, no life. Then she too sank into a coolness, a chaste calm that reduced the indefinable desire (was it desire, was that all it was?) she felt in her stomach, her trembling hands, the frenzied murmur of blood somewhere in the region she supposed was her sexual domain, belly, thighs, groin. God, how trite, how banal it all seemed now.

And yet, that kiss was indelible, a gesture impossible to withdraw. Like Du Boise's penis, an irredeemable act of intrusion. Mikey had saved them from a truly cruel pleasure. If they had made love, there would have been terrible repercussions, unimaginable consequences – but there would also have been energy, even if it was a vile energy, filled with self-loathing and hatred. Now there is only this silence, this utter soundlessness that emanates from Mikey, who insists, when he does speak, upon being called 'Michael', an aloof name for an aloof person. It began the moment she shook him: 'Mikey, Mikey, wake up, you must go to your bed.' He rose, as if snapping out of a hypnotist's sleep, walked away without saying a word, without blinking, without a gesture of greeting, without a backward glance, as if afraid he would turn into a pillar of salt. She winces at these archetypal images of mortal sin, Sodom and Gomorrah, the biblical condemnations she is calling down on herself, perhaps in order to find forgiveness. Is that not what God and all His religions are there for, to demand repentance and grant forgiveness?

No, it is much worse. Mikey walked away as if nothing had happened. As if she, his mother, had not kissed him carnally, had not asked him into her bed, as if he had not spurned her. She sometimes hopes that he indeed remembers nothing, that the trauma has induced an amnesia in him, thus sparing him the scars of her sexual desire for him.

In her heart, she knows better, knows instinctively that his desire was as strong as hers, that there was pure lust in him, but that they were saved by his arrogance, his wish to test his self-taught ascetic discipline: the ability to withstand even the most exotic temptations. He could so easily have had sex with her just to prove his capacity for the forbidden. She sees in Mikey an enslavement to another, even more puritan God: his will.

Michael, as he has now defined himself, lives only in the future, in the world of young people and young pursuits. He has no use for the older generation, his mother and father, Kate, his grandparents, God, whom he thinks of as an old man too. Even that other old man with the smile of a mischievous child, Madiba, whom he once thought of as the saving grace of the older world: they all have the same brittle air of vulnerability, of souls fallow despite years of feverish cultivation. 'The struggle' sowed the seeds of bright hopes and burning ideals, but look at what they are harvesting: an ordinariness, but also a vanity fed by sly and self-seductive glimpses in the mirrors of their personal histories. In each is born a frantic need for a 'legacy', a need to be recognized as a 'hero of the struggle'. The world – once more – is full of monument builders and statue erectors.

Only once does he envision a future for himself that is remotely like that of his parents – a wife, a life-partner, children, a home, a garden overrun by a large yelping dog, a blue Dane. Mystified by the sentimentality of this hope, full of adult vanity, right down to its mundane detail, he dismisses it: there will be no room in his life for such calamities.

Michael has forsaken the sloppy, comfortable style of his adolescence. He wears tight black clothes and has cropped his hair so short his skull is visible, strangely pale, delicate almost. His external self reflects the coldly strident person being formed inside. He sports an earring, listens now to the hard and driving music that once inspired in him a huge and visible indifference. He has acquired the callousness of uncaring youth. He goes to clubs, comes home smelling of alcohol, sits for hours before the television, languid, lazy. Then, as if snapping out of a trance, he goes to his room, where he works on his computer, the keyboard clicking urgently but precisely until late at night.

Lydia also sees him reading the Koran, and she stands in the darkened corridor listening as he reads aloud the sonorous verses of a mystical poet. When Michael is not home, she examines this book, feeling its gold-embossed cover, its rough-cut edges, as if searching for a clue to this new and mysterious person.

He was once my son, he was once Mikey, a much simpler boy!

Because he now occupies his father's old study downstairs, the noises he makes should be drowned out by the house's strange, inverted acoustics, yet they penetrate the shadowy silence, intruding upon the sleep of Silas and Lydia, until she resorts to earplugs and he simply increases the dosage of his sleeping draught.

Michael has a feverish energy that seems to consume his youthfulness. He is taller and leaner, he acquires a dark-clothed attractiveness that strikes at Silas's indifference (he stops asking Michael, 'How *are* you?' as if casually enquiring after the health of a stranger he has not seen for years) and corrodes Lydia's still tender membrane of guilty remembrance.

All this in one month. How rapidly the quicklime sets on pauperized emotions!

The TRC report is handed over to the President. Silas is seen on TV, grey-haired and distinguished – he seems to have greyed markedly in the few weeks while he was working 'behind the scenes' – hovering on the edges of the crowd, bemused and smug at the same time. His contradictions slowly become the point of interest in him. He is an 'intriguing' man, the shadow who slips in and out of public scrutiny, always whispering to his Minister.

Lydia informs Silas and Michael that she will be starting another job in the new year, part of a research team doing 'control tests' on HIV-positive mothers. Testing the effectiveness of a drug to stop the transmission of HIV from mothers to their unborn foetuses. She speaks a new language, slick and coded. She is also rapidly being transformed, terms and thought processes that astonish everyone; her family, her estranged husband, her alienated son, her mother and father, her sister Gracie, all look at her as if she is a strange insect emerging from a cocoon they had mistakenly assumed was her permanent, incarnate being. Wondrous, fearful of her own new wings, Lydia is hesitant at times, speaks as if seeking approval and permission.

'Where?'

'At the Chris Hani Hospital . . . yes, in Soweto.'

'How will you get there?'

'I am buying a car.'

Both Silas and Michael have forgotten that she can drive, that she was the family taxi for so many years, ferrying Mikey about, running errands, compensating for Silas's neglect of home and family because of the struggle, and later because of his job in government.

The conversation is quickly passed over. Neither Silas nor Michael asks where she will find the money to buy a car. They forget, too, that she has been working for eighteen years. Another passage in the invisible rites of their separate lives.

A few days later, she tells Silas that Rachel Moss, her boss-to-be, has invited them to dinner.

'Rachel Moss? Vusi Baloyi's wife?'

'Yes, the TRC advocate's wife,' she responds. 'She has a life of her own, you know.' Silas and Mikey are invited as well. Rachel has a thing about families. Will they accompany her, out of courtesy?

She is showing signs of the combative Lydia he knows and is more at ease with.

When the Friday night of the dinner comes, Silas is ready, Michael is not home. He has not bothered to call, they have not seen him since the night before. They fret, old habits of worry die hard, but they go to Rachel and Vusi's dinner. It turns out to be a large party. Guests gather in the garden talking, congregate around tables laden with food and drink spread out on a huge expanse of flat lawn, cultivated for entertaining.

'All the usual suspects,' Silas says in an undertone, as they move through the crowd of dignitaries. He too is showing something of his old, bristling self, but Lydia will not be drawn in. They run into several Cabinet Ministers, his own Minister mercifully not among them. Silas is acknowledged, smiled at, nodded to, as is the woman at his side. She earns renewed attention: she looks different from the wife they remember. They join a group of people at a table, stand in a pool of light that illuminates the sumptuous summer darkness. A journalist who knows Silas's 'fixer' role in the 'TRC process' tries to engage him in conversation. He is after a background story. Silas sips his wine, smiles, benign in his indifference.

Rachel Moss is a wiry, energetic woman, her once fussy Jewish-English nature has been totally Africanized. Even her thin, high-pitched laugh tries to boom louder than her lungs will allow. She comes dashing out of the house, shakes Silas's hand, hugs Lydia, and takes her around to meet her guests. She introduces Lydia as part of 'her team', a real 'find', a kind of prodigal daughter stepping out of the rather dubious shadow of her husband, Silas Ali.

Silas's dubiousness is not explored. Everyone now accepts that back-room, 'fix-it' men are necessary in South African politics, that the old days of public debate are gone. Being in government is different from fighting for freedom. Things have to be managed now! Some liberation movement activists remain sceptical: aren't these shadowy men merely angling for something, creating the right profile, ready for when the new President takes over?

Rachel returns Lydia to Silas's company. Partners belong together at parties. An understandable assumption. It belies Rachel's own dilemma: her husband is about to become unemployed, he has to resuscitate his practice as an advocate. The comfort zone of the TRC, its prominence and fame will be of no help. Vusi hovers around Rachel, competitive, jostling for the attention that his wife gets.

Silas and Lydia run into Kate, who is looking gaunt and tired. She greets them both with effusive hugs. Lydia shrugs her off and walks away, leaving her alone with Silas. He does not know how to deal with the awkwardness, with her wounded silence. Impulsively, he hugs her, as if asking her to forgive his wife's abruptness. 'She is not the same person,' he starts saying, then he has a sudden realization. 'Do you know, I turn fifty next month?'

They disengage, laugh.

'Well, we must have a party,' Kate says.

She is glad for a subject as mundane as a birthday party, age and ageing, the masochism of celebrating one's own mortality. The fact that Silas is turning fifty spreads to the people around them, a jollity builds, drinks are passed, a premature toast proposed, he is pressed to organize a party. He does not take much persuading, there is already a determined gleam in his eye.

When they go home, Silas is happy, the tension drained away. He toys with the notion of asking Lydia to sleep with him tonight, sex helps bring sleep along, they need to ease each other's loneliness. But his intention, having grown firmer as they drive, is quickly undone when they get home. They hear voices.

'Well, Michael is home,' he says, aware of how strange this name sounds.

Another voice, a young woman's. Music playing, there is laughter, they hear Michael say something, his voice is muffled, a silence ensues. What is he telling her? Lydia asks herself. That his parents are home, they are old-fashioned, he has never brought a woman, a girl home before? The light under his door goes out. Silas and Lydia exchange looks.

They stand in the shadows, uncertain of what to do or say.

'I'm going to have a party,' he says at last.

'A party?'

'It will be December soon . . .'

'My God, your birthday!'

'Fifty.'

They regard each other for a minute. November has slipped away, how the year has flown. Affection flickers once more, a brief, candlewick flame that hisses and goes out. They smile at each other. She'll help, she says, then they climb the stairs and go to their separate rooms.

Lydia is restless. It is the first time Mikey has ever done this, brought someone home to sleep with. Well, except for Kate, and that was an aberration. She turns to the bedside table, finds the sleeping tablets – non-addictive, the doctor said. She is glad she has decided to see a counsellor. She presses a tablet out of its foil package, pours water from a jug into a glass at her bedside. A habit picked up in hospital.

She listens to Silas in the bathroom, imagines him standing at the basin, preparing his sleeping draught. She counts at least twenty drops – that's far too much! Her concern momentarily eases the hard knot of alienation in her stomach, and she is tempted to get up and speak to him about this habit. But she realizes how hypocritical this is, and quietly wishes him a good night's sleep. All she has to offer him now is this distant tenderness. She swallows her tablet, waits for her own dark, drugged sleep to come.

She hopes that Mikey's visitor – and Mikey himself – will be gone when she goes down into that great whirlpool of sunlight and shadow that the house becomes in the morning. It is the one pleasure she takes from this otherwise forbidding house and she does not want it spoiled. With this thought, the immediacy of the new, dislocated world she finds herself in recedes.

Silas cannot sleep. He is torn between pride and pressing sexual desire. He has not had sex for months, long before he met Du Boise at the Mall and this whole chain of events started. In his room, his borrowed room, lying down like an unwelcome, usurping guest on his son's bed, he returns to his world of the past.

He was much younger than Michael, thirteen, fourteen, when he lay awake in the darkness of his mother's house, listening to the ragged sounds outside. The time of the great removals, when Africans were forcibly moved from Newclare, which had been declared a coloured area. The GGs came late at night to load people onto trucks, the remnants of families who had refused to move to Soweto, or who had simply not found the energy to gather their belongings and relocate into the unknown.

'Soweto is so far away,' said their neighbour, Mrs Rathlogo.

And her daughter Dikeledi, his companion since childhood, and even after they had become aware of their bodies, of the attraction created by different textures and shapes, and indeed colours, said, 'You will have to marry me, or my father will kill you. Do you know what a Mosotho girl means to her father, to her brothers?'

Laughter, gentle, ribald, explorations innocent because of their mutual ignorance, in that same back room where Lydia was to sleep with him, Lydia with the immeasurable experience of her imagination.

The night the grey-suited men arrived with a sudden fusillade of doors opening and closing, escorted by soldiers, their heavy boots marching across the pavements, Silas listened to the world he knew being dismembered. Through the thin walls of the old semi-detached cottage, he could hear everything that happened next door. The Rathlogo family, roused from their beds, were given half an hour to get ready. Dikeledi, her bother Pitso, her mother and father, whose names he could not now recall, human beings and belongings would be flung together on the back of an open truck.

Silas lay immersed in his darkness, aware for the first time of the power of shame. He heard Dikeledi's voice, that indignant, spirited tone that rose up in her whenever she felt confronted by an injustice – when he cheated during a game, or later, when he discovered the power of his male body and took his hasty pleasure, without considering her mood, her need. He heard her say: 'Have you no shame?'

She was probably addressing some cross-eyed official, angry at having to be out here 'in the dark' at this ungodly hour, simply because a bunch of 'kaffirs' had refused to comply with the law. But she could have been calling out to Silas, her lover, her companion, the boy in whom she had vested her youthful dreams, her young and eager sensuality. But he was unable to rise, to go outside and show his solidarity, at the very least. Not only because his mother had come into his room and sat down on his bed, saying with her tense face and tear-filled eyes, 'There is nothing you can do, this is not our fight,' but also because of some vast weight that pressed down on him, an inertia, an indifference even.

For years, this memory, this humiliating recollection of his own powerlessness, his inexplicable sense of detachment, would be his guard against complacency, the smugness of minor success, the vanity of petty fame. But the paradox was that it became a source of comfort, the very unease that it created in his mind seemed to still other, more immediate fears and concerns confronting him.

He closed his eyes, trying to help the flow of sleep that the remedy of natural herbs sought to induce (these homeopathic concoctions always demand your active collusion!), weaving Dikeledi's voice into the murmur of sounds that always seemed to rise from the streets of Berea at this hour.

Part Two

Confession

Since in order to speak, one must first listen,
Learn to speak by listening.

Mevlana Celaleddin-i Rumi, *Mesnevi*

17

DAYS AFTER MICHAEL has finished reading Lydia's diary, an image endures in his mind, a man standing in the doorway, a man 'looming', bringing darkness to a bright summer day. But he dismisses this image as too dramatic. From what he remembers, the man is not tall enough to fill the doorway, yet he is sinister and menacing. These words suggest even greater drama, but they ring true: he remembers the effect the man had on his grandmother Angel.

Michael called her 'Ouma Angel' because 'Angelina' was too forbidding a name for his child's mind. Perhaps she also looked like an angel to him: smooth, greying hair, a face that broke up into kindly wrinkles when she smiled. He would call out to her – 'Ouma Angel!' – a sensual, delicate sound that filled their gloomy township house with sudden light, and she would hold him to her chest, taking secret pleasure at being called 'Angel', even if only by a child. Why could her parents not have had this inspiration, or a young man, wilder than Ali Ali with his quiet, insidious passion? Life might have been different had she been 'Angel' to someone when she was young. Now she only allowed Michael the liberty, everyone else was sternly reminded that she had a 'proper' name.

The day the man came to the door and spoke to Ouma Angel in the language of authority, the same language as her own, but brusque and impatient, a shadow fell across her life. Michael felt her fear, the tightness in her chest that made her breathe heavily. He looked up into the man's face and saw a pair of white-flecked blue eyes, narrowed with distaste: before him was a white woman in a black man's hovel, the dark-skinned but fair-headed young boy evidence of the white woman's whorish nature (yes, white women who cohabited with black men were whores, how else could one explain their actions?).

Du Boise, that was Du Boise. Michael knows he has seen that face before, the rheumy blue eyes that Lydia describes in her diary.

Later that day, when Lydia and Silas came home from work, Michael heard the adults talking, heard Ouma Angel telling them about the man's visit, and although they fell silent after Silas had spoken (urging them not to be paranoid? Michael wonders now), he felt their apprehension, in the way Silas rested a hand on his shoulder, and in the way Lydia embraced him, whispering, 'My boy, my boy,' as if repeating an incantation against evil.

Ouma Angel faded from his life, becoming a quiet, distant presence who smiled furtively at him (on the rare occasions when they saw one another), as if they shared a secret, or had been through something together that others would find hard to believe. He remembers the last time he visited her, days before she died. Silas had had this uncanny presentiment: Ouma won't be with us for long. She had moved away from their home in Noordgesig, relocating from township to township, until she ended up in a place close to the city, where mostly whites lived, called Charlton Terrace. The name sounded foreign and intimidating to Michael. She had white neighbours who spoke a version of Afrikaans something like her own, but harsher, like that man in the doorway.

At Charlton Terrace, the weekend noises had a different texture from those in the townships. People were bitter, unsubtle in their attempts at restraint, constantly reminding each other to 'behave like white people'. But in the end, drunkenness triumphed, and the tumult was as raucous as on any Friday night in Noordgesig or Newclare.

Ouma Angel was shrinking; each time they saw her, she had grown smaller. Her gnarled hands clutching a simple wooden walking stick, she shuffled from room to room, as if trying to absorb the warmth of the wooden floor directly through the bare soles of her tiny, little girl's feet. She spoke to Silas in a whisper, not because she meant to be secretive, but simply because her breath was failing: 'There are certain things people never forget.' Michael remembers this among all the things she said ('She is starting to ramble, it won't be long now,' Silas told Lydia later on), because of her hoarseness, and because she seemed to be addressing him, rather than his father.

A week later, she was dead. Her heart simply stopped, the doctor said. This was a month before Nelson Mandela was released from prison, and it had been her life's ambition to see him 'in the flesh' (even though she only confessed this dream when it became known that he would soon be a free man). She couldn't hold on any longer, her sad countenance said.

'At least she won't have to see the blacks take over,' her neighbour told Silas, thinking that no one with a white mother could possibly support 'majority rule'.

Michael decides to retrace their township sojourns. It is an impulse, sentimental, bizarre. It is the kind of thing Silas would do, or Uncle Alec. Michael hates dwelling on the past, looking back is such a fruitless exercise, he says. It is one thing to study history, quite another to go and search for 'meaning' in the petty annals of dusty streets. Yet he feels it is something he must do, perhaps to get away from the claustrophobic fervour of the 'new South Africa'. The new South Africa. It is a phrase his father uses, and Kate, and Julian, and, of course, Vinu's parents. Politicians of all persuasions use it whenever they feel the need to sound idealistic, whether to celebrate or to lament the way the country has changed. Michael is always amazed by the sudden drama in their voices, the way even the dullest orator takes on the tone of an actor in one of those science-fiction films about distant galaxies, and exotic and hybrid beings. This new South Africa can be as strange as Ouma Angel's Charlton Terrace, just before she died.

For once, Michael does not plan; he simply takes a Kombi-taxi into the city centre, walks to the West Street taxi rank and searches for signs reading 'Noordgesig'. He sees people queuing, wearily patient, like experienced commuters anywhere in the world. But there are no timetables or maps, and to the uninformed traveller, the constant movement of people and vehicles seems chaotic. Michael is wary of asking for help: he has heard that anyone who betrays ignorance about the rituals of the Kombi-taxi is marked as a 'moegoe' and becomes ready prey for the thieves who frequent the taxi ranks. The image of sly vultures comes to mind, their smiles fixed and deceivingly benevolent. He pauses, amused by this grotesque conception of the dangers of township travel, mythologized at dinner parties by those who have moved out of the townships and now seek justification for their migration.

In the end, he asks for directions, and is told where to wait. Soon he is in a Kombi, sitting quietly as the driver waits for the seats to fill up. The journey itself is unremarkable, frantic bursts of speed, sudden stops, people getting off and on with remarkable rapidity, destinations confirmed and fares exchanged with quiet efficiency. It is as if unseen hands direct everything, some intelligence out there, controlling this world without fuss or fanfare. Later, he will admit that this is a romantic view of the struggles these commuters face every day, that their lives are in constant danger, that there is nothing wonderful about being crammed together, breathing in each other's nervous sweat. For now, he is transported into a forgotten world, one that he suspects Silas rarely sees these days.

They leave the city, turn off towards Soweto. Michael peers ahead, looking for landmarks. He vaguely remembers New Canada station, and, when he sees the community clinic, much smaller than he remembered (and derelict, as he will discover when he gets off), he signals to the driver, who does not seem to acknowledge his request. Michael is afraid that the driver will ignore him, that he will be taken into 'deep Soweto'. He is angry with himself for this instinctive sense of dread, the continuing, stereotypical quality of danger inherent in the term 'deep Soweto', but is relieved when the driver pulls up two blocks further, at a designated taxi stop.

'This is not a stop-anywhere taxi, sonny,' the driver says, as Michael gets out. The other passengers laugh good-humouredly. Michael feels foolish, he knows that all he had to do was speak in a firm voice: 'Driver, stop, I want to get off,' and the taxi would have slewed to the side of the road. An empty space is always welcome, it makes room for another fare.

He walks back to the clinic, stops before the derelict structure. Ouma Angel used to bring him here for check-ups. It was an opportunity for her to meet other people, to talk about things, rising prices, the erratic bus service (who says the taxis have brought no benefit to ordinary people?), how the consumer boycott was making life difficult, how neither the government nor the young activists cared about the struggles of older people.

'Ja-nee, it's because they want victory or death,' Michael says out loud, trying to capture Ouma Angel's weary last word on the subject. He remembers how her friends used to caution her about mocking 'The Youth' and their slogan, it could bring reprisals. He smiles at a passer-by, who stares curiously at this young man talking to himself.

Michael turns into Smith Street, which runs parallel to Main and ends in a cul-de-sac at the edge of the Soweto Highway. Number 14 is the third house in the circle at the end of the street. He remembers the number because he wrote it endlessly on the inside cover of his exercise books at junior school (you got caned if you wrote in the

183

textbooks, because they were government property). The pride we take in our littlest universe.

Michael Ali, 14 Smith Street, Noordgesig, Soweto, Johannesburg, South Africa, The World.

That schoolteacher with the tinted specs, what was her name? – anonymous horror – told him: 'You must stop putting "Soweto" on your books! This is a coloured school and Noordgesig is a coloured township!'

At night, the headlights of cars turning in the circular dead-end shone on his window, bright but gentle kaleidoscopes that lulled him to sleep. Except for the brutal sound of Johnny Smith, their neighbour's son (thin and sharp-eyed, he immediately came to mind when Michael first read Shakespeare and encountered Cassius with his 'lean and hungry look'), coming home late at night: tyres crunching and doors slamming, making enough noise to achieve the rather unnerving miracle of 'raising the dead' (Ouma Angel's words).

Over breakfast, Lydia complained about Johnny's late-night comings and goings, saying that he was no example to young kids, especially those of an impressionable age like Mikey. Yes, he'll come to a bad end, Silas said in agreement, only to have her turn on him. 'You should never wish bad endings on people!' Somewhere inside her, a Catholic dread of what happens to people who die unsavoury deaths.

'Does the street belong to Johnny Smith?' Michael asked, when he was old enough to wonder what it was like to live in a street that bore your own name. Silas snorted, Lydia gave him an indulgent look, and Ouma Angel said it must be terrible to be named after a street.

Michael often wondered what kind of end Johnny Smith had come to. Years later, he heard Silas telling Lydia that Johnny was dead. 'Ag, shame,' she had answered, offhandedly. Michael was sure that Johnny must have gone to hell.

The house has a high, diamond-mesh fence around it. A car

parked under a do-it-yourself carport (the uprights not completely upright), a small, well-kept garden, the grass cut as closely as the uneven earth will allow. There is something jarringly new: a 'water feature' has been built on the old asphalt pathway. Water spouts from the mouth of a lion, just like at Uncle Alec's. It dominates the entrance. The door that once opened directly into the face of the morning sun is now partially obscured from the street. What a grandiose search for privacy!

A dog raises its head lazily, decides that Michael does not pose a threat, goes back to sleep. A curtain parts and someone peers at him through a window. Then the door opens, and a man comes ambling up the path. A pre-emptive form of self-defence, Michael thinks. Show no fear, and maybe the potential intruder will go away.

'Can I help?' the man asks.

'No, no, just passing,' Michael answers. 'Admiring the fountain.'

The man looks back at the fountain, admires what he imagines Michael finds admirable, his suspicion gone, his posture relaxed.

'I found it here when I bought the place. Some crazy old bastard believed it would keep the tsotsis out.' The man's laughter echoes in the growing dusk.

'Well, goodnight,' Michael says with a smile, and hurries off. He feels the man's eyes on him, as he passes through the smog-filled twilight. He inhales the smell of smoke as if testing the quality of the air. In households everywhere, fires are starting up. People still use coal stoves?

What am I doing here? Michael asks himself. Looking for Du Boise, for the ghost of Du Boise?

He walks back to the main road, waits for a taxi. It is already crowded when it arrives, and he has to perch on the edge of his seat, beside a woman who clutches her bag, more to give him room than out of fear that it will be stolen. He breathes in her familiar, intimate smell, closes his eyes and tries not to identify it. Sweat, deodorant, the kind used by thousands, millions of women, the kind his mother uses. Why does Kate smell different? Christ, is there such a thing as a black woman's smell and a white woman's smell? No, he thinks, it is not the smell of the skin or its colour, it is the odour of an occupation. He peers at the woman next to him through half-closed eyes and sees the nurse's white uniform underneath her sweater. He moves away from her, and she shifts away from him too, offended. They sit in their awkward, alienated postures until the taxi reaches West Street. He climbs out and hurries off into the ghostly darkness.

At home, he contemplates the purpose of this quest. He is like a tourist doing the apartheid heritage route. What is the point of going from one ramshackle point of reference to the next? Perhaps it is true: our memories are chained to poverty, we cannot live without our apartheid roots. What is he really looking for? For evidence that he is indeed Silas's son, that Lydia is wrong, that her usually infallible maternal instincts had been undermined by bitterness, by her fear of the worst, when she proclaimed him to be Du Boise's bastard son? What will that evidence be? Physical resemblance, the unmistakable lineage to be found in the shape of a nose, the contour of a cheek, or, even more telling, the depth of an eye, the familiarity of a glance?

He dismisses this thought. Must every pursuit have a utilitarian purpose? Is it not enough to want to discover your roots simply for the sake of it? Yes, he can write his history and the history of a whole country, simply by tracing his family's nomadic movements from one ruined neighbourhood to the next, searching through photographs, deeds of sale, engineering reports (this area is predominantly Indian or coloured or African, it is filled with noise, loud music, people congregate in the street, it is squalid, it is a slum and therefore qualifies for clearance under the Slums Clearance Act), social workers' assessments (the children beam at you with dirty faces, unaware of their suffering).

186

Ouma Angel's house in Charlton Terrace was demolished a long time ago. It is now a parking lot for the Johannesburg Athletics Stadium. There is talk of an Olympic bid. Athletes pounding over the grave of Ouma Angel's last refuge. The house in Newclare was broken down to make way for 'mass housing' flats. How easily these meaningless terms come to us, how it deadens our understanding of things; still, what was once a beautiful valley is now a squalid slum, the grass squatted on by faceless concrete tenements.

No, Michael thinks, he needs more purpose. He plans: first, find his Uncle Amin, Silas's half-brother. Learn what can be learned from a potentially hostile relative. Uncle Amin will be the true Muslim, scornful of his bastard kin – why remind yourself that your father had a 'nasara' wife, that he, the Imam, did not have the courage of his convictions and insist that she become a Muslim, take on a Muslim name, that her child – thank God there was only one – be brought up Muslim?

Imagine having to call a brother 'Silas', a nephew 'Michael', how awkward on the tongue, how jarring to the mind. But Oupapa Ali had married Angelina Pelgron, and was that not a beautiful name? She was his third wife, and he accorded her the respect this demanded. He knew the dictates of his religion, Imam Ali. He even contributed materially to the child's upbringing, given the constraints of his own poverty.

Michael considers the different scenarios: open hostility; a guarded response initially; and, the least likely of all, a warm, spontaneous welcome. He thinks about the issues they will have to confront, tries to place himself in Uncle Amin's position. He overcomes his last-minute doubts, alights from the taxi (the route more carefully researched, the time of the last taxi back to the city firmly established by sweet-talking a morose taxi driver) and resolutely follows the directions he was given over the phone.

He has an address, he has an excuse: I want to find out more about my beginnings.

187

He finds 27 Griffith Street, a large house for this area, with the appropriate high wall and locked gate. He notes that the mosque is not far away. He rings the bell, brimming with his usual brash confidence.

Uncle Amin, shorter and stockier than Silas, and darker too, sits in an old armchair. Hashim, the eldest son, sits next to him on a straight-backed chair, while Haroon, the younger one, leans up against the mantelpiece of an ornate fireplace. Purely for show, Michael thinks. Not the kind of home where a cosy fire burns on cold winter nights. Electric heaters in separate, private spaces. Silas's family all right!

A young girl comes in with a tray, smiles shyly as if she is expected to do so, but does not flee the room in the sort of clichéd, theatrical way Michael anticipates. She is introduced as Safiya. She is wearing jeans, and has her hair pinned back, giving her a high-cheeked beauty that marriage and childbearing will find it difficult to wear away. She exits haughtily, her disdain and bemusement at Michael's startled expression are obvious. They drink tea, talk politely.

'How is your father?'

'He is well, very busy, though.'

'Yes, we see him on TV all the time!'

A silence descends. They shift about like actors who have lost their cues. Finally, Michael speaks. 'I am not sure how to address you. So, should I call you "Mr Ali", or "Uncle Amin", or . . .?'

They are saved from the awkwardness of this rather hasty attempt to break the ice, by a commotion in the adjoining kitchen. A young man wearing a traditional kurta and keffiyeh bursts in through the door, followed by an older woman, chastizing him: 'Sadrodien, *you dare embarrass us!*'

Amin introduces the older woman as 'Auntie Hanifa, my wife, and their mother'. He turns to the young man. 'This is Sadrodien, my youngest.'

'Papa, look at her . . .' Sadrodien says.

'Later!' Amin says sternly.

Safiya stands in the doorway, glares at Sadrodien, then turns on her heel and walks away. They drink their tea, joined now by Aunt Hanifa and the silent Sadrodien, his face a mask of contained outrage. Michael guesses that he is about twenty-three or twenty-four. His beard is too fierce to be any younger. Aunt Hanifa creates an amiable, talkative atmosphere, histories are gently explored, the whereabouts, pursuits, well-being and occupations of various relatives and acquaintances are established. Michael has to confess his ignorance of half the people she asks about. She smiles and says, 'All that will come with time.' She senses that he is on some holy quest.

Soon two sets of wives and children join them (Sadrodien is unmarried – 'I have no time for such weakness,' he will tell Michael later), a quick succession of greetings, hugs, kisses. Michael is introduced, his presence is acknowledged, he is peeked at curiously, but the discussion is overtaken by mundane talk about the state of cars, minor illnesses suffered, plans for the evening, the routine trials of lives lived as well as possible, all in a glorious babble of musical accents that lends the gathering a beguiling warmth. The purpose of his visit, his 'search for his roots', seems pretentious to Michael now. He feels immersed in his family, these are his people, these dark-faced, hook-nosed hybrids; he longs to go and look in a mirror, seek confirmation of his desire to belong. Lydia must be wrong! How can Du Boise be his biological father?

Michael announces that he has to go, he must catch the last taxi to town. No, no, Uncle Amin says, someone will drive him home. Haroon offers, Sadrodien insists on going along. Haroon drives, quietly intent on following Michael's directions. But Michael senses that this is in deference to Sadrodien, who sits at the back, a brooding, hawklike presence.

When they approach Berea, Sadrodien leans forward. 'Brother, come and join us at the mosque on Wednesday night. You will meet some interesting people. It is the Griffith Street mosque, where our grandfather was Imam.'

Michael realizes that Griffith Street is to Sadrodien not only an address, but a holy appellation. He accepts the invitation (curious, intrigued, why the pointed reference to *our grandfather*?), confirms the time, where to meet, what to wear. He turns to give Haroon directions, sees the somewhat grim, disapproving look on his face. Nothing is what it seems to be, with this long-lost family, Michael thinks.

The meeting at the mosque is not what Michael expects. There are no formal prayers, there are no rows of worshippers sinking to their knees in ritual supplication, repeatedly touching their heads to the ground in obeisance to God, all the while emitting huge sighs, in unison with each other and in rhythm with the Imam's prayers, until there is only one great expulsion of breath, and in its aftermath, a great hush. There, in that moment of peace, you can find God.

For many years, Michael has held in his mind this image of Muslims paying homage to God, praising His infinite wisdom, the supremacy of His judgement, the glory of His Prophet Mohamed, peace be unto him. During the 1994 election campaign, a liberation movement sympathizer had invited Silas to Friday prayers at a mosque in the city. Afterwards, he would address the congregation. Why was Silas invited? Was it because of his Muslim surname or because he was the son of the renowned Ali Ali, late Imam of the Griffith Street mosque, erudite speaker, champion of the Islamic cause, fearless critic of both the apartheid regime and its 'heathen Communist opposition'? And why did Silas accept the invitation? Michael does not remember his justification (delivered to his captive son en route to the mosque), nor what he actually said in his speech, only that the atmosphere imposed a silence on both of them; here nothing extraneous or frivolous is said, here even one's thoughts are no longer private, they seem to flow into a maelstrom of unwitting confessions, guilt muttered under one's breath, carried by some gust of wind throughout the mosque.

Now, as Michael completes the ceremonious cleansing of his body, seated alongside Sadrodien, emulating his actions in exact detail, the sound of running water, the murmuring of others around him create an expectation of a hallowed experience similar to what he felt four years ago.

So he is somewhat disappointed when he is ushered into a small room, an ordinary classroom, where the desks have been moved aside and carpets laid out in the centre. The day's Arabic lesson is still visible on the blackboard. He has seen Arabic script before, right-to-left, holding the promise of guttural music. Sadrodien plays the role of formal host, takes Michael around and introduces him ('This is our brother, he is also an Ali,' carefully avoiding, it seems, the mention of Michael's name) to a small group of men, who resemble each other in their dress, their manner, their deep-set eyes, the severity of their bearded faces. They remove their shoes and seat themselves on the carpet. When the Imam enters, they rise, making way for him to walk over to Michael and greet him.

Imam Ismail Behardien has perfect teeth, his beard is trimmed, he wears a soft white keffiyeh that completes his distinguished appearance. Michael sits down, grateful for the wall against which he can rest his back. He thinks: I, too, have been conditioned. Why did I expect an Imam to have discoloured teeth, why do I associate piety with physical decay?

Imam Ismail speaks in Arabic, introductory remarks, Michael guesses, then switches to English. He welcomes their guest tonight, grandson of one of the great brothers of the tariqah, the late Imam Ali. There is a murmur of assent, welcome. Then the lights are lowered (a dimmer switch, Michael notes – where is the ancient, primitive simplicity he has come here for?). A blue glow fills the room, and he sees a stone nestling on a pillow in front of Imam Ismail. The twin of Ali Ali's stone, chipped off from the same stolen fragment?

For an hour, Michael listens to prayers being said, harmoniously guided by the Imam, who raises or lowers his voice to modulate his congregation's chanting. Like a participatory choirmaster, he sets the tone and pitch with his own singing. It is all in Arabic and completely incomprehensible to the visitor.

At the end, the participants lean back, sated, as if they have just consumed an exotic dinner. They are at peace, their faces empty, their minds still resonating with the sound of God, 'ya Allah', which they have chanted repeatedly.

A young man, the Muslim equivalent of a novice, comes in bearing a tray of hot, sweet milk and coconut biscuits. As they sip the liquid and bite into the biscuits with almost womanly delicacy, the congregants slowly resume their earthly postures, becoming heavy and awkward, and have to resort to propping themselves up on their arms.

They file out, greeting each other and the Imam with effusive hugs and warm handshakes. Sadrodien signals to Michael, who follows him out into the cool inner court of the mosque. They join the Imam, who is seated at one of the fountains. A smile, a flash of faultlessly aligned teeth.

'So, brother, what do you think of us?' Imam Ismail asks.

Michael is taken aback by the question, and by its directness.

The Imam rescues him with a wave of his hand. 'You don't have to answer. But I am always curious to know what people think of us, especially those who come from us, but who are no longer . . . well, you understand.'

Michael sips the tea that Imam Ismail has offered. They sit in silence for a while, then the Imam rises.

'Sadrodien is one of our youngest adherents, but most astute. He is an excellent judge of character. Perhaps he can explain to you what our jamaa stands for.' He greets Michael with a handshake, kisses Sadrodien on each cheek, and leaves.

Sitting at the edge of the fountain, Sadrodien and Michael talk. Mostly about the tariqah that Ali Ali founded, here at the Griffith Street mosque.

'The term "tariqah" describes the structure of a Sufi organization,' Sadrodien says, his face illuminated by a piece of received wisdom, vividly recollected.

'Is it some kind of secret society?' Michael asks.

'Well, it is an elite group, open only to the most pious; accepting the word of Allah and the authority of his Prophet Mohamed is fundamental. You must accept it absolutely. Not many qualify to join, you see.'

Sadrodien's aged air of profound knowledge, his habit of speaking in biblical voices, are wearying, but Michael remains patient. Sadrodien continues: this particular order is based on the principles of Mevlana Celaleddin-i Rumi, a thirteenth-century mystic and poet. He lived in Turkey, but was born in Afghanistan. He became the inspiration behind the resistance to Atatürk's secularization of Turkey.

'Really? But Atatürk only arrived five hundred, six hundred years later than the time you describe.'

Sadrodien's soft, prayerful voice becomes hard, acquires an ideologue's edge. 'The concept and the practice of absolute allegiance to the will of Allah, according to the teaching of Prophet Mohamed, peace be unto him, are timeless, they endure for ever.'

Michael is finally overcome with weariness, and tells Sadrodien it is time for him to make his way home.

'Yes, but you can't go home using these township taxis. I don't want the blood of such an intelligent brother on my hands.'

Michael is surprised by the range of personas that Sadrodien's voice gives him. Now he is the street-smart township clever, he knows his way about, won't let this suburbanite get hurt here. From the folds of his kurta, he produces a cellphone and summons a radio taxi.

Safely ensconced in a sedan, equipped with a fare-meter and crackling two-way radio, Michael returns to Berea. The prospect of the cold and silent house seems depressing. Lydia and Silas will be in their respective rooms by now, their faces scrubbed, sedatives ready at their bedsides. Does either of them know what it is like to kiss an unwashed mouth?

Michael realizes, quite startled, that he has not thought about Lydia and Silas for some time now, that Lydia's diary and the image of Du Boise that permeates it, seem so distant, a piece of fiction, far too melodramatic to be believable.

Michael debates endlessly with Moulana Ismail ('Imam is too ostentatious a term, just call me Moulana'). It begins with a discussion on the nature of faith.

'One either believes or one does not,' Sadrodien says, at their second meeting.

'True faith lies in its ambiguity,' Michael says, bored with his cousin's pedantry.

'How do you find faith in ambiguity?' Moulana Ismail asks.

'You are marked not by what you believe, but by what you do not,' Michael answers.

Sadrodien's strident protest is silenced, and Michael is asked to expand. 'I'm having fun, playing an intellectual game,' he confesses. Still, he has created a riddle in his own mind, one that he will need to resolve by himself. Ismail smiles, and invites Michael to come back, on his own. Sadrodien is dismissed as the intermediary. Here is an intelligence, raw, unformed, but instinctive. Michael has no entrenched beliefs, and seems devoid of the prejudices of mind and spirit that inhibit true discourse.

'He is like a desert, pure and barren, waiting for a wind to shape it,' Moulana Ismail explains to a somewhat disgruntled Sadrodien.

Michael visits Ismail, once a week, then every second day. He misses varsity, and sits with the Imam at a table, close to the fountain. They talk until Ismail has to go and say prayers or until it is time for Michael to leave. He no longer has the benefit of Sadrodien's ability to conjure up taxis, lifts with friends or family. He travels at night, on gloomy, badly lit trains, on Kombi-taxis that only go as far as the city outskirts. He walks through the deserted streets, seemingly unafraid of their dangers, or he is oblivious to them. He has that uncaring, solitary look that deters would-be robbers. In this city, it would be said that he is living on borrowed time.

Someone tells the Imam that Michael has a unique insight into the politics of the new government. Michael does not disappoint Ismail. His observations are sharpened by his knowledge of his father's work, by years of exposure to the functioning of the liberation movement and its effects on the lives of its soldiers and their families. The 'movement' is an organism rather than an organization, it has no central mechanism, but relies on a series of interlinked structures, very much like gears, to make it work. Its decision-making is slow and requires continuous refinement (at the last moment, Michael avoids making an analogy with the wheels of God, fearing that Ismail will be offended).

'What is its weakness?' Moulana Ismail asks.

'One day, someone will try to replace that elaborate wheel with a human, put a manager in its place, introduce the fallibility of the single mind.'

'You are truly your grandfather's seed, such a subtle mind. But explain to a simple priest like me. What will actually happen when they do that?'

'Decisions will no longer come from many minds, nor will they embrace the many different beliefs within the movement, it will be one person's decision, difficult to enforce, and even when it is enforced, grudgingly implemented. There is nothing more obstructive than half-believing followers. Imagine a prophet being served by sceptical disciples?'

Moulana Ismail laughs. 'That has been known to happen. But we all need good managers, whether to run a country or a religious organization, no?'

'Managers run bakeries. And all they can do is bake as much bread as possible and hope that people will buy it. Managers dull the process. They cannot make miracles, because they refuse to believe in them.'

Moulana Ismail laughs uproariously. 'Ali Ali's grandson!'

'I have a question, Brother Ismail.'

'Yes, this is trade, value for value.'

'Hypothetically speaking. If someone without the means, without the power, but with a just cause, comes to you for help, will you give it?'

'In search of vengeance?'

'Justice.'

'Personal justice?'

'Against one person, yes. But he and his actions represent an entire system of injustice.'

Ismail goes quiet. Then he says:

'What do you know about your grandfather's history?'

'Very little.'

'Well, let me tell you a story, a fable of sorts.'

They settle back, fresh tea is brought, Moulana Ismail nibbles on a date – 'The food of good men. Did you know that, above all, our Prophet was a good man?'

Michael notes that the Imam did not add the requisite 'peace be unto him', waits for the story of his grandfather, Ali Ali, to be told.

18

The promise of a fable lowers Michael's expectations. Already the truth about who he is and where he comes from seems increasingly elusive. He does not need the added confusion of boastful anecdotes, minor incidents transformed by the art of their telling into historic episodes. But Moulana Ismail Behardien proves to be a true storyteller, not just a raconteur seeking the petty adulation of a captive listener. He relates the story of Ali Ali logically, and in a largely linear fashion. Of course, there are digressions, mostly to philosophize, to sketch in 'essential background', to set markers of time and event. But the narrative marches from milestone to milestone, taking welcome rests along the way, and rarely speculates, even when confronted by the absence of certain knowledge.

Moulana Ismail sits back, speaks in an unhurried voice, beginning with the facts.

In India, in what is today the province of Gujarat, there is a small village called Kacholie. It lies north of Bombay – well, Mumbai now – and south of Ahmadabad and Surat. It is close to the great railway line that runs from Bharuch, perhaps even further, Bhilwara or Ratlam for that matter, down through Navsari, all along the coast to Bangalore.

You know, when the Hindu fundamentalists renamed Bombay as Mumbai, I was one of those who said, 'Typical, fundamentalists wanting to turn back the clock.' But think about it: what a strange word, 'fundamentalist'. Am I considered a fundamentalist simply because I am a Muslim Imam, and, as you know, Islam is a fundamental religion? I have never seen Bombay – Mumbai, whatever – why should I object to its name being changed?

Anyway, Kacholie is a small village, the home of merchants

plying all kinds of trade, up and down the railway line. That is your grandfather's birthplace, the world he was born into.

One more thing you should know, his real name is Hamed Chothia, a rather simple name, fundamental you might say. 'Ali Ali' is the kind of name only a fugitive would give himself. So fanciful, so obviously an alias, that no one whom the fugitive encounters would bother to explore its origins. But, we will continue to refer to him as 'Ali Ali', for the sake of clarity. Nothing confuses a story as much as characters with shifting identities.

Let us also understand the times in which Ali Ali lived as a young man. He must have been born in the early 1890s, and therefore grew up in a world ruled by Britain, in the British Empire. Let's be more precise: the *English* Empire, the Irish and the Scots were tools, employees, paid help. The real masters were the Victorian English. We cannot even imagine the narrowness of belief, of political, religious and racial dogma, spawned in the name of that dull Queen! And we, her Asian and African subjects, were special targets for her murderous brand of civilization.

The Queen's imperial servants brought with them a peculiar, English sense of ownership. Now, that is a vital point, one you need to keep in mind all the time. It shaped British history, their desire not just to conquer the world, but to remake it in their image. In 1914, Britain led the world into war, forget the rhetoric about German aggression – they were always aggressive, weren't they? Here was an opportunity to consolidate the Empire. The British would entice their European competitors – we did not count, we were brown and black and backward – into the mud-fields of Europe, keep them there for as long as possible, in a state of distraction, spending huge amounts of money, sacrificing a whole generation of young men. She succeeded, wily Britain,

fought the Germans on French soil, the Turks in Arabia. You never
see the English fighting wars in England, do you?

What did all of this mean for India? A stronger Britain, more
capable of ruling its dominions, of imposing unwanted institu-
tions, foreign beliefs, strange games, stranger habits. After the
cricket – and the brain-paralysing gin and tonic – came the par-
liaments, where grown men spent their time shouting at each
other in archaic, meaningless language. Drunken piety, false,
back-stabbing gallantry. But above all, it provided Britain with
an excuse to keep soldiers in our conquered countries. An army
of occupation, paid for by the occupied. It also kept unemploy-
ment to a minimum in Britain.

And that is where Ali Ali's history begins, with soldiers in his
backyard. There were British military encampments all along that
coastal spine, from Bharuch to Bombay. Now, Kacholie is close to
the Bay of Cambay, the Arabian Sea, and, as the crow flies, the
Yemen, and what is now Saudi Arabia. You could smell the desert
winds, legend says, dry air, fragrant, still resistant to the polluted
ideas that Britain had brought to the world. And, some say, you
could already hear, even then, the muttered prayers of other
oppressed people, in Egypt, Libya, Iraq, Iran.

Near Kacholie is a major British military camp, houses one of
those mounted regiments, the Royal Lancers, something obscure
like that. They are bored. The war is far away, the Turks are being
beaten – and not by the British, incidentally, but by a motley army
of Arabs: united for one brief moment in their fractious and
divided history, they defeat an ancient conqueror.

The Turks are Muslim, but back then they were Imperialists
first, and Europeans on top of it. I suspect sometimes that they
have not changed at all, they are still suffering a huge identity
crisis. Europeans with Arab noses.

In the middle of all this historical ennui – how else can I describe it? – a British officer, a lieutenant, rapes Ali Ali's sister. She is sixteen years old, one year younger than Ali Ali. Her name is Hajera, named after the Prophet's first pilgrimage. Of course, no action is taken against the soldier! He is English, white, and a commissioned officer! Untouchable! No one believes Hajera. She is known to go wandering about by herself, loves music, singing aloud, is provocative even in the way she allows her body to respond to the rhythms that inhabit her.

Now, as an Imam, I would never condone promiscuity of any sort. But does Hajera's love for music, for walking in the shade of quiet mango groves, staring at the river, does this make her anything but a little strange? I think not. The soldier denies even touching her, saying that he came across her on the banks of a river one day, where he watered his horse after a long ride, but paid no attention, did not offer her so much as a smile.

When Hajera is found to be pregnant, he accuses her and her family of trying to disgrace him, says she is a whore who gives herself to untouchables and passing beggars. Whereas he is betrothed to a young Englishwoman, they are to marry as soon as the war is over. Why would he need to rape an Indian girl, the daughter of a lowly merchant, a dry-goods wallah? You see, he knows all the defences, all the believable things to say. Why would a white officer, engaged to an Englishwoman, soil himself with the body of a 'coolie' girl?

Her family is angry with her for having disgraced them. She should have kept quiet, they would have found a nice young Muslim boy to marry her. Now they do not want to draw attention to their fallen relative. Allowing her to give birth at home, in their village, would attract all kinds of curiosity. A soldier's whore. Does the infant have tell-tale blond hair and blue eyes? Hajera is sent away, to another small village near Kholvad, her mother's brother's home. There she gives birth in a state hospital. Yes sir, the British have brought civilization to India.

Then the real tragedy. The baby dies while Hajera is feeding her. 'She choked the child,' the nurses allege. She is charged with murder, imprisoned, and interrogated, but is eventually declared insane. Perhaps she is mad, perhaps not. But there is a view that the authorities do not want her to appear in court. All the old allegations would surface again. So she is condemned to spending the rest of her life in a madhouse.

In India, in those days, there are no asylums for Indians, only madhouses.

Meanwhile, in Kacholie, the family suffers its shame, its sorrow, in silence, trying to forget Hajera, to pretend she never existed. Only Ali Ali seems to remember her, perhaps because they were close to each other in age and temperament, even if they were opposites in their habits. He recalls the predictions of a Sufi mystic: one day, evil incarnate will come in the guise of saviours, they will replace the science of the soul with the alchemy of the mind. These unbelievers will rule the world for a long time, and not only will they inflict mental and physical pain on true believers, and make them fight among themselves, but they will cause them to forsake their own children.

Now, Ali Ali is a pious young man, drawn to the growing Sufi movement, tariqahs of the faithful are springing up all over the Muslim world. He hears of Muslim fighting Muslim, right there in the Muslim Holy Land, he sees these strutting soldiers and their strident political masters trying to destroy Indians, whether Muslim, Hindu or Buddhist, all in the cause of civilization, in the name of a 'gentle and forgiving God'. What has happened to his own sister confirms his fears. She has been buried alive, as it were, while her defiler walks about free, and her parents try to eradicate her from their memories. Ali Ali decides to act.

He manages to get a message to the officer, through one of the Indian workers – a cook, a cleaner, a livery boy, a groom, a toilet cleaner – Indians are everywhere. The message hints that some forbidden knowledge has fallen into Ali Ali's hands, some memento, a cheap trinket with which the soldier tried to buy Hajera's silence, something that links the two of them. Something clutched in pain, or accepted in love, it no longer matters. The soldier has denied speaking to Hajera, or even smiling at her. How then did she come to possess the ornament? His lies will be exposed. Ali Ali proposes that the English officer meet him to discuss the matter.

The officer goes, hoping to pay another bribe. Or is it arrogance? What could the son of a merchant do to a well-trained – and armed – British soldier? Anyway, they meet in the same mango grove where Hajera used to walk, on the banks of the river where she sat dreaming of another world.

They find the officer, days after he has been reported missing, hanging from a tree, his hands bound behind his back. He has been executed. Ali Ali flees, away from Bombay, in the opposite direction to the one the British think he will take. Bombay is teeming, the natural place for thieves and murderers to seek refuge. There he would be just another Indian in a city of countless Indians. But Ali Ali goes north instead of south. On foot or by train to Navsari, by truck to Dahej? Who knows?

What follows must be guesswork, educated calculations based on where Ali Ali ended up. Because he never spoke about the route he took, the people he encountered. There is a diary somewhere that would reveal a great deal.

We do know that he was in Riyadh, in Mecca. Perhaps he takes a boat from Dahej to Jafrabad in the Kathiawar Peninsula? But this is still India, he is not safe, the British are looking for him everywhere. From there, he probably makes his way to Kodinar, up to Porbandar, then across the Arabian Sea, lands in Al-Ashkarah, in what is now Oman. By caravan into Saudi Arabia, by truck across the desert on roads that the British built for their troop convoys. Perhaps the Turks help him, perhaps the details of British forces in India buy him safe passage, perhaps, perhaps?

I think he goes to the Sudan, and then to Ethiopia, before going south to Mozambique. We know for certain that he lives for a while in a place called Amsterdam, in the Union of South Africa, on the Swaziland border. And we know that he helps to set up a mosque and establish a madressa there. Look at a map, and you see a remarkable journey, a veritable hajerah. There he should have rested. But then he does the unexpected again, veers off to Cape Town, where he marries, has children, establishes an identity. Ali Ali, student of Islam, mystic, given to spending whole days fasting and praying at the various Muslim kramats around Cape Town. Finally, he settles down in Johannesburg, a learned Imam, here in this mosque, my ustad, and the founder of a Rumi tariqah.

Rumi? Sadrodien explained all of that to you, no?

Well, yes, eventually the British must have given up looking for him. History overtook them. The Wall Street crash, another war, Lenin, Gandhi, Nehru, Jinnah, Nkrumah, Hitler, Saddam Hussein, Imam Khomeini – the British are always being overtaken by history. Have you considered why the Prophet Christ was not born an Englishman? It would have been an indifferent religion indeed.

The point of all this?

You asked me a question. Would I help a helpless man in

his quest for justice, or is it vengeance? Yes, there is a point to be made.

There are certain things people do not forget, or forgive. Rape is one of them. In ancient times, conquerors destroyed the will of those whom they conquered by impregnating the women. It is an ancient form of genocide. It does not require a Sufi prophecy to see the design in that. The Romans and the Sabine women, the Nazis and Jewish women in the concentration camps, the Soviets in Poland, Israeli soldiers and Palestinian refugees, white South African policemen and black women.

You conquer a nation by bastardizing its children.

Michael declines the invitation to stay over, to sleep within the peaceful walls of the mosque precinct. Adjacent to the school – a *madressa*, he is reminded – there is a room that Moulana Ismail sometimes uses. Clean linen is available. The water flows calmly from the fountain to the ablution blocks, where worshippers will begin to gather before dawn.

'No,' Michael says quietly, 'it is time I went home.'

He takes the last train to Johannesburg Station, wanders along deserted streets, his uncaring, reckless manner earning him fearful, sidelong glances. It is Friday night and everything is silent, somehow desolate. He heads for the noise and bustle of Hillbrow, remembers for a moment that it is by reputation the most dangerous place in the country. 'It was a wonderful place once, just after Mandela was released, mixed of race and free in spirit.' He recalls how people romanticize its past at dinner tables, an opportunity lost. Now it is full of drug dealers and illegal immigrants. That is what Ali Ali was once, an illegal immigrant. If you believe Moulana Ismail's tale.

Michael finally tires of wandering about aimlessly, courting that mythical, nameless dread of the new South Africa, and takes a taxi from outside a rowdy hotel. The driver is wary, until Michael shows him the money. Then they go unerringly to the address that Michael mumbles.

He knows that Silas and Lydia have gone out, some or other party his mother wanted him to go along to. Very busy reinventing herself. He imagines them gliding about in some vast old house, exchanging brittle smiles, far too enthusiastic in the way they greet strangers.

He sees Vinu sitting on the veranda, her legs dangling over the wall, and is tempted to tell the taxi driver to carry on. But her posture is both forlorn and full of bravado, she has a pleading look, he thinks. He gets out, pays the driver.

Vinu hugs him, asks if it is okay to sleep over.

'I have nowhere to go,' she says, even though he does not refuse.

They drink tea on the veranda, look out on Johannesburg's blurred skyline. He has seen it a thousand times, it is a meaningless thing to do, yet everyone who comes here feels compelled to sit on the red-polished steps and stare into the murky sky.

Moulana Ismail's distant smile comes back to him. Why had the Moulana spoken so bluntly? It had been so sudden and inexplicable. At the end of his narrative, he had looked at Michael, perplexed, as if he was disappointed. As if Michael had proved to be less intelligent than he had supposed, as if Michael's questions, his querulous tone, his silence at the end betrayed an incapacity to grasp a fine, delicately woven moral.

There are certain things people do not forget, or forgive. Rape is one of them.

A crass, banal statement. Who are the 'people' who do not forget or forgive? The raped? The children of rape? What does Moulana Ismail know about being a child of rape?

He is tired, he tells Vinu. They go inside. In his room, she flops down on his bed, while he sits in the chair at the desk. She is preventing him from lying down. She wants to talk.

205

Vinu declares herself a 'kindred spirit', says that she understands what Michael is going through. He looks at her through narrowed eyes, his manner challenging. 'What am I going through?' he might ask. But he does not want to engage her, does not want to hear what she thinks he is 'going through'. He dislikes the assumption in that statement, the false kinship it creates, solidarity by association. He has heard adults say, 'I've been through this myself,' or worse still, 'I am going through the same thing,' as if there is a universality about human experience, nothing is new, no form of suffering different from the other.

She senses his faint hostility, responds to it as she does to all such resistance, by becoming even more fervent. He is so 'brave' to have taken back his identity, to have dared to become 'Michael' again. He has no idea how defining a nickname can be, why does he think parents impose such things on their children?

She answers herself: because children often become what their parents don't want them to be. So they change the child's name, make a diminutive of it, in an attempt to recreate the child as they conceived it. A child's given name is an instrument of self-identity, of freedom, don't you see?

She peers at him, puzzled by his silence.

'So brave, Michael, so brave,' she repeats.

'You're gushing. I thought you hated gushers?'

She turns onto her side, squirming like an animal adept at freeing itself from traps, and throws off the tightly rolled sleeping bag that she carries on her back. She has brown eyes flecked with blue. What is the colour of her skin, he wonders? Something clichéd, like amber, honey. One day, he will write a story about her – or someone like her. A true bastard, endowed with all the exoticism of an unlikely mixture: a Hindu mother and an Afrikaner father. That much we have in common. He'll start off: 'Sashtri – ' No, something much simpler, why not 'Vinu', that's a clean-sounding name for a tragic character? 'Vinu had a rough, bastard kind of beauty.' No, too sentimental. Vinu's story has to be told in a straightforward, unadorned way.

'Michael?'

'Yes?'

'I want to tell you something.'

'Something shocking?'

'Don't mock me, please.'

'I'm sorry.'

'But I want you to listen, really listen, please?'

'Okay.'

'I have been sleeping with my father.'

He looks at her, searching for some sign that she is probing, trying to elicit confirmation of some gossip, or something guessed at, divined, expecting him to close his eyes and say afterwards: 'I know what you are going through.'

'Are you listening, Michael?'

'Yes.'

'I have been sleeping with my father since I was fourteen years old.'

'Voluntarily? I mean, because you want to or because you have to?'

She turns onto her back, stares at the ceiling. 'Because I want to, because we both do. Should I tell you how it started?'

'Accidentally, right?'

'Michael, please listen, truly listen.'

'I'm listening.'

'It started when I was fourteen, while we were in exile in the Netherlands. We were living in Amsterdam. Do know how cold Amsterdam is?'

'No, I've never been to a really cold place.'

'Well, it's very cold. It rains, and the wind blows. It doesn't snow, not huge mountains of white, but things ice up. Some winters, the canals freeze, and people go skating. You can hear the sound of their skates scraping on the ice. It's a thin sound, sets your teeth on edge. My mom loved skating, my dad hated it. You know, the inversion of roles, the way our revolutionary parents loved to become someone they were not meant to be? There they were, the "Indian" taking to the cold weather and the "European" disliking it. Well, I used to climb into my mom and dad's bed when it was cold. Only, he was always home, mom was always out or away, working for the movement – you know what that's like, don't you?'

'Yes.'

'When I was fourteen, mom was away and it was a really cold winter and there were skaters on the frozen canal and I hated the screeching sound of their skates, so I climbed into bed with my dad. He was asleep, dreaming of something, and when I lay close to him, he spoke to me in this dreamy voice. He held me, started touching me, caressing me, and I wasn't frightened, I found it beautiful, I was aroused, so I kissed him on his mouth. I think he woke up, he said, "Oh, my God, no," then we kissed again, and we fondled each other, touched each other all over, and we made love. He wept afterwards, begged my forgiveness. But I told him there was nothing to forgive, we did it out of love. It was as if he was the child and I the grown-up.'

Vinu is quiet, and Michael listens to her breathing, peers closely to see if she is asleep. But she stirs, turns to look at him, her expression distant, her eyes soft.

'It was beautiful. We slept with each other often, although after the first time we used condoms. He insisted on using condoms. I loved my father, loved him in an unbelievable way. It was beautiful. Do I shock you?'

'What happened?' Michael asks.

'He betrayed me.'

'How?'

'He slept with someone else.'

'Your mother?'

'Oh, I knew about that, but sex with her was a duty. No, with someone else. My mother's friend. Mom caught them, confided in me, weeping so bitterly. I was angry, not for her sake, but for mine. I told her: "Leave him." *I* couldn't leave him, not in that sense, because suddenly I knew he didn't belong to me, he never had. Do you know what he did when my mother told him she was leaving him?'

'Told her about you?'

'No. He went for counselling, confessed, said he had abused his daughter.'

'How do you know this?'

'He told me, we had this conversation one morning, about a month ago . . .'

'Do you think your mother knows?'

'I don't know, I don't care. It was beautiful, before he decided to fuck someone else, another woman. And now he confesses, says it was abuse. Michael?'

'Yes?'

'Do you think it was abuse, something to be ashamed of?'

'No.'

'It was beautiful . . .'

'Maybe.'

'He betrayed me, Michael, reduced our love to a case of child abuse.'

He does not answer, senses that she is sinking into a merciful sleep, deep and unfathomable. He covers her with a blanket, switches off the light, and sits in the darkness for a while. Then he removes the stone from its new hiding place behind a row of books, and by its dim blue illumination, he unrolls Vinu's sleeping bag, and lays it out the way he has seen her do it. He pulls the padded coverlet up to his chin, and with the stone's light silvery on the page, he reads from Mevlana Celaleddin-i Rumi's book, *Mesnevi*:

> *Of the secret wine*
> *All drank but just a sip*
> *So as to become*
> *So as to exist.*
> *But I drank barrels*
> *And barrels of that wine*
> *So as to become a mirror*
> *Pure.*

Michael ponders this contradiction: a Sufi poet, a mystic, immersed in God, in the Prophet Mohamed's puritan God, unforgiving of all mortal indulgence, uses wine as a metaphor for discovery and illumination. Something he should have questioned Moulana Ismail about. Perhaps the Imam would understand why Vinu could see beauty in having a sexual relationship with her father? Her father certainly saw none. And if all she was doing was to deny that he had imposed his ageing body on her, his stale lust, his vainglorious manhood, why did he, her father, not have the courage to concede to her – at the very least – her right to that beauty, even as an illusion?

Michael is filled with a quick, seething irritation. He shakes Vinu out of her sleep, she sits up, her eyes wide with fear.

'Michael . . .'

'Vinu, listen. Don't fool yourself. There was nothing beautiful about it. It was rape, Vinu, simple, crude rape.'

She pulls her legs close to her body, leans her head on her knees, weeps, the way he imagines she wept as a child, bewildered, unsure of herself.

19

This December was a month of anniversaries. Jackson and Mam Agnes would have been married for forty-two years, Silas was turning fifty, and on the fifteenth it would be ten years since Silas had first learnt that the liberation movement was negotiating with the government. 'Freedom is on the way,' someone had told them, 'the only thing that needs to be determined is when – and how – the baby will be born.' A briefing in London, senior officials speaking with the smug voices of schoolboys 'in the know'. A smell of damp warmth inside the conference room, the Imperial Hotel, dull hues of gold and brown and colonial purple.

Comrade X on the podium, lecturing the delegates on the 'new responsibilities' that awaited them at home. Silas tried to ease his boredom, and his agitation (Betty was waiting for him at a bed-and-breakfast place, 'Find your way to Oxford Circus, then take the Central Line to Shepherd's Bush station, walk along Uxbridge Road, away from the city, you'll find St Stephen's Avenue . . .'), by playing a game with his eyes. Observing the Comrade from different vantage points, dressing him in a young man's clothes, lending music to his inchoate exploration of the 'new possibilities for the future' (*Eleanor Rigby, picks up the rice in the church where a wedding has been*).

Finally, Silas made a desperate swoop along the faded carpet, between the two rows of patient listeners, like a fighter-plane locked onto its target, and, when he could see the man's face, the ageing skin, the tired eyes, fired off a burst of mental gunfire. Old-fashioned machine-gun fire, loving the brat-atat-tat noise in his head. He watched in horror as the elderly man shut his eyes, clutched his throat and fell to the floor.

Afterwards, hurrying through London's bitter December cold, and hanging onto the strap in the swaying underground train, he tried to still his trembling hands. He lay next to Betty after they had made love, wanted to tell her what had happened, to explain that the moment he pulled the trigger in his mind, he knew the Comrade was going to die. But how could he capture the utter, terrifying beauty of that moment? He looked out through the brocade curtains at the cold, tyrannical sky, and, leaning into the warm rhythm of her body, he too fell asleep.

'Hey, bra, you're very far away,' Alec said.

'Ja, well, just remembering something,' Silas answered.

He was making good his long-standing invitation to take Alec out for a drink. This was an appropriate day, the afternoon of the Oliphants' prayer-and-drinks party. A solemn affair, Silas thought it would be. Imagine that for a feat, forty-two years with the same person, more if you counted the courting and stuff like that. Did they fuck before they got married?

'Why does Jackson always do this, pray and sin at the same time?' Silas mused, more to himself than to Alec.

'Always covering his bases, God and the Devil, votes for one party nationally, another party in the province. Have you watched him having a drink? Whisky in one hand, water in the other, yin and yang. What bushies know about Eastern philosophy is dangerous.' Alec too was in mordant mood. Always had to go one better than Silas.

'Listen, I have reason to be in a bad mood,' Silas said. 'But what's vreeting you up?'

'Gracie wants to move.'

'Where to?'

'Out of the townships, anywhere, Berea, Observatory . . .'

'No, man, not from one slum to another!'

'Exactly. At least in my own slum, I'm familiar with the rats and the cockroaches.'

'We don't have rats and cockroaches in the suburbs.'

'Like hell. What do you have?'

212

'Nigerians, Pakistanis, Taiwanese . . .'

'Shit, I can see you're tired of being in government!'

'Oh, don't you go losing your sense of humour as well.'

Alec turned in his chair, looked around at the dingy décor, flaking plaster, cheap pine tables polished to a dark oak, its fakery so endearingly transparent.

'How did you find this fleapit?' he asked.

'One night on my way to you, looking for, you know, refuge from Lydia's fucken tears, I saw this place and decided to stop.'

'So why didn't you come to us?'

'I remembered that Gracie has the same kind of eyes as Lydia. Would have drilled holes in me.'

Alec waved to the waitress, a young woman with a 'new South African' mouth, he said, ivory teeth gleaming against her dark skin, ah, and those bright red lips. He ordered two whiskies on ice, water on the side, smiled at her, then turned to confide his desires to Silas.

'God, I can see my penis in there.'

'Her mouth?'

'Where else? This is the Age of HIV/AIDS.'

'So it's a penis now, is it? Not a piel any more.'

'Listen, broer, you've got to keep up with the times, be politically correct and all that,' Alec said, and moved his chair closer to Silas. 'You know, they've been phoning each other like mad.'

'Who?'

'Martha and Lydia, Lydia and Gracie, Gracie and Martha, who the fok do you think?'

'About Michael?'

'Christ, you too! When did Mikey lose his name?'

'He wants us to call him by his real name, Michael, not Mikey, like a fucken lightie.'

Alec took the drinks from the waitress, gave her a generous tip,

213

flashed a grin of tarnished teeth, knew that she was recording him in her mind: seedy, dangerous, wealthy (relatively speaking). He turned his back to her, earnest now in his conversation with Silas.

'Listen, Silas, that lightie of yours is doing some strange things.'

Silas glared at Alec over his glass, ready to tell him to mind his own business.

Alec raised a hand in defence. 'Hey, I'm only trying to help. He's been seeing people in Newclare . . .'

'Our Newclare, Maklera?'

'Yes, man, our kasie. Silas, he's been talking to some bad people, guys involved in crazy things.'

Silas breathed in, his vague anxieties about Michael finding shape, looming shadows becoming precise, harrowing forms.

'Who is he seeing?' he asked at last.

'An Imam, Imam Ismail.'

'You mean like a real Imam, someone in a mosque?'

'Yes . . .'

'You have a "but" – what is it?'

'Well, first of all, he is the Imam at the mosque where your father used to be, Griffith Street. Secondly, he is kind of cuckoo, befok, if you ask me. He has these Slamse seances, you know, where they pray and go wild and all.'

'They are Sufis, mystics.'

'I hear they are also involved with those Muslim vigilantes.'

'Pagad?'

'And worse. We hear things about Afghanistan . . . Libya.'

'Who's "we"?'

'Come on, Silas, you know I do work for some of the people at NIS . . .'

'Still helping out there?'

'Legal stuff, but sometimes they tell you things . . .'

Silas sipped his whisky in silence. The National Intelligence Service wanted him to know what his son was up to, so they told Alec, who told him. He looked around at the clientele. What traumas were they going through, he wondered, apart from agonizing continually over how they weren't white enough in the past, and how they're not black enough now? The existential dilemma of every bastard in the world.

'Listen, broer, that Imam calls himself Sheg Konya,' Alec said.

'What?'

'Ja, shows you he's crazy. They've given Mikey a name as well. After some avenger, you know, a crazy Arab who tried to kill off all of Christendom.'

'Well, Alec, you certainly know what's going on in the townships.'

'My livelihood, bra. Those people are my bread-and-butter clients. How do you say? – my "core business". If I depended on the government, Gracie wouldn't have the luxury of being ashamed of the townships.'

They fell silent, each overtaken by his own preoccupations. Perhaps they wanted to offer support, advice, think back to the days when their companionship would have allowed them the freedom to confide in each other more fully. Silas smiled ruefully, raised his hand and summoned the waitress.

'No, not the same. Pastis, you know, tastes of liquorice,' he said, explaining to the waitress that it was a French drink, that it went white when you added water, only they didn't want water in it.

'Something to celebrate?' Alec asked.

'Commiserate. My failure to get the post of Ambassador to France.'

'What?'

'My Minister refused to support my candidacy.'

'Mean bastard. But why do you want to go to France?'

'Well, because I need a change, the post is available – or was – and I thought I'd explore life a little, you know, meet new people.'

'Christ, about time!'

An uncomfortable silence fell between them once more. Alec wanted to tell Silas something important. Silas sensed it, and was ready to listen. Fuck! He hoped he wasn't going to tell him that he was HIV-positive, or something truly dreadful like that. Not good enough just to have a disastrous affair these days.

Both raised their hands to get the waitress's attention, and in the midst of all these familiar gestures, this ingrained intimacy, Alec began to speak. His voice was low and gruff, a tone that Silas had never heard him use before. Although it sounded practised, as if he had tried it out when he was alone, looking at himself in the mirror or staring out of a window at the mirage of a mirrored world, Alec seemed astonished by the strangeness of his own voice, and by its painfulness.

'Si, you know that I worked for them, the cops, years ago. I couldn't help it, I could not stand pain, not like you.'

Suddenly, the voice Silas had heard on the night Lydia was raped came back to him. Exaggeratedly low, someone trying to disguise his normal timbre, reducing it to something almost guttural. Yet it had attracted his attention, a turn of phrase, a slurred 'r', a mispronounced 'g' – at times, Alec still uses a hard, Afrikaans 'g' in words like 'gesture' – despite his pain. Three cracked ribs, he recalled, made him feel heroic afterwards.

Alec had been there! A traitor. Silas stopped himself. What a crude word. Who knows what goes on in the hearts of people who are confronted with such stark choices: work for us, betray your friends and comrades, or endure unending pain. Curiously, no one had ever subjected him to such physical and psychological torture. What would he have done if Du Boise had offered him Lydia's safety in return for his allegiance?

'Gladly, I would have given it gladly,' he muttered to himself.

He could not look at Alec, could not bear to witness the pain he knew Alec was desperately trying to hide. What did it matter in any case? We defeated them, the enemy and their agents. Well, a victory of sorts. Now we have to live with the consequences. War is like that. Who said that? Joe Slovo, with one whisky too many under his belt.

'So why are you telling me now, after all these years? Is someone threatening you, trying to use it against you somehow?' Silas asked.

When Alec looked up at Silas, his face seemed to have been wiped clean of all its grinning subterfuge, the boyish smirk that always eased the tension was gone. 'No, Silas,' he said, 'I needed to tell someone, for years I've been needing to tell someone, and I thought you would be the best person to tell.'

Silas watched Alec get up and walk away, thinking how familiar he seemed, the way he held his body, like a boxer, putting more weight on one foot than on the other. No, it did not make him look unbalanced, it made him look just right, somehow.

He turned to the waitress and ordered another whisky.

'Plenty of ice, no water.'

A mass was said for Jackson and Agnes Oliphant in Newclare's Church of St Francis of Assisi. Blessings on their forty-second anniversary. A feat that all married couples should try to emulate. Live together for a lifetime, or its equivalent in life expectancy. The priest was young, filled with enlightened jargon. He spoke about the AIDS plague, people dying all around him, how only God had the right to judge, the need for compassion. Where are all the good old sermonizers, the fire-and-brimstone preachers who asked God to fry your arse at the smallest transgression? Archbishop Tutu and his kind are responsible for this: the namby-pambying of God's ferocious legions.

Silas was glad to get out into the open air. Light flowed from the Church into the darkness, as feeble as ever and unable to defeat the woven-together shadows of a place like Newclare. Even this new breed of priest could not illuminate the human condition (whatever that was).

The place stretched before him, much smaller than he remembered.

How time seduces the memory, makes the past seem grander than it could ever have been. This was where he had grown up, where he had been shaped, where his world-view had been formed. How miserable it seemed now.

An arm was linked into his; Lydia, generous in her observation of his misery, led him away to their car. They swept off in convoy to Alec and Gracie's home for supper and drinks. In the car, he asked Lydia when last she had seen Michael.

'A week ago, the night he brought that girl home.'

'You know who she is?'

'Her name is Vinu. A refugee of sorts.'

'What do you mean?'

'I don't think he slept with her, there was a bed on the floor the next morning. He's giving her sanctuary from something.'

'You went into his room?'

'Had to. Heard her crying. Sounded like she had been crying all night. I thought that Mikey had done something . . .'

'God.'

'Yes, that's what I thought. Rape, coercion. A mother's worst fears. But she was weeping about something else. Thanked us for our tolerance, said that Mikey was so generous, so wise. So were we!'

'Does that mean she's still there?'

'No, Silas. Don't you know what goes on in your own house?'

They pulled up outside Gracie and Alec's township mansion, brick and mortar testing the frontiers of their surroundings. This is how the grand little towns in Spain and Italy are built, with their front doors opening onto the street.

'You're never going to call him "Michael", are you?' Silas said.

'Michael belongs to someone else. *Mikey* is my son,' she answered, then got out of the car, and, without waiting for him, went in to join the other guests. She had restored the distance between them.

Silas continued drinking whisky deep into the night, listening to the eager chatter of people who no longer saw much of each other. Freedom had loosened bonds forged in the ghettos. Most of the guests were friends of Jackson and Agnes, their children, and grandchildren. People with good clothes, cars, homes, gardens. The black middle class that everybody said was the future of the country. You need people with vested interests, prepared to fight for what they've got. Forget about God, about sovereignty, about justice and all that kak, they'll die for their impoverished space. Well, some of them have huge homes now, dogs with shiny coats, kids in the best schools. Viva the buying classes!

Silas took a jug of water from a table, emptied his whisky on the lawn and went to sit by himself in a garden chair. He sipped the cold water, trying to cool down the heat in his head. He should have stopped drinking earlier that day, no, a long time ago. He wondered what it would be like to give it all up, not just the food, the drink, but all of this, family, friends. Yes, give up belonging, that was the only way to free yourself.

He heard Alec, loud, hoarse, telling one of his stories somewhere in the house. Alec had been avoiding him all night, protecting himself behind a barricade of banter and raucous laughter. Silas wanted to talk to him, simply to tell him that it didn't matter that he had worked for the cops during the struggle days, he would be surprised by the kind of people who had worked for the boere, some had even believed at the time that it was the right thing to do. Stop the Commies, better the devil you know. But Silas was curious as well: had Alec really been there the night they raped Lydia? That was the only thing he would interrogate him about, given the chance.

He saw Alec approaching, leading a throng of people out into his rather fussily groomed garden. History's vaudeville procession, flowing around the stone fountain. God, what had possessed him to build a thing like that? Silas shook his head, once more, at the sight of the water spewing from the mouth of a roaring stone lion. The poor animal, doomed to vomit perpetually. So this was how Alec hid his guilt, in ostentatious stone. A true monument builder. *He* should be in politics.

Silas saw that the yelping crowd was making for him. Quite a few women in their midst, most of them past their best, sexually speaking, but drunkenness lent them renewed allure. God, what he wouldn't do for sex! A good, old-fashioned, township-style grope in the dark, hands running over smooth silk, and then a heavenly fuck up against a wall.

In the background, he saw Lydia and Gracie, aloof, disdainful. The sight of the two sisters haughtily framed in the lit-up doorway filled him with a sudden rage. To hell with you, he thought, so full of airs and graces.

Beside Alec was a balding man with the gait of a fading athlete, his strength now in his pride.

'Silas, let me introduce you to Mr Moses Manning.'

'Mapaks? My God, it *is* you, Mapaks!'

The man beamed.

Begs for recognition, even from a nobody like me, Silas thought. They hugged, Silas stoically inhaling an overpowering smell of brandy and Coke.

Moses 'Mapaks' Manning held Silas at arm's length and appraised him. 'Doing a fine job!'

'How are you, Mapaks?'

Alec intervened. This was no time for exchanging pleasantries. 'Mapaks remembers that man who got away from the Vikings.'

'He doesn't!' Silas protested.

Alec addressed the group who had followed him out into the garden. They wanted to hear a good story. 'Tell them, Silas, tell them how you fucken got away from the Vikings.'

Silas hesitated, and Alec poured a drink from the bottle in his hand, shoved it into Silas's fist. Lydia walked to the edge of the garden, where Silas could see her. She wanted to save him from himself, from the obvious need he had to make a fool of himself, and of her; he was still her husband, and wives took responsibility for what their husbands did, especially in the eyes of people like these.

He saw her and smiled, gave her one of his steady, defiant looks. Alec looked at the two of them and then grinned slyly. And suddenly Silas recalled that elated moment Alec was talking about. Lydia knew it by heart, she had heard it so often. He and Alec should have been troubadours, telling and retelling their sorry little stories, over and over again.

'Okay,' Silas said, turning to his audience. 'Well, I'm sure you remember what it was like in those days, even going to movies was a real mission. There was this movie I wanted to see, *Becket*, with Richard Burton and Peter O'Toole. But would you believe it, no one wanted to go with me. Everyone said it was one of those boring high-buck movies. Except Alec, he said he would come along . . .'

Silas turned to look at Alec, to catch his eye. He was going to say, 'Of course, Alec really wanted to get away from that Slamse chick who brought him koesisters on Sunday morning, syrupy Mona Gassiep, her lips oozing lipgloss . . .' But at that moment he saw Michael instead, and his voice trailed away, his ostentatious bard's way of remembering things coming to a mumbled conclusion. A man suddenly aware of his own loudness, as if he had just heard himself speak for the first time, acknowledging with some shame that the showy voice, with its self-important tone, was his own. His audience, observing how Silas had lapsed into an embarrassed silence the moment his son Mikey walked onto the stoep, laughed politely, then drifted away to rejoin Jackson and Mam Agnes's party, which continued its subdued celebrations inside the house.

Michael stood there, next to Jackson and Mam Agnes, watching Silas, with the same sardonic smile he used to wear when he was sent to find his father in a township backyard, or on the island of grass in Berea that had become Silas's beer-and-manhood refuge of solitude.

A young woman was at Michael's side, tight black dress, shock of bright orange hair. That must be Vinu, Silas thought. She waved at someone, an elegant, youthful movement of her hand, laughed, whispered into Mikey's ear. She glowed. The colour of dirty honey, Silas thought, a bushie goddess. Beauty honed on the same bastard whetstone as I. We will make no more like her, or like Michael, for that matter. Our ambitions are too ordinary, a house, a car, a garden. We no longer dream of painful beauty when we make love.

Only Alec tried to hold onto that captivating moment, the promise of a past to be richly recalled, a mood of nostalgia that he had hoped to provoke, but his laughter was disagreeably harsh and earned him nothing but one of Gracie's cold and scornful looks. He too fell quiet, shaking his head in one last gesture that said, 'What great times those were!' He was too preoccupied with his own disappointment to observe Silas's strange, excited expression. What others might have mistaken for misery, the self-conscious realization of his own foolishness, Alec would have recognized in Silas's beaming face: it was enthralment, blatantly sexual, an agitation not evoked in him by a woman in a long time.

Silas saw Lydia move instinctively towards Mikey, then stop when Vinu leaned close to whisper in his ear. Deterred by their laughter, by their youthful intimacy, she turned away, and, observing Silas's fascination, came up to him and said: 'Silas, you're staring!'

The party quickly broke up. Michael seemed to start the process. He tugged quietly at Vinu's sleeve, helping her to escape from Silas, who had cornered her on the stoep. 'You're Johan's daughter!' Silas had exclaimed, when Michael introduced them. Silas kept up his half-drunken patter about Vinu's parents, about how they all went back a long way, his manner flirtatious, leaning up against a wall, legs crossed at the ankle, drink dangling from a limp wrist.

Other guests quickly departed, leaving Jackson's favourite 1960s township jazz playing loudly to an empty room. Lydia said she was going for coffee with Alec and Gracie, making it obvious that Silas was not welcome; he had humiliated her and embarrassed Mikey.

'Christ! She's your son's age!' she had said.

Silas drove home slowly, not only because he knew he had had too much to drink, but because he wanted to savour Vinu's smell, her young woman's breath, warm and fragrant (some kind of gum she was chewing, a breath freshener, mint, liquorice?), the green pools of her eyes. Yet, when he climbed into bed and switched off the light, hoping to take Vinu into his dreams, Michael's eyes confronted him. That cool, disdainful stare from Alec's stoep earlier that night, the look of faint disgust. Now Michael was intruding even upon his fantasies, his imaginary – and therefore innocent – seduction of a young woman (he was too old, too tired, to masturbate anyway, he rationalized afterwards). Silas felt hatred for Michael, sudden and fleeting. When it was gone, he lay awake, full of bitter remorse.

Perhaps it was time to go, to leave this place, this house, this country and its contorted history?

20

Michael and Vinu sit under the fig tree's canopy of dying fruit, inhaling the excessive, overripe sweetness of figs abandoned to the birds, to the thunderstorms that assail the city. The overhang of branches retains the day's heat; outside of this warm shelter, the night is chilly. Johannesburg cools down quickly, because of the altitude, six thousand feet above sea level, know-it-all conversationalists say.

'This is such a fickle place,' Michael says.

'The place or the people?' Vinu asks.

'Both. They are one and the same.'

It is the sight of Silas staggering into the house that spurs their conversation. He mutters to himself, loudly opens and closes doors, bumps into things. His actions have the characteristic exaggeration of someone not only struggling against the effects of too much alcohol, but also against the tide of emotional turmoil that accompanies drunkenness.

Michael observes Silas at his familiar post by the kitchen sink, drinking glass after glass of water, and staring myopically into the darkness. What does he see in that mirror of his own eyes? A life lived as best he can, and therefore wasted, by definition. Michael resists the surge of sympathy he feels for Silas, his father in name, his keeper, mentor of sorts. Every now and then, Silas gets this wild look in his eyes, a redeeming sense of yearning, a desire for something more than mere existence.

Almost chastely, Michael sips his tea. 'How are you going to resolve your problem?'

'My problem?'

'With your father.'

Vinu has also refused the offer of a glass of wine, attracted by the ascetic ritual with which he was preparing the tea. She looks into her cup, takes a sip, swirls the liquid around in her mouth. 'Only death – his death – can resolve that problem. I have no intention of taking my own life.' She smiles. 'I could get you to kill him for me. Michael the Avenger. That title suits you.'

A pact is made, unconsciously. Vinu watches Silas turn away from the kitchen window, remembers the suggestiveness with which he leaned towards her at the party. She had been flattered, but is repulsed now by the memory of his breath, hot, whisky-laden, slightly sour, like her father's. No, she does not wish Johan dead; punished, yes, but not dead. True justice would be to deprive someone of life without having to kill them. Perhaps the guilty should be put in limbo, made to live in some twilight zone, conscious of their sins for ever? Just the kind of punishment those daughter-fucking fathers deserve.

She wishes now that Michael would ask her to have sex with him, that they could lie together, their bodies wet with raw, youthful sweat. She gulps the last of her tea, the way desperate adults down the remnants of a strong and bitter drink, aware that all Michael will offer tonight is a puritan abstinence. He is beyond us now, she thinks, beyond all women. Even his mother. She shudders.

'Someone's walking across my grave,' she says.

'It's up your spine they walk, that's the cliché.'

'God, you are perverse!'

Part Three

Retribution

Thou liv'st; report me and my cause aright
To the unsatisfied.

William Shakespeare, *Hamlet*

21

KATE HAD ARRANGED to meet Julian and Silas over lunch, to discuss the plans for Silas's fiftieth birthday party. She had recruited Julian into the cause of organizing a 'truly wonderful celebration'. Julian, she felt, had to find 'new meaning in his life' now that his marriage was over. Val had left him, suddenly, without even the courtesy of a letter or an e-mail message. She had never been one for disembodied self-justifications. She left it to her lawyer to inform Julian about her intention to sue for divorce, and the conditions under which he would be able to see his son. 'It's all for the best,' the lawyer had said, mimicking Val's unctuous tones.

Now Julian was spending aimless hours at the office, trying to formulate a 'comprehensive HIV policy' that would soon be redundant, given that the President was about to retire and his designated successor had strong views on how this 'scourge ought to be tackled'.

Julian had chosen a restaurant called 'Crucible', because it was chic and decadent, he said. It was one of those new upmarket establishments that promised both 'style' and 'the feel of Africa', as if the two concepts were usually contradictory. Nouvelle cuisine in the bush. An hour's drive from Pretoria, Crucible sat like a heavily made-up but lovable old aunt, Julian said, on a ridge overlooking the place where (it was reputed) Man had been born.

'You'll love it!'

Kate shuddered at the thought of having lunch in the midst of a brash business clientele, men in suits who still believed they owned the world. They could afford the leisure of turning away from the city for a few hours, to feast, get drunk, fortify themselves on their self-righteous, pitying sympathy for a government 'who just couldn't get things right'. She suggested somewhere closer, a place where Silas especially wouldn't feel out of place. Julian should know how uncomfortable Silas would be among the kind of people who must frequent – 'What's it called? The Crucible?'

'No, darling, just "Crucible". There is a subtle difference, you know. You can sit under a tree, enjoy the heat and the shade, hear the buzzing of insects, the splash of water. There is a brook nearby. Beauty you don't even have to see. Talk about the best of both worlds!' In any case, the place epitomized the new democratic order; it was run by former enemies – an ex-cop and a one-time MK soldier, for whom the government could find no new role. 'Isn't that just marvellous!'

Julian's enthusiasm finally persuaded Kate.

'The place is out near Krugersdorp, and it overlooks a game reserve or something like that,' she forewarned Silas, when she picked him up. She also cautioned that Julian's marriage had finally crumbled and his wife had moved out. 'But don't probe, let him tell you on his own.'

Silas seemed preoccupied with her concern for Julian, even irritated by it. Something else was bothering him. She glanced at him, saw his bitten lip and drawn face, his struggle with a question that failed to find form, a man as articulate as Silas, suffering this stultifying awkwardness.

'Kate?'

'Yes?'

She had dreaded this moment for a long time. Whenever she saw Silas, she anticipated being confronted about her relationship with Mikey, although the word 'confront' was too strong for the way he would deal with the matter. He would probe, ask oblique questions, rationalizing on her behalf even as he proceeded to question her: 'It was inevitable, you are attractive, he is such a sensuous young man . . .'

She shifted about, positioned herself resolutely, ready, she told herself, to answer his questions as directly and honestly as possible. Yes, I have been having an affair with your son, I take full responsibility, but it is over, it was a moment of foolishness, a huge mistake. Forgive me, if you can. There is no point in trying to find out why or how or where. The detail is mundane, sordid really. I hope we can stay friends, even if from a distance.

They saw the sign for the restaurant when it was almost upon them, and she had to brake sharply and make a tight turn. They were on a gravel road, and she concentrated on keeping control of the car, slowing it down, allowing the dust to settle and restore her visibility. The place was much closer to town than she had assumed.

'Christ!' Silas said, clinging to the sides of the seat.

They were travelling slowly now, ahead of them a serene, if rather contrived, view of trees and manicured lawns, and, in the distance, the restaurant nestling in the cool lee of a koppie. Hundreds of birds kept up a prolonged but not unpleasant chatter.

'You wanted to ask me something?' Kate said.

'No, not important.'

'Well, any time you want to ask, anything, I'm here.'

'What are your plans for next year?'

'Next year? I haven't even begun thinking that far ahead. I'm still in post-struggle, get-it-done mode.'

'Good God, what does all that mean?'

'I don't know, Silas. You wanted to know what I'm going to do when the Old Man retires?'

'Yes.'

'You don't think the new President will have a place for me?'

'No. He has his own team, his own legal adviser, certainly his own intelligence adviser.'

'All black, all returned exiles?'

'That's too simplistic.'

'Well, that's what people are whispering.'

He did not answer.

She was glad of the diversion, the good grace with which he had withdrawn the question he had been about to ask. Was it about her and Mikey? He had retreated from an inevitable interrogation, the aftermath of which could not be foretold. Some day, the subject would have to be broached – but not today, not this perfect, cloudless day, this hour of pleasant promise, of chilled white wine and laughter, of light, inconsequential banter between old friends. The weighty problem of morality, the deviancy of an older woman having fucked the young son of a friend, would have to wait.

When the time came, she would have to convince him that it had been random, that she had not chosen Mikey because he was Silas's son. She had convinced herself, and that had been difficult enough. All her life, she had been taught to face problems, get them behind her and out of the way, never to leave matters unresolved, especially something as personal as a sexual relationship. Now she hoped that dealing with this 'loose end' could be postponed for a long time, until today's sensational revelation would have become yesterday's mildly shocking gossip. She hoped she would never have to discuss the issue with Silas, certainly not alone. She had never realized before how difficult it was to tell the truth, to confess, to say, 'I have . . .'

But her fate, her reputation, her relationships with her daughter Ferial, with her lover Janine, with Silas and Julian, all these good people, these fucking good people, depended on Mikey. She was *his* loose end, *his* discarded little 'bit on the side'. What a fall from grace, having to pursue a mere boy, waiting for him at the gates of the university, seeing him stop dead in his tracks, then retreat, disappearing into the crowd with such an obvious, evasive swerve of his body!

There was a time when she had called him on the phone endlessly, knowing that Silas was away on business and Lydia was busy preparing for her new job. The young swine refused to answer the phone. As she sat in her car outside his home, with the cellphone pressed to her ear, he would watch her from a window, and let the phone ring urgently deep inside the house. What were his thoughts as he looked down upon her taut features, the hateful, exasperated look of an older lover spurned? Indifference, scorn, detestation, did he have any feelings at all? He had used her, then dumped her, this young bastard with his beautiful eyes and his deadly body. It was all over and done with.

But what was he going to do with the information she had given him about Du Boise? God, nothing stupid, she hoped, like attacking the man. Did young Mikey know that Du Boise had raped his mother? Had he realized that she, Kate, would know about it? That Silas would have confided in her, inevitably, because they were friends and 'comrades in arms'? How hackneyed, how unfashionably nostalgic that term had become in this sceptical age, when to believe in the beauty of comradeship and loyalty to a cause was seen as weak and sentimental.

She pulled the car up under a tree, squeezed Silas's hand. An unexpected gesture. Thank God you're not your son! But it brought Silas back to the question he wanted to ask.

'Kate, just a minute.'

Another moment of dread.

'Do you remember Du Boise?'

'Oh, Silas, I thought that was behind you . . .'

'You know he's dying of cancer?'

'How did you find out? Never mind, I don't want to hear.'

'Is that not poetic justice?'

'What kind of cancer?'

233

'The worst, skin cancer, visibly eats away the outsides, uncovers the rotting flesh.'

He spoke as if imagining a photograph he had mulled over, its shocking import absorbed in minute detail.

'Oh, not before lunch!'

'Well, I thought you might want to know.'

'I've got a better one.'

'What, who?'

'Van Jaarsveld, *the* Captain Van Jaarsveld.'

'Kaptein Duiwel?'

'Ja! AIDS, the man is dying of AIDS.'

'My God, *that's* poetic justice!'

'Come on, let's go and find Julian, I need a drink.'

They found Julian seated at a table at the end of a stone terrace, his tie undone and his shirt unbuttoned halfway down his chest. But even his lazily outstretched legs could not hide his weariness, the posture of someone desperate to relax. From behind dark glasses too small, too fashionable for his rather craggy face (already it bore the signs of patriarchal ruin, to be described in the future as 'distinguished' rather than lovely, as he might have hoped), he stared out across the smooth lawn. A sprinkler shot sprays of water into the air, and his head moved from side to side, following its intermittent rotation, entranced by its precise mechanics, oblivious to the cloud of water drifting in on the breeze and steadily soaking the jacket he had flung over the cast-iron railing.

Julian sat up with a start when Kate and Silas approached, hugged each of them in turn, kissed them on their cheeks. He was filled with the exuberant rituals of his new-found freedom. He was openly gay now, no, blatantly and hungrily so, he always corrected himself. His breath had the lemony smell of alcohol.

'Been here since breakfast?' Kate joked.

'Nothing like a gin with your eggs,' he answered.

He had a bottle of wine chilling in an ice bucket, all ready for them.

'Damn,' Julian said, as Kate retrieved his soaked-through jacket and hung it over a spare chair.

They sipped the wine that a waiter poured with practised elegance, laughed at Julian's attempts to engage the young man's eyes, scoffed at his judgement that the waiter was gay, 'and available'. Then they lapsed into a placid silence, captivated, like Julian before them, by the water-sprinkler's exactitude. The waiter came back.

'Is that your car, sir, the blue Land Rover?'

'Why, yes.'

'You've left your lights on, sir.'

'I hate you,' Julian said, in a playful, teasing tone that brought a frown to Silas's face. His mood had not yet softened enough to accept Julian's coquettish behaviour ('Camp, it is called camp', Julian would educate him later). Silas secretly preferred the quiet, if acerbic, Julian that he knew, always logical, always restrained. Julian stumbled off, his body losing the leisurely grace with which he had greeted them. The spell was broken, the voices of other luncheon patrons (Crucible did not have 'customers', the waiter would tell them) intruded, the scrape of cutlery on china, the clink of glasses, chairs being dragged across the terracotta floor. Somewhere a man laughed, a woman's voice coyly deflected what Silas imagined was an advance. From inside the restaurant, darkened to his sun-blinded eyes, a babble of voices erupted, musical, voluptuous. The season of celebration was upon them, the year-end letting go of cares and worries, a country ready to allow the spent year to ebb out of them.

How much inhibition would be lost in the heady surge of laughter, the flow of wine, how many infidelities were being shaped here today, Silas wondered? He felt a sudden wave of resentment at these nominally joyous people, at the recklessness of their petty hedonism. Julian was back, complaining that they had warned him too late, the battery in his car was flat, but what did that matter, there was wine to be drunk and – 'Why are we here again?'

Suddenly, Silas was glad for Julian, his gangly presence, his forbidding irreverence, his own innate despairing, even. He dispersed some of the inexplicable revulsion Silas had been feeling lately at the mere thought of embracing arms and sweaty bodies.

'We're here to plan Silas's birthday party, remember?' Kate said.

'It's fifty, is it?' Julian asked.

Then he rocked back in his chair and, balancing precariously on its two steel legs, recited a poem:

> *Half past twelve.*
> *How quickly time has passed*
> *Since nine o'clock when I lit the lamp . . .*

He paused, peered at his two companions through half-shut eyes.

'You know the poem?'

'No,' Kate said.

A familiar cadence of words, precise in its intermittence, like jets of water caught in the afternoon sun. But no, Silas could not identify the poem or the poet. Julian, quietly triumphant in his superior knowledge of literature, continued to recite, his voice perfectly modulated; this was obviously a well-loved and often-repeated verse. He finished with a flourish:

> *Half past twelve.*
> *How the hours have passed.*
> *Half past twelve.*
> *How the years have passed.*

236

He looked at them quizzically. 'No? Constantine Cavafy, the great poet of Alexandria. The great moffie poet of Alexandria.'

Of course! Silas said to himself. When you lose the memory of poetry, you lose your mind.

Food came, salads of smoked chicken and Malay sauce, Namibian oysters, whole trout grilled with almonds, a festive repast 'worthy of Zeus, or his concubine daughter, Aphrodite'. Julian, inspired now in his inaccurate recollections of Greek literature, ordered another bottle of wine. Silas watched a procession of serene ducks passing by, then looked at the sprinkler again, the sprays of water bejewelled in the sun. He was happy to be here, indolent, without real purpose, despite Kate's attempts to get them 'to focus'. Slightly drunk, at peace with his inner world for the first time in many months, he could even contemplate sex with someone, someone younger, agile in body and bodily imagination.

'So, what about the party?' Julian asked.

'You can use my house,' Kate said.

'No,' Silas responded, then tried to soften his abrupt refusal of the offer. 'I mean . . .'

'What's wrong with my house?' she asked, mockingly affronted.

The Kate of old, Silas thought. 'Or my own house?' he countered.

'What is wrong with both your houses is that they are lived in, they contain people and furniture. Overpopulated, if you take Kate's dogs, lovers, hangers-on . . . and as for you, Silas . . .'

'Julian!'

'No, but seriously, both of you have the kind of homes made for families, full of compromised space. How many people were you thinking of having?'

'Fifty, maybe sixty.'

'Whew!' Kate said.

'There,' Julian said, and leaned forward. 'You can have my house.

Vastly empty, half the furniture's gone, all those flouncy bits, carried off by my carpet-bagging wife. What's left is austere enough to be sat on or stood upright. You can have a kinky fuck on it, too. Good enough for an orgy. Seriously, have my house.'

Julian was serious now. His drunkenness seemed to have evaporated. 'Agree now, please. We have something more urgent to talk about.'

'Well, it *is* big enough,' Kate said.

'Thanks,' Silas said, a little chastened.

'Good. Now, you know we are all about to be booted out.'

'Out of where?'

'Out of our jobs, out of government, out of the Union Buildings.'

'What are you talking about?' Silas asked.

'Well, maybe not you. But who knows? You're not really black, you know. Look, I'm in the transitional team. Our Prez is preparing the way for the new Prez. Review of all the jobs and the people. The criteria we received are quite clear. *His* people . . .'

'That's fine, to be expected,' Kate said.

'Yes, I suppose it is,' Julian said. 'Why should I expect to be treated any differently? I am just a middle-aged, white moffie, newly out of the closet, exposed for what I am in the greying of my life. My wife has left me, I'm about to lose my privileged position, my closeness to the seat of power and all that. Why should I complain?'

He looked at Kate and Silas in turn.

'Oh, all right! Don't be so damn virtuous. Forgive me my little bit of bitterness. The problem is, I haven't had a fuck in ages,' he said vehemently.

People at a nearby table froze, offended murmurs, disapproving eyes.

'Oh, bugger them,' Kate said.

'Yes, let's do that, but first let's have another drink.'

In the waning afternoon, slants of light caught in the leaves of the trees, stirring boughs, a quiet darkening of the sky. The smell of rain in the air. A young woman in the company of the crustaceans at the neighbouring table, deep-jowled she too will be one day, but lovely now in this seductive air, appraised Silas, grey-haired and slim – for his age. Distinguished, familiar somehow, must have seen him on television, one of the new elite. She smiled, a sly gesture, then hid the slight reddening of her face with a quick wave of her hair. Silas responded in spite of the annoyance he felt. How dare she raise insurrection in his groin? In the parliament of his mind, a greyer self still tried to legislate against the turmoil of naked bodies.

'To being fifty', Julian said, glass raised.

'To being alive,' Kate said.

'To fucking, and being fucked,' Silas said, moved to bravado.

The head lobster alongside them fumed, the young woman laughed into the camouflage of her wavy hair. Kate spluttered a mouthful of wine, Julian applauded, uttering a triumphant, 'Bravo!' His 'lovely young waiter' brought their bill, unbidden, to the table. The proprietors, black and white, enemies united in their new spirit of dignified enterprise, looked on in frosty disapproval.

22

Michael is negotiating the purchase of a gun, or an exchange, at least. An untraceable weapon in return for the very expensive-looking gun that he stole from Professor Graham's house. He had slipped it out of the desk drawer, where he had seen it on a previous visit, into his satchel, while Shirley ran to the bathroom to dress. To hide her ageing body, to compose her face, to expunge from her mind the joy and the ensuing shame of her screaming climax. She had to go, an afternoon class, Michael had to hurry and dress as well.

Did he want a lift?

No, he was not going to varsity.

She had proffered her cheek, asking for a distant, brushing kiss, then drawn him to her tightly, the memory of their sex surging through her body.

Now the gun is being appraised behind a closed door. Michael sits in the tiny living room of the flat that Sadrodien has brought him to. Yes, how appropriate the term 'living room' is, the only space available to its inhabitants for living in, the rest – bedroom, bathroom, kitchen – all just big enough to accommodate their utilitarian purposes. Someone, long ago, removed the need for the 'separation of sibling sexes' from the apartheid housing specifications, Michael has read somewhere. 'Coloureds are used to living very close to each other', a member of the housing standards policy committee wrote in justification.

Explained all the abuse, the rape, a non-white disease, one of those people would have surmised, and written as well, somewhere. Not afraid to record the horrors of their thoughts. How then to explain all the incest among Afrikaners? How to justify what Johan Viljoen did to his daughter Vinu? Of course! She is coloured, she invited incestuous rape. Double sin of the doubly damned.

'Michael the Avenger.'

A ludicrous concept, a comic-book idea. And Vinu had not been serious at all when she proposed it. In fact, her voice had betrayed another intention that night: to draw him into the realm of other personas, lure him out of that asensual frame of mind that the sight of Silas staggering about drunkenly had put him into. Vinu wanted sex, unrestrained youthful sex, athletic and physical. Yes, how different it must be to have sex with the light on, without the flattering camouflage of shadows, and to wake up next to a young woman, touch her smooth, languid nakedness. No averted eyes or painfully smiling mouths when you deny them the mercy of a sheet in which to shroud themselves.

But not with Vinu. Too much of a martyr to her 'father's love'. Revels in her status as a victim.

Sadrodien emerges, alone, from the bedroom.

'Gasant knows guns. You know, every gun has an identity, a personality, even.'

Michael laughs, a self-conscious gesture. Sadrodien, a man of many wisdoms. A good definition of schizophrenia. Wonder if he knows what I'm thinking, aren't all these crazed prophets clairvoyant?

Soon Gasant comes in from his 'consulting room'. He, too, speaks in Sadrodien's rehearsed tone. The gun exchange is a concession; normally, his transactions are cash only. He is making an exception because Sadrodien says Michael ('It is Michael?') is a brother. The gun he brought will be sent elsewhere, just as the one he is receiving in its place came from elsewhere. Makes it difficult to trace.

Michael considers the gun's sudden beauty in the palm of his hand. A gleam of deadly metal. 'Feel the weight', Gasant says, and Michael weighs the gun in his hand, nods as if he knows the significance of its heaviness – or its lightness? Gasant hands him a box of bullets, enough for three magazines, but this – 'of course' – is not included in the price.

'Of course', Michael says, and pays Gasant in crisp one-hundred-rand bills. Oupa Jackson's birthday gift, something for a rainy day.

He declines Sadrodien's offer to walk with him to the taxi rank, thinks of him, without reason, as a 'misbegotten' cousin, pauses to watch him sink into Gasant's all-leather settee. Gasant lets out a conspiratorial sigh.

In the Kombi-taxi, he ponders the exotic journeys that guns make. Where does this one come from, Palestine, Kosovo, Kashmir, another home in Johannesburg's northern suburbs? He also wonders why Sadrodien was so willing to help. To demonstrate to Imam Ismail the power of youthful affinity? And will the favour have to be returned one day?

And ultimately, he asks: why am I doing this? Not to avenge Vinu. Killing her father will not eradicate his sin or her complicity, willing or unwilling.

Michael does not acknowledge that this is a 'dry run', practice for a more important mission. He runs a finger along the scar that the Kaaba stone has left on the palm of his hand, idly wonders whether this is God's mark on him. Then he leans back and dozes off. The heat is intense. Johannesburg in December. The taxi makes one of its sudden stops, then pulls off again rapidly. A murmur of voices, the shifting about of bodies wakes him up.

A young white man sits perched on the edge of his seat, determined to be just another passenger. The other commuters are intrigued by his presence, the driver is amused, but concentrates on the task of weaving through the heavy evening traffic. The young man turns, smiles at Michael, as if trying to find someone he can identify with. Michael stares back coldly, at his blue eyes (their brilliance deliberately dimmed!), his nervous smile. A pleading posture – 'Christ! I need transport, just like all of you.'

Michael looks at the interloper's pale lips, too sensuous for a man, and visualizes Johan Viljoen's face, looks down and imagines the gun in his own hand, looks up again to analyse the somewhat tanned skin (a sun-lover, he will not survive Europe, geography has altered his genetics), sees the surface exploding as the first bullet hits him. The eyes start to turn, the body crumples, he falls forward onto his face.

And Du Boise will be no different, all shattered skin and exploding blood.

23

Someone from the university calls, asks to speak to Mr Ali. He's at work, Lydia says, offers to give her Silas's number.

'Is that Mrs Ali?'

'Yes.'

'Perhaps I can talk to you, it is about Michael. I am Dr Priscilla Johnson.'

What an elegant, precise ring Mikey's name has when it is pronounced like this, with fearful profundity, an implied intimacy that immediately fills Lydia with apprehension. Dr Johnson is 'from the English Department at Wits University'. There is something about Michael's behaviour they need to discuss. No, not on the phone, it would be better if they spoke in person.

Lydia drives to Wits University, going over in her mind the kind of 'behaviour' that would necessitate a call to a student's parents. Universities pride themselves on being able to deal with student misdemeanours in an adult fashion. She hopes that Mikey's 'transgression' is no more serious than having bunked classes or missed a deadline for submitting an assignment. Something mundane, routine, easily corrected through parental attention. Whatever it is, she knows it will be difficult for her to deal with. She no longer feels capable of talking to Mikey about such everyday matters, she will have to ask Silas to intervene. As she drives, coolly, expertly, a skill she is quietly proud of, this capacity to negotiate her way through Johannesburg's busy and often dangerous traffic, she deflects from her thoughts the one subject she feels compelled to raise with Mikey: her relationship with him, sullied by her behaviour, that embrace, that kiss, its carnal intent, an act she still cannot explain, except that it came about in 'a moment of madness'.

She knows, too, that this is a rationalization; that she dare not explore in her own self the source of that sexual desire for her son, suppressed now, an uncomfortable knowledge reshaped into an agonized, intellectual concern. She does concede the perverse nature of her hope that Mikey's misbehaviour at varsity involves academic rather than sexual matters, that he has done no more than squander the prospect of a good education.

She parks the car in the reserved area where Dr Johnson has kindly arranged a space for her, considers what her response should be if some more grievous transgression is revealed: Mikey having seduced a lecturer, an older woman, perhaps even Dr Johnson herself. Lydia imagines the woman who phoned: late thirties, early forties, tall and wiry, her blonde hair streaked with distinguished grey, full of nervous energy, reaching an age when her own professional achievements do not quite compensate for the personal deprivation of being single, or divorced, or of having to live with a cold and passionless husband.

Mikey's kind of prey.

In the lift, Lydia realizes, somewhat startled, that this is a profile of herself, with the exception of the professional achievement and the blonde hair. Why are blonde women in particular attracted to him? They find him exotic, she thinks, and then considers how unkind this judgement is to white women. But she strengthens the resolve of her own prejudice: they *do* fall for black men, for the innate sensuality of black skins, those pearls of sweat on dark flanks. White women want black men simply because they are different. Are we not the same, all of us women, just like Priscilla Johnson under our skins?

Dr Johnson meets Lydia in the office of the departmental secretary. Lydia is surprised by the accuracy of the picture she has created of the woman. But there is a steeliness in her, a deep-seated sense of reserve, and of self-preservation, that would enable her to withstand Mikey's diabolical charm.

They sit down in the common room, opposite each other, each

modestly drawing in her exposed knees, sparring, probing. The secretary brings tea on a tray, sets it down on the coffee table, retreats and discreetly shuts the door behind her. Dr Johnson pours the tea, tells Lydia that the matter she wishes to discuss is delicate.

'Make no mistake, Mrs Ali, your son is a good student, brilliant even. He wrote an essay on the origins of the novel that is remarkable, and not only for a student.'

She touches a folder on the table, looks up from her teacup, sees the agitation on Lydia's face, the tightened lips, expectant black eyes.

'To get to the point. His brilliance is his problem, it has made him arrogant, made him think he is beyond reproach. It has given him special access to people and places, access other students do not enjoy. Put bluntly, he has exploited these opportunities. Now, the problem we have is rather sensitive. We could, of course, resolve it through a formal inquiry, but that would destroy reputations, unnecessarily.'

Lydia puts down the cup of tea, untouched, smooths down her skirt.

'I am acting on behalf of a colleague, informally, for now. It started off with young Michael seeing her daughter, a seventeen-year-old. She took him home, he met the family, and so on. However, one thing led to another, and somehow my colleague, the mother, invited Michael to her home when she was alone, daughter at university, husband away. What happened between them is not my concern. What is of concern is her suspicion that Michael took, without permission, something from their home.'

'You're saying that he stole something?' Lydia asks.

'Yes, stole it. I am glad you are so forthright. The problem is that this was not the first thing to go missing. There was also a book.'

'A book?'

'Yes, a rare book. A first edition of Albert Camus's *The Outsider*, signed by the author.'

'It is in French?'

'You know the book?'

'Not the French, no.'

'It is the English translation, a hardcover edition brought out in 1946, by Hamish Hamilton, my colleague tells me.'

'And she, your colleague, wants the book returned?'

Dr Johnson looks at Lydia, who observes the cold pursing of her lips, the faint contempt in her eyes.

'There is a bigger problem, Mrs Ali. After Michael's last visit, she noticed that her husband's gun was missing. Taken from a desk drawer in the study.'

'Let me get this straight, they kept a gun in an unlocked desk drawer?'

'Yes, but that does not excuse the theft.'

'How can she be sure that Mikey, Michael, took it?'

'He was there when the servant was off, the husband away on business, the daughter visiting friends in Cape Town. He was the last one, apart from my colleague . . .'

'She was alone with Michael, at her home?'

'Yes. Look, Shirley's momentary lapse of judgement does not justify . . .' Dr Johnson goes quiet, sips her tea. Her irritation at being involved becomes obvious. 'Mrs Ali, I shall not venture to question why a perfectly respectable woman, successful, prominent, an achiever in her own way, would do such a thing, get involved with a student. But the point is that even sex, wrongful sex, between student and professor, does not justify exploitation.'

'And you think that Michael exploited her?'

'Her vulnerability, an older woman, lonely . . .'

'Bullshit.'

Lydia is surprised by her own vehemence, sits back in her chair. Like two ancient and flustered parents, Lydia and Dr Johnson exchange sighs. They have between them a common weariness. They can do without this sordidness.

'Mrs Ali, Shirley's husband is a collector, he will soon miss the book, or books – she is not sure – and the gun. The book is rare, the gun lethal. Michael must be persuaded not to brag about his acquisition, or how he came by it, if he is into trophy-hunting. You know what youngsters can be like. He owes it to people not to destroy their lives, simply because of their involvement with him.'

Lydia finally sips the cold tea, her empathy with Priscilla Johnson fading. She rises from her seat. 'Tell your colleague – Shirley – I will try and find the book, and the gun, and return them. Also tell her that in future she should fuck men her own age.'

Lydia sits in their quiet backyard, a place as narrowly verdant as she imagines European gardens to be, idly wonders about the family who originally built this house. The grandeur of their dreams, pared down to suit their history, their fear of having to uproot once more, merchants with money, but always prudent, careful with their wealth.

The rage she felt when she left Dr Johnson has subsided. She imagines the Doctor of Literature – must be – still seated in the common room, long after she had left. Dull afternoon shadows on her face. Prissy Priscilla, unshockable, and unfuckable. Not so, her friend and colleague, Shirley. God, what a name. Well, Shirl's not the only one whom Mikey has seduced, reduced to a doting hanger-on. Why does he do it? To shock her, his mother, to demonstrate that he can have women of all ages, that he does not need her, that incest is such a tawdry and unnecessary sin? No, that would be too obvious a demonstration of his freedom from her, from his father, indeed, from his family and everything they stand for: conformity to religion, to the politics of the country.

She sips the tea she has made – ritually heating the teapot, spooning in the exact measure of green leaves, inhaling the jasmine fragrance – acknowledges that she was, in fact, raging at herself when she told Dr Johnson: 'Tell your colleague to fuck men her own age.' She would also sleep with someone younger now, if he – or she – could offer their bodies unselfishly as her instrument of release. From the years, the decades of sexual hunger, a simple, unadorned and unpretentious tapping of the swollen darkness, bruised and discoloured, of the place in which she has imprisoned her sensuality. She no longer needs to protect herself from her rapist, from her husband's fierce but all too transient desires. She wants now to be lowered into an abyss of the flesh, unquestioned and unquestioning, to descend as if she is drowning, she wants the death of her sexual being, and thinks it could only happen dramatically, sinful and sinned against, sacrificed like Sister Catherine on the cross of her Christ's disembodied lust.

The phone rings, jarring with the afternoon's primordial silence. She does not bother to run inside to answer it. Who could it be but her husband or her son? One of the family, perhaps, asking, 'God, Lyd, how are you? We don't hear from you any more!' She is reduced to waiting for the voices of people she has grown tired of, a husband she no longer loves and a son she loves too much.

Through an open window, she hears the answering machine click on, hears her own voice saying, 'We are unable to take your call . . .', and then Mikey saying he will not be home for a few nights, he is staying with friends, but he'll be back in time 'for Dad's party'. A concession he has made, letting them know he is safe. He, too, wants the peace of not being worried about. She goes inside, realizes that she has been waiting for an opportunity to enter Mikey's room. What was once Silas's refuge is now Mikey's citadel. Locked and barricaded against the prying eyes of his parents.

She takes the bunch of keys from Silas's tool cabinet, randomly collected, slipped onto a huge steel ring. Jingling like a jailer, she goes to Mikey's room to find a key that fits. How much dust will have collected since he moved in here, how much disorder will he have created? She is surprised, when the door finally swings open, by the room's tidiness, by the almost Spartan sense of order. Silas's books are crammed into a corner of the bookcase, arranged in strict alphabetical order and therefore easy to retrieve. His mounds of papers have been boxed and labelled, stacked up against a wall according to some plan. How happy he would be with the methodical manner in which the haphazard intellectual treasures of his life have been preserved.

In the freed-up space stands a whole new range of books, mostly novels and poetry. It is the unusual simplicity of some of the spines that attracts her, the splendour of the bold embossing. There's a copy of James Joyce's *Ulysses*, Doris Lessing's *Briefing for a Descent into Hell*, Patrick White's *The Tree of Man*, and, there, the errant copy of Camus's *The Outsider*. She pulls the book gently from the shelf, is surprised by how well preserved it is, unread, it seems. She opens it, feels compelled to bring the pages close to her nose, inhaling their dusty, fragrant odour. She sees the signature, intrigued by the rather schoolboyish handwriting. It says 'Albert Camus', but she has no way of judging its authenticity. She takes out a copy of Richard Wright's *Native Son*, and gives an involuntary cry when she sees a label inside that says: First Edition – Property of the State Library – Not to be Removed from Library Premises.

One by one, she withdraws the books from the shelf, reads inscriptions, various statements of ownership, slips them back into their places. One is a gift from Nadine Gordimer to Nelson Mandela, signed and dated. Lydia stares at the display of stolen books, most of them out of print and very scarce. All have one thing in common: they belong to other people, to individuals, libraries and museums. So, her son is a thief. He steals rare books, for the sake of it, for the pleasure of

249

possessing something beautiful and forbidden, for the simple daring of the act?

She searches through the rest of his belongings, clothes hanging from the old-fashioned picture rail, shirts, underwear, socks neatly stacked in a series of kitbags arranged against the wall. Like someone trained in the art of finding concealed things, she goes methodically through Silas's desk, pulls out the books once more and looks for hidden panels behind the row of purloined spines.

There is no gun. Perhaps it was not taken as a trophy, perhaps it was taken for some other purpose? She sits down, still clutching Camus's book. For once, she does not know what to do. Decisive, *incisive* Lydia, turned to by her family whenever a decision is needed, no matter how painful, deferred to even by Silas.

She could find Mikey. Call Johan Viljoen, or Premula. They live apart, but they'll know where Vinu is. Mikey seems to be with her all the time. But she anticipates the impenetrable expression with which he will greet her enquiries: 'Mikey, did you take a gun from Shirley Graham's study? Mikey, I've seen the books . . . Mikey?' She would be reduced to angry beseeching, to mouthing parental platitudes, how she cared about his welfare, how *much* she cared. No, she did not want to degrade herself, to offer an affectionate hug against his stiffened body, Vinu observing, intrigued, aroused by the guessed-at knowledge of suppressed carnality. The sheer force of its perversity would be enough to make Vinu irresistible to Mikey. 'Fuck me, the way you fuck your mother.' No, she did not want to become a young woman's fantasy, a crude, squatting inducer of orgasms.

She could call Silas, let him find Mikey, let him speak to his son. But Mikey is not Silas's son. Perhaps he knows, perhaps both of them know that there is no biological link between them? Why, should that matter? Silas must have guessed a long time ago.

Why should she do anything? Mikey is nineteen years old, a man, a seducer of older women; in the old days, people as young as eighteen were hanged if found guilty of murder. In Mikey's case, there are no extenuating circumstances. He should take responsibility for his actions.

The phone rings again. This time Lydia answers. It is Julian, phoning to discuss Silas's party. 'Remember, we spoke about giving him something special. Have you come up with anything?'

'Why, yes, I have.'

'Oh good!'

'It is a diary.'

'A diary?'

'Rare, really special, his father's diary. A remarkable book that his mother entrusted to me. Said Silas wouldn't appreciate it.'

'Oh wow!'

'So . . .'

'Well, let's meet and talk about how we present it to him.'

Lydia goes upstairs, retrieves the book. The hiding place is secure – that empty space behind the desk drawers, who would think of looking in there? She remembers when Angelina – Silas's mother, Mikey's Ouma Angel – gave her Ali Ali's diary for safe keeping. 'A lot of history in these pages,' the old woman had said. 'Silas will resent it, the way his father confesses his sins.'

Only women, wombed beings, can carry the dumb tragedy of history around with them. History is a donkey's arse. Who said that? Certainly not in the Bible. What's-his-name? Kazantzakis. *Zorba the Greek*. Bit of macho bullshit.

She is glad for this distraction. She will wrap the gift carefully and lovingly, find just the right kind of paper, dignified but celebratory, rich gold with a bright crimson ribbon. Imperial colours. Hand Silas his heritage, say something short but profound, kiss him on the cheek, then walk away, free of him and his burdensome past.

251

24

It is easy to fire a gun. You point the barrel at the target and pull the trigger. Even a child can do it. In fact, children do it all the time, with toy guns, with their hands – thumb and forefinger pointed with purpose – their stances, learned from films and computer games, at once balletic and athletic.

But Michael's actions – the way he squeezes the trigger rather than tugging at it, the way he aims at the heart and not the face, knowing he will never be able to shoot if the image of tearing skin and splintering bone comes back to him – should not be blamed on external influences, not even on the subliminal stimulus of TV violence that psychologists keep talking about. No, this has been carefully planned, the premeditation precise and logical, where, how, why. He has practised, over and over, the motion of stepping up in front of Johan Viljoen, raising the gun, aiming at a spot left of the breastbone, firing a single shot, shooting again only if the man does not immediately sink to his knees.

He knows that Viljoen is alone every afternoon, he has a half-day maid. At the end of the working day, he always gets up from his desk – he is writing a book, yet another unique account of the struggle – and walks to the edge of the garden. It is five or five thirty. He stops to inspect the gnarled old rose bush growing against the wrought-iron perimeter fence. One of the few houses without a high wall and electrified barriers. He bends down to examine a petal or feel a leaf between his fingers, touching the stem, marvelling at its ability to survive.

Michael will stand under the jacaranda tree, enjoying the shade, waiting for Viljoen to raise his head from his reverential examination of the rose bush, then step up and shoot him.

With luck, there will be no one around. This is a quiet street in a quiet suburb. The silencer reduces the gun's usually booming report to a soft, metallic sound, foreign to most human ears. He should be able to walk away without fuss, stroll down the street, as if he is on his way to the park. There are enough mixed families living here for him to belong, he will not stand out as the 'someone unusual' the police always ask potential witnesses to think about.

Of course, Du Boise will provide a different kind of challenge. He lives in a noisy area, and takes his walks along a busy road. But for now, it is enough to know he is capable of killing another human being.

Viljoen's body falls backwards, not forwards as Michael thought it should. A rose tumbles from a flailing hand, and lies on the grass, as if plucked and abandoned by some casual, vandalizing passer-by.

25

Silas heard about Johan Viljoen's death during a break in the weekly ministerial meeting.

'Premmie's husband?'

'Ex. They were about to be divorced,' the bearer of the tidings said.

'My God, her daughter Vinu, and my son . . .'

People looked up from their papers, waiting for Silas to complete his sentence.

'They're friends,' he said, with a shrug, and fetched a copy of the *Star* to read the details for himself. Viljoen's body had been discovered by a passing jogger at seven o'clock the previous evening. It was unclear, a police spokesman said, whether there was a political motive for the killing, or whether it had been an 'ordinary crime'.

The bulk of the report was devoted to Viljoen's political career – his prison term for sabotage, his years in exile in the Netherlands, his lectureship in history at Leiden University. There were comments from his Parkview neighbours, surprised to discover that this 'quiet man', who seemed to spend so much time fussing about in his garden, was well known in political circles. To them, he had seemed like just another Afrikaner who had 'married strangely' and been lucky enough to retire young.

Silas summoned a secretary, and asked her to send flowers and enquire about the funeral arrangements. It was something the Minister would like to attend. President Mandela himself had sent a personal message to the grieving family and promised a full investigation.

He had just started on the *Mail & Guardian's* obituary – more of a diatribe on crime and the lack of 'political will' on the part of the government to combat it than a tribute to the man himself, never mind the '*Hamba Kahle*, Comrade Viljoen' in the headline – when the Minister returned from his comfort break and the meeting resumed.

A full list of all current files had to be prepared. They had to anticipate a change in Minister and ensure that the changeover would go as smoothly as possible. The present Minister basked in the weary glow of his self-sacrificing generosity. Was he genuinely humble about the prospect of being dropped from the Cabinet or shifted to a less contentious post, Silas wondered, was he generous in his readiness to give way to 'new blood', or was there some calculation involved? Probably, word of this conscientious preparation for transition would reach the new President, and something else would be offered. Silas's speculation about his Minister's motives, and the identification of tasks – his being 'to ensure that the whole TRC process was properly documented, from the Ministry's viewpoint' – swept away the anxiety created by news of Johan Viljoen's death.

The meeting dragged on all afternoon.

Tonight was his fiftieth birthday celebration. Curiously, he had come to think of it as an 'ordeal'. Somehow, the occasion had taken on a different meaning, it was more than a celebration, it was a farewell of sorts. This year was the last but one of the century; they were facing a twilight period, an interregnum between the old century and the new, between the first period of political hope and the new period of 'managing the miracle'. In many ways, his marriage to Lydia seemed to have dissolved. Let tonight be our last night of intimacy, of true friendship.

When he got home, the house was empty. There was a note next to the telephone: 'Terrible news about Johan Viljoen. I am going to pay my respects to Premmie and then going direct to Julian's. He has asked me to help.' The note ended tersely with her signature, in its usual elliptical script. No endearment, no expression of affection. 'Paying respects.' This new and hardened Lydia, acquiring a glib new language. She had her own car now, was free to do things independently. Strange how a mechanical object like a car could hasten the estrangement between people. She no longer needed him, not even for the mundane purpose of having him drive her to her appointments – 'seeing he was going that way anyway.'

He decided to take his time, to soak in a hot bath, sip a glass of cold wine. There was no need to hurry. Why are we so eager to celebrate our own mortality?

26

To get to Julian's house on the crest of Linksfield Ridge, guests had to drive up to a boom, where the names of the drivers and the registration numbers of their cars were recorded. This was a secure area, with only one entrance manned by a private security company. Here, after dark, every black male was a suspect, a potential robber or carjacker, and rape was seen as the horrific accompaniment to 'economic' crimes.

To ensure that there would be no embarrassing incidents, Julian had requested the services of one of the security company's senior officials (white, of course!) for the night. The company obliged. Mr Solomon was a respected resident, had lived up on the Ridge for many years. He was paying for the overtime, in any case.

A procession of cars stopped at the boom, and then pressed on up the winding road. Other residents came out onto their balconies to watch a seemingly endless stream of black people making their way into one of the most exclusive areas in the country. They had heard about the party, Julian Solomon, good family, made their money on the mines. Father was solid. Julian, the son, a bit of a queer fellow, more than in a manner of speaking. Heard his wife left him. He works for Mandela. What can you expect? Plenty of Mercs and BMWs. Probably government issue. Look, isn't that the Minister of Safety and Security? Bloody give him a piece of my mind, if I had the chance!

This was a place that lived up to its clichés. The view of Johannesburg was truly panoramic. On clear days, you could see the blue humps of the Magaliesberg. On rainy days, you were almost in the clouds, surrounded by mist and mystery.

Tonight was cloudless, and it was warm on the sheltered veranda ('It can get cold here, quite high up, you know'). Waiters were serving drinks from trays, but there was also a self-service bar, where the men congregated. They liked to stand, with their drinks in their hands, refilling their glasses as and when they liked. It seemed so elitist, and inhibiting somehow, to be waited upon all the time.

Julian and Kate greeted the guests, told them where to leave the occasional – and superfluous – coat, a burdensome bag ('I carry my life around with me!'). Those who had brought gifts, put them on a table at the front door. Greetings were warm, everyone hugged, exchanged kisses (one on each cheek, in the European fashion). Names were dropped, but only in the asking.

How are you?

Well, thanks.

And how is the Minister, the President, the Archbishop?

A nation superficially well, as convention demanded. The Archbishop's assistant dared not betray his anguish and say: 'The poor Archbishop has cancer, he'll have to go for treatment, chemotherapy and all. You know what hell that can be.'

Silas found Lydia, they hugged, stood beside each other for a while, then drifted away to mix with the other guests.

'Ah! Silas Ali! How on earth did you make it to fifty? The boere couldn't kill you, but the TRC damned nearly did, no?' someone said.

'Yes, you should do what old Tutu did, go and live in America or somewhere, now that you've put the cat among the pigeons,' someone else added.

'Ag, ou Silas, in the end I think you guys did a good job, you know, juggling those TRC commissioners, the old security people and our own fellers.'

Wry, guarded comments were made about the Truth Commission, about its controversial report, and about Silas's role in it all. But this was a time to celebrate, there would be no serious talk – not just yet, anyway. Most of the guests were happy to forget the 'affairs of state' that preoccupied them in their daily lives.

Julian allowed people enough time to sip drinks, renew acquaintances, embrace old comrades, distantly kiss ex-lovers, then called the gathering to order. His peculiar brand of humour always struck a chord. 'We have come together,' he said, 'to help an old friend prepare himself for his appointment in Samara.' He made a brief speech, so did Kate; both were quick, having agreed beforehand to leave all the maudlin talk to Silas and Lydia. There was also an undeclared truce between Kate and Lydia. Earlier on, they had even made small talk about how tired everyone was, how ready for a holiday, Christmas was coming 'none too soon'. Then, the gifts that people had purchased collectively – selected according to the lowest common denominator of the contributors' tastes – were presented to Silas. His colleagues gave him a copy of the TRC report, the full set of five volumes. A gift of true irony, someone said.

Then came the surprise. Silas was a man of history, and – 'Funny, isn't it, how people who "manage" great historical processes, sometimes forget their own . . .' Julian caught himself about to lecture and hastily said, 'Well, you know what I mean.' Still, Silas had to be encouraged to remember his own rich past. Lydia stepped up, and Julian handed her the wrapped and ribboned diary that they had kept hidden from view. They had choreographed the moment beforehand. Silas must not even be allowed to guess what was in the package.

'Silas's mother,' Lydia said, 'we knew her as Ma Angel, Angelina was her real name, entrusted this rather special . . .' She paused, as if struck by a sudden thought, and searched for words. 'It is a piece of history, personal, extremely private in many ways, but it also belongs to all of us. But, let Silas show it to you himself.'

Silas took the package from Lydia, started undoing the wrapping rather delicately, and then ripped it off. She was not sure whether this was eagerness or irritation. He held the book aloft for a moment, saying almost to himself, 'It is my father's journal, my God, where did you get this?'

Lydia saw the grey face of a man suddenly uncomfortable with his surroundings. What am I doing here? he was asking himself. She knew that look: he was in danger of losing control, the sediment of a brutally suppressed self-awareness was seeping out. My father did not give a damn about me until he was on his deathbed. Shall I proclaim to the world that I am a bastard, branded by this unlikely oxymoron of a name?

For a moment, it seemed that Silas would draw in his shoulders, hand the book back to Lydia and stalk away, a tsotsi from Newclare, spurning an unwanted gift, scorning the sentimentality of it all. But just as his guests were beginning to shift about uneasily, he recovered his composure, straightened himself. 'This is all too much for me; remember, I am just a bushie lightie. And here I am, standing on top of the world, literally, among friends, among comrades, among colleagues. Now, we have to thank Julian, and Kate, and of course, my dear wife Lydia.'

He drew her close and kissed her on the lips. Then, with his arm around her waist, he looked about and asked: 'Is Michael here?' Lydia stiffened as he searched the crowd. 'I saw him a moment ago.'

Michael raised his arm, somewhat shyly. He had been standing in the shadow of an awning by the pool. People urged him to join his parents, and he made his way to the front. They stood with their arms around each other, celebrating father, proud son, loving mother, for a moment. Then Silas said in a hoarse voice: 'Enough of this. I need a drink!'

Amidst applause, they split up, each trying to find some corner to escape into, where they could recover their own separate equilibriums.

The party divided, inevitably, into the dancers and the drinkers. The latter stood on the veranda, under a canopy of smog-misted stars, drinking now with true ardour. The time for sipping, genteelly, delicately, was over. They talked, loudly, about the things that preoccupied them. Politics, the upcoming liberation movement conference.

Everyone knows, of course, who will succeed the Old Man. But he cannot run a country by himself, he needs good people around him, loyal but competent, people not afraid of taking risks, not scared of dirtying their hands. Above all, with the will to change things, transform this country in 'substance as well as form'. This is a time for passion, for going beyond hope. 'We have done our reconciling: now we must build!' someone says vehemently, creating a momentary, admiring lull around him.

Inevitably, the newly released TRC report dominates the discussion.

'After all this time, we've got a big fat report, but we're nowhere nearer the truth.'

'That's because we always put our faith in priests. They don't have it in them to hold those apartheid thugs accountable!'

'Ja, it's the same old story, the so-called need to be balanced.'

Inside, the dancers twisted and gyrated to Julian and Kate's eclectic, contrasting musical tastes. The Jazz Pioneers, Sting, Erykah Badu, even Boom Shaka. This youthful kwaito brought everyone onto the dance floor, trying to imitate the sexy movements perfected by their children – hips barely moving, trembling almost – to whoops of laughter. To be dancing, to be moved by pulsating rhythms, however unfamiliar, was a joy in itself. Never mind the lack of practice, or the fact that ageing bodies lose their subtlety, their ability to follow the mind's dictates. Good dancing demands discipline, anticipation, timing. So what? This isn't a dancing competition, this is a party, Comrade Silas's party. Enjoy! Happeeee!

For some of the party-goers, dancing was a serious pursuit, even if the opportunity seldom came along. They were naturally better than others, in touch with the music and its rhythms, able to 'read' a partner with the touch of a hand laid gently on a hip. Lydia was one of them, a good dancer, especially when the dancing demanded that the partners hold each other as they moved. She had practised that very simple but defining rhythm since childhood: one-two-three together. In coloured families, it was said, kids learned to dance before they learned to read or swim. It was a necessary skill, one that had all the saving social graces you would need.

These days, Lydia very rarely danced. The last time must have been at that party where Mikey and Mireille, showing off on the dance floor, betrayed the deeper intimacy between them. Dancing demanded a closeness that she found daunting. Especially when it came to partnering strangers. And most of the people at this party were strangers.

She was delighted when Alec and Gracie finally showed up. Jackson and Mam Agnes had stayed at home; Jackson wasn't feeling too well. Why had Alec become such a stranger lately, Lydia wanted to know? She accepted his non-committal answer ('Very busy, the holidays coming and all'), not because she believed him, but to avoid a long and intense discussion about the 'things he was going through'. Somebody, somewhere, is always 'going through' something. The law of human development.

When Gracie went to find Silas, to wish him for his birthday, Lydia suggested to Alec that they dance – in the old-fashioned way.

'Are you up to it?' he asked. 'I mean, your feet don't bother you at all any more?'

She smiled at him, offered him her outstretched arms. 'Try me.'

Suddenly, Alec and Lydia swept through the crowd, doing a foxtrot with innate skill, even though the music wasn't exactly right. Alec stumbled once, but they had about them a grace that quickly cleared the floor. The music ended, and they stood in the middle of the crowd, laughing and panting. The sheer joyousness of their sudden flourish brought spontaneous applause.

As they walked back to the seats they had appropriated close to the piano ('A baby grand!' Alec said, as if he knew anything about pianos), Lydia saw a young man looking at her, boldly, his eyes a bastard green, set deep within a dark face. She looked away, tried to engross herself in Gracie and Alec's small talk. Meanwhile, Julian, inspired by the recent display of dancing skill, had switched the music: a fast Latin American dance number.

The word 'pulsate' would later go through Silas's mind, though he would not remember whether it was a rumba or a samba. He had come in to get away from the drinkers, who kept on pressing celebratory glasses into his hands he was not in the mood to drink, and watched a young man approach Lydia, saw her decline, saw Gracie and Alec urging her to go.

Then she was on the floor with the young man, dancing with him, a curious modesty in the movement of their bodies held so closely together. You only dare to do this if you have the skill, a perfect sense of timing, the ability to blend with your partner's movements, and, if you are the woman, a willingness to abandon yourself to the man's rhythm, the demands of his body. This kind of dancing flourishes in macho societies, Silas remembered reading somewhere.

But Lydia was enjoying herself.

'My name is João,' the young man said. 'João Dos Santos Honwana.'

'That's an expensive name. I'm Lydia.'

'Call me João.'

He dances naturally, moving his hips and shoulders in a way most South African men find difficult. This movement reveals an openness, an inability to conceal one's motives. The men she knows are stiff in their hips or shoulders. A sign of coyness, they expect you to anticipate what's on their mind. Makes it difficult to predict their next move. Makes dancing with them, let alone anything else, a disaster.

They dance close to each other, not only because of the crowded room, but also because this is what their way of dancing demands, being near enough to feel the music in your partner, to remain *congruous* with each other. She repeats the word in her mind, its ostentatious ring brings a smile to her face.

João smiles back. He draws her even closer, then she deflects his attentions by taking her body into a different rhythm barely noticeable to the observer, but he feels it, knows that she is undermining his sense of control. He relents, she directs him now, until her older, more practised movements slow him down, but keep him at an appropriate distance. This subtle battle of their inner rhythms brings a new sense of grace to both of them. When the music stops, they hug each other spontaneously.

'You are beautiful, Mrs Ali,' he whispers.

She pushes him away, discreetly. She is aware that Silas is watching them. João walks her back to her seat. Such old-world manners. Not since she was a young woman at the social-centre dances in Durban has anyone walked her back to her seat. She allows him to, out of politeness, and curiosity.

He asks her to dance on two more occasions, displaying his versatility, and testing hers. Dancing a samba is very different from dancing a quickstep. They succeed beyond her expectations, are able to relax, laugh at the rare misstep, she finds herself leaning against him when the music slows.

'Hey, what's going on?' Gracie demands.

'Gracie! He's just a kid!'

'Watch it, Sis, everyone else is.'

Lydia looks around, sees Silas's stony gaze, and Kate nearby, offering him her hatchet-faced solidarity. What an ugly woman, Lydia thinks, how *could* Mikey have slept with her?

Then Julian decides to play showman. 'Time for a game,' he says. 'Let's see who can dance to *this*. Whoever makes a mistake – and we'll be the judge of that – is out. Last couple left are the winners!'

He puts on Ravel's *Bolero*, people select their partners, take to the floor, some already falling about with mock clumsiness. Lydia looks directly at Silas, inviting him, daring him to dance with her, but he turns away and is gone from sight. She shrugs, demonstrates to Alec and Gracie that it is Silas who is avoiding her. She searches for João. He stands waiting at the edge of the jostling crowd.

They start dancing, held apart, brought close by the music, slow, improvising the sinuous, gypsy steps they imagine are appropriate to the *Bolero*. Face to face. He looks directly at her.

'Lydia?'

'Yes?'

'I want you.'

'Just like that?'

'Yes.'

'Here?'

'Yes.'

The music speeds up, they have no time to conclude their conversation. They are both distracted, stumble, someone touches João on his shoulder to indicate that they are out. 'Sorry! Rules are rules, and the two of you have just made a mistake.'

João and Lydia drift off, the wild, somewhat incoherent antics continue on the dance floor. Outside, there is a cool breeze. Drinkers sit slumped in chairs, a group of talkers in a circle continue their animated debate on the merits of the TRC.

'My husband is here, João.'

'There is a coldness between you.'

'Don't you dare to judge what is between us,' she says, and walks away.

She sips water at the bar, chats to a few people, then slowly walks back to the veranda. João is leaning on the stone balustrade, staring out at the murky sky.

'João,' she whispers.

He looks around.

'Come,' she says, motioning with her head.

She leads him to a room she noticed earlier, a strange space, empty except for an old billiard table, covered with a dust cloth. It must once have been a family recreation room. TV, music centre, billiards, or is it snooker they played when entertaining guests?

She leans up against the billiard table, pulls João to her. 'How old are you?'

'Does it matter? Twenty-five,' he answers.

He senses her beginning to doubt, kisses her gently, runs his fingers over her closed eyelids.

At the end of the party, Silas was too drunk to drive home, or so it seemed. Julian found him sitting at the bottom of the steps leading down into the tropical garden. His only indulgence, modest Julian. This grand house with its grand view, the extravagance with which its separate functions had been demarcated: sleeping areas from recreation space, the 'family unit' from the 'public areas' where guests were received and visitors entertained. This had been Val's vision, to create areas of private serenity, modelled, she said, on the architecture of Moorish Spain. 'And you are so *kosherly* Jewish,' Julian had remarked, somewhat churlishly, when she first described her 'concept' for the house she wanted built.

'It's my money,' she had said. 'One day, if you ever get your inheritance, you can create a little space of your own.' Well, that inheritance had come through, and he had been able to create this little garden.

'Do you know, Silas, there are plants in here that require just the right amount of moisture, the right amount of sunlight, at the right time, for just the right period. Nature is so fucken anally retentive.'

Silas smiled his wan smile.

How did you get down here, anyway? Julian wanted to ask. You have to pass right through Val's labyrinthine mind to find this little corner. My place of exile. She made sure of that. In the end, he hoisted Silas up, and said: 'The party's over, let's go home.'

Kate drove Silas back to Berea.

'I'll be fine,' he said, in anticipation of her question: Are you okay? Lydia thus remained an unspoken, and unspeakable, presence between them. Kate had seen her disappearing with João into the back of the house. If he had not closed off the subject, Kate might have told him – as consolation – that she had seen João later, sitting by himself and drinking wine from a bottle, although she would have kept to herself the empty look on his face, the aftermath of sex, an unbearable loneliness that comes with the absence of tenderness (people 'uncouple', detach themselves from each other: how easily intimacy is lost).

'Oh God,' Kate said, simply for the sake of it.

'What are you lamenting?' Silas asked, then promptly dropped back into a drunken daze.

She knew he was pretending. She had seen him drunk before, he became boisterous, argumentative, aggressive even. Not this defeated man, resigned to his fate, to the humiliating gossip, the patronizing sympathy.

Hold on, she said to herself, don't be a hypocrite. You've done the same thing with others, including Mikey. But not while their partners were in the same house, and not when there were fifty other people milling about. Ah, what courage, what outrageous bravery, Kate thought, her admiration for Lydia's boldness grudging but irresistible.

They stopped outside the Ali household in Berea.

'Silas . . .'

He was out of the car already, and waving her off.

'I'm okay,' he said, his voice echoing in the dark street. The street lamps were out. All that he wanted was the right to sit in this living city darkness and watch the world go by – surreptitiously, of course. But all that he kept on seeing, over and over, was Lydia naked, the young man João propped up on his arms, between her upraised legs. He saw her knees the moment she pressed them against him, against his skin so black it was almost blue. An old township joke, we too have our little racist images. She drew João to her, held him as he shuddered.

Shards of moonlight on the green baize, their lovemaking – they were fucking, for God's sake – had drawn up the dust cloth the way a sheet is drawn up on a bed. On a billiard table, at a party, at his birthday party, in someone else's house.

Despite the frantic attempts of his jagged mind, he could not transform the scene into something sordid, so enabling him to dismiss it, to call her cheap, a whore. There was something so ineluctably beautiful about Lydia pulling the young man to her, embracing his black body in her lovely olive-skinned arms.

He would have to live with that. His wife had found release at last from both her captive demons: from Du Boise and from himself. Now not every man would be a rapist to her.

27

Daybreak, when the Bilal bhangs.

Michael had heard the expression from Sadrodien, a mixture of Arabic and Malay, describing the call to prayer that the 'Bilal' makes at each of the five prescribed prayer hours. Michael had since learnt that one of the Prophet Mohamed's first adherents was a black man named Bilal (a faithful servant, a freed slave?). For his foresight and courage – those were dangerous times, the first Muslims had many enemies – Bilal was accorded the honour of calling the fledgling band of faithful to prayer. Now, everywhere in the world, five times a day, a man – European travel brochures call him a 'muezzin' – climbs a winding staircase to the top of a tower, supporting his bony knees with his hands, so that it seems he has added an extra element to the ritual of worship, and proclaims to the world: Allah u Akbar! God is Great. Bilal the man has been transformed by time and myth from person into concept.

Not all Bilals are black, Michael thinks. But here in Newclare, of course, he is, a Somali émigré, poor and pious. Michael is there, at the gates of the Griffith Street Mosque, when the Newclare Bilal bhangs the dawn salaat. He watches the faithful arrive, they smile indulgently: so this is the prodigal son that Imam Ismail is trying to bring back into the fold!

When the Moulana arrives, surprise flickers in his eyes. 'Wait for me in the classroom,' he tells Michael.

Michael sits on the floor, his knees drawn up against his chest. He is exhausted, light-headed from lack of sleep. The place and the hour, as well, bring upon him a dreamlike euphoria.

He remembers: he had taken a taxi from Julian's place, long before the party ended, was dropped off outside his home in Berea. But the world beyond that door seemed small, Lilliputian. He imagined that the house had become a labyrinth of narrow tunnels, booby-trapped, rigged with concealed trapdoors through which the unsuspecting visitor might fall. Alice in Mandela's Wonderland. Why Mandela? That came later, he thinks. He had turned away from the house, carefully retreating as if trying to allay the fears of some suspicious watcher.

He had walked down the hill to Louis Botha Avenue, then to Norwood, where a street party was taking place. Dancing and drinking in the street, loud music, glass against glass like the clash of metal, a loud, mad-hatter merriment, party-goers with smiles permanently painted onto their faces.

He remembers: Lydia lying on the billiard table, that young Mozambican, João, perched above her, birdlike, a heron, uncommonly black, his awkwardness given grace by her arched body. Silver shadows lighting up the loveliness of their coupling: green upon her olive skin, deep blue against his dark, dark back. She held him, no more than that, moored him, as if to prevent him from drifting into space, his head in her hands, whispering in his ear, as if instructing him in the art of sex. On the other side of the room, lit up by a full moon, stood Silas, staring intently, like a voyeur. Then he stumbled away, as if intoxicated.

He remembers: he had wandered away from Grant Avenue, away from the theatrical, staged revelry, along dark streets, until the world was quiet again, and he could hear the wind rustling in the trees, a true and solitary peacefulness. Somewhere, what seemed like hours later, he had come upon a small convoy of cars pulling up outside a house. Some important person in a Mercedes-Benz. Blue lights began to flash on the roof of the leading car when he stopped to watch. A warning: move along. But he stood still, watching as the cars waited for gates to trundle open on a rail.

Who is the VIP? he wondered. It would be easy to assassinate him. What else are they good for but dying famous deaths? The Mercedes-Benz had darkened windows. They become famous in order to crave privacy.

Then a window in the car rolled down, and Nelson Mandela smiled at him. 'What are you doing out so late, young man, and all alone?'

He was stunned, tongue-tied. He must have walked all the way down to Mandela's residence in Houghton. He wanted to extend his hand, offer a greeting; then, incongruously, he remembered the gun in his pocket, and stepped back.

The President looked at him quizzically. 'Are you afraid of me?' he asked.

'No, sir.'

'Do you need help?'

'I'm not far from home,' he remembers stammering, before waving to the President and his increasingly restive bodyguards, and walking away. To the freeway. A passing motorist had stopped, looked him over carefully, then offered him a lift (perhaps his stooped, shivering stance, that vulnerable look he instinctively assumed when he was being examined, made him appear harmless).

Through the rest of the night, he remained aware of the gun in his pocket, pressing its presence on him. He had practised pulling it out rapidly, because that might be the only way he would get close enough to Du Boise. Would he really have shot that grand old man, he wonders now, as something in his mind was subliminally suggesting when he stood before Nelson Mandela's open window?

The shuffle of many feet, voices still solemn from the prayers they have said. Soon Imam Ismail comes in, finds Michael asleep, his head resting on his knees. Ismail takes off his cloak and lays it over the boy's shoulders. Let him dream his solitary dreams. The way to heaven is a lonely road.

Michael awakens, startled. He removes the cloak from his shoulders, sniffs the strange odour, incense and smoke. Imam Ismail rises from a desk.

'My one indulgence. The hubble-bubble pipe. How is my refugee today?'

Michael smiles. 'I need a favour.'

'Another one? Michael, how will you pay all this back?'

Michael removes a disc from his pocket, hands it to Moulana Ismail. 'A full list of the next government's legislative programmes, anti-terror measures, the creation of a special unit to monitor extremist groups, and also some references to which of their agents are inside the different organizations. You can work out who they are, a simple process of elimination.'

Ismail looks a little disappointed.

'It is all I have to offer, for now.'

'I am sure it will be of some use to someone. But it is the words you use that disturb me.'

'My words?'

270

'Young man, if you talk like them, you soon become one of them. They are all alike, these silent soldiers, not enough imagination, so they use these dead words. Now, what is the favour you need?'

'A passage to India.'

'What?'

'I found out about the Kacholie Society, they have a student exchange programme. Even send some of them to the home village.'

'You want to become a "gham" boy, a village returnee? You know that the traffic is mostly this way?'

'It will only be for a while.'

'And in the meantime?'

'A place to stay.'

'To hide.'

'Yes, Moulana.'

'And you have already done what drives you into hiding?'

'Part of it.'

'And the other part cannot be deferred or cancelled?'

'No.'

'Are' baap. Yes, I have somewhere for you to stay until we can get you to India.'

28

Silas sat quietly on the veranda, in the wobbly wicker chair that was one of the few things they had brought with them from the township. A relic from the past, but fitting for an increasingly ramshackle house. And as for this 'veranda' thing, what a lot of shit. This is a stoep; verandas only existed in places like Linksfield, where Julian lived.

The grief was in his heart now, a dull, embedded presence, as if he had just detected something wrong with its beat. But it *was* grief, undeniable sorrow, that sense of loss he had sworn he would never succumb to. Lydia had finally left him. Her car was not parked in its usual place, under the old jacaranda, which would have to come down one of these days because it was 'foreign' and invasive. That car had become the real instrument of her freedom. Gave her the ability to cover great distances without his help.

Where was she? Well, he could only hope that she was safe. Perhaps that – his concern for her safety – could be his excuse for tracking her down? No, it was too late, she was gone, that scene on the billiard table, so staged, so cheaply cinematic – or cinematically cheap – had been her public declaration of freedom. He was glad she had chosen a black man as her medium of expression, even if he was so young, so young and athletic. Involuntarily, he pulled in his stomach. God, he'd have to do something about that. Perhaps make use of that lifetime gym membership. Up there with the best of them, sweating and straining to remove the inches of flab that his body had so slyly put on over the years.

He heard a noise inside. Was Lydia home after all? Certainly not Michael. This was his night for communing with the loonies in Newclare, monking with the mystics. He had a sudden fear: did Michael see his mother slip away with black João, did he see them fucking?

God, he had to stop going on about 'black this' and 'black that'. He was surprised by this preoccupation with race. Perhaps he had been denying it for too long: who we are is still determined by what colour we are. The kid who fucked my wife is Mozambican, the son of a diplomat, training as a doctor in Portugal, off to Cuba for the work experience, some in-the-know wag had told Silas when João was dancing with Lydia. How could he hope to compete? Township Silas, civil-servant Silas, greying and paunchy, versus exotic black João?

Would he have been so philosophical if the man whom Lydia had enticed into an abandoned playroom was white? White men can't fuck. Now white women on the other hand . . .

'Stop this!' he said out loud.

The door behind him slowly swung open. A slight movement in the shadows, a woman's movement, the lisp of silk against a silken skin.

'Lydia?' he said, standing up.

Vinu emerged from the darkness, came up to him. 'I did not ask you to!' she said in a low voice, striking at him with her bunched-up fists. 'I did not ask you to!'

'Hey!'

Someone paused in the street. God, what would they think? Typical Berea residents, melodrama in the middle of the night. He held her wrists.

'Why, Michael, why?'

'Vinu! I am not Michael!'

She looked up at him, slumped against his chest. He held her, the way he would have held his daughter, the way he sometimes longed to reach out and hold Michael. He led her indoors and helped her sit down on the settee, went to make tea. Hot and sweet, said to be good for people suffering a nervous trauma. What has Michael done?

He took the tea and a packet of biscuits back into the living room. Vinu was lying on her side, staring into the swathe of shadows cast by the moon, a full and dirty yellow tonight. The city's pollution was becoming intolerable. What time was it? Did it matter? He wanted to ask: what did Michael do? But first some sustenance. He offered her a biscuit, which she took and absently nibbled on.

'Here, have some tea.'

She sat up, gazed at him. Her eyes were dry. She had no tears left, but her lip trembled, as she tried to weep.

'Please hold me,' she said.

He sat down next to her, held her in his arms. Chastely,

protectively, feeling good about being able to comfort her, a tender, fatherly warmth emanating from his chest. She put her hand into his shirt. He remembered unbuttoning it when he was examining his belly out there on the stoep. Her hand was cool, gentle, resting against his skin.

They must have fallen asleep like that, Vinu leaning into Silas, her hand on his stomach. He must have dreamed of her, her nakedness gilded by the last glow of the moon before it sank behind the rim of garbage-clotted hills, the crumbling ramparts of apartment blocks. She has a down of bastard gold, he thought, the gift of indelible beauty that we bushies carry about like a second skin.

When Silas awoke, he was glad that Vinu was gone.

29

Michael alights from the taxi in Jan Smuts Avenue, some distance from the Killarney Mall. He walks slowly, having calculated how long it will take him to reach the Mall. He'll be there at least ten minutes before Du Boise usually arrives. He stops to buy a newspaper, he does not want to hang about the place, creating a presence that a potential witness might note. He is a familiar figure on the Kombi-taxi routes now, but he has established a routine. No, we saw nothing abnormal, the drivers will tell investigators, no one we haven't seen before.

So who is François du Boise? Does he have a character, a persona, is he more than a white man, a former security policeman, a rapist and torturer? The question about Du Boise comes to mind unexpectedly. Michael tries to fight it off. He must not allow himself to be distracted. The man is a rapist, my father, yes, the 'sower of my seed', as the saying goes. But that is a mere biological detail. To dispel the growing image of a frail old man (slightly stooped, cancer-ravaged skin protected by clothes that are too heavy for this weather, an Andy Capp hat pulled low over his eyes), he ticks off Du Boise's biographical details, as if on a checklist of mundane facts.

Born April 1936 near Ficksburg, Orange Free State. The son of an impoverished farmer sub-letting a plot on the land he once owned. The predator not some foreign bank, some Jew or Englishman, but a fellow Afrikaner. A truly cannibalistic tribe. Educated in Ficksburg, then the family moved, first to Bloemfontein, then to Vereeniging in the Transvaal. His father found work in the steel mills, became a foreman. An ex-farmer making good progress in an unfamiliar trade, on the backs of the black workers he supervised.

François completed Standard Eight, went to work in the steel mills as well. Fathers opened doors for their sons. Those nepotistic dynasties that messed up this country. François completed his matric by correspondence. Showed some enterprise. Then joined the police in 1957, already twenty-one years old. Must have felt uncomfortable among his fellow trainees, pimply-faced eighteen-year-olds.

Two years' training, uniformed constable for three years, then the detective squad for another three. Studied political criminology – whatever that is – part-time. Transferred to the security police in 1965. They knew the 'war' was coming, brought the most capable of their people into the security forces. Stationed at Vaal Headquarters until 1969, then transferred to the Soweto branch.

Took him another nine years – and how many rapes? – to reach my mother. He was forty-two years old, she only eighteen. He married into a good family, that opened even more doors. Two children, one works as an advocate at the Appeals Court in Bloemfontein. Not bad for the son of a security policeman. His daughter is a housewife, married to a businessman. Lives in Cape Town.

My half-brother and half-sister! Imagine that.

Michael leans up against a pillar at the entrance to the Mall. With a little imagination, the architect could have created a colonnade, cool and mysterious, not this ugly, pillared monstrosity. He sees Du Boise taking his stooped-walk shortcut through the filling station. Now he enters the car park, walks up the incline towards the lower part of the Mall. Michael steps out from the late afternoon shadow, Du Boise is still below him.

'Du Boise.'

Du Boise looks up at Michael, pushes his cap back out of habit, the sun sinking sharply in the west blinds him. He cocks a hand over his eyes as he peers up. It is as if Michael has been given a signal, as if this is a ceremonial execution and the condemned man has had his blindfold fixed. Michael raises the gun, sees the fleeting horror in Du Boise's eyes, then the sudden look of acknowledgement. He has been waiting for such a moment for a long time now. Du Boise seems unafraid, a smile begins to form on his thin mouth.

Du Boise's complexion is unnaturally white, heavily smeared with cream. Of course, his cancer. Michael sees the bits of flaking skin, those tired, red-rimmed eyes, the bitter half-smile, sees himself mirrored in the sweat breaking through the powdery brow. That could be my face one day, my thin body (how pot-bellied and red-faced he might have been were it not for the cancer!).

My heritage, he says in a whisper, unwanted, imposed, my history, my beginnings.

Michael fires – twice – directly into Du Boise's face, forgetting his carefully worked-out plan: shoot into the heart, it is quieter, tends to attract less attention. He wants to obliterate Du Boise's face, wipe away that triumphant, almost kindly expression, leave behind nothing but splintered bone and shattered skin.

Then he hurries away, not waiting to see which way the body will tumble. He walks briskly down the road. On the corner of Oxford and Riviera there are numerous taxis. He will take one into the city, then a fifteen-minute walk to Fordsburg. He has to be at the Oriental Plaza by 6.30. At Moola's Silk Bazaar, he is to introduce himself.

'Salaam u aleikum, I am Noor.' The Prophet's light. One of his most devoted disciples.

Someone will drive him to Lenasia, drop him off at the Nurul Islam Hall. From there, he will be transported to a scholar's retreat near Potchefstroom in the North West Province. India comes later, much later, after he has learnt enough about being a Muslim to perhaps become one.

Michael does not look back, does not wait for the inevitable cry, the first frantic voice that sets off a tumult: Look, that man is bleeding! Is he dead? Oh my God, look at his face! Someone help, call the police!

He, too, is going to a death of sorts. Michael is to die, Noor will be incarnated in his place.

May Michael's truth live on after him.

30

Lydia learns of Du Boise's death from a television news report. She is in a hotel room in Kimberley, some five hundred kilometres south of Johannesburg, on the less fashionable route to Cape Town. She has just come in from a rather lonely dinner in the Steers Diner, a 'franchised eatery' attached to the franchised hotel chain. The room, with its mock Texan décor, stucco walls and stained wood, was empty, and as a consequence desolate. Such places demand noise, loud voices, the drink-driven sociability of computer consultants, today's equivalent of travelling salesmen. It is the twenty-third of December, these 'Lone Rangers' have gone home to their families.

'François du Boise was shot down in the parking lot of the Killarney Mall, in broad daylight, while thousands of shoppers thronged the centre, doing last-minute Christmas purchases. No one seems to have observed the incident, and no arrests have been made. Du Boise was this evening identified as a former security policeman who had applied to the TRC for amnesty. It is not clear which apartheid-era crimes he was seeking amnesty for.'

Lydia's heart goes cold. She turns the television off, sits in the chair, listens to the sounds outside, cars passing by at a leisurely pace, people talking, the hum of the air-conditioner. It can get really hot here, 25 degrees tonight.

She calls home, lets the phone ring for a while, and is about to replace the receiver when Silas answers.

'Lydia!'

'Hello, Silas.'

'Are you all right?'

'Yes, Silas. About Du Boise . . .'

'I know.'

'Mikey, where is Mikey?'

She listens to his sigh, pictures his weariness, the way he idly scratches his scalp, releasing tiny showers of dandruff that settle on his shoulders.

'Gone, gone I think . . .'

'Where, Silas?'

'I have no idea.' Something in him is stiffening.

'Listen, Lydia, I don't know where you are or how you are, and I don't need to be interrogated . . .'

'I'm sorry.'

'It's okay. I'll start looking tomorrow.'

'Are they looking for him?'

'You mean the police? No, at least not yet. Look, it doesn't mean that he's involved, does it?'

She wants to tell him about the gun, about Shirley what's-her-name, about Priscilla Johnson and her voice of doom, she wants to warn him: they'll hear about Du Boise's death, listen to the vague descriptions of a young man seen hurrying away from the scene, they'll tell the police. That famous liberal conscience, tell the truth in the face of a crime, even if it means betraying your own guilty secret. But Silas has other, less dreadful concerns, God bless his selfish soul.

'Look, Lydia, about the other night . . .'

'What about it?'

'I was there, I saw, perhaps Michael did as well.'

'Oh my God, no.'

'Lydia, we can sort it out. There are things I need to tell you too.'

No, no, she is not going to listen to his sordid confessions. He always goes into such detail. 'Silas, it is over, it is better this way.'

She remains quiet, hopes that her silence will signal her determination to end their relationship, this marriage that had become a farce.

'Where are you?'

'I am safe, please tell Mam Agnes and Jackson.'

'Okay.'

'Silas, I'm sorry.'

'That's okay, it is for the best, as you say.'

She fears his platitudes most of all. His clichés have a way of undermining her resolve, making him seem so human, so vulnerable.

'Goodbye, Silas, I'll call.'

She puts the phone down, lies down on the bed. She needs to rest if she is to continue her journey, it will require an early start in the morning. Or she could get up now and return home immediately. She undresses, gets into bed, throws the covers off, it is so hot. She is covered in a fine sheen of sweat. Then she remembers João, his whisper, 'I love you, oh, how I love you, Lydia!' After one fuck, he loves her. God!

She gets up, stuffs what little clothing she has with her into her bag, decides to check out and press on. She could be in Cape Town by ten or eleven in the morning. She has to pay for a full night, the clerk says. Lydia shrugs, pays in cash. She is surprised that Silas didn't ask: are you all right for money? Silas the provider, the protector. Perhaps he knows that she has withdrawn everything from their joint savings account. Most of it is hers, anyway. He never knew how to save. But he is a generous soul, materially.

At the all-night filling station, she asks the attendant which other towns have 24-hour services? 'Head for Victoria West. This little auntie should get you there on a tank.' He grins. 'Don't try for Beaufort West. Too far. And ma'am, try not to stop in lonely spots.'

She thanks him for his kindness.

Kimberley's lights disappear behind her. The road is quiet, a stiff breeze from the west tugs at the car. She has to concentrate, that will keep her awake. Soon the radio reception becomes erratic, comes and goes, more static than music. She slips in the tape that sits in the mouth of the tape deck. A compilation of greatest hits. Paul Simon and Ladysmith Black Mambazo, 'Diamonds on the soles of her shoes . . .'

She begins to fret about the distance, tries to calculate how many kilometres per litre of petrol the handbook said she would get from the car, driving at a reasonable speed. The Karoo is a desolate place. It can get very cold at night, even in summer. A semi-desert.

She thinks about the last time they passed through here, just after the exiles began to come home in 1990. A rare holiday combined with Silas's political meeting in Cape Town. Mikey asleep at the back, Silas driving. She provided the entertainment, twirled the dials, found radio stations, music, the news every hour, passed him coffee, sweets, peeled the bananas. Leaned over to cover Mikey when he stirred and the blanket slipped off.

Now she thinks about Mikey again. Where are you, my son? Are you safe, are you warm? Again the temptation to slow down, turn back.

A car overtakes, a family on holiday. BMW, going like the devil. The speeding car's lights erase the dark splendour of the world. Then it is gone from sight, and the stars are back. The voice of Leonard Cohen fills the car.

The rain falls down on last year's man
An hour has gone by
And he has not moved his hand

She puts her foot down. Says in the book that it can do one-thirty, one-forty kilometres per hour comfortably. She will concentrate now on getting through the Karoo, try to make Victoria West before morning, Beaufort West by eight or so, pass through the Hottentots Holland tunnel by midday. This is no place to be alone, despite its beguiling beauty.

Time and distance, even this paltry distance, will help to free her. Burden of the mother. Mother, wife, lover, lover-mother, lover-wife, unloved mother. Unloved, in sum, except for those wonderful, un-guarded moments, Mikey, Silas, and, of course, black João, beautiful as jet. Even Du Boise does not matter any more.

But the skylight is like skin for a drum I'll never mend
And all the rain falls down, amen
On the works of last year's man.

Carry your own burdens,
Mister my friends.
She hums, laughing at her ability to paraphrase the lyrics.
Amen, Amen.